01-01-00™

01-01-00™

A Novel of the Millennium

R. J. Pineiro

A TOM DOHERTY ASSOCIATES BOOK

NEW YORK

01-01-00™

Copyright © 1999 by Rogelio J. Pineiro

This book is printed on acid-free paper.

Book designed by Michael Mendelsohn

A Forge Book
Published by Tom Doherty Associates, Inc.
175 Fifth Avenue
New York, NY 10010

Forge® is a registered trademark of Tom Doherty Associates, Inc.

Library of Congress Cataloging-in-Publication Data

Pineiro, R. J.
    01-01-00™ : a novel of the Millennium / R. J. Pinero. — 1st ed.
      p. cm.
    "A Tom Doherty Associates book."
    ISBN 0-312-87058-2 (hardcover)
    ISBN 0-312-87339-5 (Australian paperback)
    I. Title. II. Title: Oh one oh one oh oh.
PS3566.I5215A613 1999
813'.54—dc21   99-24573
                                                       CIP

First Edition: June 1999

Printed in the United States of America

0 9 8 7 6 5 4 3 2 1

For Lory Anne,

loving wife,

doting mother,

loyal friend,

soulmate.

Thank you for your unconditional love, yesterday, today, and all tomorrows.

And,

In memory of Dr. Luis Vidaurreta and Mari Tellería.

Vayan con Dios.

Acknowledgments

This book came about in a most interesting way. Ken Walker, president of WalkerGroup/Designs and creator of the 01-01-00 licensing program, thought it would be a great idea to tie in a millennium novel with his highly successful merchandising program. With the assistance of our mutual friend and agent at William Morris, Matt Bialer, plus the invaluable help of Marty Greenberg from Tekno Books, a dialogue began among the four of us. Once we settled on an outline, we sought and received the publishing support of Tom Doherty, president and publisher of Tor and Forge Books. As with all my previous projects, I received much help during the writing and rewriting of this story. Credit goes to a lot of very talented people whose dedicated efforts helped turn this book from a mere concept to reality. It's now up to the readers to decide how successful we have been. Any remaining mistakes are mine and only mine.

Special thanks go to:

St. Jude, saint of the impossible. You have my eternal gratitude for continuing to make it possible.

My wife and compassionate critic, Lory Anne, for your honest feedback on this and previous outlines and rough drafts (and for your endless patience while I hammered out the story on nights and weekends). You are my first line of defense against embarrassing myself.

My son, Cameron, age nine, for continuing to let me rediscover the world through your innocent and unbiased eyes, and for making me so proud with your good heart, excellent grades, and awesome karate kicks.

Tom Doherty, Linda Quinton, and the rest of the staff at Tor, including Steve de las Heras, Jennifer Marcus, and Karen Lovell. Thanks for treating me like one of the family during my visits to New York City. I'm really grateful that you not only publish my stories, but also put in a tremendous effort to promote my work, including that unforgettable light show on the side of the Flatiron building. The neon lights were surely bright on Broadway that evening!

Bob Gleason, my editor and friend, for your clever feedback and support, and also for all the good times in Austin and New York.

Ken Walker, architect and visionary, for your confidence and ideas, and also for turning a simple sequence of numbers into a dazzling, worldwide millennium campaign, with the 01-01-00 logo appearing everywhere, in numerous categories of merchandise.

Matt Bialer, my astute agent at William Morris, for your support during this and other projects. It's certainly been a pleasure working with you all these years, my friend. Looking forward to many more.

Marty Greenberg and Larry Segriff from Tekno Books, for your encouragement, confidence, and excellent feedback during all stages of this project. It's always a pleasure working with such professionals.

My good friend, Dave, for your technical assistance on weapons and other subjects, and also for turning me into a gun buff.

Andy Zack, who, although not directly involved in this project, did teach me more than a thing or two about writing thrillers during all of my previous novels.

My parents, Dora and Rogelio, for your love and guidance. I couldn't ask for better moral, professional, and spiritual role models. *Su hijo los quiere mucho y nunca los olvida.*

My sisters, Irene and Dora, and your wonderful families, for always being a source of support and inspiration. *Bienvenido a este mundo, Lorenzito! Que Dios te bendiga.*

Mike and Linda Wiltz, my awesome in-laws, for your love as well as for so many wonderful memories. Places like Florida, Tennessee, and Arkansas will never be the same again. Look out, Europe!

Michael, Bobby, and Kevin, my teenage brothers-in-law. May the Good Lord grant you the courage and wisdom to fulfill your dreams, whatever they may be.

And last, but certainly not least, a very special thanks to all my buddies and colleagues at Advanced Micro Devices, including John H., Jerry V., Lisa L., Doug R., Lee R., Terry M., Bob T., Allan O., Dave B., and so many others. Also, a long-distance hello to my friends at AMD Singapore, particularly Balan, Alan T., and Bobby K. for their hospitality during my 1998 trip. By the time this book gets published, I will be celebrating my sixteenth anniversary at AMD (and what an incredible ride it's been). Together we have shared (and survived) the many ups and downs of this unstoppable roller coaster we call the high-tech industry. I'm looking forward to the challenges and triumphs waiting for us in the new millennium as we take our products to the next level of excellence.

Thank you.

R. J. Pineiro
Austin, Texas
February, 1999

Prologue

In the year of our Lord 1998, the Earth rotated along its axis relative to the Sun, just as it had done for the past 4.5 billion years, after interstellar material in a spiral arm of the Milky Way Galaxy condensed and collapsed, flattening into a counterclockwise rotating disk under the influence of gravity, triggering the birth of the Sun, followed by turbulence in the solar nebula that led to the formation of the planets.

The Earth rotated along its axis while also traveling at a speed of sixty thousand mph on an elliptical orbit around the Sun, completing each journey in just over 365 days, and repeating the cycle over and over, through the seasons, across centuries, millennium after millennium. On the surface of this blue planet, protected by a thin layer of nitrogen and oxygen, the land bustled with the activity of billions of people across all continents. Entire metropolises came alive at night, the sheen from millions upon millions of lights visible in space as the globe continued to rotate, continued its perennial, tireless journey, from sunrise to sunset, from blue skies to star-filled nights, slowing down at the rate of two milliseconds every century from its interaction with the moon. Where 900 million years ago there had been 481 eighteen-hour days in a year, now, as the Earth came close to completing a new millennium, its rotation had slowed to twenty-four hours per revolution—the length of time experienced by mankind.

The end of the millennium, the first to be witnessed by the modern world, triggered feelings of accomplishment and hope, of intrigue and fear, of renewal and celebration, touching people from every land, every race, bringing unity to an eclectic planet. The countdown to this transcendental event was displayed across the globe, from the Eiffel Tower in Paris to Times Square in New York, from Ginza in Tokyo to Piccadilly Circus in London. In Moscow and Sydney, in Rome and Singapore, in Baghdad and Beijing, massive digital clocks counted down to the most significant and unifying event in the past one thousand years. Days, hours, minutes, seconds, and hundredths of seconds, displayed high above the world's most famous boulevards and squares, reminded humanity of this nearing and remarkable moment in time. And as the planet spun, carrying along the world's metropolises, turning the present into the past, the towering clocks continued to count down, their digital displays washing the heavens with crimson light, always changing, always decreasing, always symbolizing the end of an era and the dawn of a new world. Many people lived or worked near these monumental icons, oftentimes stopping to dream, to wonder, to be reminded of the passage of time, of their own mortality, before continuing on their daily routines, as dictated by their societies, by their laws, by their personal ambitions.

In downtown Washington, one of those people worked the dark keyboard of an IBM ThinkPad notebook computer with practiced ease. The scarlet glow of the large millennium clock across the street fought the early-morning light diffusing through his eleventh-floor living-room window, splashing hues of orange and yellow-gold across the small apartment, dimming the images on the plasma color display. He adjusted the brightness on the screen and resumed his work.

He was a hacker, but more than that, he was the last surviving member of Masters of Deception, the rogue hacker group that splintered from the infamous teen hacker gang Legion of Doom during the early nineties. He was born as David Canek, a name he'd stopped using after his induction into the LOD as Hans Bloodaxe. He had eventually left the trade after the FBI cracked down both LOD and MOD operations nationwide, sending most of his colleagues to jail. Only his unmatched skills had prevented his capture. Bloodaxe vanished overnight from the Internet and joined the respectable high-tech workforce in Washington, D.C.

Now I'm back, you bastards.

He'd been up most the the night working on his masterpiece, finally collapsing from exhaustion on the living-room sofa, where he'd slept until his alarm clock woke him up minutes ago.

Two hours is enough rest, he thought, convinced that true genius did not need much sleep.

Images flashed on his screen as he launched a set of programs that retrieved a thousand lines of assembly language code from a directory buried deep in the ThinkPad's hard drive, protected by a triple layer of software shields. The hacker wasn't worried about an illegal user breaking into his system and accessing his coveted file. He feared the virulent code in the file breaking *out* of the nested software cocoons he had designed to keep it contained. The fatal sequence of instructions and data, improperly handled, could easily neutralize his system in seconds, gobbling up millions of bytes of data.

His software retrievers performed just as he had designed them, accessing the malignant strain with the caution of a biologist handling a vial of Ebola, moving it to a customized editing screen. He spent the next hour touching up the code, adjusting the virus's target address, rate of replication, and the subroutine that defined its mutation sequence.

A feeling of omnipotence descended on Hans Bloodaxe as he yawned, momentarily regarding the huge millennium clock across the street, counting down with a near-hypnotizing rhythm. He glanced at the folded edition of yesterday's *Washington Post*. The city planned additional layoffs this week. More of his friends would lose their jobs, just as the master hacker had lost his two weeks earlier, when the city no longer required his computer services.

After I spent five years working overtime to modernize their traffic-light system.

Bloodaxe clenched his teeth in anger. Although it had not taken him long to secure a position with a private firm in Portland, Oregon, he still resented the city for the way it had discarded him and a dozen other programmers the moment the new system went on-line, without even having the decency of offering a severance package to tide him over while he looked for another job.

And now it's time for the bastards to feel a little pain.

The hacker reviewed the code once more, making certain that it would act just as he had programmed it. He wanted to punish city officials, not the general population of Washington, D.C. He wanted to attack the tumor without hurting the patient. And he felt convinced he possessed the skills and determination to do it, just as he had done it so many times in his not-so-distant past, a past he had worked very hard to keep buried. The authorities no longer looked for him, giving up after two years of unsuccessful high-tech tracking. Bloodaxe knew that today's strike would renew their search. Although he didn't plan to leave a personal signature with his work, he knew that once authorities captured a copy of the mutating virus, they would be able to compare this masterpiece with his previous work and make the connection, like matching high-tech fingerprints. But that was a risk Bloodaxe was more than willing to take to teach these city officials a lesson.

Satisfied, he enclosed a copy of the string in a software cocoon, designed to keep the virus contained until it reached its target system.

The next step was finding a way to pierce the city's software defense system—designed to keep hackers like Bloodaxe out of the nonpublic directories—and deliver his deadly software packet.

Logging on to the Internet, Bloodaxe dialed into one of several modems he suspected still existed at the city's central traffic-controlling branch. These modems were used exclusively by employees who wanted to log in from home to follow up on their work. Bloodaxe had owned one of these modem accounts once, but the system administrator had canceled it upon his termination. The sys admin, however, had only *canceled* Bloodaxe's account. He had not *removed* the modem's dial-in number from the system. Paranoid that someone might suspect him if he used his old dial-in number, Bloodaxe chose a different one, belonging to Bloodaxe's former boss, the manager of technical services.

Poetic justice. The hacker smiled at the irony of using his former superior's system as the launching platform for his virus.

The beauty of modems was that a hacker could bypass the initial software firewall designed to protect a network from illegal Internet users trying to gain access through the system's "front door." Modems accessed a network through a phone line connected directly to one of the computers of the network, not through the Ethernet server used by most users.

As the log-on screen for the city's traffic-controlling network greeted him, Bloodaxe typed in a shadow password, which he had left behind in all workstations as a "back door" in case he ever had to go in unannounced, gaining access to the Unix workstation. He knew that getting to this point was only half of the battle. He could easily fire his torpedo and its enclosed deadly packet of software into this system and kill it, along with probably dozens of other workstations linked to his old boss's system. But that would not accomplish his primary goal. Beyond the network's firewall was a software vault, or second firewall, accessible only to those users with the root password, where the large servers resided. The hacker so far had entered the building, roaming its hallways, inspecting the decor, but he could not yet penetrate the inner rooms, where the computers that controlled traffic hummed along protected from the intruder by this second firewall.

Aside from the system administrator, only two other people in the building had root privilege, the chief of security, and his former boss.

Adrenaline searing his veins, Bloodaxe breathed deeply to control his growing excitement. It'd been years since he had done this, and in a way he missed the thrill of it. With a few keystrokes, the hacker tricked his boss's system into crashing, forcing the Unix workstation to perform a core dump, the flushing of its random-access memory. Core dumps were designed to enable programmers to perform an electronic autopsy of the system's digital remains to learn why the system had crashed.

Bloodaxe read this core dump and transferred it to a file in his own home directory. Mixed with thousands of bytes of diagnostics and system logs were the passwords that his boss had last entered to gain access not just to his workstation, but also to the servers beyond the second firewall, the root password. Using a custom program appropriately named Extractor, the hacker gained root privilege in a few minutes. By then his boss's workstation had rebooted, allowing Bloodaxe to log in once more using the shadow password. This time, however, he also entered his newly acquired root privilege, opening the door to the servers for a direct torpedo shot. Before firing, however, he also changed the root password, locking out the system administrator and anyone who might try to attempt to stop his attack—at least for a little while.

With a single click of the mouse, he released the cocoon, which passed cleanly through the multiple layers of security, reaching the inner room, spilling its virulent contents into the network servers, following its directive to seek out the hard drives housing the complex programs that kept the nation's capital's rush-hour morning traffic from turning into havoc.

The virus quickly began to replicate across the hundreds of thousands of files in the drive, disabling the automatic backup systems, which he himself had designed to enable the local traffic-light controllers in the event of a network failure. Next, the alien code struck the primary program of the control system, instantly forcing all traffic lights within a two-mile radius into a flashing-red pattern.

Now let's see you bastards try to figure this one out without the help of the programmers you laid off!

Bloodaxe's gaze returned to the digital display across the street, which he had grown accustomed to use as a counter while cooking or exercising. Today he used it to mark the time it took before the effects of his virus brought the city to its knees.

Ten-foot-tall digital numbers flashed crimson waves of light as the counter's two right-most digits, marking the hundredths of a second, constantly pulsated next to the steady rhythm of the seconds and the nearly constant glow of the minutes, hours, and days.

In the minutes following the high-tech strike, traffic began to back up at all major intersections as the carefully designed traffic-light system turned into four-way stops. Within twenty minutes, Washington, D.C., had come to a standstill. While city officials struggled to enable the backup systems, the traffic flowing into the city clogged all access roads, from New York Avenue to Virginia and Constitution. In Dupont Circle angered drivers laid on their horns, kicking off a cacophony of sounds and shouts that mixed with those from other sections of the city. Amazingly, the first accident didn't occur until thirty-one minutes after the sabotage, when traffic backed up a curved exit ramp from Highway 195, just out of sight from a minivan getting off the highway. The driver had taken this route countless times before on her way to Georgetown University, where she taught computer science. Although the posted speed limit on the exit ramp was thirty-five miles per hour, she usually took it at forty. Her husband, a federal agent from the Treasury Department, rode in the passenger seat. Their two-year-old daughter sat in the back. All three were wearing their safety belts.

She slammed on the brakes but could not avoid crashing into the row of stopped vehicles on the ramp. The airbags mushroomed, sparing her from fatally crushing her face against the steering wheel. The airbag system also saved her husband's life. The safety belt wrapped over her daughter's shoulder kept her from bouncing inside the family vehicle.

Unfortunately, the minivan collided while turning down the curved exit ramp. The impact did not stop the vehicle but simply deflected its momentum to the left, crashing it against a three-foot side wall, forcing it over the edge, plummeting a dozen feet to the ground below.

All three were flown to nearby Georgetown University Hospital. The husband died en route from severe trauma to the head and torso. The daughter died that afternoon from internal bleeding. The driver spent two months in a coma.

Before awakening to a nightmare.

000001

1

Washington, D.C.

The Walther PPK semiautomatic could hold seven rounds, but Susan Garnett thumbed only one into the magazine before jamming it into the gun's grip. She flipped off the safety and pulled back the slide, chambering the cartridge. Keeping her finger off the trigger, she let her robe fall by her feet before stepping into the tub in her bathroom.

Susan immersed herself in the lukewarm water, her dark olive skin momentarily goose-bumping. Inhaling deeply, she forced her mind to relax, finding it amazingly easy to do, a strange sense of peace descending on her.

"Soon," she whispered, her catlike eyes glaring at the framed picture on the small shelf over the toilet. "Soon it won't matter anymore."

The slim gun fit comfortably in the palm of her right hand, which remained steady, like a surgeon's. With surprising calmness, Susan stared at her late husband's backup weapon, the one he'd always carried in an ankle holster while on duty at the Department of the Treasury, the same gun he had used to teach her how to shoot at a range in Virginia. The well-oiled PPK reflected the overheads as Susan slowly pointed the muzzle at the ceiling before placing it under her chin, remembering a story her husband had told her about a fellow agent who'd killed himself "the right way." The officer had done it in the bathtub to avoid making a mess. He'd also used only one cartridge in the semiautomatic. When he'd fired it, the recoiling slide had extracted and ejected the spent case, but a new round had not been chambered, leaving behind a safe weapon instead of a loaded one. Lastly, the officer had fired the gun under his chin instead of against his temple, where the skull could deflect the round, preventing it from inflicting the desired fatal blow.

Susan closed her eyes, recalling that dreadful morning almost two years ago. She remembered Rebecca singing in the backseat while Tom checked his daily planner. She'd always dropped Rebecca at preschool first, then Tom at his work, before driving herself to the computer science building at Georgetown University to teach her daily classes.

The thirty-five-year-old woman began to cry, tears streaming down her cheeks. She could still see the curved exit ramp, the rear bumper of a car suddenly appearing in her field of view. She felt the initial impact, airbags blossoming with the sound of a gunshot, the sky and the ground swapping places as the minivan went over the edge. Then nothing. She could remember absolutely nothing, until she'd awakened from a deep coma.

"And into a nightmare that ends—"

The phone rang in the bedroom. She frowned at the intrusion but ignored it, keeping her eyes closed, fixing her index finger over the trigger, feeling the familiar resistance of the firing mechanism, knowing just how much pressure the PPK required to fire the cartridge. For the past two years she had controlled her suicidal thoughts by going to the shooting range and imagining that the paper silhouette hanging from the track was—

The phone rang a second time. The answering machine picked it up on the third ring.

Her index finger tensed over the trigger as she listened to her own voice in the greeting, followed by three short beeps.

"Pick up, Sue. I know you're home."

She frowned at Troy Reid's voice echoing in her small apartment in downtown Washington. Reid, an old hand at the Bureau, ran the FBI's high-tech crime unit. Susan was one of his top analysts. Following the accident and her release from the hospital, Susan had switched careers, opting to devote all of her energy and skills to catching hackers, starting with the elusive David Canek, also known as Hans Bloodaxe, the man responsible for her family's death. She had immersed herself in her work as a way to forget the pain, the memories, the faces. As a way to purge her mind from a past that was simply too painful to remember, forcing all of her energy into achieving her personal vendetta. For months she'd set up traps at thousands of Internet service providers (ISPs) in the hope of finding her hacker. She'd eventually caught Bloodaxe with one of her software traps, buried deep inside an ISP in Portland, Oregon. Susan had also nailed over a hundred hackers in just under two years with the Bureau, earning a sterling reputation as top cybercop. But all of the fame and recognition didn't prevent her from spiraling into a deep depression after Bloodaxe was convicted and sentenced to life at a federal prison three months ago. She had come to the realization that the fire of retribution burning deep inside her had been the inner power that had fueled her desire to go on after the accident. Now that Bloodaxe was behind bars, Susan suddenly found herself without a reason for living.

"We've got what seems to be a global event, Sue. C'mon, pick up the phone. I know you've put in sixteen straight hours, but this is very hot. Gotta talk to you."

Global event? Susan cursed under her breath while lowering the gun and flipping on the safety with her thumb, setting it over a sealed envelope on the shelf above the toilet, next to the picture frame. Wrapping the robe around her, she walked to the bedroom and reached for the phone, noticing a slight tremble in her hand. Taking a deep breath, she said, *"Hello,* Troy."

"You sound annoyed. Sorry, Sue. Were you sleeping?"

She sat in bed and crossed her legs, eyes looking into the bathroom, focusing on the dark weapon resting on the white shelf. Only now, after walking away from a suicide attempt, did her heart begin to pound heavily. She felt a lump in her throat. A sudden heat flash made her feel light-headed, dizzy.

"Sue? Are you all right?"

Sweat began to form on her forehead. The sheer realization of what she had almost done was finally setting in. He body was reacting to the burst of adrenaline from the short-lived event, just as it would have if a thug had pulled a gun on her, threatened to kill her, and then abruptly walked away.

Laboring to control her breathing, wiping the perspiration with the sleeve of her robe, she said, "What—what do you want?"

"Have you been listening to the news this evening?"

"I'm . . . no. Look, Troy, I'm really tired. Get to the point. What is it that couldn't wait until tomorrow?"

"Just over two hours ago, at exactly 8:01 P.M., all computer systems in Washington, D.C., froze for twenty seconds."

Her suicidal thoughts momentarily vanished as the scientist in her took over. "Froze for twenty seconds? I don't understand. Did we experience a power glitch?"

"No power glitch. This event was software driven."

The room began to spin. Susan lay down, resting her head on a pillow and closing her eyes to control her dizziness. Her temples throbbed to the rhythm of her increasing heartbeat. "How . . . how do you know?"

"Because of the nature of the event. It looks as if someone somehow managed to put every network on hold for twenty seconds, before returning everything back to normal."

Susan took another deep breath and opened her eyes. The room no longer spun. She swallowed her own spit and tried to focus on the conversation. "What's the estimate on data loss?"

"There's been no reports of data loss."

"None?"

"Nope, and no messages either, or statements, or warnings. Just frozen screens for twenty seconds and everything back to normal after that, even the system clocks skipped twenty seconds to resynchronize."

She slowly felt better. The heat flash passed. Her heartbeat became steady. "Strange."

"What's even *more* strange is that we have gotten calls from our offices around the world. London, Paris, Berlin, Moscow, Hong Kong, Seoul, Taipei—they're all reporting similar events taking place at the exact same time, one minute after eight in the evening our time."

Susan sat up in bed. "That's—"

"Impossible? I'm past denial, Sue. It's very real, and *very* scary."

Susan didn't reply. In her short but successful FBI career, she had lured and trapped many brilliant hackers, most of them guilty of releasing viruses into the Internet or illegally accessing private or government networks. In fact, the most tenacious had been Hans Bloodaxe, who'd released the virus that shut down the traffic-light system in Washington, D.C., for several days . . .

Susan's eyes drifted back to the weapon, for a moment wondering if she would have actually killed herself had Troy Reid not called when he had. She decided that she probably would have. In fact, she felt she could still do so at this moment. The feeling of emptiness that consumed her from the moment she'd awakened from her coma had only deepened after Bloodaxe was convicted. Whatever healing time had done on her emotional wounds had been wiped away by the wave of loneliness that had struck her outside the courtroom, forcing her to take such desperate measures.

"Sue?"

She blinked back to her phone conversation. Troy was concerned about this bizarre event, software driven, probably the act of a skilled hacker. *But both synchronized and global?* She shook her head in disbelief. Even Bloodaxe's strike had been contained to one geographical location. The thought of a global, synchronized strike was unheard of, nearly impossible to coordinate without substantial technical resources.

"Sue? Are you there?"

She nodded. "Just thinking. See, any hacker can release a virus onto the Internet. Most viruses, however, are detected within weeks, or even days or hours, of their original release, prompting software companies to generate treatments that get posted at numerous Internet bulletin boards, where users can download them to disinfect their systems. The virus is then methodically exterminated from the web. In order to release a virus that could infect most of the world while going totally undetected, and then strike in synchronized fashion, requires not just highly specialized skills, but also a lot of software and hardware resources spread across many countries. That's virtually impossible to accomplish. Surely someone somewhere would have stumbled upon this virus before it became active and posted the finding on the Internet for the world to see."

"Not to my knowledge. This one seems to have caught us by surprise."

"Do we have any leads?"

"No. That's why I called. I need you to start digging right away. The director got a call from the White House an hour ago. Apparently the President and his advisers were in the middle of a video conference call with some classified party in the Middle East when the networks froze, killing the satellite link."

Susan sighed. The problem seemed quite distant and irrelevant to a person about to end her life. And at the moment, for reasons that she could not explain, hearing that the strange event had disconnected the President from his call actually struck her as humorous. Maybe it was hysteria from her near-death encounter in the bathtub. Or perhaps her tired mind had difficulty separating her feelings. But before she could help herself, she blurted, "Just tell the President to stop complaining and call them back. It's not as if he has to dial the phone himself."

"Susan Garnett!"

Reid reminded Susan of her own father, who would call her by her full name only when he was angry with her. And the fact that Reid was almost as old as her father only added a level of authority to the remark. "Sorry. It's late and I'm very tired."

"Well, see, that's part of the problem. We can't wait until morning. I need you over here ASAP."

"Now? But—"

"Now, Sue. Please: I've already sent a car to pick you up. It should be there momentarily. This is a real emergency. Somebody out there appears to have the power to freeze global networks at will. What if today's event was just a test? What if the next strike involves severe data loss? We're talking global shutdown, lady. We don't need this kind of crap right before the turn of the millennium. Everyone's having a hell of a time just getting their systems Year 2000 compliant. No one needs a group of rogue programmers making a delicate transition time even more difficult. Get over here now to get things going. I promise you some sleep before dawn in one of the offices upstairs."

Exhaling heavily, she agreed and hung up the phone. She unloaded the PPK and locked it away in her nightstand. She also snagged the sealed envelope she had set next to the picture frame. It contained her final will, quite simple actually, along with an explanation of her actions.

She slipped into a pair of blue jeans, a flannel shirt, and a sweater. She folded the envelope in half and shoved it in her back pocket. The doorbell rang as she crammed her feet into a pair of hiking boots. She grabbed a jacket, a scarf, and her computer carrying case as she dashed out the door.

2

The Earth continued to rotate along its axis, marking the dawn of a new day, just as it had done for billions of years, since the creation of the Solar System. Beneath the atmosphere, the large digital displays atop the world's best known structures continued their countdown to the end of the millennium, numbers pulsating to the rhythm of their computerized brains, projecting crimson hues into the sky, sequences of ever-decreasing numbers that raced across space as the Earth continued to spin while traveling along its elliptical orbit around the Sun.

One after another the numbers came, as the blue planet obeyed the laws of physics, always spinning, exposing to dark space one continent after the next, metropolis after metropolis, all displaying the same monumental icons of the passage of time.

The clocks radiated their energy in the visual range of the electromagnetic spectrum, projecting it high into the sky at the speed of light, where it mixed with electromagnetic energy from other sources as it reached the upper layers of the atmosphere, as it broke free from the Earth's gravitational force, as it ventured into outer space. The electromagnetic energy containing the visual spectrum of those magnificent clocks traveled past moon orbit and Mars, across the asteroid ring, beyond the orbits of the outer planets, plunging into deep space.

The Earth continued to spin, continued to flash electromagnetic pulses, continued to transmit these bands of energy encoding the scarlet images of the countdown clocks beyond the Solar System, day after day, land after land, city after city, over and over, creating a pulsating rhythm that moved across space as the Earth orbited the Sun, always spinning, always releasing energy, always broadcasting the global countdown to the inevitable end of the millennium.

Chapter Two

000010

1

December 12, 1999

Catching hackers was an acquired skill, something not taught in school. Oftentimes it took a hacker to catch a hacker. The FBI knew this and kept hackers in its list of ghost consultants. Many of them had been caught by Troy Reid's high-tech warriors of the caliber of Susan Garnett. Those hackers guilty of harmless crimes, like accessing a classified government web page just to prove to a friend that it could be done, were normally given a choice: a prison term, or probation with a lifetime obligation to provide free consulting services for the Bureau, anytime, anyplace. It was a pretty easy choice for most.

Just like the Godfather calling in his favors, Susan thought as she checked her system and found the name of a hacker she had caught six months ago browsing in one of the servers of the directory of intelligence of the CIA. A few years ago the kid, a junior at UCLA, would have gotten five years at a minimum security prison. The felony would have gone on his permanent record, preventing him from securing a job in the high-tech sector after completing his jail time. Nowadays, those kinds of hackers got off easy, as long as they changed their ways and agreed to the FBI's terms.

Susan sat behind her desk at her window office on the sixth floor of the J. Edgar Hoover Building in downtown Washington. She glanced at the cumulus clouds hovering over the Washington skyline—a scene she hadn't expected to see again. Only yesterday she had stared from this very office at what she thought would be her last sunset. She had watched the hues of burnt orange and yellow-gold splash the Washington Monument, the White House, and the Capitol. Her eyes had drifted to the distant shape of Highway

195 as it snaked its way into the south side of the nation's capital, remembering, reminiscing, plotting. Then she had gone home for the very last time.

Or so she had thought.

She shook her head, not certain of what exactly she was doing here again, behind this desk, tapping the keyboard of her portable computer as dawn broke and the city stirred to life. Streetlights flickered and went off. Traffic thickened. Horns blared. Pedestrians emerged from subway stations. Susan watched it all with detachment, as if she didn't belong to this world anymore.

Tonight, she told herself. *I'll just get Troy going on this investigation and then I'm gone, for good.*

She found the number for the FBI-issued nationwide pager of Chris Logan, now a senior at UCLA and forever slave to the Federal Bureau of Investigation. She used her software to send him an alpha page, ordering him to call the FBI's Watts line, followed by her extension—immediately. The reason why she had selected Logan over all the other hackers in her file was the very reason why the kid got just a slap on the wrist before the FBI sent him back to UCLA: he was a genius. Chris Logan had managed to pierce a dozen security layers at the Central Intelligence Agency, not only cracking passive software shields, but also evading active security programs created by the finest minds in the nation to patrol the myriad of directories in Langley searching for illegal users. Using a reflection program, a piece of code that reflected the image of the programs surrounding it, Logan had managed to disguise his browsing routine from the CIA search engines patrolling the directories. But Logan had underestimated the quality of the active software police, enhanced a month before by Susan Garnett herself as part of a federal program to improve security in the most critical government agencies. The security routine randomly probed files, even if they appeared to be normal, at the rate of one every millisecond, or one thousand files per second, searching for a key binary string buried within every CIA file, deep beneath the software shell that Logan's reflection routine replicated in order to disguise itself. Susan's security program probed Logan's illegal browser beyond its chameleon skin for the secret binary string. Failing to find it, the security program immediately tagged the illegal code. A second security program made a copy of the browser and began to dissect it without warning the prowler, who continued to cruise through the directories. Within seconds a trace was created and the origin of the illegal entry tracked back to a dorm at UCLA.

Susan closed the paging software and continued checking the area's Internet service providers, using a combination of commercial software and her own custom code to comb through every public server in a five-square-mile area, searching for traces of this virus. The search programs Susan used were a combination of virus scan software and search engines. The programs pinged every disk server, comparing their binary codes with a signature file in her virus scan directory. Viruses could range in size from several bytes to several thousand bytes, depending on their ability to replicate, to hide, and to cause harm. Some macro viruses, although annoying, could be relatively harmless in nature, like the Concept Virus in Microsoft Word, which forced the user to save documents as templates. Other word-processing viruses changed fonts, margins, and paragraph formatting. Other viruses attacked operating systems, or data files. The more complex ones lurked at the entrance to a network waiting for legal users to log in, and copying their account numbers and passwords. Those viruses could be particularly devastating stalking the network of a bank or investment firm. Some of those illegal copies would yield a powerful password, like that of a system administrator, which gave the hacker unlimited access to a network.

All known viruses contained a characteristic binary string, usually no more than five to twenty bytes in length, within its body. This characteristic binary string was known in the industry as the virus signature. A virus scan program contained a signature file, where the John Hancocks of every known virus resided.

Susan Garnett probed every public server in Washington, D.C., using her virus signature file to search for instances of the telltale strings. She accomplished this by the use of a script, a program that executed the actions of logging into the Internet, accessing a specific server, and performing the checks against the signature file. Instead of performing all of those tasks manually, one server at a time, she launched her custom scripts, which automatically accomplished the same thing, but in parallel, and in a matter of a few minutes, instead of the many hours it would have taken her doing it serially and manually.

Susan returned her eyes to the clouds while waiting for the scripts to report the results of their searches. Her dreamlike state of mind returned. She once again felt indifferent about her surroundings. Like a traveler who'd missed her connecting flight and simply waited at the gate of a strange airport for the next departure, Susan Garnett regarded her environment with a short-timer's attitude.

She pulled out the folded envelope from her back pocket and stared at it.

Writing a letter to explain her death had been one of the most difficult things she had ever done. *After all, how do you actually explain to your surviving friends and relatives why you did what you did, especially after you'd gotten everyone thinking that you had managed to get on with your life?* Her mother and father had moved to Washington for the weeks that followed her release from the hospital. But even their love and support could not quench her desire to end it all. Her friends had also been quite supportive, constantly visiting her to the point that she began to avoid them to get some personal time. For those initial weeks it seemed that no one wanted Susan Garnett to be alone for fear that she might do something stupid.

And here I am, she thought, toying with the envelope. She had fooled them into thinking that she had gotten over the deaths of Tom and Rebecca and moved on to a new career and, hopefully, a new personal life. The career part she had pulled off. But as for the personal life . . . *Well, some wounds are not so easily healed.*

Susan tapped the envelope against her desk, taking a deep breath, resigning herself to the fact that she could not possibly fight the overwhelming desire to end it all immediately. She now regretted answering that phone last night. She should have ignored it and just pulled the trigger. It would have been all over by now. This envelope would have found its way to her parents' hands in Maryland.

She frowned. That was the only part of this ordeal that she really, truly hated doing. Losing Rebecca had given her a feel for what her parents would go through if she pulled the trigger. But she could not help herself. The pain for the past three months had been smothering. If it wasn't a bullet then it would be the anguish that would slowly kill her, like some form of emotional cancer, chipping away at her sanity until she would no longer be able to function on her own, possibly requiring special care, putting an even greater burden on her family than a quick funeral service and burial.

If I'm going to go, I'll do so without being a burden to anyone.

But she had failed last night. She had not taken care of the problem. Instead, here she was again, staring at the same damned skies, over the same damned city, and from the same damned office window. Deep inside, however, Susan Garnett knew the reason why she had resisted the impulse to kill herself, if only momentarily: although Hans Bloodaxe was behind bars, the desire to catch hackers apparently still ranked high on her list, obviously higher than the emotional blow she would deliver to her family. Catching hackers had a way to revitalize her resolve to remain alive.

Especially to catch someone who apparently has the power to do so much global damage.

She shoved the envelope back in her pocket as the initial results from the scripts began to flash on her screen. The scan checks had found nothing out of the ordinary, meaning there were no known viruses out there. There was, of course, the strong possibility that a new virus, with a new signature, could still be lurking out there, waiting to strike again. That was one of the greatest challenges for virus scan software companies: detecting new viruses with unknown signatures. Usually, that meant waiting for the virus to strike, capturing one of the mutation sequences, dissecting it, extracting the signature, and also releasing an antidote into the Internet. That process implied that the virus would do some level of damage before it could be caught. Really smart viruses would wait for weeks, or even months, before striking, spending that time simply replicating, copying themselves into as many files in as many networks as possible, until their activation time arrived. That also implied that virus catchers had little time to react from the time the virus became active.

Susan frowned at the information scrolling by her screen.

Nothing. Absolutely nothing.

She checked her watch and paged Logan again. She decided to give him ten more minutes before notifying the Los Angeles office and sending a car with two agents to pick him up at school. She should have paged him soon after her arrival at the FBI late last night, but at the time she had felt certain of her ability to tackle this virus unassisted.

Just as she closed the paging software, her phone rang.

"Garnett," Susan said.

"Hello, Miss Garnett."

"It's about time, Chris. What took you so long?"

"Ah... it's only four in the morning here. I didn't hear my pager go off the first time."

Susan closed her eyes. She had forgotten about the time difference. Seven in the morning in Washington was only four in Los Angeles. Still, the deal cut by the FBI was for twenty-four hours a day, seven days a week. She did not apologize.

"Are you calling about the event?"

"What do you know about it?"

"Nothing. I've been keeping clean, as promised."

"Don't bullshit me, Chris. What do you *really* know?"

"I'm dead serious. I'm concentrating on my schoolwork and staying off hacking. All I know is what's been on the news. It certainly looks like a nasty one."

Susan regarded her unpainted fingernails while considering her next question. She remembered this kid, short, slim, freckle-faced, but damned smart. In fact, too smart for his own good.

"All right, Chris. Let me try another angle. If you were trying to release such a global virus, how would you go about it to succeed while also avoiding getting caught?"

"Hmm . . . I would write self-destructing code to cover my tracks."

Nothing new there. Self-destructing code had been around for many years. "Keep talking."

"Well, this is how it could have happened. This hacker must have injected the code into specific addresses, because according to the news, the virus went many places around the globe, but not everywhere, right?"

"Go on."

"Okay. So, the virus makes it into a significant portion of the world. That in itself is a major accomplishment. This hacker is some artist. It must have taken him months to get the code straight, get it debugged, run some test cases in some small city, manage to stay undetected while checking it out, doing more debug, tuning up, until he's ready to cut it loose. He tacks Internet addresses to each copy and shoots them off one by one. I would have timed them to GMT to keep them all in sync. Then, I activate them all at the same time after giving them about a month to reproduce, make plenty of babies, really dig themselves in."

Susan was quickly getting bored, her eyes on her fingernails, which she had stop polishing some time back, when she had stopped caring. "I figured this much on my own, Chris. What do you know about self-destructing code?"

"Self-destructing code's not that difficult to write. Just put in a snippet of code at the end of the virus to erase every line after execution of its prime directive. I'm pretty sure that the hacker must have used the twenty seconds when the screens were frozen to destroy all evidence of his work."

Susan Garnett sighed. "Chris, if you don't stop quoting me undergraduate-level computer stuff I'm sending agents to pick you up right now and throw your little butt in jail."

"But—but, I haven't done anything wrong!"

She smiled. "Then you'd better start telling me something I don't already know."

Silence, followed by, "You promise you won't bother me for a while?"

"I promise you that if you don't level with me I will have two agents at your dorm in fifteen minutes. They will cuff you and throw you in jail with a couple of big-ass inmates. Need I say more?"

"No. The only way you have a chance of bagging this hacker is if he tries to do it again."

"How?"

"By settin' up software traps at the entry points of the Internet for one of the affected cities, like Washington, D.C."

"I thought about that, too. How do you make certain that the virus doesn't self-destruct inside the software trap?" A software trap was sort of like a hunter's trap, sprung along the trail, or Internet service provider, where the prey or virus might travel. The trap remained open until the prey came along. It would then close, keeping the prey from escaping.

"I'd write the trap so that it makes a passive copy of the virus the moment the trap closes."

In spite of her current state of mind, Susan Garnett grinned. A passive copy of the virus within the software trap meant creating a copy that lacked all of the links of the active virus and therefore would be incapable of destroying itself, like its active sister.

Susan, however, was disappointed in herself. She should have thought of it on her own, and six months ago she probably would have. But lately, she'd had other stuff on her mind aside from developing software. Susan thanked the young man, warned him to keep his nose clean, and hung up.

A software trap with a built-in passive replicator.

Susan dove into her laptop, accessing a library of short general purpose programs that she had created over the years to quickly patch together scripts, or custom programs. She spent the next few hours immersed in her work, tapping keys, dragging the cursor, clicking her way through hundreds of files, cutting and pasting, rearranging, reformatting, adding, deleting, creating, tuning. Slowly, the software trap began to take shape. She had designed it to behave like a vault. The door would remain open until a program tried to attach itself to it, like a virus normally would. Then the door would shut, trapping the virus inside by making a copy of it and hiding it from the original. This artificial replication method had a different effect than when the virus replicated willingly, according to its original programming. During replication, all of the mutating elements of the virus, including its primary directive, would be transferred in their active state to the clone, including the ability for further replication. By copying a virus already attached to a file, the active portions of the virus, like the ability to further replicate, or the ability to follow its primary or secondary directives, remained in a dormant state because, unlike mutation, simply copying a virus did not increase the mutation sequence, which acted like a checksum, or internal validation check, prior to the activation of the virus. If the checksum within the virus didn't add up, then the virus would remain dormant, even after it was given the order to become active.

Susan checked her software cocoon with a "test" virus from her library. She did this in a secured directory, and only after physically unplugging her Ethernet cable from the side of the laptop to avoid inadvertently releasing a virus into the network. In addition, she had already set up a directory within her system as a "petri dish," capable of processing and containing viruses. If something went wrong and the virus managed to start replicating, the secured directory would be her first line of defense in containing it. If somehow the virus managed to expand beyond the secured directory, the isolated system would keep it contained, unable to reach the network.

The petri dish held a dozen decoy files, placed there by Susan for the purpose of luring the virus. One of the decoy files contained her software trap. The virus immediately attached itself to the closest file and began to replicate, infecting every file in the directory within a millisecond. This particular test virus was highly toxic, the brain child of a Florida hacker now working at Microsoft but forever in debt to Susan Garnett and the FBI for cutting him some slack after catching him a year ago. Following its primary directive, the virus consumed every file it touched, turning them into random strings of ones and zeroes. In the midst of the destruction, her special file turned into a cocoon, trapping the virus inside, immediately making a copy, and further isolating it from the trapped version.

Got ya.

Susan nodded, satisfied with her work. She stretched and yawned. Her stomach rumbled. She had not eaten a thing in almost twenty-four hours. She had planned to kill herself on an empty stomach as a courtesy to the people who would have to clean up her mess. Her husband had told her that gunshot victims typically voided their bowels.

Returning her attention to the screen, she wrote a script that automatically made copies of her software cocoons, each with a different Internet address, but all in the Washington area. She tried to cover as many entry points into the capital city as she could find.

As the cocoons made their way across the local network, forming a ring around the city, she also sent an E-mail to her entire list of FBI-owned hackers asking for help. So far, she was aware of at least a dozen other security agencies in this country, and many more abroad, also trying to track down the origin of this peculiar virus. No one had reported a breakthrough so far.

Hoping that a soda might calm her stomach, Susan headed for the vending machines, on the way walking by Troy Reid's office a few doors down. She stuck her head in the doorway. "Knock knock."

His back to the Washington skyline, Reid lifted his wrinkled face from the documents sprawled across his desk. He regarded Susan over the silver rim of the spectacles perched at the tip of his nose. Looking ten years older than his age, Reid was an old hand at the Bureau, having started his career during the final months of J. Edgar Hoover. He had an engineering degree from the University of Virginia and a second degree in criminology from Georgetown University. His blue eyes, although encased in dark and wrinkled sockets, still gleamed with bold intelligence. Ten years behind a desk, however, had turned his once athletic body into a mass of fat, which he still managed to carry reasonably well due to his height. His bald head and deeply lined face, combined with his bulk, reminded Susan of her father. Reid was due to retire next year.

"What did you find?" he asked in the hoarse voice of a chain-smoker. He waved the unlit cigar in his right hand toward one of the chairs across his desk.

"Not much, actually," she replied, walking in and sitting down, feeling the envelope in her back pocket, forcing it out of her mind for the time being. She took a few minutes to explain her current tactic.

Leaning back in his swivel chair, Reid exhaled heavily and ran a hand over his gleaming head. Probably a handsome man in his youth, three decades of stress and hard living as a field agent and then as a desk agent had taken a severe toll on him.

"These hackers scare me, Sue. Bastards are learning new tricks every day, and we can't seem to keep up."

Susan crossed her legs. "I'd say we're right on their heels, especially since we started turning them instead of putting them behind bars."

"That was part your idea," he said, pointing at her with the cigar.

She shrugged. It really didn't matter. Nothing mattered anymore. Once again, she questioned why in the hell she was here, sitting in this office, discussing yet another high-tech crime with her boss. She had sworn to herself that yesterday would be her last day. She had paid all of her bills, bought a plot at the city's cemetery, put all of her affairs in order, and even included the numbers of all bank accounts in her will. The total amount would not only pay for her funeral services, but it should also cover the expenses her relatives would incur by coming down for the funeral. She had even packed her personal belongings to make it easy for her parents to haul it all off to their house in Maryland.

"So what's next?" Reid asked.

"We wait for the hacker to strike again."

"That's something else that's been bothering me," Reid said, setting down the cigar and interlacing his fingers before resting his arms over the papers he had been reading. "What was this guy trying to do? Why just freeze the systems? If he had the power to freeze them, he could have also displayed a message on the screens, said something. There was also no loss of data. No real damage done. I don't get it. And why freeze systems for only twenty seconds instead of an hour, or longer? Is there any significance in that?"

Susan had not thought about the hacker's reasons for doing what he or she had done. After catching so many of them, she had long ago stopped questioning their motives. And in this case, she cared even less. Still, she felt she owed Troy Reid her attention in return for his support and encouragement over the past eighteen months. Reid had been more than fair to her, which maybe was part of the reason for her sitting here today, instead of lying naked in a morgue awaiting identification by her parents.

An image of herself, covered with a sheet, stuffed inside one of those refrigerated cubicles, probably without a face, after the bullet had done its intended damage, chilled her.

Is that what you really want?

She forced herself back to the conversation. Reid was talking about the possibility that this attack could be the result of a terrorist trying to disturb the delicate state of the Internet at the turn of the millennium. "I mean, Sue, look at the statistics. Only the United States has achieved a ninety percent compliance level with Year 2000 policies. France and Germany are still at the seventy percent level. Japan is up around eighty. Southeast Asian nations are just barely breaking the sixty percent level. And God help countries in South America and Eastern Europe, which at our last count were barely past the fifty percent point. Perhaps one of those countries is out to sabotage our efforts in order to level the playing field a little."

Susan thought about the possibility and decided that Troy Reid had a valid concern. "I think you're on to something here. But I still hope it's just a rogue group of hackers trying to get noticed."

"If that's the case, why aren't they advertising their objectives? Why didn't they send us a message during the event?"

She tilted her head. "Well, message or no message, they sure got our attention."

"That, I'm afraid, they did. And not just ours. The director got two more calls from the White House this morning. The President's been on the phone with the leaders of a dozen nations already, all of them quite troubled by the event. Some countries are blaming their enemies for the attack on their networks. In fact, Iraq and Iran have already issued statements blaming Israel. North Korea is blaming South Korea. China is blaming Taiwan. Japan is blaming China. Even the CIA is now suspecting someone."

"Who?"

"They wouldn't say. You know how the spooks are about these matters."

"Maybe that's just what they're trying to accomplish, Troy. Maybe they want to create confusion, make everyone suspicious of everyone else."

Reid bit into his cigar while inspecting his ego wall to the right of his desk, where, in addition to his college diplomas, hung a number of training certificates, commendation plaques, and several framed pictures of Troy Reid shaking hands with important people, including a couple of presidents. The chief of the high-tech crime unit nodded. "Maybe you're right. It sure looks like this strange event stirred up quite a few world leaders."

"Well, it's all speculation for now anyway. If there's ever another event, we should at least be able to learn something from it." Her stomach rumbled.

Reid grinned and stood. "When's the last time you ate?"

Susan shrugged.

"Let's go to the cafeteria. I'll buy."

She exhaled and also stood, not really knowing what to do or think anymore. She was obviously starving, but didn't want to eat because that went against her ground rules for a clean suicide. On the other hand, if she didn't eat something soon, she might pass out. This morning she had already seen dark spots a couple of times and had to sit down to regain her strength.

Resigned to the fact that she would have to live just a little longer than expected, Susan followed her superior to the elevators.

2

La Serena, Chile

Dr. Ishiguro Nakamura rushed inside the main building at the Cerro Tolo Observatory, in the Andes Mountains, climbing the circular stairway two steps at a time, reaching the main platform nearly out of breath. Two years of intensive graduate work, plus three more of specialized studies to earn his Ph.D. in astrophysics from Stanford University, plus the intense work of up-grading Cerro Tolo to a world-class radio telescope facility, had left the native of Osaka, Japan, with little time for exercise. Ishiguro, although still lean thanks to a sensible diet of fish and vegetables, was hopelessly out of shape, in sharp contrast with his undergraduate days, when he had jogged regularly at Stanford while pursuing a B.S. in computer engineering, before discovering an affinity for astrophysics he never knew he had.

He stormed inside the central observatory room, illuminated only by the pulsating glow from the monitors of a dozen Hewlett-Packard 735 work-stations. Modern deep space observatories did not use regular telescopes.

"Ishiguro-san! Ishiguro-san! What is happening?" asked the corporate li-aison from Sagata Enterprises, the Japanese conglomerate currently leasing the large observatory from the Chilean government. The young executive, Kuoshi Honichi, unaffected by the long climb, had tried to catch up with Ishiguro outside the building, where the whiz kid from Stanford had dropped his two-way radio and run inside the building. Kuoshi spent about one week out of every six at Cerro Tolo at the request of Sagata executives to monitor the team's progress. The rest of the time he spent either at their headquarters in Osaka, or at three other Japanese-controlled sites engaged in the search for extraterrestrial intelligence (SETI).

"When . . . did it happen?" Ishiguro asked Jackie Nakamura, his wife, also a Ph.D. from Stanford. The rest of the SETI team was formed by technicians from Sagata Enterprises.

Jackie glanced at Kuoshi and shook her head while sipping from a can of diet Coke. She returned her attention to the screen. "At one minute past nine in the evening local time today. One minute after one in the morning GMT." She checked her watch. "About two hours ago. The automatic scanner picked it up. I've just noticed it while browsing through the day's telemetry."

"Ishiguro-san! What is—"

"Hold on, Kuoshi-san," Ishiguro snapped at the young executive before turning back to his wife. "Where . . . where is it? *Show me.*"

"Right here," she said while two technicians glanced over from their stations. She continued to point at the large color display of her HP workstation. Jackie Nakamura was a second-generation Japanese living in northern California. The glow from the screen washed her soft features. Her slanted eyes belonged to her Japanese mother. Her brown hair, rounded cheekbones, and full lips were her dad's, a native Californian. Ironically, Jackie and Ishiguro had not met through their studies but during their sophomore year at a marathon in Mountain View, California.

Ishiguro tried to control his breathing as much as his growing excitement. The prospect of a SETI breakthrough increased his heartbeat as much as the strenuous climb. Sagata Enterprises, the same company that had awarded him the scholarship that had financed his entire education at Stanford, had hired him and his wife four years ago to lead the Japanese SETI effort. As the millennium came to a close it seemed that every country had an effort out there to search for intelligent life outside our Solar System. The Americans had NASA's Deep Space Network. The Germans ran their research at the legendary Max Planck Institut fur Extraterrestrische Physik. Project Phoenix, a privately funded project to search for extraterrestrial intelligence, operated in Australia using the Parkes 210-foot radio telescope in New South Wales. The Russians and the Chinese had also mounted their own independent efforts. Japan could not be left behind. In addition to the massive radio telescopes at Nobemaya, Kashima, and Mizusawa, the Japanese government, with the financial assistance of Sagata, had not only leased Cerro Tolo for a period of ten years from the Chilean government in an effort to bolster its capabilities in the Southern Hemisphere, but had also invested heavily to outfit the aging facility with state-of-the-art technology.

While Kuoshi mumbled something in Japanese, crossing his arms, Ishiguro grabbed a stool and sat next to Jackie, his dark eyes absorbing the graph on the screen. Sagata had recently built two radio telescopes at Cerro Tolo, one of them with a diameter of 350 feet, larger than the Parkes in New South Wales, making Cerro Tolo the world's most sensitive and comprehensive observatory of its kind.

Unlike regular telescopes, which were only useful for detecting radiation at wavelengths that could be seen with the human eye, radio telescopes covered a wide range of the electromagnetic spectrum, of which light was but a small part. The concept of radio astronomy was invented in 1931 by Karl

Jansky, an American engineer, following his discovery of the background radiation that originated from the thermal residue heat of the cooling Big Bang. Since their invention, radio telescopes had opened the door to the cosmos, allowing scientists to probe deeper into the far reaches of the universe, limited only by the ability to process the billions upon billions of bytes of information downloaded from their instruments. Until recently, this had been a crippling limitation for radio telescopes. While old-fashioned astronomers gazed through their telescopes and were rewarded with the instant gratification of live images, radio astronomers trained their sophisticated equipment on the stars and then had to wait for hours, days, or even longer, as the computers crunched away at the electromagnetic data and transformed it into an image. With the advent of the high-speed microprocessor and parallel computing, those waiting periods had been drastically cut down to the range of a few seconds, or even less, overnight making it the preferred tool of the deep space astronomer.

Armed with this sophisticated equipment, Ishiguro and his high-tech team scoured the sky, listening for microwave signals that might be deliberately beamed their way, or were inadvertently transmitted from another planet. The Japanese team focused their search in the 1–4 gigahertz (GHz) frequency range, encompassing the 1.420 GHz frequency emitted by hydrogen atoms. The accepted theory was that since hydrogen was the most abundant element in the universe, another intelligence would logically choose this frequency to communicate. Ishiguro's team divided their frequency search range into very small increments, or channels, 20 hertz wide, starting at 1 GHz up to 4 GHz—skipping bands used for digital cell phones and other high-tech equipment—resulting in billions of radio channels that had to be monitored simultaneously by their networked computers. This frequency search could only be focused on one spot in the cosmos at a time. At a monitoring, or scanning rate of one billion channels per second—which equated to searching through an *Encyclopaedia Britannica* and picking out a three-word phrase in one second—it took the system just over ten seconds to scan through all of the channels in the 1–4 GHz range.

Ishiguro Nakamura had selected 210 Sun-like stars within a distance of 140 light-years from Earth as his target area. Each star system ranged in size from one to a hundred times the magnitude of our Solar System. Depending on its size, Ishiguro assigned it a number of hits. Each hit represented a full frequency scan of ten seconds. Under Ishiguro's model, a star system the size of our Solar System would get ten thousand hits evenly scattered across the entire system in the hope of intercepting a stray radio signal between planets. That translated to just over a day of high-speed monitoring. Ishiguro wished he could spend more time on each system, but using this model, which certainly left a lot of uncharted territory, would still take his team almost seven years to complete the entire project.

"This is the signal," Jackie said, moving the cursor to a series of lines on a graph in the middle of the glaring screen, one of a dozen high-resolution monitors arranged in a circle inside the old observatory building, in the middle of which stood the observation post for the visual telescope. "It only lasted twenty seconds and we intercepted it at a frequency of 1.420 gigahertz."

He barely suppressed a smile. "Dead on the frequency of hydrogen."

"And quite strong." Jackie grinned.

"I see," Ishiguro said, his scientific poker face accentuating his sharp features. "That bandwidth is much narrower than the narrowest natural maser lines, suggesting that it could be artificially generated."

"And the signal was also pulsed and highly polarized, further supporting its artificial origin." Jackie pointed at the screen.

"Have you checked for terrestrial interference?"

Jackie nodded, taking another sip of diet Coke. In addition to the 350-foot-diameter radio telescope at Cerro Tolo, Sagata Enterprises—at the request of Ishiguro—had also built a second radio telescope fifty miles to the south. This remote-controlled radio telescope was only seventy feet in diameter and served the purpose of filtering out Earth-generated signals. Anything from microwave ovens to satellite downlinks made this naturally quiet section of the electromagnetic spectrum highly noisy. The seventy-foot radio telescope, with its limited range, could not pick out the distant signals emanating from Ishiguro's target search area. Therefore, all signals acquired by the smaller radio telescope were assumed to be of terrestrial origin and were filtered out of the acquired signals from the main radio telescope, leaving only signals generated in deep space.

"I didn't call you until after I had filtered it. It's definitely from our target area."

"Have you found a signal? Where is it?" asked Kuoshi. The young corporate liaison seemed quite nervous.

Ishiguro ignored him. "Have you mapped it?" he asked, even though he already knew the answer. His wife was the only student at Stanford who could match Ishiguro's vast knowledge of modern astrophysics. She was not only a superb scientist, but also a phenomenal researcher, and very thorough in her analysis of field observations. She was also gorgeous and in prime shape. Unlike Ishiguro, who had collapsed into the sedentary life of a scientist, Jackie never stopped jogging, which she did as a way to keep herself crisp and fight the dullness that often plagued this type of long-term research.

"Ishiguro-san! Are you going to tell me what this is all about?" demanded Kuoshi.

Ishiguro shot him a look. Out of all the weeks for him to visit, he had to be here during their first interesting observation in months.

"Chill, Kuoshi," said Jackie before Ishiguro got a chance to reply. "Why don't you go fetch us some drinks from the fridge?"

The corporate liaison stomped away cursing in Japanese.

Ishiguro smiled and winked at his lovely wife. She threw him a kiss. One of the main reasons he had fallen in love with her was because although Jackie looked Japanese, her personality was everything *but* Japanese. "Gotta keep those Jap bureaucrats in their place."

"Please do remember that they're footing this bill."

"And if they want their money's worth, they better keep out of *our* research." She dropped her voice while adding, "And out of our marriage." Sagata Enterprises had requested transferring Jackie to run the operation at Nobemaya. She had turned it down and also reminded their superiors that Ishiguro and she worked as a team. When Sagata had threatened to terminate her employment unless she transferred, Ishiguro had turned in his resignation. Sagata came back with an apology and a request that they continue their research at Cerro Tolo.

"Nobody's separating us." She ran a hand through Ishiguro's hair, just as she did when they made love, narrowing her eyes as she did so. Lovely, brilliant, and passionate. Jackie Nakamura warmed what would otherwise be a desolate and remote location in the cold Andes Mountains.

Ishiguro cleared his throat when he caught two technicians glancing their way. "So, *dear*, do you have a point of origin?"

The petite scientist, dressed in faded jeans and a Stanford sweatshirt, nodded, finishing the soda and dropping it in a wastebasket by her feet. "I'll have to check my results with the computers in Osaka in the morning, but my current analysis pinpoints the origin of the transmission to a point in space between HR4390A and HR4390B, two stars of the southern constellation Centaur, 139 light-years away, just barely inside our search envelope." She selected a couple of options from a pull-down menu and the powerful Hewlett-Packard workstation translated the billions of bits of data into an image of the faraway galaxy. She typed in the coordinates and a small red X appeared on the screen. "Right *here*."

Ishiguro stared at the thousands of stars making up one small fraction of the vast constellation. "Zoom in."

Jackie clicked her way through a few more menus, not only directing the radio telescope much closer to the two star systems, but she also used a custom software package to enhance the magnified image, sharply improving its quality.

Ishiguro stared at the screen long and hard, his mind considering the possibilities. But before he could contact Sagata and claim to have received an artificially generated signal from deep space, he first had to make certain that the signal was real by detecting it consistently from the same star system. "Have you checked our logs from—"

"Yes, and the answer is no. These two star systems are each roughly five times the size of ours, that translates to about six days of searching at fifty thousand ten-second hits per star system. We had finished our search in HR4390A and were two-thirds through the search on HR4390B when this signal came along. I've checked the logs for the search done to date and there is no indication of this signal ever being present."

Ishiguro nodded, staring at the monitor. "Well, let's extend the search of this system, focusing on this frequency and start hitting around the point of origin."

"You know that's going to require a decision record to deviate from our standard operating procedure, and only Bozo the Jap over there can approve it." She extended a thumb over her shoulder toward Kuoshi, speaking on a cellular phone at the other side of the room.

Ishiguro smiled. "He's probably calling Osaka to complain about your politeness, again."

She shrugged. "It's not my problem that the chauvinistic pig doesn't know how to treat a woman."

"He's not chauvinistic. He's just Japanese."

She exhaled heavily, extending her lower lip as she did, ruffling the bangs dangling over her forehead. "Thank God Mother married an American. Had it not been for Dad, I would have been raised just like her, submissive, subservient, and spending the rest of my life washing your underwear, pressing your suits, and being your sexual slave."

He shrugged. "I like the last part."

She made a face. "Lucky me." She reached for a drawer beneath the workstation and pulled out a blank decision record form. "Too bad right now I have to write a DR."

"I'll get it signed off. Kuoshi's just a rubber stamp around here."

"For how long do you want the DR?"

"Twenty-four hours. See if it surfaces again."

Ishiguro kissed his wife on the cheek and she patted him on the rear as he headed off to have his chat with Kuoshi Honichi, still blasting Japanese on the phone. Based on the look on the corporate liaison's face, the scientist knew that it was not going to be a pleasant conversation.

Chapter Three

000011

1

December 12, 1999

There are certain events that have a profound effect on some people's lives, when things may never be the same again. Marriages, births, divorces, deaths, even new jobs and layoffs become pivot events for many. Susan Garnett considered the untimely deaths of her husband and daughter such a transforming event, when life changed for the worse in a fraction of a second, altering her outlook forever. She began to measure everything according to this new perspective, finding that her world had indeed changed much since awakening from that long coma. The sun shone a little less brightly. The skies didn't seem quite as blue. Colors appeared bleached, food tasted blander, sounds seemed muffled, friends were distant, even her own parents didn't seem real anymore. In this surreal world, where nothing remained the same, where she could no longer cope with everyday events, when the fear of breaking down governed most aspects of her life, Susan Garnett had actually survived thanks to an even stronger force burning deep inside her.

Retribution.

The word had echoed in her mind over and over, again and again, bouncing off the outer walls of her consciousness, keeping her focused, keeping her alive, helping her ignore this alienlike world in which she now lived, where nothing, not even the most fundamental of feelings, had survived unscathed. She no longer loved, no longer felt, no longer cared. She had simply kept on to honor her family, to put the one person responsible for their deaths behind bars, to give him a taste of the personal loss that had stripped her of everything she considered vital in life. And now that she had achieved this personal vendetta, anger—the last human emotion still burning in her heart—had flamed out, leaving her core empty, dark, alone, with nothing left to live for.

And so Susan Garnett found herself in her apartment, sitting up in bed, the phone off the hook to keep Reid and the rest of the FBI from bothering her. She contemplated her life, her options, the shiny Walther PPK on the nightstand, the magazine in her right hand, a single bullet in her left.

She had left the FBI building at three in the afternoon, when she could no longer keep her eyes open. She had not felt guilty for leaving Troy Reid in their current situation, with the phones ringing every minute and everyone from the President down demanding answers. After all, she had done everything she could to catch the hacker. It was now time to wait—something Susan had found quite difficult to do these days, for it meant letting her mind go idle, encouraging dangerous thoughts. A Bureau car had dropped her off in front of her apartment building, and she had immediately gone off to bed, waking up thirty minutes ago, wondering what to do next.

Yesterday she had seriously contemplated pulling the trigger. Tonight she was no longer certain if that was the right thing to do.

Setting down the magazine and the bullet next to the gun, Susan grabbed the remote control and began to channel surf without really looking at anything, her mind revisiting her options. Her eyes landed on the clock display of the VCR over the TV. It flashed 7:59 P.M., almost twenty-four hours after last night's global event.

2

Troy Reid sipped at his coffee while going through the motions of reviewing several field reports before drafting his daily update to his superior, the associate deputy director of investigations of the FBI, who would further condense Reid's report, along with those generated by the criminal investigative division, the intelligence division, the laboratory division, the training division, and the office of liaison and internal affairs, before submitting his update to the deputy director. At that level the deputy director would also take inputs from the associate deputy directors of administration, and send a "big picture" report to the director, who would in turn brief the President.

He glanced at the computer screen on the corner of his desk, quickly reviewing the two paragraphs he had managed to write so far. Unfortunately there wasn't much to report at this time. Almost twenty-four hours after the bizarre event the FBI still didn't have one clue. And the Bureau wasn't alone. Susan's E-mail to the entire hacker community owned by the FBI had returned nothing beyond what she already knew. Either the hackers were holding back, or like the FBI, no one had any idea who had triggered the event last night. The two-hour-old CIA report on his lap indicated that the Agency also had nothing, and strongly suspected that the intelligence services of several friendly nations were in a similar state of ignorance.

Reid leaned back and rubbed his eyes. He had been here almost thirty-six hours and couldn't wait to wrap up the report for his boss and head on home to his wife of thirty years. She had called him an hour ago to see how he was weathering the storm.

He stretched and yawned, feeling fortunate to have such a loyal and understanding wife, who had stuck by his side through the years, putting up with his second love, the Federal Bureau of Investigation, where she was used to him working long hours. As a young and tough field agent in the seventies and eighties he had been on assignments for weeks at a time, on many occasions sleeping in the backs of cars or in the street. And his wife had always been home waiting for him, as well as sitting by his bedside when he had been hospitalized twice with pneumonia from exposure, and several more times after he had been kicked, stabbed, punched, and even shot once in the shoulder from behind by a twelve-year-old punk. The round had broken his clavicle before exiting just above his left pectoral, nicking the bottom of his chin, chipping the bone, and shaving a square inch of flesh. But Reid didn't care. He wore the scars of his profession with pride. The strain on his wife, however, had been pretty severe, which was part of the reason he had applied for retirement at fifty-five instead of sixty, to try to make up for some of the lost personal time. His wife was already counting down the days until his retirement next summer. Oddly enough, he found himself looking forward to a change of pace, figuring that three decades at the Bureau was long enough.

Reid rubbed the discolored tissue on his chin while glancing at his report. He leaned forward and began to tap the keys to conclude his daily update but the system did not respond. He pressed several keys with no effect. The system had hung up. He frowned and was about to press the CTRL, ALT, and DEL keys to reboot it when he noticed the frozen time on the system clock: 8:01 P.M.—the exact same time of yesterday's event.

Damn! It's happening again!

He grabbed the phone, but the line was dead. By the time he stood, walked around his desk, and reached for the door, his phone rang.

Puzzled, Reid turned around, staring at the black unit next to the PC. The event must have ended already. He picked it up while checking his system. The PC was alive again.

"Sir, we've just had another—"

"I know. Get Sue on the phone right away. Let's see if her software traps caught anything."

"Yes, sir."

Reid returned to his desk, sitting down. "Bastard," he said, staring at his screen. "Who are you? What do you want?" He tapped the side of the monitor with a finger while he considered the significance of this second event. The hacker had been cocky enough to try it two days in a row and at the exact same time. And, like yesterday's event, Reid could see no apparent damage done to his system. He browsed through his main directories, looking for signs of data loss, but found nothing abnormal. Next, he launched his virus scan software, which checked every file in every directory in the PC, also coming up empty-handed.

The phone rang.

"Sue?"

"It's busy, sir."

"Must I have to do everything myself?"

"But, sir, she is not—"

"Forget it. I'll call her. Get back to work. I want answers on this damned hacker!"

"Ye—yes, sir."

Reid slammed down the phone and dialed her number, cursing when he got a busy signal. He dialed the operator, but she could not pry into the line. Susan had the phone off the hook. He slammed the phone down again and buzzed one of his assistants.

"Yes, sir?"

"Send a car over to Sue Garnett's, *NOW*."

"Yes, sir."

3

Heavy knocking on the door pulled her away from her thoughts, the TV tuned to some sitcom rerun.

"Miss Garnett? Miss Susan Garnett? Open up, this is the FBI."

"You've got to be kidding me," she mumbled, switching off the TV and shoving the gun, the magazine, and the single bullet in the drawer of the nightstand. "Why can't you all just leave me alone?"

More knocking, followed by, "Miss Garnett? Please open up. This is an emergency."

"It's *always* an emergency," she said, putting on a robe over her pajamas as she walked toward the door, tying a knot across her waist.

Brushing back her short brown hair, she opened the door, scolding the two young agents standing in the doorway with her gaze. One agent was Hispanic-looking, the second blond with blue eyes.

"Let's see some ID," she said.

Both men reached inside their coats and produced laminated FBI ID cards. Special Agents Steve Gonzales and Joe Trimble.

She barely glanced at them. "You people don't know when to leave someone alone, do you?"

"I'm sorry, Miss Garnett, but Mr. Reid . . ." began Gonzales in a voice a bit soft for the large FBI agent. He was quite tall for a Hispanic, almost six three, with a slight receding hairline. He reminded Susan of actor Jimmy Smits.

She cut him off. "I've worked almost forty-eight hours without a break. What does he want to do? *Kill me?*" She thought of the irony of her remark after she had blurted it out.

"Look, ma'am," tried Agent Trimble, as tall as Gonzales, but with wider shoulders and a baritone voice, palms facing Susan. "There's been another event. Everyone's in a frenzy back at the office. We tried to call you but no one answered. That's why Mr. Reid sent us to—"

"Yeah, yeah, yeah," she said, "give me a minute." She closed the door and went through the motions of dressing, grabbing the first thing she could find. It turned out to be a pair of faded jeans, a white T-shirt, and a heavy woolen sweater. She opened the door a minute later, her laptop carrying case hanging from her left shoulder. "Let's go, boys. Don't want to keep Mr. Reid waiting, do we?"

The agents exchanged glances as she rushed past them. They followed her out of the apartment building. Agent Gonzales opened the rear car door for her. She tossed the carrying case across the backseat and got in, staring at her apartment complex, wondering when it would all end.

The sedan pulled onto the road. Trimble drove. Gonzales also sat in front, placing an elbow on the back of his seat while turning sideways, attempting a smile. "We'll have you back in no time, ma'am."

Susan nodded absently, her eyes still on the old brick building, where she had moved in after selling her Bethesda home—along with many other items from a life too painful to remember. She had tried everything to forget about her past, including going from traditional furniture to contemporary, from conservative clothes as a college professor to jeans, shirts, and sneakers as a hacker catcher; from a leather attaché to a backpack laptop carrying case; from long hair to her punkish cut. But the past would not let go of her. The memories refused to fade away, suffocating her, haunting her, torturing her. She dreaded the midnight hours, sleeping alone, on her side, hugging a pillow, missing Tom's embrace, his warm breath caressing the back of her neck as he hugged her from behind.

Soon, she thought, wiping away a tear.

"Are you okay, ma'am?" asked Steve Gonzales.

Susan nodded. "Got something in my eye, and the name's Susan."

"Yes, ma'am."

Susan sighed and continued staring out the window.

4

Cerro Tolo, Chile

Ishiguro Nakamura sat on a field of grass separating the observatory building from the massive radio telescope dish, atop a peak in the Andes Mountains, in the heart of Chile. He zipped up his sky jacket. Although December was the middle of the summer in the Southern Hemisphere, temperatures still dropped to the forties at night because of the altitude.

A starry night enveloped the long mountain range. The lack of city lights plus the high altitude made for spectacular star-gazing sessions. This was the reason why Cerro Tolo had been erected here many years ago, high above the cloud coverage that often blocked the view of the green valleys leading to the Pacific Ocean in this long and narrow country. The peaks of a hundred mountains projected through the clouds, their jagged outlines still visible in the night as trillions of distant stars shed their minute light on the planet, like a field of candles, pulsating in a surreal universal dance, radiating their energy on the majestic Andes.

Using a ten-inch telescope mounted atop a tripod, Ishiguro inspected this breathtaking sight, focusing on the southern constellation Centaur. This galaxy was 139 light-years away, which meant that the light reaching his telescope at this moment in time had traveled for 139 years.

He looked down at the Toshiba portable computer on his lap and used the pointer to select an icon on the screen. He clicked it, starting a slide show. The first image on the color screen was of the same constellation but as viewed by Cerro Tolo's main radio telescope at full power last night, when Jackie had zoomed in to get a closer view of the origin of that mysterious twenty-second signal. Ishiguro admired the constellation as it had looked 139 years ago.

This was the beauty of star-gazing, especially with the new generation of telescopes. By probing deep in space, Ishiguro actually looked back in time. But 139 light-years was insignificant relative to the vastness of the universe. He shifted his telescope to a point in the cosmos a little farther out, the nebula of Andromeda. To the naked eye it looked like a wisp of faint, hazy light shaped like a curlicue, near Andromeda's knee. Through his telescope, the hazy light became a swarm of churning stars, over a hundred billion of them, some young, others shining with amazing brightness, prior to their inevitable deaths. A star spent its life battling the gravity that pulled all of its mass toward the nucleus. These nuclear reactions at its center, resulting in incredibly high temperatures and outward pressure, kept the star from collapsing, balancing the inward gravitational pull for billions of years. The star's nuclear reactions, however, slowly evolved its mass into heavier elements, until it no longer had a source of nuclear energy to hold itself together, seizing in convulsions, swelling, vomiting its outer layers in spectacular displays of scorching interstellar matter, before spilling its white-hot heart across the cosmos, seeding the universe with carbon, oxygen, and hydrogen, the basic elements for life.

Ishiguro admired this galaxy, roughly 2.7 million light-years away, still quite close relative to other galaxies, but far enough for Ishiguro to take his next trip back in time. He advanced the slide show to an image of the nebula of Andromeda, taken by the radio telescope, noticing stars that no longer existed but from which light continued to shine through the vastness of time and space. He admired the enlargement in the center of the spiral galaxy, swelled by blue-white blazing suns, creating a stellar rainbow toward the outer edges of the nebula, feathery rings of violet, green, and dull red fading in the hazy distance.

Ishiguro continued on his journey through time and space, focusing next on the Pinwheel Galaxy, fifty million light-years away, a faint smudge of light through the ten-inch telescope, but a magnificent sight when viewed on his screen. He held his breath in silent admiration of this celestial cloud, alive with supernovas, imploding stars whose vast energy caused gas and elements to condense, then ignite again in a violent cycle that triggered the formation of new stars.

For a moment the astrophysicist felt like a cosmological archaeologist, digging through the layers of history, inspecting the relics from times past, preserved by the vast distances that light had to travel. He compared the electromagnetic energy across the entire spectrum, as captured by the radio telescope, from the time galaxies were formed to the present, making observations, taking notes on his engineering notebook, proposing theories of universal expansion, of the fading glow from the Big Bang, wondering, admiring, thinking, dreaming.

The Stanford graduate shut off the PC and lay back on the grass, gazing at the stars, dreaming about the birth of the universe, about how it all begun, about the Big Bang, the moment in time when the infinitely small universe, compressed into a space many times smaller than a proton, burst outward with the power of a trillion stars, setting time and space to zero, marking the cradle of the heavens. Shaped by the forces of gravity, electromagnetism, and nuclear fusion, this infant cosmos began to expand. Quarks, electrons, and antimatter formed. Matter and antimatter collided. Quarks combined, creating protons and neutrons, farther expanding the universe, shaping the laws of physics that Ishiguro had mastered at Stanford. Electrons combined with nuclei, triggering the birth of the first elements, hydrogen and helium, which, shaped by the enlarging forces of the universe, molded the first stars. The nuclear fusion of those first-generation suns formed heavier elements, beryllium, iron, zinc, copper, incorporating them in second-generation stars, and continuing in a perennial nova-supernova cycle that formed the first galaxies, the first nebulas, always expanding, always growing, always changing.

And it's still expanding, he thought, suddenly frowning when hearing hastening footsteps on the cobblestone walkway between the radio telescope and the observatory building.

"Ishiguro-san! Ishiguro-san!"

The scientist sighed, peering at the intrusion. Ishiguro considered his time alone with the stars sacred. These short periods of isolation, away from the drudgery of the daily problems of running Cerro Tolo while keeping his corporate sponsor apprised of their progress, was really the reason he had taken on the study of the universe as a career. He needed this time alone to think, to look inwardly, to absorb the vast knowledge that was out there for the taking, for the interpreting, for the analyzing. If only he had more time, like Galileo Galilei, Nicolaus Copernicus, and Johannes Kepler, to be alone, to let his mind wander, to consider new possibilities, new concepts, to appraise new philosophies, to ponder on past theories and formulate new ones that fit the most recent observations. If only—

"Ishiguro-san!"

"*Yes*, Kuoshi-san?" the scientist asked patiently, forcing control into his intonation. He had come to dread these week-long visits from the corporate types. At least Kuoshi wasn't as inflexible or radically bureaucratic as the last corporate liaison, who got transferred to another job eight months ago. But there was something about Kuoshi that troubled Ishiguro, though he couldn't figure out what. It seemed that there was more to Kuoshi Honichi than the role he played as corporate liaison. "*What* is it now?"

"We tried to radio you, but—"

"I never take my radio on my nights off, and *this* is precisely why." Ishiguro stood and began to collect his gear. "So, tell me."

"Another one!" the corporate liaison hissed. "We've detected another signal . . . from the same origin!"

Ishiguro suddenly forgot all about his contempt for the corporate robot standing in front of him. Leaving the telescope and his laptop behind, he snagged his engineering notebook and headed toward the walkway.

"What about this equipment?" he heard Kuoshi screaming from the field.

"We'll get it later!"

"But this is expensive hardware! What if it rains?"

Ishiguro smiled inwardly. How typical of a corporate executive to worry about a thing like that while on the verge of making the discovery of the millennium. "You haul it in then!" he shouted while going inside.

This morning, during one of her daily Internet excursions, Jackie had discovered that the timing of last night's signal from the southern constellation Centaur coincided with what appeared to be a worldwide computer freeze event, blamed on a new type of virus. Fortunately for Ishiguro and his team, the virus had not reached their systems in the Andes, not only sparing them from this dangerous event, but also allowing them to capture the incoming signal from outer space. Had their workstations been frozen, like so many other systems across the globe, the radio telescope would have stopped acquiring signals during that portion of time, missing what now seemed to be one of the most important cosmological events of the millennium.

Scrambling up the observatory's steps two at a time, he reached the main floor. The lights were off. Jackie and three technicians huddled around a glaring monitor, its pulsating glow forking through the spaces in between their bodies, casting a wan hue inside the large room. The clicking of his shoes broke up the silence, mixing with the humming of dozens of small fans cooling the HP workstations.

Ishiguro peeked in between two technicians, who politely stepped aside after noticing him. Jackie worked the mouse, clicking her way through layers of menus on one window while another window displayed the signal from yesterday's event in red and what had to be today's signal superimposed in blue. Beneath that window, a close-up map of the southern constellation Centaur displayed two X marks, one in red and another almost on top of the first in blue, their overlap shade reminding him of the violet hue of the nebula of Andromeda's feathery ring.

"They're not technically from the exact same origin," Jackie said, zooming in to the point in space between HR4390A and HR4390B. "But awfully close, about two million miles apart."

Ishiguro thought about that for a moment and suddenly opened his engineering notebook, making a few notes. "Hmmm, that's interesting."

"What are you doing?" asked Jackie.

Ishiguro closed the notebook. "Let's assume that the signal originated from a planet circling the smaller of the two stars, HR4390A, roughly five times the size of our Sun. If we also assume that this planet circles the sun at about the same speed as our Earth, sixty thousand miles per hour, that would translate to just under 1.5 million miles in a twenty-four hours pe—"

"What's going on?" asked Kuoshi, struggling inside the room while hauling the ten-inch telescope and the laptop.

"Hold on, Kuoshi-san. Anyway, the fact that the signals are two million miles apart should be expected if the transmission is coming from another planet. Can you zoom in as much as possible and clean up the image to see if we can spot the planet?"

Jackie shook her head. "I tried the strongest setting, but all I get is this." She clicked the mouse a few times and the image on her screen changed to one of near total darkness, save for a dimmed violet-white haze on the right.

Ishiguro leaned closer to the screen, trying to make out the round shape of a planet in the vastness of space. He could not.

"There's a few more interesting things about this event," Jackie said, tapping her screen with a pen. "Yesterday's signal pulsated for twenty seconds. Today's pulsated for only nineteen."

"Like a—"

"Countdown?" she said.

"Maybe. It could also just be interstellar noise altering the original transmission. Have you been able to make any sense of its content?"

Jackie shook her head. "That's another thing that seems unique about the signal. It's so polarized and of such narrow beam that you almost need to be right on the intended target on Earth to pick it up."

"So you can detect it but can't get a clean download of its contents?" asked Kuoshi Honichi.

"Right," she said. "Sort of like watching a car with tinted windows drive by. You see the car but not the driver or what's in the trunk. You need to be at its destination in order to see all of that."

"Where is this point on Earth?" asked Ishiguro.

Jackie made a face. "That's the last issue. Since we weren't sure if this signal would ever come again, we focused our efforts on scanning the sky around its point of origin. We know that the signal's headed for our planet. In fact, it looks like it's being beamed down somewhere in the American continent, north of the equator and south of Canada."

"Great," said Kuoshi, throwing his hands up in the air. "That sure narrows it down! What am I supposed to tell Osaka now?"

"Hey!" Jackie began to get up, her index finger cocked at the corporate liaison. Ishiguro put a hand on her shoulder while rapidly adding, "We're scientists, Kuoshi-san, working on what could be the discovery of the millennium. The only way to be successful is by cooperating with each other and understanding the difficulties of the task. Now we need your help. We think we have a good fix on the point of origin, but we need to nail down the destination. For that we will need a minimum of three satellites to perform a terrestrial triangulation."

Jackie exhaled heavily and remained seated, seemingly satisfied with Ishiguro's diplomatic intervention. Kuoshi nodded.

"All right," Ishiguro said, pacing in front of the group. "We have to do this by the numbers. Protocol is to contact another researcher with a suitably equipped radio telescope to confirm the event."

Kuoshi nodded. "Nobemaya. They have the best radio telescope in Japan."

"Okay. What about satellite coverage of the next event?"

"Which should occur tomorrow," added Jackie. "Assuming that the event is following a pattern."

"I'll have to contact Osaka and set it up with our own satellites."

"Okay. Now, Jackie, get on the phone with Nobemaya and follow it up with a detailed E-mail. If the contact is confirmed, we'll need to inform the

International Astronomical Union, as well as the secretary-general of the United Nations, again following international protocol rules for extraterrestrial contacts."

"No," Kuoshi said. "One step at a time. First the contact confirmation. Then we wait for instructions from Osaka."

Jackie stood next to her husband. "What do you mean?"

The corporate liaison crossed his arms, prepared to stand his ground on this one. "This operation is financed by Sagata Enterprises. Our executives will decide on the appropriate course of action once the contact has been confirmed by Nobemaya. Those are the rules. If you deviate, your employment will be terminated. Now I must contact Osaka."

The Japanese technicians from Sagata lowered their gazes. Ishiguro held Jackie back as Kuoshi left the room.

"Those . . . those *bastards*! I knew they would do something like this if we ever came across a signal!"

Ishiguro held her from behind. "Easy, there. Easy. Let's take it one step at a time. First the confirmation of the contact. Tomorrow we'll also find out about the origin. Come. Let's go get some fresh air before you have to contact Nobemaya."

They left the building not just to get out of the stuffy observatory room, but also to have some privacy. Ishiguro didn't trust the technicians from Sagata any more than he trusted Kuoshi Honichi.

A crystalline sky greeted them, having a soothing effect on Jackie Nakamura. She took a lungful of some of the cleanest air on the planet. It was cold and dry. The distant, snow-covered peaks of the highest mountains in the Andes looked down upon them beneath the starlight.

"This signal wasn't beamed for the exclusive monitoring of Sagata Enterprises' executives," she complained after a minute of gazing at the stars.

"Let's *play ball*, as you Americans like to say," said Ishiguro. "That way we're kept in the game. Our options remain open. Once we learn enough, we can apply some pressure to get this released."

"Why do I get the feeling that they have already thought of that possibility?"

Ishiguro patted her cheek. "You're worrying too much. Right now you should be ecstatic that it was you who first detected the signal yesterday. Do you realize that you could be the very first person on the planet to ever have picked up a signal from outer space—with scientific data to back it up, of course."

Jackie considered that for a moment and then smiled. "When you put it that way ... I guess you're right."

"You bet. And don't worry about Sagata. Kuoshi is simply following orders. Sagata can't contain this for very long, and when word gets out, you'll be the one on the covers of *Newsweek* and *Time*. Heck, maybe they'll even take your picture next to Jodie Foster. The actress next to the real thing." He grinned.

"That's why I love you," she said. "You've always found a way to calm me down, even back in college, when I couldn't sleep before an exam or a dissertation."

"I'm always here for you."

Ishiguro embraced his wife and gazed at the stars.

Chapter Four

000100

1

December 12, 1999

"I tried to call you," Troy Reid said the moment Susan stepped into his office, "but the phone—"

"I took it off the hook. I was hoping to get a good night's sleep and come in fresh in the morning." She made a face while sitting down. "*Obviously* you had other plans."

Troy Reid regarded her haggardly from behind his desk. He actually looked pretty consumed himself. Dark and puffy skin encircled his bloodshot eyes. A salt-and-pepper stubble reflected two days without shaving, and Susan thought she could smell his perspiration.

"Looks like our friend's back," he said in a voice hoarser than usual.

"That's what your two boys said, but couldn't provide me with any details," she replied.

"Same time as before, exactly eight oh one in the evening, local time."

"Did it also last twenty seconds?"

Reid slowly shook his head. "That's what I thought at first, but the official time was *nineteen* seconds."

She raised an eyebrow. "Nineteen, huh? *Exactly* nineteen?"

"On the nose." Reid locked eyes with her.

"You don't suppose . . ." she stopped.

"A countdown?"

She nodded. "Why do I get the feeling that tomorrow there's going to be another event at the exact same time?"

The aging Bureau officer frowned. "And it'll probably last *eighteen* seconds. I know. That's the first thing that came to my mind. That's why I sent for you."

Susan stared in the distance, the intriguing finding overshadowing her

55

exhaustion as well as her annoyance at being here again. She abruptly stood, snagging the carrying case next to the chair. The sooner she got started the sooner she could think about something other than killing herself. "I'd better go check the contents of the cocoons."

"Let me know what you find. It's obvious I ain't going anywhere."

2

Susan Garnett's system finished booting up, and she launched a program to access the information in all deployed cocoons.

SEARCH COMPLETE. WOULD YOU LIKE TO VIEW CONTENTS? Y/N

Susan pressed the Y key and the script automatically read the target address of each cocoon, mapping it to a string of binary code that acted as an access key, allowing her to view its contents. There was only one file inside each cocoon, just as she had suspected. The original virus had pierced each of her hundreds of software traps, infecting a decoy file inside each trap. The moment the decoy became infected, the trap's software automatically made a copy of the infected file and placed it in a separate directory within the software trap. This directory then cocooned itself, isolating the copied file from the original virus, which self-destroyed during the event.

Susan ran a script against the file in each cocoon, comparing a copy of the original, untainted decoy file with the infected version inside the cocoons. The difference between the two files yielded a passive copy of the virus itself. Susan dumped this inactive version of the virus trapped in each cocoon into a secured directory that acted as a petri dish to keep the code contained in case for some unanticipated reason it decided to wake up. She had to be cautious. She was obviously dealing with a highly skilled hacker, probably the best in the world to be able to pull a stunt like this one.

The custom petri dish software performed a comparison of the viruses, searching for differences in their signature strings. The process took less than one second of real time. She read the results on the screen.

PETRI DISH SOFTWARE
FEDERAL BUREAU OF INVESTIGATION
© 1999 BY SUSAN J. GARNETT
12-13-99   21:05:00
CC1 01011010.10101010.01011001.01110100.10111010.01000110.11010101
CC2 01111011.00101000.01011001.01110110.01111010.01000110.11010101
CC3 01001010.11101010.01011111.01101100.10111011.01000110.11010101

CC4 01101011.10101010.01111001.01110100.00100010.01000110.11010101
CC5 01110010.10101100.01001001.01111100.11111001.01000110.01010101
CC6 01111110.11101010.01111000.01110100.10111010.01000110.01010101

She inspected the signatures of the viruses from the first six cocoons for several minutes, the extreme complexity of the virus making her hold her breath. She browsed down and glanced at three more screens of signature files before going back to the top. The lines under specific bits within a byte highlighted the differences between the strains trapped in each cocoon.

"Here you go," Susan heard Troy Reid say from behind. Her superior placed a cup of coffee on her desk.

"Thanks." She picked it up and took a sip. Black and very hot.

"Got anything?"

Setting the cup next to the mouse pad, she pointed at the screen. "Sure do, but it doesn't look good." She took a minute to bring her superior up to date.

Looking over her shoulder, Reid said, "Damn. Looks like the signature string of the virus is different in every cocoon."

"Yeah," she said. A virus that mutated so much between replications was nearly impossible to catch, especially with such a long signature, because the possible combinations were nearly astronomical. Although the situation looked quite hopeless, Susan didn't get upset about it. "There's no way to clean it even if we knew the mutation pattern."

"What about writing a prescription to handle all possible permutations?"

She shook her head and wrote down some numbers on a piece of paper. "That won't work. Look."

> 1 Strain Byte = 8 Bits
> 7 Bytes = 56 Bits
> POSSIBLE COMBINATIONS = 2^{56} OR 7.2×10^{16}

"Astronomical," she hissed. "There are . . . how big is this number . . . one trillion repeated seventy-two billion times?"

"I get the point," said Reid.

"It's as close to infinity as we're ever going to get. I can certainly write a treatment to kill the few hundred strains that we've managed to capture, but there's no way to kill *every* strain out there. The next time the virus strikes, it will do as it pleases because it mutates every time, making it quite impossible to stop it from executing its directive . . . which brings me to the next step. Let's find out how much we can disassemble from the main body of this virus. Maybe that'll give us a clue."

She activated a custom disassembler, a software engine that used the ones and zeroes that all computers understand—also known as binary or machine code—and translated them into assembly code, a low-level program that showed the ones and zeroes as operation codes, or "opcodes," strings of instructions and data that a human can understand.

The screen changed to:

STATS
LENGTH: 1270 BYTES
COMPOSITION: 7% ASSEMBLY CODE 93% UNKNOWN
ORIGIN: UNKNOWN
HOST STATUS: INTACT
UNFILTERED STRAIN FOLLOWING . . .

100010110101010010110011111010101010100110001110001110101010101100110 11
01011010111010110010101010101010010101110101011001010101011010101011010
10011011010010101010010101111100101110010101010111010011011011101010 0010
01101010010100101001010010101101111110010100101001011100101010100100010
01011001101101011010111010110010101010101010010101110101011001010101 0111
01010101101010010110110100101010100101011111001011100101010101110100110110
11101010001001101010010100101001010010100101011011111100101001010100 1111001
0101001101101011010111010110010101010010101010010010110111010110010101010111
0101010110101001011011010010101010010101111100101110010101010111010011 0110
11101010001001101010010100101001010010100101011011111100101001010100 1111001
100010110101010010110011111010101010100110001110001110101010101100110 11
01011010111010110010101010101010010101110101011001010101011010101011010
10011011010010101010010101111100101110010101010111010011011011101010 0010
01101010010100101001010010101101111110010100101001011100101010100100010
01011001101101011010111010110010101010101010010101110101011001010101 0111
01010101101010010110110100101010100101011111001011100101010101110100110110
11101010001001101010010100101001010010100101011011111100101001010100 1111001
0101001101101011010111010110010101010010101010010010110111010110010101010111
01101010001001101010010100101001010010100101011011111100101001010100 1111001
100010110101010010110011111010101010100110001110001110101010101100110 11
01011010111010110010101010101010010101110101011001010101011010101011010
10011011010010101010010101111100101110010101010111010011011011101010 0010
01101010010100101001010010101101111110010100101001011100101010100100010
01011001101101011010111010110010101010101010010101110101011001010101 0111
01010101101010010110110100101010100101011111001011100101010101110100110110
11101010001001101010010100101001010010100101011011111100101001010100 1111001
0101001101101011010111010110010101010010101010010010110111010110010101010111
01101010001001101010010100101001010010100101011011111100101001010100 1111001

CONTINUE BROWSING? Y/N

"Not much got translated," she said, sipping coffee.

"Seven percent is better than nothing," Reid commented while Susan typed N.

A moment later short sections of opcodes and data browsed down the screen, in between long sections of machine code that the disassembler was not able to translate. She scrolled up to the first section that was translated.

"What's that doing?" asked Reid, pointing at the lines of opcodes of the highly customized assembly code. It could be read only by Susan—plus the two assistants she had trained to avoid leaving Reid hanging after she had killed herself.

She inspected the opcodes for a minute before saying, "This section's a straight counter that keeps the code in a loop." She reached for her engineering notebook and a ballpoint pen. "It's essentially doing this."

```
10 START
20 A = PREV
30 A = A + 1
40 IF A > 86400 THEN GOTO 70
50 PAUSE 1 SECOND
60 GOTO 30
70 CONTINUE EXECUTION
```

Then she added, "If you assume for the time being that the value in PREV is zero, then register A gets initialized as zero and begins to increment by one. As long as the value in register A is less than or equal to 86,400, the virus will remain in this initial loop, unable to go any further in the program. And each loop is essentially one second long."

"What defines the value in PREV?"

Susan shook her head. "Don't know. Maybe something later on in the virus." She typed a couple more commands and extracted the current value in register A. It was the number 86,400, meaning the loop had completed and the virus program had proceeded to the rest of its code.

"So, this code is sort of a delay circuit in the software, right?"

"That's *exactly* what it is." Reaching for her calculator, Susan punched in several numbers, repeated the operation just to be safe, and then looked at him. "The delay is set for 86,400 seconds, or twenty-four hours."

"This explains why it occurs only once per day."

Susan nodded. "It must reset itself somehow after execution and start over, ticking away until the following day."

Susan scrolled down, past many rows of machine code that the disassembler had been unable to decode, and reached another section of opcodes.

"Can you make this out?"

She nodded while scribbling in her notebook,

```
START
WAKE = MASTER. DATE
IF WAKE = 12.12.99 THEN GOTO FREEZE.20
IF WAKE = 12.13.99 THEN GOTO FREEZE.19
```

```
IF WAKE = 12.14.99  THEN GOTO FREEZE.18
IF WAKE = 12.15.99  THEN GOTO FREEZE.17
IF WAKE = 12.16.99  THEN GOTO FREEZE.16
IF WAKE = 12.17.99  THEN GOTO FREEZE.15
IF WAKE = 12.18.99  THEN GOTO FREEZE.14
IF WAKE = 12.19.99  THEN GOTO FREEZE.13
IF WAKE = 12.20.99  THEN GOTO FREEZE.12
IF WAKE = 12.21.99  THEN GOTO FREEZE.11
IF WAKE = 12.22.99  THEN GOTO FREEZE.10
IF WAKE = 12.23.99  THEN GOTO FREEZE.09
IF WAKE = 12.24.99  THEN GOTO FREEZE.08
IF WAKE = 12.25.99  THEN GOTO FREEZE.07
IF WAKE = 12.26.99  THEN GOTO FREEZE.06
IF WAKE = 12.27.99  THEN GOTO FREEZE.05
IF WAKE = 12.28.99  THEN GOTO FREEZE.04
IF WAKE = 12.29.99  THEN GOTO FREEZE.03
IF WAKE = 12.30.99  THEN GOTO FREEZE.02
IF WAKE = 12.31.99  THEN GOTO FREEZE.01
IF WAKE = 01.01.00 THEN CONTINUE MAIN EXECUTION
```

"Damn," Reid said, shaking his head. "This is a damned countdown to the year 2000."

"The virus checks the date in some master clock to see which day it is. It does so once a day, according to the opcodes at the beginning, and depending on which day it is, it goes to a different subroutine, which freezes systems for a specified time according to which day it is."

"But the first event took place on December eleven. This program shows the twelfth."

"You're right. This probably means that the virus is synchronized to a time zone east of ours, where the date has already changed," Susan said.

"It first happened at one minute after eight on the eleventh, which is one-oh-one in the morning on the twelfth, Greenwhich Mean Time."

Susan nodded, doing the math in her head. "So it's either synchronized to GMT or another time zone east of GMT."

"Right."

"So, on December twelfth, GMT, the event lasted twenty seconds. On the thirteenth, nineteen seconds, and so on. The question is: what happens on January first?"

She bit her lower lip, feeling her stomach knotting. The emotion momentarily confused her. She hadn't really cared about anything since her family died, except for catching Hans Bloodaxe. That carefree attitude had boosted her career at the FBI because Susan Garnett was never afraid to speak her mind. After all, what did she have to lose? Her superiors always knew she would provide them with a truthful assessment of a situation, free from personal biases or secret agendas.

So, why do you care now?

"Good question," she said. "Looks like as long as it is *not* January first, the main program is not being executed. The software bypasses it and orders another global computer freeze."

"What would happen if you advanced the system clock to January first? Would that force at least this system to experience what the world would on January first?"

She shook her head. "According to this code, the virus doesn't care what date is stored in the system clock. It gets its date from a master clock, probably from some central location. The only way to force it to show what would happen on January first is to advance its original clock, but in order to do that we also need to know its origin."

"Too bad."

"Actually, I would have been disappointed if this hacker, who has gone to such extreme measures to come up with this global virus, would have made such an obvious mistake by allowing anyone to just advance the clock and see what would happen on January first, which would then give us insight into how to protect our systems from such an attack."

Reid exhaled. "You got a point there."

She nodded and scrolled down to the next section of disassembled code. After reviewing the opcodes, she jotted down the translation for one of the freeze routines.

```
10 FREEZE.20
20 A = 0
30 EXECUTE LOCKKEYS
40 EXECUTE DISPLAYLOCK
50 A = A + 1
60 IF A > 20 GOTO 90
70 PAUSE 1 SECOND
80 GOTO 50
90 EXECUTE RELEASE KEYS
100 EXECUTE DISPLAY RELEASE
110 PREV = 20
RETURN
```

"So this is where PREV gets defined," commented Reid, rubbing two fingers against the two-day white stubble on his chin, making the raspy sound of sandpaper.

"Yes," replied Susan, working the keyboard and the mouse. "It provides an offset to the daily counter to compensate for the duration of the event, so that every day the virus occurs at exactly one minute after eight in the evening, local time. Pretty ingenious."

She scrolled down to the bottom of the file and found no other sections translated.

"So," Susan said, browsing through two pages worth of notes. "All we know is that it strikes once per day at the exact same time, one minute after eight in the evening. The initial event started yesterday, and it lasted twenty seconds. The second event, which happened today, lasted nineteen seconds. That information matches our findings in the disassembled virus."

Reid nodded, pushing his glasses up the bridge of his nose with an index finger. "The countdown starts twenty days before the end of the millennium with an event that lasts twenty seconds. Then nineteen seconds for nineteen days before January first."

"And so on. Also the freeze algorithm is fairly straightforward, locking the keys and the display while the internal counter in the virus regulates the length of the event depending on which day it is. And we know nothing else."

Reid leaned back. "Great. So we have confirmed what we already suspected about the countdown, but have no idea what will happen on January first."

"That about wraps it up."

"How do we figure out where it came from?"

She shook her head. "This is how I've done it in the past. I've even caught Bloodaxe this way. I trap a virus, dissect it, release a potion to the Internet, and ninety-nine percent of the time it also leads me to the source. This time, however, I have nothing. I get the feeling that my cocoons will capture the exact same thing tomorrow, and the day after."

"Any word of advice from our hacker community?" Reid crossed his legs and frowned.

She shrugged. "Everyone who had input has given it. There's nothing beyond the usual."

"What about Bloodaxe?"

Susan Garnett froze, before slowly turning to face her superior. "What about him?"

"Do you think he might know?"

A lump formed in her throat. She swallowed, acid spurting in her stomach at Reid's insinuation. "We didn't make a deal with him, remember? The man is a—"

Reid put a hand on her shoulder, his lined face softening. With his white stubble, round face, and large bulk, he began to resemble Santa Claus. "I know what he did, Sue. I'm the one who convinced the director not to make a deal, remember?"

Susan managed a slight nod.

"We all want to see the bastard rot in jail. But this problem is beyond all of us. The high-tech world is at its most vulnerable moment in history. You know there's going to be a lot of unexpected problems popping up all over the place when the clock turns from nineteen ninety-nine to two thousand. The last thing we need is some global virus corrupting files at the worst possible moment. This is a matter of national security. We must figure out what this thing is going to do and how to stop it. We need to get to the very bottom of the problem and we only have eighteen days to do it."

Susan Garnett stared in the distance, contemplating her situation, remembering the last time she had seen Hans Bloodaxe, cuffed, escorted out of the courtroom by two policemen after the jury found him guilty on all counts, sentencing him to life in prison for the murder of her family, as well as three other people in the Washington, D.C., area, pedestrians run over by automobiles. The bastard Bloodaxe had gotten what he deserved, not only condemned to spend the rest of his days in a federal prison, but also banned from ever accessing a computer system again. That latter punishment had been far more severe than the jail time, for it meant robbing the hacker of his purpose in life, like denying a musician access to a favorite instrument, or a pilot an airplane, or an artist a canvas and oils—forever.

Susan had stared into Bloodaxe's blue eyes as the judge pronounced the unexpected twist to the sentence. His face, quite composed during the delivery of the life sentence, had gone ashen. The hacker would have collapsed had it not been for the officers flanking him. The knowledge that she had inflicted so much pain on her family's murderer had finally quenched her desire for retribution. Now Reid was considering making a deal for information.

"Sue? You okay?"

"You know what's he's going to ask for, right?" Susan snapped, a finger cocked at ther superior. "The bastard could care less about the jail time. He's spent most of his life inside some dark room hacking anyway. He was already a hermit. Being in jail doesn't bother him. What's *punishing* him is the fact that he's a high-tech junkie, and now he's not getting his fix. *That's* the real punishment that Hans Bloodaxe received for killing my family. You ask him to help us out and he'll demand access to hardware and software in return. Are you seriously considering giving him that?"

Troy Reid removed his glasses, breathed on them, and kept them on his lap while pushing out his lips, obviously pondering his response. After a moment he said, "If he can help us prevent this virus from doing whatever it is that it might do, I'll consider allowing him some access under close supervision, to make certain that he's not concocting a high-tech reprisal. Personal issues aside, in my own judgment I consider that a fair business deal for vital information on this case. It's no different than previous deals the FBI has made with convicted criminals."

"Well," Susan said, crossing her arms, "have you considered the possibility that Bloodaxe's the one who set this whole thing up as an insurance policy in case he ever got caught? It's quite a coincidence that a few months after his conviction this virus suddenly comes out of nowhere, and now here we are, considering lessening his sentence in return for help in cracking another one of his viruses."

Reid made a face while contemplating that scenario, and then almost laughed. "I've got to hand it to you, Sue. You sure know how to put doubt in a man's head. You think he could have done this?"

"He's brilliant—no, he's *beyond* brilliance. Bloodaxe's in a class of his own. I can see how he could have worked secretly for months—maybe years— slowly creating his ultimate masterpiece, a virus that would be released in the event of his capture and conviction, a virus that no one else could break except himself, forcing the authorities to go back to him and offer him a deal for his assistance."

"Damn. I'm beginning to think that you just might have something there."

"For all I know, this could be one of a number of contingency viruses he's stashed away at secret Internet locations. Perhaps he's planning on releasing them one at a time to give him negotiating leverage. In a year or less he may have negotiated his way out of jail."

"An interesting, and somewhat scary, theory. But . . . can you *prove* it?"

"There's only one way to find out," she said, finishing her coffee. "Only one way."

Chapter Five

000101

1

The large millennium clock atop the National Gallery, overlooking Trafalgar Square, in the heart of London, England, washed the dawn skies with its crimson hues, its pulsating glow mixing with the city's gleaming holiday decorations.

Antonio Strokk stepped out of a black cab where Northumberland Avenue met Trafalgar Square, by the Charles I monument, blending with a mob of early-bird tourists already snapping pictures of the old king's equestrian statue and the impressive Nelson monument across the street. Its large stone lions flanked a granite column and bronze capital rising 185 feet high, with the statue of Nelson, England's greatest naval hero, at the top.

Strokk glanced up at the millennium clock, its nearly hypnotic rhythm momentarily distracting him. Christmas music flowed out of unseen outdoor speakers, attempting to brighten an otherwise cold and gloomy December morning in the English capital.

He zipped up his leather jacket before producing a city guide from his back pocket, pretending to study it while surveying the crowd. An Asian woman dressed in a business suit and holding a small colorful umbrella milled aimlessly about the square, pointing at the large lion statues while speaking Japanese. Two dozen tourists, mostly elderly couples, aimed their Sony camcorders at the sculptures, chattering among themselves and following her.

Strokk frowned, then walked across the street to inspect Nelson's statue, absently staring at the bronze reliefs on the podium, which illustrated Nelson's major battles in the Napoleonic wars.

The request had arrived three hours ago—reaching him only after being relayed through the normal channels—in the form of an address jotted on a napkin at a café on the other side of town. Obeying professional habits, Strokk had memorized the number before pocketing the napkin, which he had later torn up and dumped in a sewage drain. He had taken one underground trip and three taxicabs before emerging here, feeling confident that he had not been followed. Still, you could never be certain. The last cab had dropped him off four blocks from his destination, but Strokk would take a much longer route to get there. In his business it paid to be paranoid.

He leaned against the pedestal supporting one of the lions and continued to inspect the river of humanity crossing the famous square. Gloved businessmen in dark trench coats walked briskly by, holding briefcases, visibly annoyed at the slower tourists, particularly those stopping abruptly to snap photos destined to fill forgotten shoe boxes in attics or basements. A red double-decker bus cruised up Northumberland Avenue turning right on Strand.

Strokk clutched the small guide while walking down Strand, past Charing Cross Station, turning right two blocks later on Carting Lane, going across the Victoria Embankment Gardens, reaching the crowded embankment itself. Tourists and locals filled this area, many sitting on the benches facing the Thames.

According to the instructions, the pay phone was located by Cleopatra's Needle, London's oldest monument. First erected near Cairo by Pharaoh Thotmes III around 1475 B.C., the obelisk was relocated, along with its twin, to Alexandria in 14 B.C. One of the obelisks eventually made its way to London. The second stood today in Central Park, New York.

He reached his destination exactly fifteen minutes before nine o'clock, giving himself a buffer in case the phone was being used.

The phone was indeed being used. Two young American women were trying to make a collect call to the United States. For a moment Strokk shared the businessmen's irritation at the tourists.

Briefly considering his options, narrowed down to one when he spotted a pair of policemen patrolling the embankment, Strokk chose to stand a short distance from the Americans, far enough away to give them privacy, yet close enough to let them and others know that he was next in line. Shoving the guide in a back pocket of his jeans, Strokk rested against a lamppost, feeling the 9mm Sig Sauer pistol pressed against his spine, beneath his jacket.

He became anxious after a couple of minutes went by and the women didn't appear to make any progress. He felt exposed standing here, at a location known by at least a dozen people, half of them his own, the other half business associates who contracted his services on a regular basis. Still, Strokk didn't trust them. He barely trusted his *own* people, much less voices on the phone who made requests and transferred funds to Strokk's Swiss accounts upon delivery of services.

The anxiety made him shift his weight from one leg to the other, rubbing the Sig against the post, subconsciously trying to get reassurance from the weapon secured in a holster clipped to the inside of his jeans by the small of his back. Failing to do so, he checked his watch as the girls toyed with the phone for another minute before one of them turned to him.

"Sir?"

Strokk regarded her briefly. A college girl. Medium height, slim, blond with blue eyes, and dressed in a pair of denim jeans and a matching jacket, which she wore over a turtleneck sweater. He gave the two policemen another glance and decided to be polite. He didn't want to draw unwanted attention to himself. Although his face had been altered by the finest surgeons in Germany and his credentials described him as a Venezuelan businessman on holiday, Antonio Strokk could not take chances.

"May I be of assistance?"

"Yes. My girlfriend and I are trying to—"

"Call home collect?"

She smiled. "Do you mind showing us how? We can't figure out the instructions."

Strokk hid his amazement. The instruction plate on the booth had been designed for a five-year-old. That observation, however, triggered his answer. "The problem is that this phone is only for local calls. The international phones are located on the other side of the embankment."

The girl exchanged a glance with her friend before turning back to him and slapping the side of her thigh. "Well! That explains that!"

The other girl brought a hand to her face. "I feel, like, sooo stupid. I told you we should have called from the hotel."

Strokk smiled, hiding his growing annoyance. "Actually, that's the best place to make international calls. Pay phones are too unreliable."

The college kids thanked him and walked away.

Strokk checked his watch. Four minutes before nine. Keeping an index finger pressing down the phone's hook, he lifted the receiver and held it against the side of his face, pretending to be listening while surveying the embankment. An old lady was selling flowers from a white bucket. The two policemen chatted with a tourist pointing to a map. A couple held hands while watching the vessels on the Thames. He remained tense, having much to fear from this particular customer, who was just as demanding as his Libyan, Colombian, or Irish clients, but equally generous. His clients often commissioned him for tasks needing a lot of casualties, like the mission he'd completed three months ago in Colombia, which had required him to kill over fifty people, some of them American tourists, at a crowded nightclub in Bogotá, just a month before the country's presidential elections. He had done this to convince voters that the current president could not guarantee their safety. Four weeks later the president lost the election to a younger candidate owned by the political party who'd hired Strokk as an insurance policy during the elections. Unlike the old days, when a government faction would openly cheat to get in power—or to remain in power—nowadays the Colombians had learned the art of manipulation and deception to achieve their political goals—a lesson learned from more developed nations.

The phone rang at exactly nine o'clock. Strokk released the metal hook.

"Is it raining in London?" asked a voice tinged with a French accent.

"No, but it is storming in Paris," Strokk replied, completing the code.

"The National Gallery," continued the voice, "behind the wastebasket between Monet's *Water Lilies* and Van Gogh's *Sunflowers*."

The connection was broken. Strokk calmly hung up and made a brief phone call before returning to Trafalgar Square, stopping on the way at a sidewalk café for a cup of espresso and a toasted bagel, which he ate while watching the traffic thickening on Strand, as well as on Northumberland.

Having operated out of London for the past ten years, Strokk knew that the National Gallery didn't open until ten. At nine forty-five, he left the café and continued down Strand, taking a left on Ducannon, walking past St. Martin's church, and stopping amid a dozen tourists admiring the equestrian statue of George IV, the first monument erected in Trafalgar Square. Children played beyond the monument, one of them, a girl not older than five, clung on to her father's leg while glancing oddly at the gentleman atop the horse wearing a Roman toga.

Strokk regarded them with the stoic indifference of someone who could kill without remorse, of someone who had laughed at men, women, and children bellowing in agony, of someone who had never needed friendship, of someone who trusted not loyalty but *fear*. His small army *feared* him. He paid them handsomely for their services, but they obeyed and never betrayed because of *fear*. They all had seen firsthand what happened to those who dared break faith with Antonio Strokk, often provoking the most inhumane of punishments.

Ten o'clock.

Strokk turned away from the soft tourists and ascended the steps leading to the National Gallery's main entrance, for a moment glancing at the huge millennium clock atop the ornate structure. The massive numbers, almost ten feet tall, had been flickering for over a year.

He looked about him. A small crowd had already gathered there. A woman wearing black jeans and a dark brown jacket approached him from the side, brushing against him, her left hand moving too fast for anyone but Strokk to see, before briskly walking away. Strokk verified that his operative had removed the Sig Sauer clipped to his back before stepping into the gallery's lobby and going through the metal detectors installed years ago to protect the priceless works of art from the bullets of a madman. He would retrieve his weapon after obtaining his instructions. In the event that he needed to defend himself while inside the building, Strokk's hands and feet qualified as deadly weapons, as well as the fiberglass blade strapped to his left ankle, or the garrote he could strip off his belt in seconds.

He reached Gallery One a few minutes later, walking down a wide hallway flanked by some of the world's finest paintings. Rembrandt's *Self-Portrait*. Da Vinci's *The Virgin of the Rocks*. Rubens's *Le Chapeau de Paille*. He finally found Monet's and Van Gogh's works, his dark eyes zeroing in on the trash receptacle against the far wall. This early in the morning only three other people were visiting this section of the gallery, a couple engaged in low-level conversation while pointing at someone's artwork, and a security guard standing by one end of the hallway.

He had observed six surveillance cameras, two at each end and two toward the center of the long and wide corridor.

Strokk walked up to Monet's *Water Lilies*. He had never cared much for the work of the French artist but pretended to enjoy it nevertheless while inspecting the metallic receptacle just a few feet to his right. He walked casually toward the wastebasket and leaned down, while pretending to tie the laces of his sneakers. Peeking in between the wall and the receptacle, he spotted a manila envelope, which he quickly slipped into his jacket before proceeding to the nearest exit.

Once outside, he retrieved his weapon from the same female operative. Together they walked straight to a nearby underground station, Embankment Station, catching the yellow Circle Line to High Street Kensington Station.

"*¿Lo encontraste?*" Celina Strokk asked. She was as tall as her brother, with closely cropped blond hair, and a gaunt face that made her brown eyes and full lips quite pronounced, giving her a somewhat unrefined but appealing look. Her pale skin came from her Russian heritage, but her Latin features made her look more Hispanic than Slavic. Celina could pass as either not just because of her physical appearance, but also because, like her brother, she was fluent in several languages, including Spanish, Russian, and English.

"*Sí,*" Strokk replied while patting the right side of his jacket. Together they often reverted to their native tongue.

The ride on the "Tube," as the London underground was locally referred to, was uneventful. They got off at the High Street Kensington stop. Walking up the oval-shaped tunnel—its brick walls layered with advertisements—they reached a long escalator leading to the surface. Strokk and Celina went up, reaching the street, heading down Kensington High Street, toward Holland Park, taking a left on Earl's Court Road.

Strokk kept a safe house three blocks away, a two-story brownstone near the intersection of Pembroke and Earl's Court Road.

Once inside, he sat at the kitchen table while Celina made some coffee. He tore open the envelope and inspected its contents, a couple of typed reports, a city map of Washington, D.C., and vicinities, and a half-dozen photographs taken with a telephoto lens. He studied the first brief, a report from the European Economic Community relating to software preparations for the year 2000. By the time Celina brought two cups of dark Colombian coffee, he had already moved on to the second brief, which described the global virus and the ongoing investigation at the FBI. He glanced at the photos, the reverse side of each containing an explanation.

Celina sat down next to her brother and asked, "*¿Quién es ella?*"

Strokk stared at one of a handful of photographs of an FBI analyst named Susan Garnett. "The lead investigator at the FBI on the strange computer virus that's causing all of the commotion."

Celina reached behind her and removed her pistol, a Beretta 92FS, and set it on the table. She planted both elbows on the polished mahogany surface and brought the cup of coffee to her lips. "And our mission is?"

"Same drill as the executive from California a year ago."

Her right eyebrow rose. "Yes . . . I remember."

He pointed at the laptop on the small desk in the open living room. "Log in. Check the account."

Celina brought the cup of coffee with her and began to pound the keyboard.

As he heard the laptop's modem dialing, Antonio Strokk returned his gaze to the photographs. A medium-height, slim woman in her mid-thirties. The brief dossier on the back of the largest photo, a color eight-by-ten, mentioned the deaths of a husband and a child a couple of years back, victims of a traffic accident caused by a computer virus. Strokk would have felt sorry for her, but he had no such feelings left in him. This was just another job for the former Russian Spetsnaz officer, and the thumbs-up that Celina gave him while pointing at the screen officially initiated this operation.

As Celina logged off the system, Strokk stood. "Gather the team. We're leaving immediately through the usual route."

2

Paris, France

A wave of Fiats, Renaults, BMWs, and Mercedes rushed past the tourists gathered by the obelisk in the center of the Place de la Concorde, at the south end of the Champs-Élysées. The wide boulevard, known to Parisians as the Voile Triomphale, or Triumphal Way, began at the Louvre, passing through the lush Jardin des Tuileries, across the Place de la Concorde, and up the Champs-Élysées to the Arc de Triomphe.

The Paris vista known the world over bustled with activity during the lunch hour. Horns blared. Street vendors shouted. The mellow tunes from a sax player outside the American embassy blended with the sounds of children singing Christmas carols on the steps leading to the terrace overlooking the Louvre and the Seine. Beyond the Arc de Triomphe, down Avenue Kléber, across the Seine, rose the Eiffel Tower, completed in 1889. High up on this world-class monument stood a millennium clock, its constant flashing marking the passage into a new era, a new one thousand years of human history. Its powerful display stained the steel beams with its crimson light, pulsating upon them, bringing them to life, the surreal effect visible even beyond the Louvre and the world-famous Hôtel Crillon, past the gardens surrounding the Palais de l'Élysée, home of the Ministère, the various ministries of the government.

Philippe La Fourche, minister of industry and economy, stood by the windows behind his desk, gazing at the Palais de l'Élysée, the presidential residence across the Boulevard Saint Honoré. The elderly politician, dressed in a fine Italian suit, kept his hands behind his back while contemplating the arched entryway to the elegant palace. The president was not home today. He was traveling to Brussels to meet with the leaders of the other EEC nations to discuss final preparations for the transition into the year 2000. Included in the discussion would be the level of preparedness of Europe's vast computer networks.

La Fourche pressed his wiry lips into a frown at the state of his country's computer systems, the result of negligence on the part of his president for failing to dictate stern policy to force corporations and government offices into a unified plan to get Year 2000 compliant, like the Americans had done.

"Quel imbécile," La Fourche mumbled, his eyes gazing at the palace. His president, as well as the presidents of the other European nations, had underestimated the task, and had further ignored the severe economic consequences of such neglect. While the United States led the Y2K-compliance race with their systems approaching the ninety-five percent compliance mark, France was still in the low eighty percent range.

La Fourche, whose future as minister of industry and economy depended on how well France survived the millennium bug, had spent the past months desperately searching for ways to get his country higher up on the compliance ladder. But he had found that there was no quick way to fixing France's remaining Y2K problems, mostly in embedded computer chips—those controlling equipment ranging from elevators and copy machines to medical monitors, traffic lights, fuel-injection systems, and a variety of military applications. The mighty United States had invested hundreds of billions of dollars in the past three years to get to where it was today. France didn't stand a chance this late in the game to get past eighty-five percent, even with so much help pouring in from the United States and England.

And the president is going to let me take the fall for this, even though it was his negligence that got us in trouble in the first place, he thought, anger swelling up in his gut at the thought of the many times he had requested his president to take action. A week ago, frustrated, La Fourche had been on the verge of resigning, having explored all viable avenues and seeing no way out of his predicament.

But then this global virus had struck, threatening all countries, regardless of their level of preparedness—in a way, leveling the playing fields. And a thought had struck him: Control of the potion that killed this virus meant control of one of the most powerful pieces of software in the world. The value of such software was beyond his imagination. If America spent hundreds of billions of dollars fixing Y2K problems, it would not blink at spending a fraction of that to acquire the cure for this potentially dangerous virus.

And so, Philip La Fourche, resigned to the fact that he would be politically ousted, had opted to use his last days in office to find a way to get his hands on that potion.

Turning around, La Fourche faced a man in his early fifties sitting across from his desk.

"All set then?" the minister asked, also sitting down and crossing his legs.

Henri Jourdain, the corpulent chief of the Direction Générale de la Sécurité Extérieure (DGSE), the French version of the CIA, gave him a slight nod. "The contractor should be on his way today, monsieur."

La Fourche shifted his gaze from Jourdain's square face to the computer on the corner of his desk. "Is the mission clear?"

The seasoned spy nodded. "The contractor's mission is three-fold. First he will spy on the FBI as it struggles to crack this global virus. Second, in the event of a breakthrough, he will be ready to steal the potion from the Americans and deliver it to us. And third, he will make sure that the Americans can't reconstruct the potion, leaving them at our mercy."

Philippe La Fourche nodded, keeping his eyes on his computer system, not wanting to know exactly how this contractor was going to achieve all of that in such short time. "Have you used him before?"

"*Oui, monsieur.* With the most satisfactory of results last year in California."

La Fourche nodded, remembering an operation that had resulted in the recipe for manufacturing a faster video controller. The contractor had forced the Sunnyvale executive to yield the schematic database, before killing him and setting his company ablaze. "That was him?"

"*Oui, monsieur,* and he will deliver again. This time his results will benefit us directly." Like La Fourche, Henri Jourdain was equally motivated to use his last days in power to set up his future. Jourdain, as well as several other close friends of the minister, would all be politically banished following La Fourche's downfall.

The minister locked eyes with the DGSE chief. "He can not fail us, or we lose everything."

"He *will* deliver, monsieur, regardless of the cost. And then we will have the power to name our own price. Many countries will pay dearly for the code. We will be set for life."

Exhaling heavily, the fourth most powerful man in France returned his attention to the windows, to the presidential palace, to the lush gardens leading to the Champs-Élysées, to a country that would soon betray him, outcast him, disgrace him. As Henri Jourdain left the office, a passing cloud momentarily blocked the noon sun. The elder official watched it in silence.

Chapter Six

000110

December 13, 1999

Susan Garnett sipped coffee while waiting for the guards to escort Hans Bloodaxe to one of the visitor's rooms at the Haynesville Correctional Institute in northern Virginia, just an hour's drive from Washington, D.C.

Windowless walls of peeling off-white paint washed by the grayish glow of fluorescents surrounded the FBI analyst as she contemplated the single metal door. A metal table bolted to the concrete floor stood in the center of the room. A steel hook had been secured to the table with thick bolts. Susan eyed it, momentarily wondering its purpose, while sitting on one of four metal chairs nervously crossing and uncrossing her legs. The murderer of her family would soon walk through that door and Susan feared that she would not be able to contain her deep-rooted hatred for that man.

She set the cup of coffee on the table and shook her head in amazement. *Exactly what are you doing here, Sue? What do you expect to accomplish?*

Leads, clues, suggestions, anything! Troy Reid had shouted before sending her off to Haynesville. *Just be sure to come back with something to keep this investigation alive! The White House is on our asses demanding answers!*

She took a deep breath and checked her watch. *Almost five o'clock.* The virus would strike in another three hours and she had no idea what to do different from the day before to learn something new. Her software traps were already deployed and—

The door creaked open. Susan sat upright, hands on her lap, shoulders aching with tension, hazel eyes zeroing in on the handcuffed figure dressed in a gray jumpsuit flanked by two corpulent security guards, their bulging biceps stretching the short sleeves of their khaki uniforms.

The figure in gray raised his head, brown eyes flashing instant recognition.

Bloodaxe abruptly stopped, but his lanky frame could not match the forward momentum of the guards, who lifted him off the ground with ease and sat him in a chair across from Susan.

She took a deep breath, hiding a mix of anger and apprehension at meeting with this man. The smell of cheap cologne assaulted her nostrils.

"You—what in the *hell* is going on?" Bloodaxe, who had grown a beard in the months since the trial, turned his gaunt face to the guard on his left. "Hey, man! What in the fuck's going on? I thought it was my lawyer coming to see me! I don't want to see *her!*"

The guard he was addressing, a large African-American, slapped Bloodaxe in the back of the head, not very hard, but firmly enough to get the inmate's undivided attention. "Quiet, moron. Warden's orders. Now, be nice to the lady, or I'll whack you again."

"Lady? You're calling *her* a lady? She's the reason I'm stuck in this—"
Whack!

"All right, all right! Just stop that, would ya?" Bloodaxe said, rubbing the back of his head as he stared suspiciously at Susan Garnett. The African-American guard planted himself right behind the inmate. The second guard left the room.

The FBI analyst remained calm and expressionless while watching the show. Bloodaxe's nervous reaction to her presence injected Susan with confidence.

She addressed the guard. "Could you give us some privacy, please?"

Bloodaxe's eyes narrowed.

"Are you sure, ma'am?"

She nodded.

"All right, but I'll be right outside if you need me." He walked next to the hacker. "Okay, moron. Assume the position. Hands on the table."

Bloodaxe sighed and complied, spreading his legs while resting open palms on the table. Susan now understood the purpose of the large metal ring on the table. The guard released one of Bloodaxe's hands, ran the cuff through the hook, and cuffed him again. With the table bolted to the floor, Bloodaxe could not reach Susan Garnett sitting across from him.

The guard stepped out, leaving the master hacker and the FBI analyst staring at each other.

"So, to what do I owe the pleasure?"

Susan forced her personal feelings aside, struggling to remain professional in front of this man. "I need a favor."

He laughed and then became serious. "You've *got* to be kidding me, lady."

"I've never been more serious in my life."

The hacker shook his head while smiling. "You people are amazing. You put me in here, remember?" He raised his hands as much as his restraining hardware allowed him. "You bastards made deals with every other damned hacker out there, but chose to stick me in here and throw away the key. Give me one good reason why I should help you."

"Because you killed my family?"

His narrow face beneath the beard tensed. He regarded Susan for a moment before saying, "I didn't mean to kill anyone. I stated that many times during the trial. I merely released a virus to screw up traffic lights, but in a way that they would not cause accidents. I wanted to punish those city manager bastards for what they did to me. I despise those corporate types. Hire you one day, use you, and then fire you when they no longer need your services. And then they turn around and do it again to someone else. I had to teach them a lesson."

Her temples beginning to throb, Susan remembered quite well the angle Bloodaxe's lawyers had taken during the trial, trying to make him look like the victim of corporate greed—a pathetic attempt at justifying his actions. The jury had still found him guilty on multiple counts of manslaughter. The judge, with a little encouragement from the Federal Bureau of Investigation, had sent him to prison for life without parole. In the end, the master hacker had gotten just what he deserved.

Breathing deeply, trying to remain calm, refusing to let herself get dragged down into this useless argument, she said, "I didn't come here to discuss your views on that incident."

"Oh?" Bloodaxe raised an eyebrow.

"I'm here to talk about a different incident."

"Really?" He leaned back, a smug grin surfacing on his face. "Don't tell me. Like a virus you can't figure out on your own?"

"There's been a global event," she added, ignoring the remark. "It started two days ago."

"So I've heard. Everyday program. Same bat time, same bat channel. What else is new?"

"So you know about it," she stated.

"Just because you bastards don't allow me to use a computer doesn't mean I haven't been keeping up with the business."

"What do you know about it?"

"Not so fast. First you tell me what *you* know."

"Not much beyond what's in the papers."

Bloodaxe smiled. "Don't insult me."

Susan contemplated her next sentence. If he was indeed the owner of the virus, he was apparently trying to learn how much the FBI had figured out so far. If he wasn't the owner, then his questions were justified. Either way, it was obvious to him that the FBI had to know much more than what was printed in the papers. She offered, "We were able to trap a copy of the virus."

"I figured that much already." He leaned forward. "And?"

"We found a twenty-four-hour counter, which explains the daily events." "And?"

She told him about the freeze routines counting down to January first. "And?"

"And that's it."

"What about the signature file?"

"Changes with every mutation."

"Have you figured out the sequence?"

She shook her head. "The number of combinations are astronomical. Our systems can't break it. It appears truly random."

The easy-knowing grin had vanished. Bloodaxe's face became rigid, his eyes staring in the distance, like those of a doctor listening to a patient's symptoms before issuing a diagnosis. He was either truly interested or was pretending to be interested in order to get information.

"Did you find a random number generator?"

"No."

"Then how do you know it is random?"

She pressed her lips for a moment. "It's either random or very nested."

"Nested," he said.

"If it's nested, then we're talking several nesting levels, which is just as bad as being random, unless we happen to come across the nesting key. Otherwise, it would take centuries for today's systems to check all possible permutations for the master sequence."

The hacker grinned. "Multiple nests. A sequence within a sequence within a sequence. And you're right. It could be multiple levels deep. Given what you've said so far, I'd say it's a minimum of seven to eight deep. It gives the appearance of a random sequence but it's really not. The problem's that, like you said, with today's machines it will be impossible to counter it without the key. How did you catch it?"

She told him about how the virus would self-destruct after each daily event, forcing her to release software traps to grab a passive version.

He frowned. "Of course. I should have known. What else were you able to disassemble?"

"Not much more, I'm afraid. After the last freeze routine, which will occur on December thirty-first, the code will execute one final routine. I'm speculating that this sequence will trigger a destructive global event at a time when the world's networks would be at their most vulnerable point: January first, 2000."

"A virus strike on zero one, zero one, zero zero. That's beyond genius," he said, marveling at the thought. "Now that's one mean, and smart, son of a gun you've got there, lady—assuming, of course, that the virus actually does something more than just blowing smoke."

"I have to assume that it's something much worse than simply someone trying to show off skills."

"Of course you do. You Feds always think the worst of people." He lifted his cuffed wrists.

"So, are you going to help us?"

Bloodaxe placed both forearms on the table, flanking the metal hook limiting his movements. "Why should I?"

Susan also leaned forward. "I've already told you why."

"You don't understand. What's in it for *me* if I help?"

"The knowledge that you will be paying back society for all the pain and suffering that you've caused."

The hacker made fists of his hands. "I'm already doing that!" he protested, an edge developing in his voice. "At least that's what the judge told me when he delivered that sentence, plus the cruel twist that must have originated from the FBI . . . from *you*."

Susan was running out of options. She had promised Troy Reid that she'd offer computer privileges to the hacker in return for information leading to the antidote of the elusive virus, as well as capture of its originator. But she had not promised him that she wouldn't try another angle first, like appealing to the hacker's sense of decency. "Maybe you will sleep better at night knowing that your skills actually helped society, probably even spared it from chaos if this virus turns out to be as damaging as I'm assuming it'll be."

"You're going to have to do better than that. I sleep like a baby already, and you have only one last chance to tell me why I should help you." He leaned forward, dropping his voice a few decibels. "And *think hard.* Otherwise I'm calling for that head-slapping gorilla outside to take me back to my cell."

She closed her eyes, knowing that granting him computer privileges was the same as commuting his sentence. Susan considered her options. If Bloodaxe was not the source of the virus, but he *did* help, and his assistance prevented this global virus from causing pandemonium at the end of the millennium, then it would seem fair—as much as she personally hated the idea—that Bloodaxe be granted supervised computer privileges. On the other hand, if the little bastard had created the virus as a way to get himself some leverage, then Susan would make certain that she used the information Bloodaxe gave her to not only kill this virus of his, but also find a way to turn that around and prove that he had been the originator.

"We're prepared to offer computer privileges in return for your assistance."

The master hacker leaned back on his chair, his haggard face beneath the unkempt beard relaxing, his eyes blinking excitement. "*Now* you're talking."

"This will be a supervised privilege, of course."

He nodded. "Of course. Don't want you guys to think that I'm going to abuse it by creating a retaliatory virus, right?"

"Let's just say that you're going to have to earn our trust."

He considered that for a moment. "Fair enough."

"Now it's your turn," she said, crossing her arms and tilting her head. "Tell me something I don't already know."

"You took the obvious first step and you caught a passive version of the virus that essentially confirmed the information which you already had. The countdown. The freeze routine. But you didn't really *learn* anything that will help you kill this thing."

Susan slowly shook her head. "I hope you're going somewhere with this."

"The problem is that you're not a hacker. In order to catch hackers you have to *think* like one. Over the years you've obviously recruited enough of us to help you nail others, building up a machine whose product is not really a result of your technical brilliance but the brilliance of others."

Susan frowned. "If I didn't know any better I would say that you've just insulted my technical skills."

"Don't get me wrong. You're quite smart. In fact, smart enough not just to teach at a university, but to learn enough from your previous FBI cases to figure a way to trap me. But again, professors and FBI analysts are not hackers. You don't know how to bend the rules. That's why you need us. But you seemed to be bothered by me stating the truth."

"The truth?" she said, inhaling deeply. "Exactly what do you think you know about the truth?"

Bloodaxe leaned forward again, locking eyes with Susan. "You came here today, Susan—as personally difficult as that may have been—because *none* of the hackers on your staff were able to provide you with options beyond this vanilla-flavored cocoon. You have probably been struggling with this unavoidable visit just as you have been struggling with your feelings since that judge pronounced that sentence, sending me here, in the process quenching your desire for retribution. But the problem is that me being here is not going to bring them back. They're dead, and whether or not I had something, albeit involuntarily, to do with their deaths is irrelevant. So you find yourself suddenly without meaning, without a reason to go on. You joined the FBI to catch me. Now you have and you don't know what to do next, where to go, what to do to fill that emptiness that eats you alive every night. How is that for the truth, Susan Garnett?"

If Susan had her Walther PPK in her hands, she had no doubt she would have pulled the trigger, blowing this monster out of her life forever. Flashes of her last seconds before the accident filled her mind. Rebecca singing . . . Tom reading . . . the impact . . . the sky and the exit ramp swapping places. Then nothing, just emptiness, loneliness, desolation—feelings she had replaced with the unyielding resolve to catch this bastard.

Taking another deep breath, controlling her emotions, she kept her gaze leveled with Bloodaxe's inquisitive stare. "You see a lot, Hans Bloodaxe. But can you see enough to help us kill this virus?"

His face suddenly becoming somber, the master hacker nodded. "Yes, I can."

Chapter Seven

000111

1

Inside a cold warehouse several blocks north of Dupont Circle, Antonio Strokk sat on the stained concrete floor with his back resting against one of many wooden crates occupying the majority of the floor space of a hardware distribution center.

Strokk was not alone this late evening. Scattered around the unloading area were three of his subordinates, plus his sister, Celina, all wearing black nylon jumpsuits, skintight gloves, and black sneakers. Terrorist-style hoods lay by their sides.

They had arrived at Dulles International aboard three separate flights from London throughout the day, converging at this location, a safe house for DGSE operatives. Just as his instructions back in London had indicated, three of the crates housed the equipment his team would need to carry out the current contract.

Strokk reached for an Uzi submachine gun and held it in his right hand in an upright position, pointing the muzzle at the warehouse's corrugated metal ceiling. As his right hand depressed the grip safety, Strokk used his left hand to pull the cocking handle of the unloaded weapon all the way back, keeping his index finger off the trigger, testing the resistance of the cocking lever spring, trained ears listening to the latching mechanism.

The weapon felt right, balanced, powerful. Pressing the trigger released the cocking handle, which remained in its original, uncocked position because there was no round in the firing chamber. Had there been one, the pressure of a detonating 9mm Parabellum round would have pushed the slide back, ejecting the spent cartridge and loading a new one from the magazine, leaving the Uzi ready to fire again.

Strokk performed a basic field strip. He used very fine oil soaked in a soft cloth to clean the different sections meticulously. His eyes looked for imperfections or hairline fractures in the weapon. He checked for barrel bulging, problems with the extractor, the return spring, and the general integrity of the breechblock. Satisfied, he reassembled the submachine gun, inserted a forty-round magazine, rested it on his lap, and screwed on a bulky silencer.

Strokk eyed his troops, all former Russian special operations forces—Voiska spetsial'nogo nazacheniia, or Spetsnaz for short. Most of them had been operatives or officers of any one of several special-purpose units. Strokk himself had belonged to a Spetsnaz unit within the old KGB umbrella, charged with gathering intelligence and acting on that information for the benefit of the Rodina. Other members had been assigned to Spetsnaz units affiliated with the Russian Ministry of Internal Affairs (MVD). Two of his men had belonged to the Vitiaz', one of the finest special groups within the MVD. After the collapse of the Soviet Union, however, many of these Spetsnaz teams had been disbanded or merged with other units to better serve the new Russia. But Antonio Strokk chose to capitalize on his talent, on his training, selling his services to the highest bidder. At first he had gone solo, becoming a contract assassin, operating mostly in the former Soviet republics. Then he'd expanded into Germany and France when Celina joined him. Over time his reputation grew, attracting new members, eliminating larger targets, expanding into new territories, eventually going global, climbing to the upper echelons of the international terrorist community.

In spite of his field experience, Strokk felt a tinge of excitement. Tonight's mission would allow him not only to eliminate some Americans, but also to penetrate the FBI's computer network—with the handy technical assistance of Celina, his skillful sister also field-stripping her silenced weapon.

Antonio Strokk was the product of a one-night stand between Nikolai Strokk, a colonel in the KGB serving as military attaché at the Soviet embassy in Caracas, Venezuela, and a local woman working the embassy's switchboard. Strokk only shared the same father with Celina. Her birth had been the result of another one-nighter with a local street dancer a few months before Strokk was born. Apparently Nikolai Strokk had a weakness for beautiful Latin women, but he also had the sense of accountability, paying for their education in private schools. When his kids reached the age of nine,

Nikolai Strokk took them with him to Russia, against their mothers' wishes, and completed their education at the finest schools in Moscow. Antonio Strokk chose the military path, joining the Spetsnaz. Celina went technical, earning an engineering degree before being recruited to spy for the technical division of the KGB, until its dissolution in 1989.

Strokk rose to his full height of six feet, slinging the Uzi across his broad back, and verifying that his Sig Sauer pistol was safely holstered, as well as the ten-inch knife strapped to his left ankle. "Ten minutes," he said, rubbing a gloved hand over his pockmarked face.

At exactly 7:30 P.M. the warehouse's garage door automatically lifted and a single Ford Aerostar van headed down Sixteenth Street, toward the White House, turning left on M Street, and then right on Ninth Street, stopping in a dark alley near the corner of Ninth and H Street, just three blocks from the J. Edgar Hoover Building. The street was nearly deserted, even at this early-evening hour, mostly due to the high crime rate plaguing the nation's capital.

"Equipment check," said Strokk, breathing the cold night air, his ebony eyes surveying the dark alley, condensed air curling up as he spoke. Opening a Velcro-secured pouch on his jumpsuit, just above his waist, he removed a pair of miniature headphones. A dark wire connected the headpiece to the two-way radio safely tucked inside the pouch. A flexible, voice-activated microphone extended from the side of the headphones. Strokk adjusted it so that it barely touched his lower lip.

"Radio check," he whispered. The response of his team members came clearly through the miniature headphones.

Reaching for his dark cotton hood, he slipped it over his head, taking a few seconds to line up the holes with his eyes, momentarily enjoying the warmth the cotton hood brought to his face.

The operatives accompanying him did likewise.

"Time," he said, cueing his team to start their digital chronographs. Strokk expected to complete this phase of the mission in eight minutes. No more and no less. One operative remained with the van. The rest, Celina included, followed Strokk.

The foursome moved out swiftly, quietly, blending with the cold and humid night, their dark silhouettes racing down the filthy alley, reaching the deserted street, cruising past a small basketball court enclosed by a chain-link fence. Their silenced Uzis leading the way, the team dashed over an unkempt field bordering a red-brick building next to the court. A pair of pines shaded the twenty feet separating the chain-link fence from the back of the small building. Beyond the small field projected a small parking lot, which at the moment held a half-dozen automobiles.

Strokk pointed two fingers in that direction. Celina and one operative cut right, disappearing behind the trees as Strokk and another operative raced around to the front, briefly stopping at the side of the building, next to a bundle of ISDN high-speed modem lines running down the side of the house and into the ground.

"One minute," Strokk spoke into his mouthpiece. "Measure your fire. Do *not* damage the equipment."

His pulse quickening, his lungs expanding as he inhaled through his nostrils and exhaled through his mouth, Antonio Strokk slowly walked up the wooden steps, reaching the front door. A sign that read CAPITOL.COM hung next to the entrance. Putting an ear to the wooden door, right hand clutching the Uzi, which he had set to single-shot mode, Strokk listened to what sounded like a television.

"We're in position." Strokk heard the voice of Celina, covering the rear door.

Stepping back, he let his companion pick the lock, before slowly turning the knob.

"Commence elimination phase," Strokk hissed into the microphone as he rushed inside the small lobby. A security officer munching on a sandwich while sitting in front of a small television set abruptly stood, eyes wide in surprise. Dropping his dinner, the guard reached down for his holstered sidearm.

Strokk fired twice. The silent rounds made a soft clapping sound as they tore into the guard's chest and neck, shoving him back into his chair, blood jetting onto the cluttered desk.

The dark silhouettes rushed across the foyer, furnished with weathered chairs, a sagging sofa, and walls lined with bulletin boards under gray fluorescents.

Strokk removed the keys from the security guard and used them to unlock the thick door leading to the interior of the building, which housed the servers for the local Internet service provider. He burst into the main room, expecting chaos at the sight of hooded men bearing automatic weapons. Multiple screams echoed inside the murky interior, illuminated by the pulsating glow of a dozen color displays, the sound mixing with footsteps and hastily spoken words.

Bodies rushing between desks, humming servers, and glaring monitors filled his field of view. Many screamed, others cursed, some dove for cover behind desks and filing cabinets. A few raced toward the back door of the building.

Strokk lined up the closest figure and fired twice, a cloud of blood and foam erupting from his chest and neck as he fell on the carpeted floor while thrashing pathetically. Another shot to the head and motion ceased.

Strokk switched targets, automatically pressing the trigger, taking out the technicians one at a time with surgical precision, without damaging the equipment, with the satisfaction that he was delivering a powerful blow to the Americans and their high technology. The former Spetsnaz officer carried out his contract with icy efficiency as skulls burst, as chests exploded, as figures collapsed over the carpeted floor, on their desks, against the walls.

A man reached the rear door, opening it, trying to escape, but an invisible force shoved him back into the room, victim of Celina's deadly accurate fire.

It was over in thirty seconds. As Celina cleaned up a terminal and began to work the keyboard of a Unix workstation, Strokk and the other two operatives set up a defense perimeter. One of them wore a security guard uniform beneath his black suit. He took the place of the dead guard, whom Strokk dragged inside the main room while the second operative cleaned up the blood splashed on the desk and chair.

The front lobby secured, Strokk's second operative took a position behind the building, hidden in the shadows of the pine trees, the perfect vantage point to cover their getaway.

Strokk gave his handiwork one last glance before pulling up a chair and watching his sister perform.

2

Three blocks away, Susan Garnett sat quietly in her office, working her keyboard, trying to get everything ready prior to her deadline, the time when the virus would strike again: one minute after eight this evening. The time was now fifteen minutes past seven and the seasoned FBI analyst had her door closed. A DO NOT DISTURB sign hung from the doorknob.

Night had fallen on the nation's capital. A moon in its third quarter diffused its wan light through the half-open blinds covering her windows, providing the only illumination in the murky room, aside from the glare radiating off her laptop's color screen.

Bloodaxe's basic idea was to include a "Scent" string at the beginning of each software trap deployed across the Internet service providers not just in the Washington area, but also across the nation. As normal Internet traffic flowed across the ISPs, Scents, transparent to the network, would tag onto programs containing the countdown sequence Susan had disassembled from the passive virus trapped in one of her software cocoons. That conditional attachment algorithm guaranteed that a Scent would attach itself only to the mysterious virus as it replicated its way across multiple networks in preparation for the next event. Bloodaxe had speculated that the virus infection rate was exponential in nature, doing most of its growth across systems in the final minutes prior to the event, climaxing to maximum expansion the nanosecond before systems froze.

At 7:40 P.M., Susan Garnett wrote a program in C++ that automatically loaded thousands of Scent files into a larger program that resembled a Trojan horse. She released tens of thousands of Trojan files onto the Internet, reaching Internet service providers across the United States, covering every possible path in and out of the country, including a dozen Teledesic satellites in low Earth orbit and all eight Hughes Electronics' Spaceway satellites in geostationary orbit, used heavily by Internet traffic.

Each of the Trojan horses released its pellets upon entering their assigned ISPs, "scenting" every virus crossing their network. Another one of Bloodaxe's theories was that not all of the mutations automatically erased themselves during the freeze routine, leaving the authorities without any leads to follow after the event. The master hacker believed that among these "warrior" self-destructing mutations were "queen" mutations, highly sophisticated versions of the warrior virus tasked with monitoring the deployment of the troops prior to the strike. Bloodaxe had proposed that while the warriors used the event to self-destruct, the queens used that time to return to the source. The Scents would make a trail for the FBI to follow by using a "Sniffer," another brainchild C++ program of Hans Bloodaxe. Susan had found Sniffer and Scent, and dozens of other custom programs, in a remote ISP in Oregon, where the hacker kept his most coveted programs. Bloodaxe had given her the ISP address after they had signed an agreement to allow him use of a personal computer under the supervision of a local software technician. The privileges would be removed if his help did not result in the eradication of the virus.

At 7:50 P.M. Susan leaned back in her swivel chair and rubbed her temples. She had done it. The feedback from the ISPs indicated a successful deployment of Scents. Now it was time to wait.

Susan stood and stretched, yawning. She stepped outside her office and into an ocean of gray cubicles under an array of fluorescents, heading for the rest rooms on the other side of the open area, but she didn't get that far.

"All set?"

Susan turned around, regarding Troy Reid, leaning against a gray cubicle wall, arms folded. He wore the same pair of slacks and white shirt from this morning. He looked worse, still unshaved, and probably with a body odor that matched her own.

"Looks that way." She checked her watch. "It's now just under ten minutes to show time. I'm going to fall asleep unless I sprinkle some water on my face and get some coffee. Be right back."

"I'll walk with you."

She brought him up to speed on the way, stopping at the entrance to the ladies' room. "I think I can manage in there by myself."

Reid waited for her with a mug of steaming black coffee when she got out. She sipped it as they walked back to her office, sitting side by side in front of her laptop. The time was 7:59 P.M.

"All right," she said, checking the digital timer that was synchronized to the last virus strike. "Here we go. Fifteen seconds . . . ten . . . five . . . three . . . two . . . one."

Her screen froze, triggering the start of a new event. Susan kept her eyes on the digital clock next to the laptop.

"Eighteen seconds," she said the moment the system returned to normal. She had her fingers ready and tapped the commands required to release tens of thousands of Sniffers to go after the queen viruses. "Let's hope Bloodaxe was right."

The Sniffers expanded radially into every ISP in the area, resembling an army of hound dogs following the prey's scent, searching, smelling, tracking. The packets of C++ code spread across New England in the first few seconds, reaching the southern states and the Midwest five seconds later. California and Washington were last, roughly ten seconds after Susan had released them.

"Got one tracking in southern Colorado," she said moments later, when one of the Sniffers E-mailed a small file, or "Bark," back to her, announcing a hot trail, a direct match between the code in Scent and the code in Sniffer. The Bark included the coordinates of its current ISP in longitude and latitude. A surge of confidence suddenly swept through her. The hunt was on.

In the next thirty seconds her electronic hounds were barking from hundreds of ISPs all over the United States, following the scent left behind by the queen viruses returning to the source. She could track their progress visually on an electronic world atlas, which read the incoming coordinates and automatically mapped them on the screen, also recording the event in digital video in memory for future review.

Susan had selected a map of North America as a starting point, ready to pan around depending on where the Sniffers went. Black dots representing Sniffers tracking prey moved about on the light blue map in seemingly random fashion, hopping from ISP to ISP, many of them crossing paths, separating, and doubling back, before slowly heading south. The dots began to cluster on a Hughes Spaceway satellite in geostationary orbit over southern Mexico and Guatemala. Susan scrolled down to position the icon representing the Hughes satellite in the middle of the screen. The map in view now covered all of Mexico, the Gulf, and portions of Central America. The dots moved from the satellite down to a location in the middle of the Yucatán Peninsula.

And then they disappeared, marking the original location of the virus.

"Where is that?" asked Reid.

"According to the last recorded Bark, the virus originated at . . ." She zoomed in on the location where the dots had converged before vanishing. "Looks like longitude ninety degrees and thirty minutes west. Latitude seventeen degrees and four minutes north."

She zoomed in some more, clicking an option to add names of regions, cities, rivers, and mountain ranges.

"But that's in the middle of nowhere. There shouldn't be any ISPs down there."

"Middle of the jungle," Susan added, disappointed. "The lowlands of the Petén, to be exact." She pointed to the name on the screen. "In Guatemala, around sixty miles from the border with Mexico."

"Where is the closest large city?"

"That would be either Belmopan to the east, in Belize; Guatemala City, two hundred and fifty miles to the south; or Campeche, to the north in the Yucatán Peninsula. The closest towns are El Subín, to the east, or Tenosique, to the west, by the Río San Pedro, both around fifty miles from the coordinates."

"Something went wrong," Reid said, getting up. "This doesn't make sense. How can the world's most sophisticated virus emerge from such a remote location?"

Susan remained sitting, dragging the mouse to an icon on the top left corner and double-clicking it. A window opened up that resembled a VCR remote control. She clicked on the PLAY button and watched the digital video of the short event. The Barks originated from hundreds of ISPs within seconds, moving in a random pattern before heading south, hopping from one ISP to the next, then beaming up to the Hughes satellite, and back down toward the Petén jungle. "I don't know what to say. The Sniffers all converged on only one location."

"I'm not buying it," Reid said, rolling up the sleeves of his shirt to his elbows. "You might want to make a call to Haynesville for more help. Looks like something may have fooled the Sniffers, sending them astray."

Susan remained silent, staring at the screen as she replayed the event a second and third time. "Do you think that the queen virus has a scent of her own? Perhaps something that overpowered our own scent?"

"Possibly. But how can we tell?"

Just then a notification appeared on her screen. HANSB@HAYNES.GOV wanted to start an Internet chat with her.

"That's strange timing," said Reid, leaning down.

"Not really. He said he would check in right after the event." She clicked on it.

HANSB@HAYNES:	HOW DID IT GO?
SGARNETT@FBI:	I SEE IT DIDN'T TAKE YOU LONG TO GET ONLINE.
HANSB@HAYNES:	JUST LIKE RIDING A BIKE. WHAT'S THE STORY?
SGARNETT@FBI:	I THINK THE SNIFFERS FOLLOWED THE SCENT TO THE WRONG PLACE.
HANSB@HAYNES:	WHAT DO YOU MEAN?
SGARNETT@FBI:	I THINK THAT THE QUEEN VIRUSES HAD A SCENT OF THEIR OWN, OVERPOWERING THE ONES WE TACKED ON TO THEM.
HANSB@HAYNES:	IF THAT HAPPENED, THEN THE SNIFFERS WOULD HAVE BECOME ERRATIC, GOING TO NO PLACE IN PARTICULAR. IS THAT WHAT HAPPENED?
SGARNETT@FBI:	NO. THEY ALL CONVERGED ON A SINGLE LOCATION.
HANSB@HAYNES:	THEN THEY WERE NOT FOOLED. IT'S IMPOSSIBLE FOR THE SNIFFERS TO CONVERGE ON A LOCATION THAT DID NOT ALSO HAVE THE SCENT. THAT'S THE NATURE OF THE SCENT-SNIFFER PROGRAM. THEY DEPEND ON EACH OTHER. THE SNIFFER ONLY HAS ONE DIRECTIVE: TRACK AND FIND THE

	SCENT. NOTHING ELSE. THAT VIRUS ORIGINATED WHERE THE SNIFFERS TOLD YOU IT ORIGINATED.
SGARNETT@FBI:	IN THE JUNGLE IN THE MIDDLE OF THE YUCATAN PENINSULA?
HANSB@HAYNES:	I SEE. TELL ME EVERYTHING THAT HAPPENED.
SGARNETT@FBI:	WHY DON'T I SHOW YOU INSTEAD? HOLD ON.

Susan launched her E-mail software and sent Bloodaxe the video clip.

HANSB@HAYNES: GOT IT. GIVE ME A SECOND.

Susan played the video on her screen once again, pointing at the images while saying, "He's right, you know. If the Scent had been altered or over-powered, then the Sniffers would have remained roaming the continental United States, like now." She tapped her finger on the plasma screen. The black dots were spread all over the map without a pattern, like a shotgun blast. "But now they are converging, see? They have found their match and are going after it, all the way to the origin . . . right here." She zoomed even more, selecting an option on the top menu to add all labels to the map, including sites of historical significance.

"Interesting," she mumbled.

"What is?"

"This." She placed the cursor on the exact coordinates transmitted by the Sniffers before they vanished. "The coordinates are right in the middle of the Tikal ruins."

"Tikal? That's the Aztecs?"

She shook her head. "No. The Maya."

"How do you know?"

"From my Georgetown University days. In addition to my teaching re-sponsibilities, I managed the university's Web page, with the assistance of several grad students. We set up Web pages for many departments, including the department of natural science. In order to do justice to each department, we would do some research first. Two of my kids spent a couple of weeks researching pre-Columbian history, including the history of the Maya and the Aztecs. Although we did this about five years ago, I do recall that the Maya populated the Yucatán Peninsula, including portions of southern Mexico and most of Guatemala. The Aztecs were primarily located in central and northern Mexico, not in the south."

Before Reid could reply Hans Bloodaxe sent a new message.

HANSB@HAYNES:	NOW I'M MORE CONVINCED THAN BEFORE. AS BIZARRE AS IT LOOKS, I'M WILLING TO BET ANYTHING YOU WANT THAT THAT'S THE ORIGIN.
SGARNETT@FBI:	I BELIEVE THAT THIS IS THE PLACE WHERE THE SCENTS WENT. BUT WHAT IF I TOLD YOU THAT THE COORDINATES PUT IT RIGHT IN THE MIDDLE OF THE MAYAN RUINS OF TIKAL?
HANSB@HAYNES:	THAT WOULD BE STRANGE. THERE IS ANOTHER POSSIBLE EXPLANATION. I'M THINKING THAT THE QUEENS SOMEHOW RECOGNIZED THE SCENTS AND EJECTED THEM, ALONG WITH A BOGUS DESTINATION, SENDING ALL OF MY PUPPIES TO BANANA LAND. I SUGGEST YOU GET YOUR GOVERNMENT PALS TO TAKE SOME HIGH-RES SHOTS OF THE AREA ANYWAY. SEE IF SOMETHING SHOWS UP. TOMORROW WE'LL TRY SOMETHING A LITTLE DIFFERENT.
SGARNETT@FBI:	WHAT'S THAT?
HANSB@HAYNES:	A MUTATING SCENT THAT CAN ONLY BE TRACKED BY A SNIFFER PROGRAMMED TO THAT MUTATION SEQUENCE. KIND OF LIKE FIGHTING A VIRUS WITH A VIRUS. THERE IS A CHANCE THAT THE QUEENS ARE ALL SUPPOSED TO BE MUTATION SEQUENCES THEMSELVES, MEANING EACH IS DIFFERENT FROM THE OTHERS. ATTACHING THE SAME TYPE OF SCENT TO EACH ONE MAY HAVE TRIGGERED SOME KIND OF GENERAL ALARM, PERHAPS DEFAULTING INTO A ROUTINE THAT EJECTS THE COMMON CODE AND SENDS IT TO A BOGUS LOCATION. MAYBE WE'RE JUST DEALING WITH SOME FIREWALL MECHANISM BUILT INTO THE QUEENS TO PREVENT EXACTLY THIS TYPE OF TRACKING.
SGARNETT@FBI:	IF THAT'S THE CASE, THE OWNER OF THE VIRUS MUST HAVE DETECTED THIS GENERAL ALARM AND IS PROBABLY EXPECTING A COUNTERATTACK.
HANSB@HAYNES:	THAT'S ALWAYS A POSSIBILITY. WE DON'T HAVE A CHOICE, THOUGH. I'LL PREPARE THE VIRUS THIS EVENING AND SEND IT TO YOU BY MORNING.
SGARNETT@FBI:	BE WAITING FOR IT. ANY LUCK BREAKING THE CODE I COULDN'T DECIPHER ON THE VIRUS PROGRAM?

HANSB@HAYNES:	WORKING ON IT. IT RESEMBLES NONE OF THE KNOWN ASSEMBLY LANGUAGES. SO I'M TAKING A SLIGHTLY DIFFERENT ANGLE.
SGARNETT@FBI:	WHAT'S THAT?
HANSB@HAYNES:	NOT QUITE SURE YET. JUST DIFFERENT FROM WHAT I'VE TRIED SO FAR. LET YOU KNOW WHEN I GET SOMETHING. GOTTA GO NOW. DON'T FORGET TO GET THE PENTAGON TO START LOOKING AT THAT LOCATION. THERE'S A CHANCE THAT WE MAY HAVE FOUND THE ORIGIN ALREADY.

Susan broke off the connection.

"Sounds like he's cooperating," commented Reid, still standing next to her.

The combination of tension and exhaustion pressed down on her like a ton of bricks. Keeping her arms to her sides, Susan raised her shoulder as much as she could and rolled her neck, eyes closed, trying to relieve some of the stress. "Seems that way. So far he appears to be keeping his end of this deal. This whole thing is still very difficult for me. I can't believe we let him use a computer again."

"I know it is difficult, and I commend you for putting your personal feelings aside and keeping it professional. Do you still think he could be behind this virus?"

"I don't know what to think anymore, Troy. On the one hand he appears to be putting in an honest effort to help us out. On the other hand . . . how can you trust a person who was responsible for the death of your family?"

Reid didn't respond. He simply patted her back, his tone of voice fatherly as he said, "Hang in there, kid. You're doing just fine. We'll be out of the woods in no time."

Susan nodded. "What about contacting the NPIC to get some satellite shots of the region? Plus it would be a great idea to scan that area for any signs of electronic equipment," she said, referring to the national photographic interpretation center.

"I'll give them a call. With some luck I should have some prints in the morning."

"Let's give our new virus a quick check," she said, pulling up the passive version and loading it into her petri dish to check the mutation sequence.

PETRI DISH SOFTWARE
FEDERAL BUREAU OF INVESTIGATION
©1999 BY SUSAN J. GARNETT

12-13-99 21:15:00
CC1 01011010.10101010.01011001.01110100.10111010.01000110.11010101
CC2 01111011.00101000.01011001.01110110.01111010.01000110.11010101.
CC3 01001010.11101010.01011111.01101100.10111011.01000110.11010101
CC4 01101011.10101010.01011010.01110100.00100010.01000110.11010101
CC5 01110010.10101100.01001001.01111100.11111001.01000110.01010101
CC6 01111110.11101010.01111000.01110100.10111010.01000110.01010101

"That looks pretty familiar," she said to herself, launching her disassembler and running it against the body of the new virus. "Now, let's see if we can learn anything new."

STATS
LENGTH: 1270 BYTES
COMPOSITION: 7% ASSEMBLY CODE 93% UNKNOWN
ORIGIN: UNKNOWN
HOST STATUS: INTACT
UNFILTERED STRAIN FOLLOWING . . .

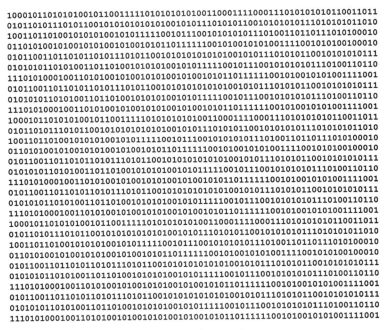

"Looks the same as yesterday's," Reid noted.

Susan frowned. The disassembler had decoded the exact same percentage as the night before, meaning that she would not be learning anything new. "Let's see if any of the undecoded sections have changed since last night."

Using a custom script, she performed a DIFF between the sections of the virus that had not been decoded. To her surprise she found that a section of 260 bytes had changed drastically, starting at Byte 367 to Byte 627. The rest of the virus, including the section that defined the routine to be executed at one A.M. GMT on January 1st, had not changed.

"What do you make of it?"

Susan shrugged. "Hard to tell without knowing what it does in the first place." She rubbed her eyes and leaned back, suppressing a yawn.

"Why don't you go home and get some sleep?" said Reid. "I'll have a car waiting for you out in front in a few minutes."

Susan nodded as her superior left, her eyes staring at the skyline of the nation's capital, uncertain of what she would do once she got to her apartment and once again found herself alone. As she was about to close her laptop, she noticed a blinking icon on the top left-hand corner of her screen.

"Shit!" She immediately clicked on it, pulling up a window controlled by the network's sentry, charged with detecting illegal breaches of the FBI's network's firewall, which Susan designed a year ago to keep Internet users from accessing sensitive FBI files without permission. Internet transmissions followed certain rigid protocols. A sender transmits an initial message containing a SYN flag, a string of ones and zeroes used to synchronize the upcoming communication. The intended receiver reads the SYN and replies to the sender with an ACK, acknowledging the request. When the sender receives this ACK flag, it sends an ACK of its own, acknowledging that it understands that the receiver is ready to begin accepting data. The three-way handshake completed, the actual transmission begins. At the end, the sender issues a FIN flag, signaling the end of the transmission, and the receiver responds with a final ACK, closing the electronic correspondence.

Susan's sentry had detected an Internet user issuing premature FIN flags into every port of the FBI's network. Idle ports had replied with resets, or RSTs, in the process letting the hacker know that no one was guarding them. Three of the ports belonged to users who had failed to log off the system before going home, in serious violation of FBI computer policies—leaving the door wide open for an illegal user with the correct FIN scanner. After remotely crashing one of the ports to get a core dump—along with the critical network passwords—the hacker had logged into a second port, named Leonardo, and used the stolen passwords to get past the firewall and gain access to the core of the network.

Susan began to remotely log off the users, but she knew that the damage had already been done. Someone had penetrated the system. She pulled up a system log, dreading what she would find. The log provided her with the electronic record of the activity of every port in the system, including the three that had resembled open portals to the hacker using the FIN scanner. One port reported a crash, followed by a core dump. The second port reported no activity. The third, Leonardo, had performed a network search for *GAR-NETT*. The system had responded with SGARNETT@FBI.GOV, Susan's E-mail address. Leonardo had then made a copy of the E-mail directory in her account, as well as her Internet chat log, which contained a transcript of her Internet chats for the past week.

Susan felt weak. Someone now knew as much about this global virus as she did, including the probable location in the Petén lowlands.

She slapped a hand on her desk. *"NO!"*

Angry, she logged off the illegal user, but not before dumping Leonardo's log file into her own directory, reading the Internet Protocol (IP) address of the illegal user, which belonged to an account in a nearby Internet service provider, Capital.com. She grabbed the phone, fingers trembling as she dialed the number that appeared on her screen.

The line was busy.

Susan raced out of her office, finding Reid, alerting him of the intrusion, of the implications. The elder FBI agent immediately sent a car with agents to Capital.com, the origin of the FIN scanner.

Five minutes later the phone rang in Reid's office. Susan stared out of the window, a mug of coffee in her hands.

"Yes?" Reid said after pressing the speaker box next to the phone.

"Sir, I've just called for an ambulance. One of them is still alive, but barely."

Susan turned so fast that she spilled some coffee on her jeans. She momentarily cringed from the stinging burn. Wiping it off with her hand, she reached Reid's cluttered desk.

"Still alive? What—what are you talking about?" Reid asked.

"It's . . . it's a bloodbath in here, sir. A damned bloodbath."

3

Antonio Strokk sat in the passenger seat of a rented Ford Taurus clutching a pair of commercial field binoculars, which he used to survey the entrance to the J. Edgar Hoover Building from a block away. Snow peppered the sidewalk, accumulating next to walls and around the bases of light posts and fire hydrants.

"¿Es ella?" asked Celina, hands on the steering wheel. Like her brother, she now wore plain clothes, blue jeans, and a leather jacket. A tourist map spread on the backseat, the American traveler's checks in their pockets, and their passports corroborated their claim to being a Mexican couple on their honeymoon. Their dark uniforms, as well as their weaponry, were on their way back to the safe house, where two of his operatives would spend the next hour extracting intelligence on the information Celina had stored in a half-dozen diskettes before leaving the building thirty minutes earlier. Ten minutes ago Strokk had received the first phone call from his team, informing him of the Internet chat Susan had with Hans Bloodaxe, including their progress to date on the investigation of the daily global events.

Strokk nodded. "That's her." He put the binoculars down.

4

Susan Garnett shivered on the sidewalk while watching the FBI sedan pull up to the curb. She got in the rear, sitting down, momentarily closing her eyes while enjoying the warmth.

"Back home?" asked Agent Steve Gonzales, sitting in the front passenger seat while Agent Joe Trimble drove. In light of the recent killings, Reid had decided to take zero chances and assigned both agents to escort Susan everywhere she went.

She provided them with an address that was different from her home address.

"*Where* do you want to go?" asked Agent Gonzales while Trimble's blue eyes regarded her through the rearview mirror. "That's not your—"

"I've already cleared it with Reid. Somebody's on to us. We're stepping up security and speeding up the investigation."

The agents exchanged a glance.

"We ain't got all day, boys. Let's get moving."

Trimble drove off. Gonzales sat sideways, resting an elbow on the back of his seat. "Who lives there?"

"A friend of a friend." Staring out the window, Susan put a finger to her left temple and rubbed. She was still terribly disturbed by the events in the past hour. Someone had wanted to spy on her bad enough to kill eleven people at the local ISP. The only survivor had died on his way to the hospital.

Eleven people! Susan closed her eyes, forcing back the shock. All shot to death like animals.

Poor bastards never had a chance, Reid had said. *It was a professional hit. The equipment wasn't damaged.*

A professional hit? What kind of people are we dealing with?

"Excuse me?"

Susan blinked. Agent Gonzales was staring at her. "What?"

"You said something about the kind of people we're dealing with?"

"Ignore me. Just thinking out loud."

The Hispanic agent turned back around. Susan shifted her attention to the snowflakes drifting onto the sidewalk.

5

Neither FBI agent noticed the Ford Taurus leaving the curb after them from the opposite side of the street. Celina Strokk kept a reasonable distance in the late-evening traffic, far enough away to avoid detection, yet close enough to keep her quarry in view.

Antonio Strokk relaxed. His sister had done this many times before in dozens of countries, with exemplary results, never once losing her prey.

He retrieved a miniature laser audio surveillance system, with a range of five hundred feet. The unit fed off the vibrations on glass windows created by normal conversation. He had requested a specific brand and model number from his contractor because it was the most reliable, having yielded outstanding results in Moscow, Sunnyvale, and Tokyo within the past year.

His cellular phone rang. Strokk picked it up on the second ring.

"Mr. Holland?" he asked.

"This is Mr. Wharton. Mr. James Holland is busy," the voice replied, completing the code. His subordinate proceeded to spend five minutes updating him on the information in Susan Garnett's E-mail account, including her request for help from many hackers across the country. Some of them had replied, providing some level of technical assistance, but none to the level of Bloodaxe. In the end, all of the FBI detective work to date pointed to the Tikal ruins, in the lowlands of the Petén.

The former Spetsnaz operative exhaled in disappointment, expecting the Americans to be much further along than that. Although they had been skilled enough to capture a passive version of the virus and decipher sections of it that matched the daily observations, the American analysts had failed to decipher the most important portion of the code: the routine that would be triggered on the final day of the sequence. Still, he reminded himself not to underestimate the Americans. He had done so once before and had paid dearly for his mistake.

As his sister drove them through downtown Washington, Strokk stared at the snow-covered sidewalk, remembering Afghanistan. Strokk had participated in the 1979 strike against President Hafizullah Amin's palace at the beginning of the invasion, killing the president and his bodyguards. He had later operated in the mountains, planning and executing strikes against the Mujahideen. His Spetsnaz unit, codenamed Skorpion after the Czech CZ65 Skorpion machine pistol used by its members, distinguished itself by using medieval torture methods to force information out of locals, yielding the intelligence that allowed them to hunt down numerous Mujahideen strongholds. But then the Americans began to get involved in a war that did not concern them. The CIA armed the rebels, providing them not only with sophisticated weapons, including Stinger antiaircraft missiles, but also with satellite intelligence on the movement of Russian troops in the region.

Anger swelled inside the half-Russian, half-Venezuelan operative as buildings rushed past, snow striking the windshield to the rhythm of the wipers, the same rhythm as the main rotor of the Mi-24 Hind helicopter as it had transported his team to the mountains south of Baghlán, in northern Afghanistan.

The intelligence on the hideaway was solid, confirmed both by satellite and high-altitude surveillance. The native guerrillas thought that they could hide in the high mountains following their hit-and-run strikes on Russian convoys headed for Sayghan. They believed that the narrow, mountainside trails, inaccessible to tanks and trucks, would provide them a safe haven. He planned a surprise attack by helicopter. His contact in the GRU, Russia's military intelligence division, cautioned the Spetsnaz about a recent report of sophisticated American weapons being infiltrated into the ranks of the Afghan rebels. The message from Moscow was to exercise extreme caution when flying over terrain controlled by the guerrillas. Strokk, unwilling to believe that the Americans could provide sophisticated weapons to the Mujahideen that fast, much less train the savages on how to use them, disregarded the warning, feeling confident that no rebel armed with an AK-47 could pose a serious threat to a Hind, one of the finest gunships in the world, armed with a 30mm twin-barrel cannon and a multitude of missiles under its stub wings.

The strike went on as planned.

The two Hinds came in from the north, their dark shapes closely following the uneven terrain. Antonio Strokk sat by the side door, peering out of a square window, scanning the terrain below, the sparse vegetation, the jagged hills, the desolate land. The lead chopper flew just ahead and to the side, its main rotor reflecting the morning sun.

A beam of light arced up from behind a clump of boulders, striking the lead Hind's left turbine. The craft caught fire, crashing against the mountain, disappearing behind a bright sheet of orange and yellow flames.

Before anyone could react, Strokk saw a second flash of light coming from the same boulders. The impact was as powerful as it was unexpected. In the seconds following the explosion, Strokk spotted several guerrillas on the ground, their rifles up in the air in triumph. One of them still had the Stinger launcher mounted on his shoulder.

Smoke filled the cabin, stinging his eyes, searing his throat. He felt the intense heat as the pilots screamed, their bodies in flames. The craft hovered for an instant, before plummeting to the ground, less than a dozen feet below. He braced himself for the impact, rolling across the Hind's floor as it struck the ground, kicking open the side door, rolling once more as he exited the scorching craft. Three of his men did likewise, their faces blackened, but their eyes clear, alert, weapons clutched tightly against their chests. They ran several dozen feet before the flames reached the fuel tanks.

The craft broke apart with a spectacular flash, followed by a thundering blast that shoved Strokk and his men against the wall of the mountain.

He stood, dazed, light-headed, blinking rapidly to clear his clouded vision, seeing shapes dash across his field of view, hearing nothing but a loud ringing—the result of the blast crashing against his eardrums. It would be minutes, if not longer, before his hearing returned.

Another silhouette crossed in front of him, zigzagging past a large rock. *Rebels!*

He shouted to his men to seek cover, even though he doubted they could hear him. He could not even hear himself! But his ears did detect the slow rattle of AK-47s, drowning his warnings, ripping across two of his men. The survivors, Strokk and a young private from Serpukhov, dove for the cover of a ravine, landing among dried and tangled brush, the ground exploding above them in clouds of stones and dirt that fell over them.

Caked in white dirt, his heart pounding his rib cage like a piston, Strokk kept his Skorpion in single-shot mode to conserve ammunition. He glanced at his subordinate, whose eyes were wide in fear. They had been warned about the fate of Russians caught alive by the Mujahideen. They both carried a suicide pill in their breast pockets, but a bullet in the head was equally effective.

The ringing in his ears persisted, forcing him to rely on his sight to detect the enemy. He could only hear the distant, clapping sounds of the assault rifles. The smell of cordite assaulted his nostrils. His eyes continued to tear from the smoke.

The AK-47s went silent. Strokk signaled the private to follow him up the ravine to reach a vantage point, to get a chance to fire back at the savages, to avenge their comrades.

They moved in unison for fifty meters, their weapons ready, their determination to remain alive strong. A shape loomed beyond a rocky bend in the ravine. Strokk leveled his weapon at a dark man in gray clothes and a turban swinging an AK-47 in his direction.

The Spetsnaz commando exhaled as he pressed the trigger. The Czech weapon fired once, the 9mm Parabellum round striking the guerrilla in the middle of the chest. He dropped to the ground a corpse.

Two more rebels replaced him. Strokk thumbed the fire selection lever to full automatic fire and released two shorts bursts. A third burst of fire preceded his subordinate clutching his chest, falling on his back in convulsions, blood and foam oozing from his mouth and nose.

Strokk swung the Skorpion up, toward the source of the fire at the top of the ravine, releasing a burst. The Mujahideen warrior arched back. In the same instant, two more rebels appeared. Strokk pressed the trigger but the Skorpion had jammed.

An invisible force lifted him off the ground, flipped him in midair, and shoved him against the side of the dry creek. Bouncing, he collapsed on the bottom of the creek facedown. His back stung, as did his shoulder and left thigh. Pretending to be dead, he ceased all movement, except for his right hand, which reached for his side arm, a Russian Makarov pistol. He held it close against his chest, out of sight from someone inspecting the bottom of the ravine.

The ringing in his ears intensified. He realized that he would not be able to hear them coming to rob him. The Mujahideen stole everything from their Russian victims, from watches and wedding bands to gold crowns. Out of options, Strokk counted to ten and rolled over, his eyes locked on the Makarov's sights, desperately searching for a target, finding one, two. The rebels were caught by surprise, their weapons pointed in the wrong direction. Strokk fired two rounds at each target. One in the heart and one in the face. The rebels dropped unceremoniously.

Then he grabbed his subordinate's side arm and just lay there for several minutes, a pistol in each hand, waiting, determined to take as many of these savages as he could with him. The lack of activity told him that he had survived them all, but not for long if he didn't stop the blood flow and call for help.

He used his subordinate's first-aid kit to apply a dressing to his thigh. He used his own to do the same to his left shoulder, feeling lucky that both rounds had gone through clean, without damaging any bones.

In pain, but elated to have survived, he staggered up the side of the ravine, feeling light-headed from the loss of blood, from the scorching sun, from the high altitude. He made it to the top on pure adrenaline, finding a radio on one of his slain comrades, calling in a rescue helicopter.

Then he waited, trying not to doze off, forcing his eyelids open. But he drifted away, slowly, almost imperceptibly, to be woken up by a blow to the side of his face.

He stared at a group of women and children carrying baskets of supplies. It didn't take but a second for Strokk to realize that these people were related to the men he had killed. They were bringing supplies to the rebels, to their relatives, to their fathers and husbands.

Terror struck him when he realized he no longer held the weapons. A woman in a dark garment cloaking her from head to toe pointed a Skorpion at him, her eyes alive with anger. A kid not older than ten or eleven held his Makarov, burning him with his stare. Another woman clutched the second Makarov. Two older women cried next to fallen rebels. The rest—a dozen of them, and all dressed alike—made a circle around Strokk.

He scrambled to his feet, placing his palms in front of him, pretending that he was willing to reason with them, but looking for an opportunity to snag one of the firearms. A stone the size of a baseball struck him square in the chest. The blow weakened his knees. He collapsed on his side as the women began to make high-pitched shrieks while lifting the stones clutched in their hands. The noise chilled him, sounding like witches from hell, all dressed in black, all scourging him with their evil stares, with their wicked wails.

He assumed a fetal position, covering his head as stones rained on him, numbing his arms, his ribs, his legs, his back. A stone ricocheted off his wrist, striking his temple. He felt dizzy, the circle of dark figures closing in, like vultures, their devilish song rising to an ear-piercing crescendo.

He floated in a sea of pain, the excruciating agony making him wish for a quick death, his throat-scorched sobs hovering over him. He felt hands grabbing his wrists, forcing them over his head, binding them. Others pulled on his feet, securing him to stakes driven into the hard soil with anger. Then he felt hands on his waist, unbuckling his belt, lowering his pants.

Through the inconceivable pain, through the racking torture, he understood what they were about to do and he screamed in terror.

6

Strokk jumped in his seat. The streets of Washington continued to rush by.

"Are you all right?" Celina asked without looking at him.

Strokk didn't reply. He inhaled deeply and forced the nightmare out of his mind, checking his watch, angry at himself for having let the past distract him.

Exhaling, he inspected his surveillance gear once more before returning his attention to the road.

Chapter Eight

001000

1

**December 13, 1999
Cerro Tolo, Chile**

Ishiguro and Jackie Nakamura sat side by side in front of a Hewlett-Packard workstation staring at a color map on the high-resolution monitor. The cooling fans of the workstations purred inside the large observation room, mixing with their steady breathing, and with the distant chatter of Kuoshi Honichi as he talked on his cellular phone with headquarters in Osaka while making exaggerated hand gestures, and occasionally bowing while listening intently.

Outside, a light breeze swept through the rocky Andes, carrying the cooler temperatures of the high peaks. Tonight's signal had lasted eighteen seconds, and it was in full synchronization with the worldwide daily computer freeze events, which, according to Jackie's most recent Internet excursion, were affecting about seventy percent of the world's computers, with emphasis in the larger cities. In addition, the origin had moved another two million miles down the orbit that Ishiguro and Jackie had projected around HR4390A based on the location of the first two signals, plus the calculated velocity based on the distance traveled in a twenty-four-hour period. This third point, landing right on the estimated orbit, gave more credibility to Ishiguro's theory that it was coming from a planet.

"It looks like the beam is focused on southern Mexico," Ishiguro observed while Jackie drove the workstation.

"More like northern Guatemala."

A map comprising the Yucatán Peninsula and the northern portion of Central America filled the screen. She used a magnifying feature of the software to zoom in around the area of interest.

She frowned. "Nothing but jungle."

"Let's add text."

Jackie superimposed the text for cities, lakes, rivers, and other significant sites.

"You're right. That's in the middle of nowhere. Are you sure of the coordinates?"

"See for yourself." She opened up a window and retrieved a file downloaded from one of their satellites after completing the triangulation following tonight's event. She keyed in the latitude and longitude and the software rewarded her with a red X on the same spot in northern Guatemala.

"I don't get it," he said. "There's nothing down there, at least according to this map."

"The closest thing is this." She used her mouse to direct the cursor to a site marked TIKAL. "Looks like the location is about fifty miles west of it."

Ishiguro nodded. "So we have a repetitive event, three times now, that's synchronized with the daily computer freezes, and that appears to be counting down." The two scientists had already made the connection between the duration of the events and the days left before the end of the millennium. "And this beam, which we can't decipher unless we're at the intended target, is right in the middle of the jungle?"

As Jackie was about to reply, Kuoshi returned. His angular face was tight with apprehension.

"Something wrong?" asked Ishiguro, not certain that he wanted to hear the answer. By now, some elements of the Japanese government had gotten involved in the discussion of how to proceed with this finding, including the secretive Japan Defense Agency, which considered the coincidence between the extraterrestrial signals and the global computer virus a matter of national security as nations struggled to get Year 2000 compliant. It was no secret that many nations had mounted efforts to break this global computer virus, and that no one really knew if anyone had made significant progress. Ishiguro feared that the JDA would try to take advantage of the extraterrestrial contact detected at Cerro Tolo to get an edge over the other nations.

"We have big problems," the corporate liaison said, shifting his weight from leg to leg as he spoke. "There is great fear in our country about what this global virus will do at the turn of the millennium, when our systems will be at their most vulnerable state. Knowledge of how to break this virus is vital for our nation as it positions itself to become a major economic power in the next century. Our government believes that the message encoded in this signal may possess clues about the virus. We must capture this signal at its intended target and convey it to our scientists in Osaka and Tokyo in time to stop the virus."

This was exactly what Ishiguro feared, that Japan was going to be Japan and not share this with other nations for some time. "What about the rest of the world, Kuoshi-san? What will the other nations do if they are attacked by this virus and their systems are disabled?"

"I was told that we will do everything we can to assist them."

He frowned at the typical Japanese answer, indefinite, noncommittal. "How exactly?"

"Our government is working out those details."

Jackie stood. "Let me ask a more specific question, since you appear to have gone vague on us. Are we intending to share the results of this research, including the extraterrestrial contact and the cure for the virus—if there is one—with the rest of the world before December thirty-first, while they can do something about it?"

"Our government is working out those details."

Ishiguro turned to Jackie. "That means NO, dear."

Jackie crossed her arms and looked away. "Incredible!"

"Kuoshi-san. You must understand that the protocol established by the International Astronomical Union is very clear regarding possible extraterrestrial contacts. We accomplished the first step by getting Nobemaya to confirm the contact this evening." He grabbed a faxed sheet of paper, which had arrived shortly after the event. "The next step is to inform the IAU. Then we present our data, our evidence, to a panel of scientists from the IAU, followed by a press conference."

"There is *nothing* I can do," Kuoshi said, looking away. "This project is the property of Sagata Enterprises, a government-subsidized corporation. They decide what we do with the information."

"That's it," said Jackie. "I'm posting the finding on the Web."

"You will be discredited," said Ishiguro, knowing where this was headed. "Sagata will deny the finding, refuse to release the proof, and call you a fraud. I've seen it happen before."

"I'm sorry, Ishiguro-san. I'm just following orders."

"Where does that leave us?"

"We also discussed this. As long as you're willing to accept your place, you will be allowed to continue your research."

"Accept our *what*?" Jackie blurted.

Ishiguro clasped her hand and held it tight as he said, "Then we need to visit the Yucatán Peninsula. We need to capture and interpret the signal."

Kuoshi Honichi bowed slightly. "That is acceptable."

"And at the right time we want the credit of making first contact with the extraterrestrial signal."

"That will also be acceptable. I must now call Osaka again and confirm our arrangement." Kuoshi bowed. Ishiguro bowed in return before pulling Jackie outside.

"What kind of crap was that?" she asked after they had left the building.

"It was our only chance to remain with the project. Had we been perceived as noncooperative, we would have been fired . . . or worse."

"Worse? What do you mean?"

"Even with their fumbling economy, Japan still has a lot of power and influence. We might have been fired only to find out that no other school would take us for research, that no company would sponsor any of our projects. Doors that were previously open would be suddenly closed. When you work for a Japanese company, like we do now, you must be extremely careful about how you act, what you say."

"This is . . ."

"Unbelievable? It's quite common in Japan. You just never had to experience it. You grew up in America. Your father is American. He worked at an American corporation, took you to baseball games, dressed you in blue jeans and sneakers. In Japan it is very different. Take me, for example. If I were fired, not only would it be practically impossible to find another job in the field because Sagata would use its power to prevent it, but my family back in Osaka would be shamed. My younger sisters would never find suitable husbands. My mother would be insulted in the street, denied some services. She would become persona non grata. That's part of the reason why we can't simply quit, or just post our findings on the Web. The only ones we would be hurting would be ourselves, and my family."

Jackie stared at him for a long time. "All right, then," she said after a long pause, "when do we leave?"

2

Washington, D.C.

They drove up Massachusetts Avenue and turned left on P Street, crossing over Rock Creek and Potomac Parkway, heading into Georgetown, toward the university campus, a place Susan had avoided for the past few years.

"Where do I turn?" asked Special Agent Trimble, steering down a tree-lined residential street dominated by two-story brownstones.

Susan inspected the Post-it note in her hand. "Right on Wisconsin. Left on R Street. The number's thirty-seven fifteen."

They reached the brownstone a few minutes later, parking by the curb. Dozens of cypress trees planted on both sides of the street projected their leafless canopies over the asphalt, merging in the middle of the road. Streetlights filtering through naked branches spotted the asphalt, creating islands of light in between ragged shadows. The sparse late-evening traffic had allowed some snow to accumulate on the street.

"Stay here. I won't be long," she said, stepping out, snow pelting her coat.

As Susan closed the door Gonzales rolled down his window. "You sure you don't want us to come in?"

"Nothing harmful in there. Just an old college professor. Besides, you two being in there might intimidate him."

"All right," replied Gonzales. "We'll stay put. Call if you need us." The automatic window rolled back up.

She opened the gate of a waist-high wrought-iron fence. Beyond it a narrow cobblestone walkway was flanked by a small garden. Everything but a few evergreens had lost its foliage to the frozen soil. She shuddered while filling her lungs with chilled air, wondering if she was trembling because of the cold or from being back on campus.

Careful not to slip on the light frost layering the bedrock, Susan reached the front door, ringing the bell once.

Shivering, she pulled up the lapels of her coat before bracing herself, glancing backward at the FBI sedan, engine running, smoke coiling from the exhaust.

The front door opened. A man in a colorful shirt and blue jeans greeted her. He was around forty, athletically built, with a ruggedly handsome face and a full head of dark hair, save for a little gray over the temples. The top three buttons of his shirt were undone, revealing well-defined pectorals and a curious relic hanging from a plain silver chain around his neck. It looked like a small aboriginal stone head. The stranger smiled softly, looking more like a retired gymnast than a professor of pre-Columbian history. For a moment Susan wondered if she had gotten the wrong house.

"Dr. Slater?" she asked tentatively.

He nodded, looking directly at her, still smiling. Susan felt something stir inside. "And you must be Susan Garnett. Metcalf called. Said you would be dropping by."

"My apologies for the late hour."

"No problem." He extended a hand. The sleeves of his shirt reached just below the elbows, exposing his forearms. A narrow leather band etched with glyphs hugged his left wrist. He wore no wedding band or watch. "I was just working on some papers."

Susan shook his hand firmly. "Pleasure to meet you."

"Please come in."

The man didn't look like the eminent Dr. Cameron Slater, author of a number of textbooks on the Maya, the Aztecs, and the Incas—according to Jonathan Metcalf, the school's chancellor, with whom Susan had become close friends during her professorship days. But this was the correct address and he did mention that Metcalf had already contacted him regarding this last-minute meeting. Still, now that he'd turned out to be anything but an old man, Susan had second thoughts about going inside the stranger's house alone, and for a moment wished she would have let Gonzales come along. Something about Cameron Slater disturbed her, but she suddenly realized that it did so in a way that drew her in.

"Just for a minute," she said, extending a thumb over her left shoulder. "I have people waiting for me in the car."

Slater peered out toward the street. "Tell them to come in. No one should be outside when it's this cold."

She shook her head while stepping inside the warm foyer, his remark easing her concern. "They're shy."

Slater closed the door behind them.

Susan stopped in the middle of the foyer admiring a tall stone statue of a hideous-looking creature, half man and half breast. The carved stone stood next to a set of tall clay vessels from which projected some of the most beautiful feathers she had ever seen. A low glass table next to the pots held smaller artifacts of apparent pre-Columbian origin, mostly made of stone. A mountain bicycle resting on the opposite wall seemed out of place with the unique decor, which took her by surprise, until she remembered that he was an archaeologist.

She became conscious of Cameron Slater beside her.

"That's Kinich Ahau, jaguar god of the Sun in Mayan mythology," observed Slater, pointing at the statue. "Or at least a hollow plaster replica," he added, pushing it with a finger. It budged. "The real one's where it belongs, near Tikal. This little thing is real, though." He pointed to the relic dangling from his silver chain, which upon closer inspection resembled the head of the pagan god. "It's supposed to keep me safe from the wrath of Kinich Ahau." He winked.

Susan grinned, relaxing a little around him.

"But the vases are the real thing, as well as the quetzal feathers."

Susan had obviously come to the right place to learn about the Maya. "Quetzal?"

"A tropical bird, worshiped by the Maya." He picked up a two-foot-long hunter-green feather with streaks of violet and gold. It looked dazzling under the light of the foyer's chandelier.

"It's beautiful," she said, running a finger across it.

Slater frowned, replacing the feather. "Beauty can be a curse sometimes. The poor creature has been hunted into near extinction. I pulled those feathers from a young male shot dead near Tikal last year."

She followed him into a living room that resembled a museum. Glass cabinets lined the two side walls, enclosing artifacts of various shapes and sizes, some carved out of rock or wood, others shaped by clay artisans. Many of these figures sported heads that bore a similar resemblance: oversize foreheads, high cheekbones, pronounced noses, and full lips. Some wore feathers, others ceremonial hats. French doors in the back of the living room led to a small courtyard enclosed by a brick fence. A single sofa chair, covered with the skin of a brown animal, faced a cocktail table cluttered with old maps, a notepad and pen, a phone, and more relics. It became obvious to Susan that Slater used the living room as his workroom. However, a peek at the breakfast room to the right also revealed more artifacts on the table and two overstuffed bookshelves. It looked as if the entire house was his office.

"Can I get you something to drink? Hot tea? Coffee?"

"No thanks."

Slater extended a hand toward the sofa chair. She sat on it before realizing that it was the only place to sit in the living room. He grabbed a plain wooden chair from the breakfast room, turned it around, and straddled it, resting his elbows on its back.

"So, Miss Garnett?"

"Susan."

That smile again. "Susan. How can I be of service to the Federal Bureau of Investigation?"

"Well, it may sound like a cliché, but what I'm about to tell you is considered a matter of national security," she began. "Are you familiar with the recent computer virus that's paralyzing networks around the globe?"

He nodded. "It's all over the news."

"Right," she said, feeling a little stupid for having asked that.

Standing, he walked over to the kitchen and returned with a small basket of apples and a small steak knife, setting them on the corner of the cocktail table. "Hungry?"

"No thanks."

He snagged one and the knife. As she spoke, Susan noticed his forearms flexing while slicing a wedge and putting it in his mouth. He chewed it slowly.

She told him a little about the ongoing investigation, including the software Sniffers that had led her to the lowlands of the Petén. Slater listened without interruption, consuming two apples in the process.

"Has it really started?" he said more to himself than to Susan, staring in the distance, before mumbling something she couldn't make out.

"*What* started?"

"How certain are you that the virus did originate in Tikal?"

She shrugged. "As certain as the accuracy of the programs that I used . . . what has started?"

"I'll tell you in a moment. Now, please, tell me everything that you've learned regarding the accuracy of your observation."

She proceeded to explain the caveats with her findings, which included the possibility of the Sniffers being fooled by the queen virus. "So we're going to try a different approach tomorrow night. See where that takes us. But assuming that it's to the same place, I'm trying to get a head start by learning as much as I can about Tikal and the Maya to shed some light on this mysterious virus. There has to be a connection somewhere that might tell me how to kill it."

Slater stood, walked over to one of the bookcases in the breakfast room, and returned with a thick leather-bound tome. He set it on the cocktail table, sat cross-legged on the hardwood floor next to the sofa chair, and began to leaf through it. "So, these events started two days ago, right?"

She leaned forward, her face only inches from his while he browsed through yellow pages with cracked edges and packed with text and drawings. "That's right. Twenty days before the end of the millennium."

Cameron Slater smiled. "You know that's not technically accurate, right? The end of the millennium is the end of the year 2000."

She nodded. "From the computer world's perspective it is when the year changes from 1999 to 2000."

"Makes sense, I guess. But in any case, why did the countdown start twenty days from zero one, zero one, zero zero?"

"Excuse me?"

"Zero one, zero one, zero zero is January first, two thousand, the first day of the new millennium, if you ignore the technical accuracy. Why did the countdown start twenty days before this date and not sooner or later?"

"We haven't been able to come up with any theories that explain the significance of the twenty days."

"Let me offer one. The Maya considered the number twenty quite sacred."

"They did?"

"Our decimal system was created after the number of fingers that a human can count on, ten. The Maya just went a little further, including their toes to get up to twenty, making it a vigesimal system. See here." Slater ran a finger across the middle of a page, showing her a table of Mayan symbols counting from zero to twenty. Zero was represented by a shell. One by a single dot. Two by two dots in a horizontal sequence. Three by three dots. Five became a horizontal bar. Six was represented by a single dot over a horizontal bar. The sequence continued, with nineteen shown as four dots over three stacked bars. Twenty was a shell with a single dot on top. "Also," he added, "their months, or *uinals*, are twenty days, or *kins*, long."

Susan thought about it for a moment before saying, "That certainly gives the coordinates from the Sniffers some credibility. Tell me about Tikal."

Slater leaned back against the sofa chair. Susan sat sideways to face him. "Tikal is the greatest of Guatemala's three thousand sites. It was once a bustling city of almost fifty-five thousand and one of the primary centers of learning in mathematics and astronomy, and also dominated commerce during the Classic Period, which extended from A.D. 200 to A.D. 900, when Tikal began to decline."

"Why?"

"For reasons that still remain unexplained, the Maya abandoned some of their greatest cities around that time. The entire civilization stopped progressing, almost as if they lost their purpose in life."

"Was it because of the Spanish conquerors?"

Slater shook his head. "No, that came much later. Around A.D. 1600. By then the once-glorious Maya had declined into rather primitive groups spread across the Yucatán Peninsula and southern Mexico. Something else prompted the Maya to stop advancing. They lost their inner fire. After several centuries of explosive growth, they just went belly up for no obvious reason."

"Any theories?"

"Plenty. Some scholars believe that around 900 A.D., slaves and the common people revolted against despotic rulers. However, I don't quite see how such a solidly established civilization could be overturned so easily. Besides, if the slaves and commoners were dissatisfied, there is certainly zero evidence of that in the centuries preceding their decline."

He went back to the breakfast room and returned with another book, this one more recent. He opened it to a section of color prints. "This is the way Tikal pretty much looks today. Here we have the sets of twin pyramids built facing each other across the Great Plaza, with its numerous stelae and altars. That one over there is the Pyramid of the Giant Jaguar. Other pyramids included the North Acropolis, the Temple of the Masks, and the Temple of the Lost World, which was used as an observatory by the Mayan priests. The whole place is part of a national park with plenty of wildlife on-site, including one of the last collections of quetzals in the region."

Susan stared at the photos while listening to him, all the while wondering how on earth such a virus could originate from a place like the one shown in Slater's book.

She leaned back. "This is all very interesting, Professor, but—"

"Cameron, please."

"All right. Like I was saying, this is all quite fascinating, but I'm not making any connections. We're talking about the world's most advanced computer virus, something that appears to be a generation ahead in sophistication from anything we have to fight it. And I'm supposed to believe that it came from a primitive place like Tikal? Also, you still haven't explained what you meant by your comment about something having started."

He regarded Susan like a father regarding a teenager who thinks she knows everything but who in reality has *everything* left to learn. "In order to truly understand the Maya you have to stop thinking like a Westerner," he started.

"In the eyes of our modern world, the Maya do resemble a stone age society, nothing more than another ancient, pyramid-building civilization. They had no metallurgy, no wheels aside from those used in toys, no weaponry beyond knives and spears. J. E. S. Thompson, the admirable compiler of two large tomes on the Maya, essentially regarded them as idiotic scholars, skilled in mathematics, architecture, and astronomy to the point of obsession, but to no apparent practical or meaningful end. Thompson, in all his expeditions and research, was never able to explain why. Why did the Maya go through the trouble of creating such civilization and then suddenly decline? Where did the astronomers and the mathematicians go? What legacy did they pass on to the generations after them? Why did they abandon not only Tikal, but also other great cities, like Palenque, Uxmal, and Chichén Itzá, leaving behind nothing but the ruins you see in these pages, and the glyphs and codices which have kept historians and archaeologists busy for decades trying to decipher?

"You see, Susan, the problem is not with the Maya. The problem, according to this theory, is with *us*, with the way we measure—have measured—their accomplishments."

She frowned. "Now you have *totally* lost me."

"For many decades now, we have measured their civilization using the yardstick of Renaissance European values, which are based on the invention of material technology, the innovations that essentially have continued to the modern day, from the steam engine to the space shuttle, from a crossbow to nuclear missiles, from vacuum tubes to the silicon chip. In that light, Thompson was right, the Maya were indeed quite primitive."

"But you seem to believe otherwise," she said, intrigued to see where he was headed.

Slater rubbed his eyes and tried to suppress a yawn. "It's not a belief, really. I'm simply considering other theories that may explain why they did what they did. Think of us archaeologists as detectives at the scene of a crime. We inspect what's left and try to put it all back together again. Many times we can't be certain, so we opt for possible explanations, or theories."

"Tell me."

Slater went back to the first book, finding a two-dimensional array made out of squares, each containing a different number written in Mayan. Susan made a quick count. There were thirteen squares across and twenty down. After Slater's crash course on their number system, she was able to read the numbers in the squares. Some of the squares were white with black numbers.

Others were reversed. The black and white tiles formed a strange pattern that resembled a crossword puzzle.

"The theory that I'm going to propose is quite controversial, and you'll soon see why. But I'm offering it to you because some observations do seem to match it. This is the Tzolkin, a matrix of thirteen numbers and twenty symbols created by the Maya as a harmonic matrix to achieve galactic synchronization."

Susan narrowed her eyes, puzzled. "Harmonic matrix to achieve galactic synchronization? I'm afraid you're going to have to be a little clearer than that. I have no idea what that meant."

Slater smiled. "Very few people do, and those who do understand it are quite reluctant to accept it. What I'm about to propose is going to seem far-fetched and, in layman's terms, downright crazy, because it goes against our modern-day acceptable scientific state of mind, which is based on physical evidence—proof—to back suppositions. The reason why Thompson and many other archaeologists before and after him failed to understand the Maya is because they were never able to transcend their way of thinking from the Western mind to the mind of the Maya. They were incapable of seeing beyond the material evidence left behind, and thus were unable to answer the most fundamental question about the Maya: why? Why did they do what they did? Why create such large cities, develop such great mathematics, architecture, astronomy? Why? There is no evidence that they were able to apply their knowledge in the way Western culture would have: to advance the standard of living, to improve transportation, communications, health, physical life. Had they applied that knowledge in the way that we would have, in the way that *we* did, the Maya would have grown into an advanced society in a matter of a few hundred years, certainly way before the Spanish conquerors arrived. Actually, the Maya would have been the ones *discovering*, and possibly even conquering, Europe."

"Do you really think that would have been possible?"

"Absolutely. Look at our own civilization. Four hundred years ago we had very little in terms of technology, medicine, communications. Look at us now, just four centuries later, or one *baktun*. We evolved quite rapidly, and the evolution has taken an exponential form. We have accomplished more in the past one hundred years than in the last millennium—as measured by our ability to create an incredible array of creature comforts. But the Maya did nothing of the kind with their science, and then, in their glory, at the peak of their scientific accomplishments, they suddenly regressed to a very primitive society, starting around A.D. 830, the beginning of the eleventh *baktun*. By A.D. 900, they had declined so much that it marked the official end of the Classic Period."

"What's a *baktun*?"

"A measure of time in Maya. About 395 of our years. The theory is complicated, but you'll understand its concept shortly."

"All right. Go on."

"The Maya, this theory offers, had a different reason for being on this Earth. In simple terms, there's been enough evidence to theorize that their mission was to place the Earth and its Solar System in synchronization with a larger galactic community. Once that purpose was achieved, around 830 A.D., the Maya departed. Some remained here as caretakers, overseers of the code left behind by the Classic Maya to describe their purpose and their science. That's the Tzolkin, the harmonic matrix used by the Maya to achieve galactic synchronization."

Susan regarded him long and hard. "And you really believe this?"

Slater smiled graciously, obviously used to getting such a reaction. He continued. "Like I said at the beginning, Susan, I'm just a scholar who is providing suppositions that may or may not help explain the phenomena that we've experienced in the past few days. Think of this as a free lecture. The Maya do challenge our science, requiring us to open our minds to a new level of thinking. When you heard me say, 'Has it started?' I was referring to the beginning of a new Mayan Great Creation Cycle. Like us, the Maya measured time in intervals of ever-increasing size, like our seconds, minutes, hours, and days. Western civilization measures time according to the Gregorian calendar, which has 365 days per year, marking one circle around the Sun. After that, it follows our decimal system: 10 years per decade, 10 decades per century, 10 centuries per millennium, and so on. The Long Count Mayan calendar is different only because it's based on the vigesimal system. A *kin* represents one day, measured just as we do, a complete revolution of the Earth. A *uinal* represents their month, made up of 20 *kins*. A *tun* is their year, made up of 18 *uinals* or 360 *kins*, quite close to our 365 days. A *katun* is equivalent to our decade, only twice as long because their system, again, is vigesimal. Twenty *tuns* form a *katun*, which is around 19.7 years. A *baktun* is made up of 20 *katuns*, or close to 394.5 years. The start of the last Great Creation Cycle, according to Mayan scribes, who kept a record of time with good accuracy, is around 3129 B.C. These cycles last 13 *baktuns*, or 5129 Gregorian years. The ninth *baktun* ended around A.D. 830, when the decline began. The thirteenth *baktun* comes to a close at the end of the year 1999, if you assume the year 3129 B.C. as your starting point."

"Are there any other starting points?"

He grinned. "Now you're getting to some controversy. Some scholars feel that the end of the thirteenth *baktun* is more around 2012 because of evidence that the cycle started around 3116 B.C. instead of 3129 B.C."

"But you seem to believe otherwise."

"It seems like an incredible coincidence that after 5129 Gregorian years the two calendars would miss each other by a mere thirteen years. My theory, which is 99.766 percent accurate, is also more exciting, more intriguing, more Mayan than my colleague's stolid and narrow-minded views. That also means that my translation of dates from Mayan Long Count to Gregorian differs from my colleagues' by thirteen years, something that drives some of my friends crazy, but so do some of my other theories."

"Well, there seems to be some validity to your suppositions."

"I was actually beginning to wonder the other day if we would indeed start seeing any signs that marked the conclusion of this cycle. The daily computer events, all at the exact same time, one minute after eight in the evening local time, and starting on the first day of the last *uinal*—month—of the last *tun*, of the last *katun* of the last *baktun*, suggests that we are being contacted."

Susan shook her head and stood. "Contacted? This is . . ."

"Bizarre? I know how it sounds, believe me. Problem is, as an archaeologist, I must consider all of the evidence and try to piece together a reasonable theory. This one, as crazy as it may sound, does fit the observations."

"Well," she said, "I'm having one hell of a time not only understanding everything that you're telling me, but also trying to digest it, to make some sense of it."

He smiled again, his dark eyes regarding her warmly. She felt something stirring inside again and quickly looked away. "I'm having difficulty visualizing the relationship between the Mayan calendar, our own, and this Great Creation Cycle."

"It's all actually quite simple, once you write it down. Here, let me show you." Ripping a piece of paper from a pad, Slater wrote:

BAKTUN#	MAYAN/LONG COUNT	GREGORIAN PERIOD	EVENT
1	1.0.0.0.0	3129 B.C.–2734 B.C.	STAR PLANTING
2	2.0.0.0.0	2734 B.C.–2339 B.C.	THE PYRAMIDS
3	3.0.0.0.0	2339 B.C.–1944 B.C.	THE WHEEL

4	4.0.0.0.0	1944 B.C.–1550 B.C.	THE EGYPTIANS
5	5.0.0.0.0	1550 B.C.–1155 B.C.	HOUSE OF SHANG
6	6.0.0.0.0	1155 B.C.–761 B.C.	HORSE WARFARE
7	7.0.0.0.0	761 B.C.–366 B.C.	MIND TEACHINGS
8	8.0.0.0.0	366 B.C.–A.D. 28	THE SAVIOR
9	9.0.0.0.0	A.D. 28–A.D. 422	THE ROMAN EMPIRE
10	10.0.0.0.0	A.D. 422–A.D. 817	THE MAYA
11	11.0.0.0.0	A.D. 817–A.D. 1211	THE CRUSADES
12	12.0.0.0.0	A.D. 1211–A.D. 1606	WORLD CONQUEST
13	13.0.0.0.0	A.D. 1606–A.D. 2000	INDUSTRIALISM

"Okay," he said, "we are close to completing one entire Mayan cycle, from the first *baktun* to the thirteenth, and those are the periods as measured in our own calendar."

"How do you read this?" She tapped a finger on the rows of numbers separated by periods.

"To read the Mayan Long Count, look at the five numbers separated by periods. Each number represents one time interval, as follows." He wrote beneath the table:

BATKUN.KATUN.TUN.UINAL.KIN
KIN = 1 DAY
UINAL = 20 KINS
TUN = 360 KINS
KATUN = 20 TUNS (7200 KINS)
BAKTUN = 20 KATUNS (144,000 KINS)

"With that you can simply multiply the number in the date times its respective time interval and come up with the actual number of days. You then add that number of days to your reference of 3129 B.C. and you have your Gregorian calendar equivalent date."

The information was pouring in too fast for Susan to keep up with it. "Wait," she said, also sitting on the floor next to him, placing her elbows on the cocktail table. "You're telling me that we have gone through this cycle, and its end coincides with midnight on January first?"

"The event is even more significant than that. It will be the first time in history that both the Mayan and the Gregorian calendars line up at the *baktun*-millennium level. In addition, there are two other significant observations that tie into this theory. The first is the decimal equivalent of zero one, zero one, zero zero. Do you know what that is?"

Susan stared into his dark eyes, gleaming with bold intelligence. A part of her felt intimidated by his knowledge and the ease with which he recalled specific events and dates. The rest of her felt annoyed that he had just given her a test.

"All right," she said. "The binary system is based on the number two, just like the decimal system is based on ten. I need a pen and paper, please."

Amusement softening his features, Cameron Slater gave her the notepad and his pen.

"Each numeral one in the binary sequence indicates a place where the number two has to be multiplied by as many times as the position of the one in the binary sequence, with zero being on the right-most position. Then each number is simply added, yielding the decimal equivalent of the binary number."

She wrote:

BINARY	POSITION	DECIMAL EQUIVALENT
0	5	0
1	4	16 ($2 \times 2 \times 2 \times 2$)
0	3	0
1	2	4 (2×2)
0	1	0
0	0	0
		Total: 20

Susan didn't say anything. She stared at her results for several seconds, almost in denial, amazed at the parallels. The damned number twenty seemed to be everywhere.

She turned to Slater, who wore a pensive mask. Her eyes drifted to the hundreds of ancient artifacts crowding the shelves covering the walls of the living area. They seemed to look down upon her. She studied their faces, the pronounced features, their ornate headdresses, the glyphs carved in stone, etched in wood, painted on molded clay vessels. Could this be true after all? The coincidences were simply too many for Susan to ignore, to push aside to consider a more plausible theory. She suddenly found it difficult to breathe.

"There is yet another observation," Slater said.

"I don't know how many more I can actually take tonight, Cameron."

"The time of the events."

She rubbed her chin. "One minute after eight every evening?"

"Local time, yes. But as a planet, we have one central time, from which all time zones are referenced."

"Greenwich Mean Time?"

"Correct. The events occur at exactly one minute and zero seconds after one in the morning, Greenwich Mean Time."

"Or zero one, zero one, zero zero," she added in marvel.

"Or twenty. It's actually quite remarkable how everything is just falling into place, just as the theory suggests."

She stood, crossing her arms, walking to the French doors, absently inspecting the small courtyard, turning to look at one of the booksh.lves. "This is..." She shook her head. "Everything so far fits this theory of yours. In fact, everything fits it *too well*, almost as if it has been planned that way." She crossed her arms and stared into the distance. "The Maya were from outer space. They came to this world thousands of years ago to do some kind of galactic synchronization of the Earth and the Solar System for a purpose that you have yet to propose. Do you realize how far-fetched that sounds? Do you really believe this?"

"Susan, you're getting me all wrong here. This is just a theory. I have many others I could share with you, but none fit the observations as well. Remember, we're just detectives at the scene, gathering information, making stipulations, seeing how those theories match up with the observations. We still have a lot more digging to do before we can go down any path with a reasonable degree of confidence."

She returned to the sofa. "All right, then. Tell me, how do you propose the aliens arrived? Aboard a vessel? Is there any indication of space travel in the physical evidence left behind by the Classic Maya?"

Cameron Slater calmly flipped a few pages of his tome and pointed at a drawing of the Earth at the bottom and the cosmos at the top. The Sun was in the middle. A row of squares, each with a Mayan number in it, projected from the Earth, through the Sun, and into the center of this cosmos. "There are two terms that you want to become familiar with. The first is Hunab Ku. Translated literally, it means One Giver of Movement and Measure. It is the principle of life beyond the Sun, the galactic core, from where all things come. The second term is Kuxan Suum, which means the Road to the Sky Leading to the Galactic Core, or the Hunab Ku." He pointed to the center of the cosmos on the drawing, where the row of squares formed a path through the Sun and into the stars. "This is where the Hunab Ku is located. In modern astronomical terms, the Hunab Ku is a point in space between HR4390A and HR4390B, two stars of the southern constellation Centaur, 139 light-years away. The connection between Earth and this distant galaxy is the Kuxan Suum. In modern astronomy, however, the term "galactic core" is used in reference to the center of our own Milky Way Galaxy, which is much further away. But the Maya use this term in reference to the point in space between those two stars."

"So is the Kuxan Suum how they came and left?"

He shrugged. "If you believe in this theory. Let me show you another drawing." He flipped through dozens of pages, stopping at a drawing of a Maya, wearing a colorful skirt and a feathery headdress, sitting in what appeared to be the seat of an object shaped like a space capsule. His hands operated the controls inside the vessel. Fire came out from the bottom, propelling him skyward.

Susan examined the incredible detail of the pre-Columbian drawing. "Is this real?"

He nodded, staring directly at her. "Susan Garnett, meet Pacal Votan, the greatest Mayan chief that ever lived. The Mayan Classic Period reached its peak during his reign. He died in A.D. 683. This drawing is an exact copy of the reliefs on the lid of his sarcophagus, discovered in 1952 in an ornately decorated tomb inside the Temple of the Inscriptions at Palenque, in Chiapas, Mexico. Some scholars call Pacal a galactic agent, who used the Kuxan Suum to reach the Hunab Ku after completing his work here."

"What do you think?" she asked him.

He grinned. "I think it makes for an interesting debate at seminars and banquets."

"Why the Maya, Cameron? Why not the Egyptians? Or the Greeks? Or one of the early civilizations from the Orient? Why is the origin of the virus pointing to the Maya?"

"All I can offer here is the fact that the Maya appear to have influenced other civilizations, even those on the other side of the globe."

"How?"

"Well, Maya, for example, is a key Hindu philosophical term meaning Origin of the World. The word Maya in Sanskrit relates to concepts meaning Mind, Magic, and Mother. Maya is the name of the mother of the Buddha. In the Vedic classic, *The Mahabharata*, Maya was the name of their most noted astronomer and magician. The treasurer of the renowned boy-king of Egypt, Tutankhamen, was named Maya, while in Egyptian philosophy the term Mayet means universal order. In Greek mythology, the seven Pleiades, daughters of Atlas and Pleione and sisters of the Hyades, number among them one called Maia, also known as the brightest star of the constellation Pleiades. Finally, the month of May is derived from the name of the Roman goddess, Maia, the Great One."

Susan took a deep breath, running a hand through her short auburn hair, her engineering mind absorbing every bit of information and cataloguing it to find its place in this puzzle she was trying to piece together. "One thing I don't understand, though, is what did you mean by galactic synchronization? We've talked a lot about the significance of the observations and how they fit into this theory, but what did the Maya accomplish, or try to accomplish?"

"Galactic synchronization is subject to many interpretations. One of them suggests that the term is not associated with a historical event, but with a state of mind. It implies a mental attitude that makes people want to live in harmony with the environment, with those around you, just as the Maya and other ancient civilizations did, without the waste and pollution created by our modern world, by technology. Under this theory, the Maya came here to teach us how to live in peace, in harmony with nature, how to achieve a perfect society, how to use science to advance the human spirit without the waste created by our industrial world. Only then, after we transform our way of thinking from one of material gain to one of harmony and spiritual gain, would the human race be ready to take the next step in the transformation: the development of the power to connect directly with the energy of this beam called the Kuxan Suum, emanating from the Hunab Ku, the Galactic Core."

Susan grabbed one of the apples in the basket and took a hearty bite, holding it up in the air, her elbow tucked in. "This energy beam . . . how do you know it exists at all? What proof is there beyond the drawings you showed me?"

"The proof is everywhere, in scientific journals, even in the newspapers. For some time now physicists have been able to detect density beams sweeping through the galaxy. Many of them, scientists claim, influenced our own evolution. These density waves at some point in time ignited a giant star, creating our Sun, and therefore our Solar System. Do you see how we are all connected here? So the Maya calls it Kuxan Suum and a professor from Harvard labels it a density beam that dominates the galaxy's dynamics. This theory proposes that both are the same, Susan. These beams of energy, which astrophysicists claim have swept through the cosmos for the Sun's entire existence of some 4.5 billion years, pass through the Sun, which alters their dynamics, changing their composition as they bathe the Earth with radiant energy, bringing life beyond that which can be measured by today's science. The Maya believed that this beam of energy sparked new ideas, convictions, visions. Where scientists of today focus on measuring the composition of materials, breaking them down into its basic elements, the Maya focused on qualities that are dismissed in today's physics, like emotions and feelings. Where scientists detect energy beams that influence the birth of stars and entire galaxies, the Maya detected energy beams that triggered the birth of ideas. The beams are the same, only interpreted differently. For example, music is nothing but sound waves propagating through space. A machine can detect those signals and display the music in the form of a number of waves on a screen. A human, however, can hear that same music and experience an emotional change because of it. There're two very different reactions to the same wave forms. You asked for proof of the Mayan claims? I challenge you to open your mind, like listening to music, and see the proof that has always been there, in front of you, only you didn't know how to recognize it for what it was."

Cameron Slater closed the books. "And that, my dear Susan, I'm afraid wraps up your first lesson in Ancient Maya 101. Remember that there will be a test on Friday." He grinned and returned to the kitchen to replace the books on the shelves.

She blinked, a bit dazzled by his eloquent explanations, and also by his innate ability to go up on a podium and deliver such revolutionary thoughts and then mix in the right amount of humor.

She checked the time. It was almost midnight. "I didn't realize it was this late. I do have one more question, then I'll leave you alone."

"Not a problem. Shoot."

"What do you think is going to happen on zero one, zero one, zero zero?"

Slater dropped his gaze to the floor, frowning. "Good one. Some scholars believe that on the day of total alignment, when the Mayan Long Count calendar aligns with our Gregorian calendar at the *baktun*-millennium level, our eyes and hearts will recognize the distorted sensibilities under which we have been living during our fifty thousand years of Homo sapiens' existence. We will become empathetic with a world that shouts out in anguish from all the abuse, all the death, all the suffering of past millenniums. That day we will all go through a new birth of spirit and awaken to the full gamut of human emotions."

Susan didn't know what to say. Her eyes returned to the relics on the shelves, to the ancient remnants of a long-lost civilization, to the clay vases, the carved rosewood, and the sculpted stone objects that she felt somehow held clues to the undecipherable binary code embedded in the virus. But how all of this tied together was beyond her current comprehension, as well as

Slater's ideational descriptions of what kind of event might be triggered at the end of the millennium. "I'm having difficulty taking those abstract concepts and applying them to our current dilemma of this virus counting down to zero one, zero one, zero zero."

"That's because you are thinking in the same way that you have been trained to think from the time you were a little girl, in the same way your parents think, and your grandparents before them. This theory proposes that a time of transformation is nearing, when we will transcend from a civilization that values the accumulation of personal wealth, to one that values the strength of the spirit, just like the Maya did. Anyway, I hope you don't take all of this stuff too seriously."

She smiled. "Don't worry."

"I also hope you don't discard it, either. I think there are some undeniable observations that match the theory. If you're interested, I may have a couple of small books that provide good insight into the mind of the Maya. Perhaps they can be of help?"

"Absolutely."

"Come. Let's see what we can find." He headed up the stairs next to the foyer, leading to a small open room, also filled with not only artifacts but also with a wooden bench resembling a two-headed jaguar. Susan was mesmerized by the shine on the wood and the level of detail.

"That's beautiful."

"Isn't it?" Slater sat on it and patted the space to his left. "It's also quite comfortable."

She sat, feeling as if the chair somehow pushed up on her upper body, maintaining it erect. "You're right," she said.

"It's the angle. The bench is tilted just enough to align your spine with the angle of your hips when you sit, giving you great posture. The Maya were phenomenal architects."

"That's amazing. What's its purpose?"

"It's a ceremonial bench, for marriages. The bride and groom have to sit here for hours while the shaman goes through a lengthy process to unite the couple forever. In fact, we're sitting in the correct position. The man on the right, the woman on the left."

For reasons she could not explain, Susan blushed when looking at Cameron Slater. He cleared his throat and quickly stood.

"Anyway," he said, gesturing her into the bedroom, "I think I have a couple of books about basic Mayan mythology and beliefs."

She followed him inside, where more bookshelves flanked an unmade bed. Susan noticed a khaki vest with many pockets and zippers perched on a hook on the door that probably led to his bathroom, next to a long and narrow glass table displaying more relics. Beneath the table she spotted two pairs of hiking boots, also quite worn.

"Do you do much traveling?" she asked, also noticing an old backpack with several airline tags dangling from the top; most of the names rang South American.

"All the time. In fact, I've just returned from Peru. I spent a month in the jungles under a grant from the Museum of Natural History in New York, looking for evidence of a tribe of Ixmatzuls, a distant cousin of the Inca."

"A month in the jungle? Alone?"

"With a couple of local guides, although I couldn't convince them to go past a certain point in the mountains. I was alone for two of the four weeks."

Susan regarded him quizzically, not certain if she admired him or felt that he was totally crazy. "What did you live on for two weeks?"

"Some beef jerky, but mostly from the land. I'm used to it," he said, too naturally for Susan to believe otherwise. "It paid off, though. I was able to collect enough artifacts to fill two crates. The museum's preparing a special exhibit for the spring." He squatted next to a bottom shelf and pulled out two books.

"Are you heading out again soon?"

"To Brazil. This time courtesy of *National Geographic*. They want me to study the Mamelucos, a native tribe from the lower Amazon region. I'm leaving in two weeks . . . here we go." He pulled out two small books and handed them to her, both on Mayan mythology.

Susan stared at the colorful covers.

"There's several illustrations of some of the concepts I described today, including a couple of maps of the cosmos showing the location of the Hunab Ku."

"You have been most helpful, Cameron. Right now I need to head back to the office and try to sort this out."

"I'm glad I was able to help out." He walked her to the foyer, where she put on her jacket.

"Again," she said, extending a hand, "many thanks. I'll make sure these books find their way back to you."

"Don't rush. I won't be needing them for a while."

"Would you be available if I come up with something else?"

"Absolutely." Cameron Slater took her hand in his, firmly shaking it while locking eyes with her. "Call or come back anytime."

Susan smiled before heading back to the sedan. The cold air tingled her cheeks. She had been gone for a total of one hour, but somehow it felt much longer than that. She got in the rear of the sedan and watched him standing in the doorway until they had pulled away. For a brief moment, Susan no longer felt alone.

She closed her eyes. Exhaustion, combined with the complexity of the Mayan connection, gave her a headache, which rapidly increased in intensity as she thought of the slain crew at the local Internet service provider, further complicating the scenario.

Who is after my data?

She yawned, her thoughts becoming cloudier, difficult to keep focused. Suddenly losing the desire to head back to the FBI, Susan asked her body-guards to take her home. She could use a good night's sleep so that she could start fresh in the morning. Right now she was no good to Troy Reid.

Special Agent Gonzales turned around. "You sure you want us to take you home?"

"If I don't get some sleep you'll be taking me to the hospital next."

3

Antonio Strokk removed his headphones and unplugged them from the laser surveillance device he had attached to the top of the brick fence enclosing the courtyard. The vibrations on the glass panels of the French doors had provided him with an excellent frequency response, enabling him to capture most of the conversation.

He returned to the sedan, parked across the street, where Celina waited behind the wheel.

"Let's go. Follow her."

"What did you learn, *hermano*?" she asked, darkness hiding her Hispanic-Slavic features as she put the car in gear and sped to the end of the block, turning the corner and coming back around the other side, in time to catch the taillights of the FBI sedan as it came to a stop at the corner.

"Much more," he replied, watching the Bureau car head out of Georgetown, spending a few minutes summarizing the amazing conversation he had heard.

"So," she said. "It appears that Bloodaxe's Scent-Sniffer program may have led the FBI to the right place?"

"Looks that way. It also looks like this Hans Bloodaxe is the only one skilled enough to get to the bottom of this problem."

"If that is the case—"

"We need to get to Bloodaxe without delay." Strokk peered at the snow-covered sidewalks. "Our employer wants a solution to this virus right away."

"But he is in prison," Celina said.

Strokk remembered the information extracted from the diskettes. Bloodaxe was serving a life sentence for a previous crime. But that didn't mean that he was unreachable. Antonio Strokk operated in a circle of international contractors, all of whom relied on an infrastructure of informants and subcontractors, many of them with contacts in various government agencies, including the Justice Department, which ran the federal prison system in the United States. "There is *always* a way," he said, grabbing his cellular phone. "Keep following them. I'll make the request, along with a handsome compensation. There will be many takers."

Chapter Nine

001001

1

December 14, 1999
Washington, D.C.

Susan Garnett drove under blue skies through downtown Washington. She could smell her husband's aftershave, could sense his presence next to her in the minivan, could hear Rebecca singing in the rear seat. She saw the exit sign over the highway and put on her blinker, just as she had done countless mornings, slowing down as she approached the exit ramp, which curved as it descended to the street level. Her eyes saw the speedometer, stuck on forty, her usual speed. Then her windshield filled with the rear bumper of a car. The initial impact was sudden, powerful, mixed with Rebecca's screaming. Time seemed to slow down as an explosion of air preceded the airbag deploying, as her forward momentum shoved her face forward despite the safety belt, as she immersed her face in the cushion of white, before jerking backward, crashing the back of her head against the headrest. Then came the incessant spinning, the world turning in an uncontrollable blur, steam hissing from the busted radiator, Rebecca's screams turning to cries, Tom shouting to hold on. Although it only lasted a second or two, time seemed to stretch indefinitely, her mind absorbing every sight, every sound, every smell with uncanny detail. Then a second jolt stopped the spinning, turning it into a tilt, as the side of the minivan slammed against the guardrail, going over the edge, plummeting while turning upside down. The screams and cries intensified. Tom's hand reached out to touch her, one final time, one last brush of his skin against hers, before the impact came, before the roof collapsed on his head, crushing it as the unyielding concrete stopped the falling object in one brief moment, turning its energy into a deadly, compacting force.

A period of darkness was followed by pain, agonizing, unbearable pain, which vanished at times, relieving her at first, but then terrifying her, making her wonder if she had died. Pain meant she was alive, and she fought vehemently to reestablish it, to force it back into her system, somehow, from somewhere, for it meant hope, the possibility of seeing her loved ones again. And the pain returned, stronger than before, consuming, intolerable. But Susan welcomed it, embraced it, no longer wishing for it to end. Then she awakened, and through the physical pain clutching her broken body, she learned of her family's death, of the funeral she had missed, of the farewells that destiny had denied her. She cried that afternoon, and the following week, and the week after that, until her swollen eyes dried up, until her sorrow turned to anger, and the anger into an overwhelming desire to achieve retribution, to avenge them, to honor their memories, to give some sense of significance to the mortal remains buried beneath the frozen soil of northern Virginia.

Susan found herself in a snowy graveyard, sitting in a wheelchair, her body riveted together by enough titanium to set off metal detectors a mile away. She had insisted in doing this alone, her nurse remaining behind, by the tree line overlooking endless rows of tombstones. Hands trembling, snow falling on the two roses on her lap, she steered herself through the upright slabs of granite and stone marking the final resting places of so many different names, so many strangers, all sharing a common bond with her loved ones. Then she reached a pair of new marble stones, one gray, one white, side by side, the names etched into their surfaces stabbing her eyes, tunneling her vision, making everything spin around her. A demon came alive deep within her, rapidly gaining strength, spiraling upward from the darkest corner of her gut, reaching her gorge, like a lump of hot coals, burning her throat, scourging her. Susan wrenched out a heart-crushing howl, an angered scream, the desperate cry of a desperate woman.

Soaked in perspiration, Susan sat up in bed screaming, suddenly realizing that it was a dream, taking a deep breath, staring at the murky interior of her bedroom, her heart pounding behind her ears.

She glanced at the clock on the nightstand.

Almost six in the morning.

She had been sleeping for nearly seven straight hours, a luxury compared to the last few days.

She blinked the graveyard memories away, breathing deeply again, forcing the nightmare out of her mind. Wiping the sweat off her forehead, Susan got up, walked to the kitchen, and drank from a cold bottle of Evian, staring at the star-filled sky beyond the windowpanes of her fifth-floor apartment, calming down, her heartbeat returning to normal. Kicking off her nightgown, she walked into the bathroom, abruptly stopping in front of the mirror to study her figure, still quite slim in spite of her thirty-five years. Her breasts remained firm, as well as her stomach and legs, thanks to the few hours each week that she'd spent at the FBI gym, something she had done not because she cared about her appearance, but just because it was one of the few things that actually made her feel good, pumping her with enough energy to face her otherwise taxing days.

She stepped into the tub, suddenly realizing the unfamiliar lack of a desire to end her life. Quite the opposite, she looked forward to getting the refined Scent-Sniffer programs that Hans Bloodaxe should have generated by now.

What is happening to me? Why the change? Am I really getting over their deaths? What about the recurring nightmare?

After towel-drying her hair and putting on a fresh pair of jeans and a sweater, she powered up her notebook and logged into work, launching her E-mail software, and browsing through the day's mail messages, instantly recognizing one from Bloodaxe.

Just as she was about to open it, she received a notification that HANSB@HAYNES.GOV wanted to start an Internet chat.

HANSB@HAYNES:	JUST SAW YOU GET ON-LINE. DID YOU GET THE FILE?
SGARNETT@FBI:	DO YOU EVER LOG OFF?
HANSB@HAYNES:	WHAT ELSE IS THERE ASIDE FROM BEING ON-LINE?

Susan shook her head.

SGARNETT@FBI:	I HAVEN'T READ IT YET. IS IT ANY GOOD?
HANSB@HAYNES:	ONLY THE BEST, AND IT'S READY TO BE DEPLOYED. THE SCENTS NOW MUTATE, CREATING INDIVIDUAL STRAINS THAT CAN ONLY BE MATCHED WITH A SINGLE SNIFFER. QUITE A WORK OF ART.

I bet, she thought, staring at the color screen, deep inside still considering the possibility that Bloodaxe was either the creator of this virus or perhaps was using it as a way to meet some other goal or secret agenda.

SGARNETT@FBI:	ANYTHING SPECIAL I SHOULD BE AWARE OF?
HANSB@HAYNES:	NO. JUST LAUNCH IT LIKE YOU DID THE LAST

ONE. IT WILL AUTOMATICALLY REPLICATE AND ATTACH ITSELF TO INDIVIDUAL QUEEN VIRUSES DURING THE EVENT. YOU CAN LAUNCH THE SNIFFERS AFTER THE EVENT AND SEE WHERE THEY TAKE YOU.

SGARNETT@FBI: WHAT IF THE RESULT IS THE SAME AS LAST NIGHT'S? THEN WHAT?

HANSB@HAYNES: THEN YOU'LL KNOW FOR CERTAIN THE ORIGIN OF THIS VIRUS. SPEAKING OF WHICH, DID YOU CHECK OUT THE LOCATION WITH SATELLITES?

SGARNETT@FBI: WORKING ON IT. SHOULD HAVE SOME IMAGES WAITING FOR ME AT WORK THIS MORNING.

HANSB@HAYNES: TERRIFIC. LET ME KNOW WHAT YOU SEE. IN THE MEANTIME, I'LL KEEP WORKING ON THE SECTION OF THE VIRUS THAT DOESN'T SEEM TO MATCH ANYTHING. IT STILL RESEMBLES A RANDOM BINARY SEQUENCE.

Susan remembered the section of code in the virus that she had been unable to translate, the one that would be executed on 01-01-00. She had E-mailed that section to Bloodaxe the day before in the hope that he would be able to decode it.

SGARNETT@FBI: HAVE YOU BEEN ABLE TO FIGURE OUT ANY SECTION?

HANSB@HAYNES: NOPE. TOUGH COOKIE TO CRACK. WILL LET YOU KNOW WHEN I DO. REALLY GOTTA GO. BREAKFAST TIME.

She broke the chat connection and proceeded to review her E-mail, importing the C++ program containing the refined Scent-Sniffer programs. Launching her system's C++ compiler, she converted Bloodaxe's source code into an executable file, and ran a test case in a secured directory of her hard drive, monitoring how the Scent code infected the files in the petri directory. Unlike the previous Scent, this one mutated every time it replicated itself. She then launched the Sniffers, which also replicated themselves, just as a virus would, but instead of attacking any file at random, its execution subroutine commanded the Sniffers to seek out their individual Scents, matched by a two-byte-long mutation code. Given the proximity of the Scents, the Sniffers immediately began to bark, converging onto their targets in a millisecond.

Susan decided that the code seemed ready, and she deployed it across the Internet before logging off and preparing to head into work. It was going to be another long day.

2

Hans Bloodaxe stood patiently in the long breakfast line formed along a narrow, poorly lit corridor leading to the mess hall. The food lines at Haynesville sometimes lasted for an hour or more, depending on the number of fights among the inmates, which had a tendency to slow things down. Hungry inmates from various cell blocks took turns at lining up for their daily meals. Bloodaxe's group was next, roughly one hundred men, most of them serving sentences ranging anywhere from twenty years to life.

Someone whacked him in the head.

"Hey!" Bloodaxe turned around.

"Hey, moron."

The hacker frowned, rubbing the back of his head. The large African-American guard had apparently taken a special liking to him. Bloodaxe had learned during his first week here that the guard had lost his savings because a hacker had wrecked the company he had invested in.

"Yes, sir?" he muttered.

"Come with me."

"How about my break—"

Whack.

"All right, man! Damn!"

The corpulent guard led him through one of the cell blocks, a long, damp, and murky corridor flanked by two-man cells, each with its own sink and toilet, many of which got backed up every day. The putrid stench struck him like a moist breeze as the guard made him step up the pace, exiting at the other end of the quiet block, through a thick metal door that screeched after he unlocked it.

"Where are we going?" Bloodaxe asked.

"Shut up, moron. Keep walking."

Bloodaxe complied, heading into the large warehouse building connected to the kitchen. Then a sharp object struck him behind the head and all went dark.

The prison's main entrance and visitor's center faced north. The south end of the prison grounds was bordered by double chain-link fences separated by a gravel walkway patrolled by guard dogs, Dobermans. A single gate connected the access road curving up from the highway a mile away to the central kitchen and storage buildings. Used mostly by delivery trucks, the gate was lightly guarded and only used on weekdays, like today. No one questioned the blue and gold dairy truck that approached the rear gate, its arrival time matching that of the day's log. The double gates slid back and the guards waved it through. It continued on to the single delivery dock behind the kitchen building, where it made its normal delivery. Before it headed back, two guards loaded a large box onto the rear of the truck and covered it with a canvas. One of the guards was the African-American, who that day would become twenty thousand dollars richer, four times the amount of money he had lost two years ago to a hacker.

3

"He's *what?*" Susan Garnett leaned forward on her chair at work.

"Gone, ma'am," replied the warden's assistant at Haynesville, where the FBI analyst had just phoned to set up another appointment with Bloodaxe.

Susan clutched the phone tight against her ear. The noon sun shone bright in the clear skies over Washington, D.C. "Gone? How? When?"

"We're trying to figure that out. It happened sometime this morning. He didn't report during roll call after breakfast. That's when we first took notice that he wasn't inside the prison grounds."

"This is . . . amazing. I can't believe this!"

"We started a manhunt in Virginia an hour ago. The office of the U.S. Marshal is involved. We're hoping to find him in the next twenty-four hours."

"Do you have any leads? *Anything* at all?"

"Nope. There's also the issue of the dead guards."

"Dead guards?"

"Both shot in the back of the head. Execution style."

Susan stood, a hand on her forehead, her mind trying to catch up with the shocking news. "Where?"

"Right outside the south perimeter. We found them a couple of hours ago."

"And no one heard the shots?"

"The police investigators are still at the scene. No details have been released yet."

Susan urged him to contact the FBI if they got a break in the investigation. Then she thanked him and hung up, trying to size up the implications of Bloodaxe's escape. Did he break out on his own, or did he get help from either the inside or the outside, or both? Was it possible that he used his computer privileges somehow to get himself out of jail? It sure seemed like an incredible coincidence that he'd vanished less than forty-eight hours after getting access to a computer. Was he really *that* talented? Did she grossly underestimate his skills?

Just then Troy Reid walked into her office wearing a fresh look after going home and getting a decent night's sleep. "What's new?"

"You don't *really* want to know." Then she told him.

Sitting on the edge of her desk while Susan paced in front of him, he asked, "Do you think it had anything to do with last night's slaughter at the local ISP?"

Her arms crossed, Susan shook her head. "I don't know *what* to think. First he agrees to help us, and his help leads us to a most unusual place in Yucatán. Then we have the killings at the local ISP. Then I do a little digging to learn more about the Maya, and find some very incredible coincidences between the event and that ancient civilization. Then this morning, after having a brief Internet chat, where everything seemed normal, he just vanishes, leaving behind two guards shot dead plus a million unanswered questions. And in the meantime, we have made zero progress on this virus."

"I wouldn't call it *zero* progress, Sue."

"You're right. It's not zero progress, it's *negative* progress. I'm getting a really bad feeling that Bloodaxe has been playing us all along. I'm thinking that this is either his virus or he took advantage of the virus, using it not only to bargain a more pleasant stay in jail, but to gain access to a computer and use it as an escape tool."

"We still have to crack the virus, one way or the other, with or without Bloodaxe's help."

"You've got that right," she said, returning to her laptop and invoking the last source code given to her by Bloodaxe, the refined Scent-Sniffer programs. "And the best way to get a fresh start on cracking this virus—which is still my highest priority—is to use code carefully checked by no one but myself."

"What about Bloodaxe?"

"I frankly don't care what happens to him anymore. If he escaped, then I'm sure the U.S. Marshal's office will eventually capture him. In the meantime, I've got an event coming up in less than eight hours, and I'm not anywhere near ready."

"Will you be ready?"

"I can't afford *not* to be."

4

Antonio Strokk watched his sister backhand the lanky hacker across the face. It was four in the afternoon and he couldn't wait any longer to get his information. By now the authorities would have found out about his disappearance and a manhunt would be on its way. Although he had covered his tracks efficiently, eliminating the closest buffer to the target, thus breaking the linkage to the kidnapping, Antonio Strokk remained alive in this business by being overly cautious. And besides, he had paid over fifty thousand dollars to get this man out of prison and delivered to his safe house, an abandoned building on the outskirts of Washington, D.C. While two armed subcontractors guarded the stairs of the decrepit brick building—at one point in its life a bustling banking center—Strokk and Celina had dragged the unconscious hacker up to the fifth floor, secluding themselves in an empty office with a distant view of the city's skyline beyond a pair of wood-framed windows.

It was time for Antonio Strokk to get his money's worth.

Hans Bloodaxe, hands bound behind his back, sat on a chair in the middle of the room. A lamp dangled over his head from a cord as he peered at his captors. "Who—what do you want?"

"Information," said the international terrorist, grabbing a chair, sitting in front of him.

"In—information? What kind of information?"

"To control the virus."

"Control it?"

"That's right," replied Strokk. Control of the virus meant power, and his client was willing to pay handsomely for such power.

"I don't understan—"

Celina slapped him hard.

"Please . . . don't hurt me," he said, a trickle of blood flowing from the corner of his mouth to his chin. "I'm just an inmate . . . I—"

Celina got in his face. "Don't lie, *puto*! Or I'll cut off your *cojones*." She produced a knife and showed him the long steel blade.

The bearded hacker went ashen at the sight, his eyes widening in fear.

"We know about your tracking programs and your arrangement with the FBI, so stop pretending," said Strokk.

"I . . . I'm helping Susan Garnett find the origin of the virus."

"We know that," said Strokk while Celina walked behind him. "What else?"

"The initial program led us to the Yucatán Peninsula."

"And?"

"And I've written a more refined program to make sure that the tracking program wasn't fooled by a decoy from the virus."

"And?"

"And that's it."

Celina cupped his chin from behind and jerked the hacker's head back, pressing the sharp blade against the stretched skin of his neck, right beneath his Adam's apple. "I told you not to lie to us, *puto!*" she hissed, leaning down, her face only inches from his. "Stop playing with us!"

"It's useless to resist," added Strokk. "You will tell us everything we want to know, it's just a matter of how much pain you're willing to endure before you do so. Now, why don't you tell us how it is that such an advanced virus could originate from such a remote location?"

Celina released him. The hacker coughed, clearing his airway, breathing deeply, coughing again, blinking rapidly. She abruptly grabbed his groin. "I'm going to start squeezing unless I hear something interesting."

The hacker lowered his gaze to the daggerlike polished nails at the end of long fingers in between his legs. "I'm not being totally honest with the FBI," he said quickly, shifting his gaze between his groin and Celina.

Strokk stood to the side, watching with half amusement at his sister at work.

"The pigs," he continued. "Bastards put me in jail and specifically ordered no computer privileges for me. Do you know what that meant? I'd rather get executed than not be allowed to get on the Internet, to write code. *That's my life!* And those pigs took it away, and only when they needed me did they come back and offer to grant me those privileges in return for my assistance."

"So you gave them the initial version of your tracking code," stated Strokk. "But with a slight twist."

"Damned right. I added an offset to the coordinates reported by the Scent-Sniffers to have some fun with the bastards and keep them busy for a little while to give me time to retrieve some of my old code and trigger a virus that I can use to hold them up for ransom later on."

Strokk waved Celina off and squatted in front of Bloodaxe, leveling his gaze with the hacker's. "To trigger a virus that you can use for ransom? What about the virus that's striking every day now? Where did *that one* come from?"

Bloodaxe shrugged. "I have no idea. I'm not responsible for it, though the program I released to the FBI this morning should help get them. I eliminated the offset. The revised Scent-Sniffers would yield the true coordinates, which should still be somewhere in the Yucatán jungle because my original offset wasn't that significant, just enough to keep the FBI from getting to the source of the virus right away, which they'll be able to accomplish with the Scent-Sniffer version, but by then it would have been too late. My *own* virus would have been all over the Internet, waiting for my signal to strike . . . but I didn't get a chance to release it. I was going to do it after breakfast. Then I was kidnapped." He made a face.

"Do you know the significance of this virus coming from the jungle?"

"I have no clue . . . and that's the truth. I just created the Scent-Sniffers. I didn't tell them where to go, except for the small offset."

Strokk exchanged glances with Celina. If the hacker was telling the truth— and they would soon find out—then all they knew was that this daily virus did originate in the Yucatán Peninsula, and that it may have something to do with the Maya, according to the conversation between Garnett and Slater.

They left Bloodaxe alone in the room to have a private chat in the next one, another empty office with a view of the capital in the distance through large fifth-floor windows.

"This is not going to be that simple," Celina commented when they were alone. "We're going to have to increase our electronic surveillance of Susan Garnett to see where the unaltered Scents lead her to."

"What about having the hacker do the same for us right here?" He checked his watch. They still had over three hours before the virus struck again. "You can set him up with a computer, can't you?"

She nodded. "I could, but I don't trust him. What prevents him from tricking us just like he tricked the FBI? There is no way for me to monitor his work simply by looking over his shoulder. Hackers are a strange breed of people, *hermano*. They can accomplish much more than the average programmer with the same number of keystrokes. Instead of deploying his code to track the origin of the virus, the little bastard could just as easily accomplish that while also sending a flash message to the FBI about his abduction. They'll track us down the phone line in minutes, and the building would be surrounded with pigs before we knew it."

"What options do we have?"

"Not many," she said.

"What good is he to us?"

"We still must learn if he has been lying. Beyond that..."

Strokk nodded. "All right, then. Do what you must. In the meantime, I'm going to set up a new surveillance post."

5

Susan Garnett was used to deciphering other people's computer code. She had first done it as a senior at Harvard, while majoring in computer engineering, where she got the unenviable job of translating programs from one language to another—mostly from Pascal or Fortran to C^{++}—as part of a modernization effort at the computer department to get all of its programs in C^{++} instead of the ancient Pascal and Fortran. Susan continued to take programs apart while earning a master's degree in computer science at Yale. While working on her Ph.D. thesis at Yale on advanced computer algorithms, she had spent months consulting for Honeywell and later on for Siemens on the translation of complex control systems algorithms used by the oil and chemical industries as those corporations switched to newer and more versatile software.

Susan now performed a similar task, combing through thousands of lines of codes, probing, examining, dissecting, just as she had done for most of her career. Only this time she did it not to translate into another language, or to correct malfunctioning software, or to improve the efficiency of a control systems program. Today Susan performed high-tech surgery on a complex C^{++} program to find evidence of Bloodaxe's trickery.

First she reviewed the original Scent-Sniffer algorithms that Bloodaxe had given her two days before, following their initial meeting. After checking the short Scent code, whose job was to attach to the queen virus during the seconds before and after the event, Susan pulled up the Sniffer code, frowning after the first few minutes. The hacker had not followed proper programming rules, failing to create a structure that flowed smoothly from top to bottom. Instead, the program jumped all over the place depending on the values of a number of variables, including the Sniffer's current physical location on the Internet, its last location, the expected new location according to the last known location of the nearest Scent, and the calculated quickest route to that new location. The program performed a constant loop through these variables, using the last set as input to the new loop, constantly adjusting its route to follow the Scent to the source of the virus.

On the surface, the code appeared to perform as programmed, but Susan had been around hackers long enough to know to look for subtleties in the code, for minor anomalies usually overlooked by the average programmer. The basic body of the Sniffer program consisted of a tracking section, where the variables were computed over and over as the Sniffer made its way toward its target, and a message section, where the location of the virus, in longitude and latitude, was coded and sent back to Susan for monitoring. Within the message section there was a unique snippet of code chartered with the delivery of the final message, or Bark, to mark the origin of the virus, the results of millions of iterations of the tracking section. Susan paid special attention to this last area, the place that told her where the virus was located, the spot she suspected Bloodaxe may have altered to fool her into thinking that the virus had originated in Tikal.

As she jotted down the essence of the code on a notepad next to her laptop, Troy Reid walked into her office.

"There's still no news on Bloodaxe," he said, pulling up a chair. "Any news on your end?"

"I'm not sure yet," she said, tapping the screen with the eraser of her pencil. "This is the section that generated the final set of coordinates for the origin of the virus."

"Which pointed to Tikal, right?"

"That's right. Now, look here, this is how it works."

```
ROUTINE ADJUST
IMPORT ADJUST1, ADJUST2
LONG = LAST_LONG + ADJUST1
LAT = LASTLAT + ADJUST2
CALL MESSAGE LONG, LAT
```

"The new longitude and latitude of the virus is calculated by making adjustments according to the most recent location of the Scent code attached to the queen virus. ADJUST1 and ADJUST2 mark the difference between the last location and the new location in degrees, minutes, and seconds, providing an accurate position within a dozen feet. Once the adjustments have been done, the set of variables, LONG and LAT, are transferred to the MESSAGE routine, which fires them directly to me."

Susan tapped the PAGE DOWN key and browsed to the MESSAGE routine, inspecting the cryptic C++ code, and then writing:

```
ROUTINE MESSAGE
IMPORT LONG , LAT
```

```
RLOGIN SGARNETT@FBI.GOV
PASSWORD ******
FTP LONG
FTP LAT
LOGOFF
RETURN
```

"It's pretty simple, actually," she said. "Just grab the last set of coordinates, remote log into my account, and FTP the coordinates into my account before logging back off. I have a script that automatically reads the E-mails and maps them to my tracking chart." FTP was a Unix command to transfer a file from one location to another.

"I don't see any evidence of wrongdoing," commented Reid, the wrinkles of his face moving as he frowned.

"On the surface," she said. "But you're forgetting about blank spaces to the right of the variable name. Did you notice the blank space between LONG and the comma? There's a blank space there. Watch."

She ran the snippet of code through a program that recognized all blank spaces not being used for actual spacing of instructions and data, marking them with a $ sign.

```
ROUTINE MESSAGE
IMPORT LONG$, LAT$
RLOGIN SGARNETT@FBI.GOV
PASSWORD ******
FTP LONG$
FTP LAT$
LOGOFF
RETURN
```

"Now let's run the same blank space identifier on the adjustment routine."

```
ROUTINE ADJUST
IMPORT ADJUST1, ADJUST2
LONG = LONG + ADJUST1
LAT = LAT + ADJUST2
```

"No dollar signs," said Reid.

Susan nodded. "That means that this section is truly doing what it's supposed to be doing, adjusting the location as the virus moves across the Internet. But it never transfers the outcome of the computation."

"Instead you get whatever values are stored in the variables LONG$ and LAT$."

"Let's find out where those variables are being generated."

Susan did a massive search through the Sniffer code for any matches to LONG$ and LAT$. The search routine took her to a new section of code:

```
ROUTINE 586RH
IMPORT ADJUSTı, ADJUST2
LONG$ = LONG + OFFSETı
LAT$ = LAT + OFFSETı
CALL MESSAGE LONG$, LAT$
RETURN
```

Susan turned to Reid. "That bastard," she said. "He was just messing with us, adding an offset to the coordinates to keep us from getting to the right place."

"It makes sense," commented Reid, pointing at the plasma screen. "He is taking the true longitude and latitude coordinates and adding a constant offset. On the surface, the Scent-Sniffers appear to be doing their job, tracking the virus, only the final coordinates will not be exact. Can you tell how much this offset was?"

She browsed down the screen and nodded. "Here it is. It looks like a fifty-mile offset, which means that the true coordinates should still be in the jungles of the Petén."

"Brilliant," said Reid. "But also puzzling. He should have known that eventually we would have combed through this code and figured out his trick. Why do it and risk losing his computer privilege?"

Susan stood, checking her watch. One hour to go before the next event. Dusk had already fallen over the nation's capital. Hues of burnt orange and gold washed the indigo sky, splashing buildings and monuments with dazzling colors, before fading away, giving way to grayish streetlights and the crisscrossing halogen beams of evening traffic.

She stared at the magnificent sight, but in her mind she saw Bloodaxe, finally understanding his true motive for cooperating. "He was buying time," she finally said.

"Time?"

"To escape. He knew we would eventually figure out his scheme, but not until he had used his skills to break out of jail. And we fell right into his plan. Damn him."

"What about the program he sent you this morning, the one already deployed across the Internet to intercept the virus after today's event?"

Susan returned to her laptop and spent thirty minutes searching through the new program, largely based on the one she had already dissected. This most recent version of the Scent-Sniffer code appeared clean, at least based on the checks Susan knew to perform. There was always a chance that Bloodaxe had introduced a programming element that Susan was not familiar with. But if there was one, it must have been quite revolutionary because she didn't see it.

"Looks clean," she finally said, checking her watch once more. "But then again, there's no way to be certain with Bloodaxe. Just to be sure, I've introduced a new routine to Bloodaxe's Sniffers. We'll find out if we've been tricked in another fifteen minutes."

They watched the clock count down to 8:01 P.M., and as expected, the screen froze for seventeen seconds. After her system returned to life, she released the new version of the Sniffers, which scrambled after the Scents attached to the queen viruses, converging south, on the same Hughes satellite, which pinpointed a location in the Yucatán Peninsula.

Susan leaned back, sighing. "Not again."

"Hold on, though," Reid said. "Look at the location. The coordinates are different from last night's."

She inspected the new longitude and latitude. "That looks to be to the west of Tikal . . . roughly fifty miles."

She typed a set of commands and a new window appeared on her screen.

"That's the true coordinate sequence from Sniffer serial number zero zero one. That's the output from a program I tacked to about ten percent of the Sniffers just to double-check their reported results, in case Bloodaxe decided to play another trick on us. There's forty-five entries per Sniffer, reporting the physical location of the closest ISP within a one-second interval, or forty-five sets of coordinates before convergence."

"They're converging south," observed Reid.

"Just like the reported results on my map."

"So does that mean this time this is for real? Is that the origin of the virus?"

Susan shrugged, once again not certain what to think. Bloodaxe had a way of injecting uncertainty into the clean logic of computer software, leaving her questioning the validity of results that otherwise she would have taken at face value.

Reid continued. "According to your conversation with the archaeologist from Georgetown University, there were quite a few parallels that cannot be ignored about these bizarre events. It could still make sense if it did originate in the lowlands of the Petén jungle."

Susan exhaled heavily, running fine hands through her brown hair. "Now that even my own code is pointing in that direction I'm not sure what to believe."

"What's that?" Reid asked, pointing to the bottom of the window on her screen. "That last set of coordinates looks strange."

Susan inspected the row of numbers following entry number forty-six, an additional set of coordinates transmitted after convergence. "You're right. There's not supposed to be an entry number beyond forty-five. The numbers are also not longitude and latitude. They look more like . . . damn!"

Susan quickly accessed the American Astronomical Society's Web page and used their interactive map of the universe to locate the point in the cosmos marked by the coordinates in her program.

Feeling a lump in her throat, she reached for one of the books that Cameron Slater had loaned her, flipping through the pages, finding the Mayan drawing of the cosmos.

"Oh, God, I have to call Cameron. This is . . . *incredible*," she mumbled more to herself than to Reid when matching the image on her screen with the drawing on the book, which showed the same two stars of the southern constellation Centaur that Cameron Slater had mentioned the night before. She remembered the Kuxan Suum, the umbilical cord that connected Earth to the Hunab Ku, the galactic core. "And this is no Bloodaxe trick. This is the output of my *own* code."

"Is this the location you mentioned from your conversation with the archaeologist?"

She nodded, the implications of her finding chilling.

Reid stood. "If this is all true . . . God Almighty, I need to reach the director. There is a chance that someone is trying to make contact with us."

6

Darkness enveloped the garbage Dumpsters lining the red-brick wall of an alley a mile from the White House, behind a strip of restaurants. Rats fed on what had been fine cuisine just hours before, their whistling sounds mixing with those streaming out of a club a short block away.

The stench nauseated the busboy dragging out a garbage bag, which he threw into the nearest Dumpster, landing with a heavy thump, splattering debris into the alley. The college kid, working nights to put himself through school, watched it with revulsion. The revulsion, however, turned to nausea when he spotted a forearm sticking out of the pile of trash, a rat nibbling on the flesh by the wrist. His eyes shifted up, recognizing a human face surrounded by refuse. Another rat had its entire head inside an eye socket, its furry tail sticking up in the air.

He stepped back, a hand on his mouth as he leaned over, vomit reaching his gorge, tears clouding his vision. He tried to scream for help, but another convulsion forced the rest of his dinner to his throat. Somehow, he staggered back inside. Two waiters helped him to the manager's office, where they called the police.

Chapter Ten

001010

1

December 15, 1999
Northern Guatemala

The helicopter flew in from the north, high above the hot and humid expanse of lush jungles projecting in every direction as far as the eye could see. This majestic ocean of green, sporadically broken by meandering rivers and crystalline lakes, merged with the blazing horizon as the crimson sun disappeared behind the volcanic glacier mountains to the west, spreading shadows across the limestone shelf of the Yucatán Peninsula.

The glistening craft cruised over a land surrounded by many legends, site of the rise and fall of one of the world's greatest civilizations, stretching from the scrub vegetation and thin soil of the northern peninsula down to the lowlands of the Petén and the lush jungles of the highlands, to the Pacific Coast, covering 120,000 square miles.

Deep within the natural protection of this tropical rain forest, abundant with fertile land and fauna, the Classic Maya developed complex mathematics, charted the heavens with superb accuracy, developed the only true writing system native to the Americas, measured the passage of time with a precision matching our own Gregorian calendar, and built vast cities with an astonishing degree of architectural perfection and harmony. This enchanted land, filled with fabled temples and palaces, marked by a legacy of stone and glyphs, witnessed the cycles of rise and fall that characterized the Maya, true believers of the influence of the cosmos on human ideas, on the very essence of human life. City-states emerged in prominence out of the jungle according to that belief, rising high above the trees, reaching toward the heavens. While Europe still slumbered in the midst of the Dark Ages, places with names like Palenque, Copán, Chichén Itzá, Tikal, and Uxmal blossomed out of the jungle, out of blocks of hand-cut limestone that evolved into astonishing works of architectural perfection.

Yucatán. Land of Turkey and Deer.

Cameron Slater recalled the Mayan name given to this land because of the abundance of edible wildlife.

He watched the remnants of that legendary world as the U.S. Navy Sea Stallion helicopter cruised over the ancient ruins, its streamlined shadow pulsating across temples and stone courtyards, climbing up steep pyramids, like a Mayan winged god rushing up to claim its human offering, before disappearing in the beyond, soaring over silvery streams and hunter-green canopies. The craft glistened in the dying, bloodstained shafts as the distant rimrock swallowed the sun, staining the blue sky with hues of violet and burgundy.

Cameron turned to Susan Garnett, curled up on her side in a corner of the cargo area. She had fallen asleep shortly after the helicopter made a refueling stop at a Navy vessel in the Gulf of Mexico. Cameron was amazed that she could sleep through the rough ride and the intense noise of the main rotor reverberating over his head, but apparently the former college professor was exhausted from the nonstop activity of the past few days, since the first event wrestled control of a significant portion of the computer systems around the world.

Cameron's eyes gravitated to their official escort into this remote section of jungle: eight SEALs from the naval base at Virginia Beach, one of two training camps for Navy SEALs, as Cameron had learned from the squad leader, Lieutenant Jason Lobo. The SEALs were all awake and staring in the distance, face paint blending their features with their jungle camouflage fatigues. The warriors resembled green statues, displaying neither excitement nor fear, professionally waiting for the mission to begin. He found their serene attitude comforting.

Both Susan and Cameron wore similar jungle cammies but had passed on the guerrilla makeup.

The seasoned archaeologist shifted his attention back to the darkening horizon. He would have preferred to have arrived at the site during the day, but Lieutenant Lobo would not hear of it. All SEAL deliveries were conducted at night. No exceptions. When Cameron had started to argue that this mission was of a scientific nature, he had been reminded of the recent presidential decision to militarize it. Susan and Cameron had had no choice but to comply. The SEAL team's orders were to deliver the scientists and their hardware to the exact coordinates that Susan said marked the origin of the global virus. They were then to set up a defense perimeter to protect the site. Not that they expected any problems from local authorities. The right phone calls had already taken place between the American embassy in Guatemala City and the Presidential Palace. The Guatemalan president had been politely reminded of the economic aid his country received from the United States every year.

Cameron checked the weathered watch he took with him during field trips, an old Seiko. Almost seven in the evening. His apprehension increased as the craft approached the drop zone. He was used to working alone, or at the most with a couple of local guides. Not only was he stuck with the SEALs, but Lieutenant Lobo had also confiscated Cameron's gun, an old Smith & Wesson .38 Special, the pistol that had accompanied him through a dozen trips to Central and South America. He missed the weapon he had used once to scare off a wild boar in Guatemala, and again to spook a black panther in Brazil. He had used it in Peru to kill a small deer during his two weeks of isolation, and in Venezuela to discourage a group of teenage kids from robbing him. Now he had the mighty SEALs to protect him, but he still couldn't suppress the knot in his stomach he'd always felt whenever a situation developed beyond his control.

Cameron Slater sighed. Everyone was armed except for him. Even Susan Garnett carried a small pistol, which Lobo had allowed her to keep after she had shown him her FBI credentials.

He tried to calm himself, gazing at the last of the day's light fading into the indigo tint spreading across the sky, followed by an ocean of stars slowly coming into focus. The sight was always the same once Cameron left civilization behind and ventured into the wilderness. As artificial lights receded, the universe came alive with an impressive display of celestial magnificence, washing the forest below with a grayish light.

He sat next to Susan and nudged her.

The beautiful computer scientist stirred to life, yawning, sitting up, regarding Cameron with sleepy eyes.

"We there yet?"

Cameron nodded. "For a moment there I thought you were going to sleep through the whole mission."

She rubbed her eyes and blinked. Leaning over, she whispered, "Have the macho men smiled yet?"

Cameron grinned. "Not a chance."

"How long have we got?"

"Should be there in ten more minutes."

Together they gazed out the side window.

2

Under a crystalline sky, Joao Peixoto walked slowly over the flat rocks protruding from the water along the banks of the Rio San Pedro as it flowed
northwest, through the lowlands of the Petén, snaking its way to the fertile
valleys leading to the Gulf of Mexico.

His eyes remained fixated on the shallow and narrow stream formed by
two long boulders running in parallel for almost twenty feet. Joao was careful
not to fall in the clear stream, but not for fear of leeches or caimans, the
latter preferring the twilight of dusk to hunt their prey along the shores of
the long river. The Maya feared the candirú, a tiny catfish of the Central and
South American tropics that had the peculiar habit of swimming directly into
the bather's urethra and extending its thorny spikes outward to attach itself
to the inner walls of the urinary track. Two of his people had died from the
ensuing infections caused by the microscopic fish.

Joao Peixoto kept his balance as he walked barefoot over the moss-slick
rocks, a five-foot-long string attached to an arrow and also to his right wrist.
He pressed the end of the arrow against a second string, this one made of
boar intestines, that bent the mahogany *atl-atl*, or bow, he held in his left
hand. Pulling back hard, he aimed and released. The arrow bolted toward the
rippled surface reflecting the moonlight. A second later a fish splattered water
in all directions in a desperate effort to free itself from the arrow impaling it.

Joao smiled as he pulled on the string and inspected the fish, large enough
to feed three, perhaps four. He removed the arrow and threw his catch in a
sack by the shore before returning his attention to the stream.

Joao Peixoto was a *nacom*, Mayan military leader, guardian of the high
priests, descendants of Pacal Votan, the greatest Mayan chief from the Classic
Period. But Joao was also a mestizo—an ethnic group created by the interbreeding of natives and Europeans, typically from Spain or Portugal. European colonists cohabited freely with Mayan women during the colonization
period, creating the Indian-Caucasian mixture reflected in Joao's fair skin and
light green eyes. His facial features, however, were native Guatemalan—a
round face with a predominant wide nose and full lips that always seemed
to drop at the edges, giving him a permanent frown that went well with his
eyes, which also dropped. His features had intrigued the British missionaries

from Belize who had visited his village when he was young, and with whom Joao had spent a portion of his youth, before being assigned the lifelong duty to protect the Mayan priests that lived deep in the jungle. And just like his father, Joao had to discover the outside world in order to become a better protector of the secrets of their ancestors. He did that by accepting the hospitality of the missionaries and moving to the outskirts of El Subín—a city in central Guatemala—for a few years during the mid 1980s. But he soon discovered that the highlands to the south were torn by left-wing guerrillas fighting government soldiers. When British missionaries tried to assist two wounded guerrillas, government soldiers had shot them all and set their mission ablaze. Joao had managed to escape north, across the mountains, reaching the Petén lowlands, and his village, where he was initiated into the lifelong duty to protect the elder priests, an honor among the Maya.

Joao spotted another fish approaching and readied himself for a strike when he heard the whop-whop sound of a helicopter. Puzzled, he tiptoed over several rocks and a large root from a nearby rubber tree, reaching the shore. He picked up his sack and headed in the direction of the noise.

3

Cameron exited the Sea Stallion, then helped Susan, who hauled a backpack as large as his. The SEAL unit had already formed a protective circle by the tree line of the small clearing, weapons held with both hands, reminding Susan of some old CNN footage.

They raced away from the craft, under the downwash from the main rotor, reaching the jungle just as the chopper took off, disappearing in the night.

Darkness surrounded Susan Garnett as a sudden sense of abandonment filled her when the helicopter noise faded in the distance. She inspected the small patch of rocky brush in the middle of the jungle, just barely large enough for the helicopter to drop them off, but still a few miles from their objective, just as Lobo had planned it to avoid telegraphing their position.

Telegraphing it to whom?

She shook her head, closing her eyes, wondering what in the world she was doing here. But things had happened too fast for the computer engineer. The moment she had found indisputable evidence of the connection between the virus and Mayan mythology, she had rushed to the phone to contact Cameron Slater, who had arrived at the FBI headquarters within the hour. By then Reid had gotten ahold of the FBI director, who'd agreed to send a search party to the region. Somewhere along the way the White House had found out and had militarized the operation, sending the SEALs along for protection, especially after the mysterious murders surrounding Susan's investigation. Bloodaxe had been the latest victim of this killing spree, found by a busboy emptying the trash from a Washington-area restaurant. His body was missing both eyeballs, all fingernails, the tongue, and the genitals. Plus it had been further maimed by rats. Autopsy results, however, attributed the cause of death to internal bleeding due to a small caliber bullet fired up his rectum. The report indicated the likelihood that the hacker had been alive when dumped in the trash. Rats had fed on him while he slowly bled to death.

Susan shook the thought away, in a strange way feeling sorry for him, even after everything he had done to her. She also got a sudden appreciation for Lobo's extremely cautionary behavior, like the night insertion at a distance far enough from their objective to avoid flying into an ambush.

And here you are now, in the middle of nowhere.

She frowned. Everything seemed surreal, like it belonged in some dream. Susan watched the SEALs moving across the clearing under the dim moonlight, weapons ready, intensity in their motions as they surveyed the surrounding jungle.

Her boots sank in soggy mud. She felt the warm humidity and the wetness of leaves by the edge of the clearing. Mosquitoes buzzed around her face.

She reached down and unfastened the small night-vision goggles that Lobo had given her on the way over. The battery life would be enough to get them to the objective before dawn.

"Are you all right?"

Susan turned to face Cameron Slater, his grin relaxing her. He wore a chocolate-brown floppy hat and the same weathered light jacket she had seen hanging in his Georgetown brownstone. His goggles hung from his neck.

"Just need to get acclimated, I guess."

"These sudden changes in environment can be intoxicating at times, particularly if you don't have much time to prepare. Give it a day or so and you'll get the hang of it."

She shrugged. "I just hope it's all worth it. I hope we find something of substance that helps us understand what's going on."

Cameron leaned closer, whispering, "If you're dissatisfied with the trip, you don't have to tip the tour guide." He motioned toward Lieutenant Jason Lobo, inspecting a handheld global positioning system unit.

She elbowed him lightly in the ribs.

"You're point," Lobo told one of his men, a bulky African-American.

The soldier nodded as Lobo continued to examine the LCD screen.

Cameron put on his goggles and switched them on. Susan did the same. The night suddenly changed to palettes of green as the small units amplified the available light.

"That way," the SEAL commander said before addressing the rest of his platoon. "Move out. Single file. Five feet spread. I'm covering the rear."

Seven soldiers disappeared in the jungle. Then Lobo nodded at Susan and Cameron.

"Relax," Cameron whispered as he led her into the thick bush, past towering trees heavily draped with moss and twisted vines. "One way is by listening to the natural sounds of the jungle."

Susan Garnett inhaled deeply, filling her lungs with the moist and fresh fragrance of the tropics while listening to it. The sounds of birds chirping or squawking from the high branches rang in her ears—along with a dozen other sounds adding to the choir; ceiba trees with wide leaves grazing against the trunks of rubber trees; the noise made by crawlers of some sort dragging themselves over the leaf-covered terrain; the peaceful splashing sound of the Rio San Pedro in the distance; monkeys screeching and howling while jumping from limb to limb.

Susan continued to move through tangled brush, the goggles showing her the way in the pitch-black jungle. She kept her distance with the soldier in front of her, occasionally glancing over her shoulder to make certain that Cameron was behind her. The archaeologist had warned her about some of the local wildlife, particularly caimans, jaguars, wild boars, and eyelash vipers—the most poisonous snake in the region.

Susan suddenly felt demoted to the bottom of the food chain, carefully scanning the flanks for anything that remotely resembled a predator. At least she had her Walther PPK.

The Walther PPK.

Susan sighed at the irony. The gun that she had used in her failed suicide attempt was the same gun upon which she now relied to preserve her life in an emergency.

In addition to the danger posed by the local wildlife, she also had to worry about the possibility of encountering those responsible for the recent assassinations. Troy Reid now suspected that Bloodaxe had not escaped but was abducted from prison. There was a greater than average chance that the hacker had told them everything under torture, before being killed. And even if he had not, someone still had managed to break into the FBI network and stolen her E-mail records, which contained information on the origin of the virus.

The group kept on the march for two straight hours, crossing ravines filled with knee-deep muddy water, across shallow streams, up rocky hills covered with hanging vegetation, and through twisted vines. Totally drenched in sweat, Susan followed the soldiers upstream in a parallel course with the shores of the river, which flowed almost a hundred feet to their right. Relief swept through her when Lobo allowed them to have a brief water break.

Sitting down over the leaf-littered ground, she set the backpack next to her, resting her back against a fallen log, which had flowers growing out of its decayed bark. She couldn't tell their color because everything looked green through the goggles.

"Goggles off," ordered Lobo.

Cameron sat next to her and removed his goggles. Susan did the same, the jungle turning pitch-black for a moment, before a glowing stick in Lobo's hand painted the surroundings green again.

The archaeologist sighed while removing his boots. She noticed some of the SEALs doing the same.

"What's wrong?"

Reaching inside one of many pockets on his fatigues, Cameron produced a pack of Camels and a lighter.

"I didn't know you smoked."

"Used to."

She narrowed her eyes at him.

He lit one up and offered the pack and lighter to a pair of SEALs to his left. One of them accepted his offer. The other had already produced his own cigarettes.

Cameron applied the burning tip to a black spot on the instep of his left foot. The black object jumped off his foot and into the cushion of leaves.

"Tick check," he said, removing a second one, and a third, before working on his right foot.

Susan made a face. *"Ticks?"*

He nodded. "Forgot to tell you."

"Ticks?" she repeated. "That's just great. Don't you get Lyme disease from ticks?"

In the green glow, Cameron grinned, eyes filled with dark amusement. "If you survive that long." One of the SEALs grinned, his gleaming white teeth contrasting sharply with his dark olive war paint.

"I don't find that funny."

"Take off your boots," he said in a voice that conveyed both amusement and authority. "Let's see how many visitors you have in there."

She did, and the sight of a half-dozen quarter-inch parasites sucking on her feet, ankles, and lower calves made her sick.

"Don't move," he said, lifting one of her feet and setting it on his lap. "The trick to removing new ticks consists in applying the red-hot end of the cigarette right on the head, not the body of the parasite, which, sensing the life-threatening heat with its antennae, will immediately release its grip on the host's skin and jump off . . . just like this one. See?"

"Little bastards," mumbled Susan, reaching down with her fingers to pull one off her other foot.

Cameron stopped her, putting a hand over hers. "If you try to peel them off, the head will break off the body and eat its way into your skin, where it'll grow a new body."

"That's comforting to hear."

"Relax. I'll take care of you." He winked.

Susan crossed her arms, watching as he rubbed his fingers over her ankles, carefully applying the tip of the cigarette just to the tick. His movements were fluid, practiced, hard hands against the soft skin of her calves, of her ankles. Susan's mind began to wander, imagining Cameron in the jungles of Peru doing the same thing by himself, surviving off the land.

Embarrassment suddenly prompted her to pull her foot away, but he seemed to have anticipated her discomfort and gently released it while smiling. "I'll bill you."

She said nothing, watching him put the cigarette to his lips and take a drag, eyes closed, drawing obvious pleasure before exhaling through his nostrils. A sudden craving awoke inside of her, dormant since the years before Tom, when she had smoked regularly, eventually giving it up under his constant criticism. But the feeling passed. Cameron took a second drag and passed it on to her, pointing at a pair of ticks on her other leg.

"You'd better hurry," Cameron whispered, pointing at a fat parasite feasting on her lower calf.

She nodded and focused on ridding herself of ticks.

A few minutes later and a few dozen ticks lighter, night goggles back on, they marched through dense foliage. The soldiers abruptly stopped. Something was whispered from the point back through the single file.

"Black palms," the SEAL in front of Susan whispered.

Cameron extended an index finger at a cluster of waist-high palms to their immediate right. "Careful with those," he told Susan. "Their foot-long spikes are quite capable of impaling any creature unfortunate enough to accidentally bump against them."

"That's right," said Lobo from behind. "During training exercises at Fort Sherman, in the Canal Zone, some of my men had to be airlifted because of close encounters with those deadly palms. Not a pretty sight."

Great, Susan Garnett thought. *Just great.*

4

Joao Peixoto was puzzled. He couldn't understand what the English-speaking strangers, less than fifteen feet away, were doing in his land. From their accents he knew they were not British.

While standing behind a thick rosewood covered with moss—some of which he had pulled off and wore like a long cape—Joao felt fortunate to remember enough of the English the missionaries had taught him to follow most of the conversation. The soldiers moved toward the secret temple of Kinich Ahau, protector of the Sun, a place still to be discovered by the wave of archaeologists and tourists crowding the region near the coast and around the highly commercialized Tikal. Aside from the secret ruins, and the small village an hour's walk away, there was nothing but wildlife there, plus the traps the seasoned native hunter set up to complement his village's corn, beans, yucca, and fish diet.

Have they spotted the sacred temple with one of their airplanes? Joao could not imagine how. The entire site was under the protection of the jungle's canopy, as it had been for a very, very long time, certainly long before his father and grandfather had protected the high priests.

Why, then, were those strangers here, marching toward the secret site carrying those weapons and moving as if trying to make little noise? Joao found the latter question actually amusing. He could hear them coming from a hundred feet away, but they could never hear him, even as he closed the gap to ten feet.

5

An hour later they reached a small sandy clearing bordered on one side by the wide Rio San Pedro. Susan felt a bit queasy from the heat and the humidity, but otherwise she had endured the long trek fairly well—though not without a fair amount of effort on her part to keep up with the SEALs, and also with Cameron, who seemed to be in excellent shape.

Perspiration filmed her face. A cool breeze coming from the river swept the small beach. Susan closed her eyes, welcoming it.

Lieutenant Jason Lobo decided to stop for a water break. They removed their night goggles and the SEAL commander cracked another light bar, its greenish glow diffusing across the small beach.

Susan felt the canteen strapped to her waist. It was nearly empty. Following Lobo's instructions, each member had been steadily sipping water to avoid dehydrating.

She glanced at the spring-fed Rio San Pedro's crystalline waters. Moonlight reflected off its rippling surface.

"The water should be quite pure," Cameron said. "But you'd better use a water purification tablet anyway."

While Lobo checked their position on the GPS, two of the SEALs approached the water to fill up their canteens. Susan and Cameron sat side by side and browsed in their backpacks for their purification pills.

6

For Joao the strangers grew more interesting by the minute. Eight were soldiers, judging from their weapons and the manner in which they moved. The couple was not, although they did wear the same camouflage clothing. Their tactics reminded Joao of left-wing guerrillas from the 1980s.

The more he observed them and listened, the more curious he grew. What was their mission? They seemed well trained for jungle warfare, but there was really no war to be fought here. Even during the worst years of the civil war between the leftists and government forces, the fighting never made it past the highlands separating the Petén from the valleys leading to Guatemala City to the south. This was worthless land as far as the world was concerned. Yet, the soldiers' sense of urgency, and the determination with which they plowed forward, could only mean they were after an important target. But what it was, Joao could not guess.

Now the strangers rested by the water's edge, and he wished he could warn them about the dangers lurking below the surface of the river's deceivingly peaceful waters. But for the moment, the Mayan guardian chose to remain hidden from view.

7

Standing sideways to the water's edge, Cameron applied the tip of a lit cigarette to a tick attached right below Susan's left knee. The parasite fell off instantly. While he worked on two more ticks on her left ankle, Susan absently watched another one of Lobo's men lean down by the shore and dip his canteen into the water. In that same instant, she noticed the strange five-toed prints on the brownish sand.

"Look, Cameron," she said, pointing at the strange tracks.

He leaned forward, eyes narrowing. "Ah . . . Lieutenant?"

Lobo looked up from his glowing GPS receiver. "What is it?"

"Tell your men to be care—"

Abruptly Cameron bolted to his feet, rushing across the sand just as a long and dark creature surged from beneath the water in an explosion of foam and sand, jaws wide open. The canteen flying in the air, the soldier jerked back, but not far enough to avoid the oncoming beast. Cameron collided with him with the force and speed of a seasoned linebacker, shoving him away from the shore, missing the snapping jaws by inches, rolling in the sand as the beast disappeared below the boiling surface.

There had been no warning, no scream, just a flash attack that left zero time for any of the soldiers to react, to reach for their weapons, to fire at the reptile as its tail thrashed for a second before disappearing beneath the water.

"Oh, my God!" Susan shouted as Lieutenant Lobo and two of his men helped Cameron and the stunned SEAL to their feet. Many pairs of ruby eyes, like hot coals, broke the surface.

"Caimans," Cameron said with amazing calmness. "The river's full of them."

One of the SEALs pointed at the torsos and tails of several reptiles a dozen feet from shore.

Susan approached Cameron. "Are you—" she began to ask.

"I'm all right," the archaeologist replied, brushing off the gray sand from his gear vest.

She put a hand to her mouth.

Visibly shaken, Lieutenant Lobo walked over to Cameron. "Thank you, sir." He shrugged. "Got lucky."

"Luck my ass," the SEAL commander replied, his eyes no longer conveying indifference, but respect.

8

Guatemala City, Guatemala

"El equipo es muy, muy importante. Lo nesesitamos para nuestro trabajo en el Petén. ¿Entiendes?" explained Ishiguro Nakamura to the two customs officials as he stood next to Jackie in a poorly illuminated hangar at the crowded airport, where a Learjet owned by Sagata Enterprises had dropped them off at dusk. Kuoshi Honichi stood to the side looking impatient because he could not follow the conversation. Unlike Ishiguro and Jackie, who'd learned Spanish after spending four years running Cerro Tolo and shopping in nearby Santa Maria, the corporate liaison did not venture beyond the very essentials, and his pronunciation had already drawn laughs from the customs agents.

The lead inspector, a short and stubby man in a light green uniform, sporting a beer belly and a mustache, regarded Ishiguro from behind his glasses.

"¿Y para qué es el equipo?" What's the equipment for?

Ishiguro relaxed, having rehearsed the answer to that question multiple times in the past twenty-four hours. *"Es un equipo sísmico, para medir los temblores en esta región."* Seismic equipment, to measure tremors in the region.

"Ah, okay," said the agent. *"Está bien, pero tienes que pagar impuestos de importación."* All right, but you have to pay import tax.

"¿Cuánto?" How much?

The official glanced at his assistants before looking in the distance while smoothing his mustache with an index finger. *"Como . . . mil quinientos dólares."*

Ishigoro turned to Kuoshi. "Need fifteen hundred dollars."

"*What?* Fifteen hundred dollars? Why?"

"To let us take our gear to the helicopter. Import tax, he calls it."

The corporate liaison turned red with anger. "That's preposterous! I checked with my people before coming down here. There's no such thing as an entry tax on research equipment when the equipment will not remain in the country for more than two weeks." He pulled out a small booklet in Japanese titled *International Customs Laws*. "It's right here."

Ishiguro looked at Jackie, who shrugged and said, "You don't get it, do you, Kuoshi? This guy doesn't give a damn about your little booklet in Japanese. First of all, he can't read it. Second of all, even if he could, he would still come up with some excuse to make some money today. These guys are way underpaid, and they want Sagata Enterprises to subsidize their income today. So, you better fork out fifteen Ben Franklins now or the equipment is not going anywhere."

With a heavy sigh, the corporate liaison pulled out a company checkbook for a bank in the United States.

"No, no," the customs agent said. *"Cheques no. En efectivo, por favor."*

"What did he say?"

"No checks. He wants cash," said Jackie.

"I can't believe—"

"Now, Kuoshi. Or you'll piss him off," said the female scientist. "And don't expect a receipt."

Fuming, the liaison pulled out a manila envelope and extracted fifteen crisp one-hundred-dollar bills.

Five minutes later the customs official, and his three smiling agents, assisted the Japanese trio to the waiting helicopter, patting them on the back as they climbed inside.

As their chartered craft left the ground and headed toward northern Guatemala, Ishiguro said, "I hope you brought plenty of bills. You're going to need them to pay the local guides once we get to Tikal."

"Plus whatever bribes we might need to offer local officials to stay out of our way," added Jackie.

Ishiguro had called ahead and found out that there were a few Mayan settlements around Tikal, mostly tour guides, vendors at the large souvenir markets, and street performers—all catering to the affluent tourists taking a break from their Caribbean scuba-diving vacations in neighboring Belize. They planned to pick up a couple of locals as guides and also to help them haul their gear to their destination, near the Rio San Pedro, about fifty miles west of Tikal.

"Ready?" Ishiguro asked Jackie, sitting next to him in the rear of the craft.

"As ready as I'm ever going to be."

"Nervous?"

The northern Californian gave him a slight nod, her Asian eyes widening as she smiled. "A little. Are you?"

"I guess. I've never been in the jungle before."

"Great," she said. "It'll be a new experience for both of us, and we'll do it together."

"Don't forget *him*," he whispered into her ear. "He's the eyes and ears of Sagata Enterprises, sent here to make certain that we do things right."

Jackie stared at him long and hard before saying, "The right thing, my dear husband, is *precisely* what I intend to do."

Chapter Eleven

001011

1

December 15, 1999

Natural wonders always have a way of making people feel small, meek, insignificant. The Grand Canyon, the Himalayas, Niagara Falls, the Amazon rain forest, Mount Everest, Yosemite National Park, the Great Barrier Reef, Mount Fuji, natural marvels that for centuries have dazzled the human race with their grandness, their splendor, their vastness.

These magnificent sights, unfolded as the surface of the Earth changed over hundreds of millions of years, captivated the imagination of the civilizations of the ancient world, sparking their ideas, feeding their dreams, fueling their determination to leave their marks on the world. It was these natural wonders that inspired the Greeks, the Egyptians, and the Romans to create marvels of their own, monuments to the will, the passion, the skill, and the strength of their cultures. This man-driven desire to leave his legacy on an ever-changing world created such magnificent sights as the Seven Ancient Wonders of the World, all of them now a memory, save for the Great Pyramid of Giza. But the human race continued to build, continued to create beyond those ancient architectural marvels. Civilizations sought to leave behind silent testimonies of their existence, of their legacy. Across the globe, beyond the lands of Homer, Cleopatra, and Julius Caesar, other societies converted their dreams into edifices of stone. Wonders such as the Great Wall of China, the Taj Mahal in Agra, and the Temple of Angkor in Cambodia changed the landscape of the Old World forever.

But while those architects, artists, and skilled laborers transformed stone into legacies, across the ocean, in what was to become the New World, other civilizations carried out their own immortal works of architecture. The Incas built the city of Machu Picchu high among the clouds in the Peruvian mountains. The Aztecs erected their monumental temple in Tenochti-tlán, which later became Mexico City. The Maya created their vast cities across Mesoamerica, filled with monumental structures, like the Temple of the Inscriptions at Palenque, the Pyramid of the Giant Jaguar at Tikal, and the Kukulcan Pyramid at Chichén Itzá. And man continued this monument-building legacy across the millennia, erecting larger and taller structures, shadowing the works of their ancestors, pushing the envelope and the laws of physics to create breathtaking masterpieces like the Eiffel Tower, the Statue of Cristo Redentor overlooking Rio de Janeiro, and the Petronas Towers in Malaysia, the world's tallest buildings. Other structures challenged the imagination, like the epic sculpture at Mount Rushmore, in South Dakota's Black Hills, one of the world's greatest mountain carvings, testament to the ingenuity, dedication, and God-given talent of its creator. Great works of engineering combined the elements of beauty, ingenuity, and man's ability to transform the landscape in the name of progress, to improve the quality of life, to serve his own needs, like the Panama Canal, the English Channel tunnel, the Suez Canal, the Golden Gate Bridge, and the Hoover Dam.

New marvels. Old marvels. Silent affirmations of man's relentless desire to leave behind symbols of times to be remembered, to be admired, to set a standard for future generations to challenge.

And the Earth continued to spin, bringing ancient and modern marvels through periods of light and darkness, through the years, the centuries, the millennia. The new became the old. The old became the ancient. The ancient became just a memory, like most of the wonders of the ancient world. But one wonder had remained intact from pre-Columbian times, surviving the destructive colonization period, enduring the passage of time, hidden deep within the jungle's protective mantle, out of reach to all but those who knew of its precise location.

Tonight, washed by the greenish glow of her night-vision goggles, Susan Garnett saw this unique marvel concealed beneath the array of branches of towering ceiba and mahogany trees crowding the lowlands of the Petén. They had found this site only because Lieutenant Lobo's handheld GPS claimed that their destination lay beyond a wall of densely packed trees cluttered with vines, moss, and other hanging vegetation, requiring the use of machetes to cut through fifty feet of thick greenery, carving out a narrow gap between trunks that forced the team to constantly twist their bodies to conform to the winding, humid corridor.

"Dear God," Susan muttered, staring at the vastness beyond the natural barrier.

The American team stood at the center of a large stone courtyard overlooking a huge, craterlike pit. A small palace stood to the east of the crater. A pyramid stood to the west, adorned by dozens of freestanding stone slabs along the front of the structure. A large temple, its many columns rising twenty feet in the air, its domelike roof grazing the canopies of ceibas and mahoganies, spanned the entire north side of this hidden site, opposite to where they stood. The branches of dozens of trees projected over all structures, reaching the edge of the crater, their canopies forming a circle that matched the shape of the pit below. Beyond this break in the canopy Susan could see the evening stars.

"Amazing," Cameron said. "No one can see this place from the sky. The opening in the trees is just large· enough for the pit. The rest is hidden from view."

Standing next to Cameron, Lobo nodded. "That would explain why no one has spotted it before."

"But someone definitely knows of its existence."

"Why do you say that?" asked Susan.

"Because that someone's been keeping this place up."

"Keeping it up?" asked Lobo.

"This kind of jungle would swallow a place like this within twenty-five years. The trees you see today would shed their seeds over the entire site in the spring, creating new trees. In fifteen years those new trees would have grown twenty feet high, their branches doing as much damage to the walls as their roots would to foundations, making the whole place crumble. In another five to ten years mud and vegetation would have covered the ruins. Even that pyramid would look like a hill covered with vegetation and trees. You'd never know what it was. Instead, there's just a few vines lacing columns and some shrubbery on the pyramid's limestone." The archaeologist nodded. "It's a pretty safe bet to say that somebody's been keeping this up."

"Who do you think has been—" Susan began.

Cameron clapped his hands once, the cracking sound bouncing off the limestone structures, creating multiple reports echoing in the night, before slowly fading away.

Susan and the SEALs jumped. The soldiers instantly pointed their weapons at the structures.

"What—what *was* that?" asked Susan while Lobo motioned to his men to lower their weapons.

"What a civilization," he said in awe, walking to the edge of the courtyard. "The priests and nobles had these temples built with remarkable acoustical resonance. They did this to impress the people, who could only come to the temples during ceremonies. They called these places cities of voices. In fact, this whole place is built like an outdoor theater, and this large courtyard is the main stage. Listen. *Suuusssaaannn!*" Cameron hissed in a sinister voice.

Her skin goose-bumped when her name echoed among the ancient structures, like some spirit coming alive from the stone, slowly vanishing after several seconds.

She slapped him on the shoulder. "*Stop that.* This place is creepy."

"Breathtaking is the word. This is *the* find of the century. Forget discovering Pacal Votan's tomb at the Temple of the Inscriptions in Palenque back in 'fifty-two. This one's in a class of its own."

Lobo asked Cameron to refrain from making any more loud noises. The SEAL commander expressed concern about having given his position away. Cameron told him that whoever kept this place up probably had heard them hacking their way through the mangled brush and vines and probably knew they were here. That comment didn't make Lobo feel any better, and he ordered his men to form a defense perimeter around the courtyard.

"We'll set up camp right there," he said, pointing to the edge of the jungle, by their hacked entrance.

"I'm going to check out the place," said Cameron. "Be right back."

"We have to conserve batteries. Please turn off the goggles in ten minutes," said Lobo. "And don't venture too far until we get a chance to secure the entire site in the morning."

While the SEALs set up their defenses, surveying the area around the tree line, Cameron dropped his backpack next to the rest of the team and ventured toward the other end of the courtyard, by the edge of the crater. Susan followed him, catching up with him halfway, amused at the excitement displayed on his face. With the goggles on she could see a grin painted across his face, reminding her of a child on Christmas morning.

"Are you all right?" Susan asked. "You have this strange look."

"A cenote," he said, pointing at the oval-shaped crater, roughly the size of one basketball court, filled with water up to around twenty feet from the edge.

"Excuse me?"

"A cenote. A sinkhole. They're very typical of these regions. Rain seeps through cracks in the limestone bedrock, dissolving areas of softer rock beneath the hard surface crust. Over thousands of years this process creates vast underground caverns roofed with only a thin layer of limestone. This weak roof eventually collapses, leaving this water-filled hole. Cenotes provided an ample supply of water for Mayan settlements away from rivers or streams."

He walked to one of the freestanding slabs by the corner of the stone courtyard, near the base of the pyramid. It showed an elaborate carving of two men wearing what appeared to be thick pads around their groins, waists, shoulders, elbows, and knees. They both had the same exaggerated profiles and elongated heads that Susan had seen in Cameron's books. One of them held a ball. The carving was inlaid with stones that looked green, but then again, everything looked green with the goggles.

"Jade," Cameron said, running a finger over the large diamond-shaped piece adorning the headdress of one of the players. "This is priceless."

"Why did they exaggerate their heads and facial features?"

"That's no exaggeration. The Maya practiced skull deformation. Infants' heads would be locked in wooden frames to distort the development of the skull and achieve the elongated head and flattened brow favored by the royalty and the high priests."

She made a face. "That sounds sick."

He shrugged. "Not really. It was just their tradition. They also favored crossed eyes, oftentimes hanging a ball of wax in front of a child's eyes for long periods of time to force the effect. The royalty also filed their teeth to points and filled the spaces with jade or gold."

"Amazing," she said, staring at the sculpted limestone. She pointed at the pads on the men and also at the ball. "Is that some kind of Mayan football?"

"Pokatok," Cameron said, running a finger over the aged surface, admiring the intricate detail of the relief. "A ball game the Maya played, but not quite for recreation. They used a heavy ball made of rubber, from the area's rubber trees, about half the size of a basketball. They played on a I-shaped stone court. Like soccer, they couldn't use their hands, having to propel the ball with their feet, knees, hips, and waists. I played it once at Copán, on the border between Guatemala and Honduras, with a few of my students and some locals during a research trip several years ago. Very difficult and very bruising. Got our butts kicked by the local Mayan team. During pre-

Columbian times, the game had significant religious and political implications."

"What did they play for? Land? Political advancement?"

Cameron shook his head. "For the right to live. It was played mostly by warriors. The object of the game was to bounce the ball off parrot-head sculptures on the sloping walls flanking the court. The losing team was sacrificed to the gods."

"I don't really think I want to know how."

"The victim's back would be broken in order to render him or her immobile. Then the high priest would carve out the victim's heart and hold it up to the gods while it was still beating."

She kept her eyes on the carvings. "Thank you for sharing that with me."

"From the perspective of the Maya it made perfect sense. See, our industrial world promotes the accumulation of wealth, which indirectly makes us fear death because we know we can't take anything with us. It leads us to be too attached to material things, to this world. The Maya, on the other hand, valued the enhancement of the spirit and the birth of ideas. They all knew that life on Earth was a very temporary stage. Dying was considered an honor, particularly if one died while protecting Mayan traditions or being sacrificed to a god. They had nothing to fear, nothing to leave behind but the knowledge that they had served their purpose on Earth and it was now time to travel to the Hunab Ku to achieve galactic synchronization."

Before Susan could reply, Lobo approached them. "Bedtime, folks. We'll check out the entire site at first light."

Cameron scanned the area, gave a heavy sigh, and followed Susan to pitch their tents.

2

A light fog lifted off the slow-flowing waters of the Rio San Pedro, hazing the shoreline as a cool breeze blew it into the jungle. A moon in its first quarter hung high from the crystalline, dawning sky, staining the mist with its wan gray light. The indigo tint gave way to shades of crimson and burnt orange as morning broke. Birds chirped. Monkeys howled. The jungle came alive, its sounds mixing with the soft purring of three outboards.

Slowly, like an apparition arising from the grayish cloud hovering over the surface in the twilight of dawn, three rubber vessels broke through the foggy veil, water lapping their sides. A lone figure stood at the front of the lead vessel, inspecting the shoreline with a set of binoculars.

Antonio Strokk concentrated on selecting a landing zone for his team, twenty-five of the most seasoned and loyal operatives he could find, many of them former Spetsnaz operatives—in addition to his sister Celina, who sat next to him in the lead Zodiac reading the amber display of a handheld GPS receiver.

Strokk checked his watch. According to his calculations, the Americans should have reached the target coordinates in the past few hours. Of course, the Americans had the advantage of using helicopters to get closer to the objective—something that the resourceful Celina had been able to figure out through another Internet breach at the FBI, where she had also learned that a team of U.S. Navy SEALs would be escorting the scientists to the site. The short notice, however, had not given the terrorists the time required to set up their own helicopter transport, settling instead for a turboprop cargo plane from an obscure field in south Florida to a strip near the Mexican town of Tenosique, by the border with Guatemala, where he easily bribed local authorities to look the other way while his men deployed the Zodiacs and transferred their gear into the boats.

Now, after ten hours cruising on this winding river, enduring a dozen close encounters with caimans, a snake dropping into the tail boat from an overhead branch, and the unending buzzing of mosquitoes, Celina's GPS receiver finally indicated that they had reached their destination—at least as close as they could get using the river without reaching the Agua Dulce Falls and its majestic but deadly fifty-foot drop. Strokk could hear the distant rumble of the falls.

It was time to get off and start walking.

"How far is it?" he asked when the coxswain cut off the engine as they neared a sandy section of shore, lifting the rear of the engine to keep it from getting tangled in the roots and debris lacing the murky bottom.

Celina looked up, her eyes glistening in the early-morning light. She had dyed her blond hair dark brown to help her blend in with the jungle. "Less than two miles to the northeast."

The sandy bottom broke the boat's forward momentum as it got within a dozen feet from shore, shortly after entering the murky shadows created by the green canopy projecting over the water. Two of his men were about to jump off to push the rubber vessel ashore when Strokk stopped them. Instead, the former Spetsnaz operative produced a halogen light and flashed it at the dark water, highlighting a half-dozen pairs of coallike eyes on the surface.

"*Caimanes,*" said Celina.

Strokk glanced at his nearest operative, a native from Moscow who had never seen a live crocodile in his life, until today. Strokk had found it amusing to watch him inch to the center of the boat when a pair of caimans had gotten too close to the boat around dusk, while the team was just beginning its journey upriver. He now reacted the same way. Strokk grabbed him by the arm. "Your weapon, Petroff."

The tall and stocky operative, almost twice the size of his superior, handed over a silenced Uzi, which Strokk aimed at the reptiles.

He fired, the multiple spitting sounds matching the splashes that tuned the river's calm surface into a boiling frenzy of dark tails and torsos rushing away from the boats, toward the opposite bank.

He handed the weapon back to his subordinates. "Now get out and push."

The extra-large operative stared at the weapon in his hands, smoke coiling from the muzzle, before complying.

It took the team ten minutes to disembark, hide the Zodiacs with branches and other debris, and begin to move toward their target.

The seasoned Celina Strokk was point, guiding the group with her GPS as well as her innate ability to operate in the jungle. Five years providing technical assistance to Central American rebels during the late eighties had taught her more than she would ever want to know about jungle warfare.

The morning breeze sweeping through the thick jungle caressed Antonio Strokk's face and neck with the same rhythm as the moss swaying overhead. Strokk, his face painted with camouflage paste, moved through the forest quietly but swiftly, the rest of his team following single file.

Sunlight filtered through narrow breaks in the thick canopy, providing enough illumination for their silent advance. Strokk concentrated on the mission. The longer he spent in the region the more his senses tuned to its sounds, and the easier it became to imitate them. But never as well as Celina, who walked in a deep crouch a few feet in front of him, advancing through dense jungle without using a machete—and without the associated hacking noise it made. Celina swiftly moved branches aside and sneaked through them by twisting her slim body to correspond with the bends in the heavy foliage. As she slipped through openings in the greenery, Strokk would quickly take the branches that she had brushed aside and mimic her body movements, gently passing them to the man behind without letting them snap back, and grabbing the next set of branches that his sister was now using. They continued in this fashion for nearly two hours, covering roughly two-thirds of the distance to their target.

Strokk felt his machete safely strapped to his thick utility belt, and he wished he could use it instead of his bare hands to move the vegetation out of the way—particularly the black palm leaves—but they were too close to the target now. Even though the chance of anyone hearing them chopping foliage was slim, Strokk would not risk giving away their position—particularly to a team of deadly U.S. Navy SEALs.

The price they paid for their silent approach, however, was the stinging cuts that lacerated Celina's and Antonio Strokk's hands and wrists, in spite of the racing gloves everyone in the team wore. He would have liked to wear more protection, but that would have had impaired his ability to use his MP5 submachine gun. Strokk, whose head now throbbed from a nasty headache, also had a few facial cuts from some of the branches that had swatted him across the face when he had missed the—

"Hold on," Strokk whispered as he raised a fist, signaling his team to stop. He dropped to a crouch and swept the jungle around them with the silenced MP5.

Celina turned around in the thick vegetation, her camouflaged face almost lost in the darkness around them. Her eyes seemed to float in the murky jungle as they turned to face him.

"What is it, *hermano?*"

"I think someone's watching us."

She immediately looked about them, then closed her eyes and listened for several seconds. She shrugged.

"Maybe it is just this headache," Strokk said, rubbing the tip of his index finger against his left temple.

"Probably the humidity," his sister offered.

Strokk nodded and reached into a Velcro-secured pocket on the front of his fatigues and pulled out a small airtight bag with ten extra-strength Tylenol caplets. He popped two in his mouth and downed them with a sip from his canteen before motioning his team to move forward.

As the mercenaries complied, Strokk kept a watchful eye on his flanks, still sensing someone stalking them. He continued for another five minutes, before once more raising a fist high enough for his team to see.

"Hold," he whispered to Celina.

"What's wrong?" she asked.

"I still feel stalked." Strokk inhaled and slowly scrutinized the thick forest around them, but saw nothing. He closed his eyes and listened, but again, the forest told him nothing. He looked at Celina and shook his head.

Celina frowned. "I don't like this, *hermano*."

"I'll take the lead," he said. "Stay behind me."

Strokk walked around his sister and began moving toward the target, scanning the thick underbrush in front and to both sides of him.

3

Joao Peixoto exhaled slowly. The warriors were skilled, he reflected, increasing the gap by several feet. He had to be careful. Their ears seemed fine enough to discern human noises from those of the jungle, even when Joao had imitated the sound made by snakes by slowly dragging his feet. Now he moved only when they did. While in motion the warriors made enough noise for all of them.

He had been following them for the past hour, when one of his sentries had detected them as the strangers got within a hundred paces from his village. For a brief moment over twenty Mayan warriors had the team in the sights of their deadly and silent blow tubes. But the armed men had not stopped. Instead, they had continued toward the temple of Kinich Ahau, where the first team had spent the night.

Joao's shoulder accidentally pushed a branch forward, and as he walked by, it flung back and swatted another. The noise wasn't that loud, but it didn't sound natural.

4

Strokk froze. He'd *definitely* heard something this time, and he brought the MP5 in front while his finger caressed the trigger. He wasn't sure exactly what had tripped the alarm in his head. The noise from the birds and the screeching monkeys had not stopped.

That's not it.

His ears had already tuned that out. He detected no sounds of reptiles crawling on the ground like he'd heard before ... *so what was it?*

He turned around and lowered the palm of his right hand. His team dropped to the ground and vanished from sight, except for Celina, who approached him. Strokk pointed at her and then made a half circle in the air with his index finger. She nodded.

5

Joao Peixoto saw the soldiers split up and decided it was time to go up. Still wearing the moss cape, he reached for the closest tree and skillfully made his way up the rough trunk, careful to keep an eye on the encircling soldiers below.

6

Five minutes later brother and sister met at the same spot they'd started.

Antonio Strokk was confused. "I don't understand."

"Maybe we're not used to the sounds of this jungle yet."

Strokk shook his head. "I'm telling you, someone is *watching* us."

Celina exhaled. "Well, whoever in the hell it is obviously doesn't want to show his face."

Strokk sighed and clicked twice the two-way radio strapped to his belt. Like shadows detaching themselves from the sides of the tangled bush, his team materialized back on the trail.

Celina took up the point spot again, with Strokk and the rest of the team following close behind. They continued moving for another hour before Celina pointed at a hair-thin wire partially covered by moss from a nearby cypress.

"Trip wire," she said.

Strokk nodded. If he listened very carefully, he could also hear voices, which his training told him were not more than a hundred feet away.

Chapter Twelve

001100

1

December 16, 1999

"Señorita Jackie," said Luis, one of the two Guatemalan guides in the *cayuco*, a long and narrow boat made from a hollowed-out mahogany trunk. Luis Arroyo, a short and wiry Guatemalan of Mayan ancestry, manned the small outboard purring along as they made their way down the Rio San Pedro. *"Aquí todo es pura selva." There's nothing but jungle around here.*

Kuoshi Honichi looked at Ishiguro. "What did he say?"

Ishiguro's face turned solemn. "There are big caimans in this part of the river."

Jackie suppressed a laugh while regarding the corporate executive, nervousness tightening his angular features as he sat at the front, peering at the dark waters slapping the sides of the boat.

"Continúa, Luis," she replied. *"Tenemos que llegar al punto que te enseñé en el mapa, antes de las cataratas." Keep going. We have to get to the spot that I showed you on the map, right before the falls.*

Ishiguro sat next to his wife in the center of the long and narrow boat. Luis played coxswain in the rear. Porfirio, the second Guatemalan guide, sat toward the front between Kuoshi and them. Porfirio, tall for the region and quite muscular, only spoke a local dialect, which Luis understood. According to Luis, Porfirio knew the region well.

Their gear was evenly distributed beneath the wooden seats. Jackie had covered the vital equipment with plastic and secured it to the boat with ropes, in case they capsized. No one but the two guides was allowed to stand, lest they take an unexpected dip in the river. And even when one of the guides did stand, the boat often rocked precariously.

Ishiguro wiped the sweat off his forehead. The noon sun beat down on the tiny boat, roasting them while they sat unprotected in the middle of the river. The guides had refused to steer the boat closer to either bank, where the trees hanging over the water would provide some protection. Luis had claimed that deadly black mamba snakes were known to drop into the river from the branches to cool off. Some had dropped right into boats, forcing passengers into an unavoidable emergency evacuation drill.

The back of Ishiguro's neck was already glowing red by the time he'd decided to drape an extra T-shirt over his head, covering his shoulders. Now it hurt every time he moved. Jackie, on the other hand, had developed a golden tan, which accentuated her brown eyes. She now wore a silk scarf over her head, plus a pair of dark glasses that gave her a Jackie Onassis look. Ishiguro suddenly wished that he was alone with her, instead of sharing this boat with the two Guatemalans and Kuoshi.

"How much longer?" asked Kuoshi, slapping the back of his neck after a horse fly settled on him. As he did that, his shirt rose above his waistline. Ishiguro caught a glimpse of a small gun tucked in the executive's pants. He was about to say something but chose to wait until he was alone with Kuoshi.

Jackie held a small GPS receiver—the only way to tell where you were in the jungle. Ishiguro wondered how the old conquistadores had found their way around this place, surrounded by nothing but dense jungle, with the flatness of the land not allowing for landmarks. Besides, once they left the boat, they would definitely lose track of any outside reference. He doubted they would even be able to see the stars at night in case they got lost.

"Another couple of miles downriver," she said, shifting her gaze between the GPS unit and the folded map on her lap. "Then we begin our trek. That will be about another two miles."

"Will we get there in time for the next contact?" asked Kuoshi.

"Only if we manage to reach the location before sundown. According to the guides, the jungle is quite dark during the day. At night it is pitch-black, even during a full moon."

Ishiguro nodded. "If we don't get there before night falls, we'll have to set up camp and continue in the morning."

Wildlife thrived in this section of the Petén jungle. Ishiguro saw dozens of assorted birds flying overhead, and many more perched atop trees hugging the wide river. A flock of flamingos crowded the left bank. He also spotted a few caimans basking in the sun—and he made certain to point them out to Kuoshi too.

According to the guides, this whole area was part of the largest wildlife preserve in northern Guatemala, home to six hundred species of birds and one of a handful of jaguar sanctuaries in the world.

The river's slow-flowing waters began to gather speed as they neared the Agua Dulce Falls. Jackie let the guides steer them to shore.

"Not the closest spot, but close enough," she said as Luis directed the cayuco toward a rocky section of the shore.

"*Mira,*" said Ishiguro, pointing at a patch of beach a few hundred feet to the right of the rocks. "*¿Por qué no vamos allá?*" Why don't we go there?

"*Por los caimanes, señor.*"

"What is going on?" asked Kuoshi.

Ishiguro narrowed his eyes, noticing at least a dozen reptiles resting on the sand, their charcoal hides blending in the gray river sand. He turned to face the corporate liaison. This time Ishiguro didn't have to lie.

2

Susan Garnett set up her equipment by the edge of the courtyard, just a few feet from the *cenote*, the circular sinkhole in the center of the ancient site. The noon sun beamed into the area through the circular opening, its luminous rays washing the limestone structures with a yellow glow that gave them the appearance of being made out of gold.

Gold.

The computer scientist sighed. During the one-hour tour of the area with Cameron and a couple of SEALs, Susan had seen more gold and jade than in her entire lifetime, particularly at the large temple across the *cenote*, the steps of which Cameron now sat while reading glyphs etched in the stone and taking copious notes in his field notebook. Three of the stelae of Kinich Ahau guarding the ceremonial structure had masks of gold with obsidian eyes and teeth made of jade. Thick gold bands covered the base of each stele, as well as the bases of the square columns at the front of the temple. Susan had touched the shiny metal, feeling its pliability. The metal actually wasn't gold, as Cameron had explained, but something called *tumbaga*, an alloy created by mixing gold with copper, which had a lower melting point. The craftsmen made it look like solid gold by removing the surface copper with acid, leaving a film of pure gold. The bands of *tumbaga* adorning the columns were also etched with glyphs.

Glyphs.

Now, that was also something that seemed to be everywhere. Glyphs ruled this place. She saw them carved in stone and wood, painted on masonry, etched into slabs, on columns, even on the twenty steps leading up to the temple. The number twenty also seemed to be quite common. In the number of stelae in front of the temple. In the number of steps of the small pyramid. In the number of columns supporting the porch in front of the temple, which they had thoroughly checked for anything that resembled an entrance, failing to find one. The archaeologist had even convinced Lieutenant Lobo to let him borrow some of his SEALs to look around. But the search had yielded nothing. The building appeared to be completely sealed.

She watched Cameron use a brush to clean a step, before running a finger over the relief on the limestone. The archaeologist was now dressed in khaki shorts, a white T-shirt, and the khaki vest with multiple pockets that she had spotted in his room a few days ago. He topped off his outfit with a dark green floppy hat. He was still making notes and inspecting the glyphs, while moving across the entire length of the second to last step by the foot of the temple. Then he stood, glanced at his notes, at the temple, back at his notes, and then climbed up the steps and walked beneath one of the corbel vaults in between the columns supporting the large mansard roof, also decorated with stucco figures of various Mayan gods, many of them adorned with gold and jade. The corbel vault, as Cameron had explained, had no keystone, like European arches, making them look more like narrow triangles than archways.

The archaeologist squatted and touched the limestone floor, under a corbel vault, brushing it, and touching it again. Then he moved to another section of the floor, beyond the vault. His movements were automatic, with purpose, projecting the fluidity of repetition. He had obviously done this before many, many times. From the moment they had left the helicopter, Cameron had seemed more at ease with the tropical environment than even the SEALs, always anticipating, always realizing what had to be done well ahead of everyone else. It was almost as if everybody but Cameron moved in slow motion, like they didn't quite belong in the jungle. But he did, and that reality made Susan want to remain close to him. The unarmed Cameron Slater emanated a natural sense of security that even the well-armed SEALs could not match.

Susan sighed, waving a hand in front of her. Mosquitoes buzzed nearby but did not settle, thanks to the repellant she had brought down from Washington. But they still annoyed her. She glanced at the elite Navy unit, deployed in pairs around the site. Two stood by the foot of the pyramid, partly hidden by the underbrush. Another pair guarded the area near Cameron, glancing at the intricate bas-relief carving on a large pillar that stood by itself in front of the temple across the cenote. The ornate pillar marked the main entrance to the site from the jungle, through a cavelike path carved out of the jungle but covered by a layer of moss to hide it from outsiders. A third pair patrolled the palace to her right, a single-story structure built like the temple but on a lower platform, without any steps, and protected by a roof comb, a simple lattice of limestone and stucco laced with the vines dropping from the canopy overhead. Lobo sat by himself on the stone courtyard by the tree line fiddling with the knobs of his satellite communications gear.

Everyone had settled into their roles. Susan returned to her work, interfacing an electromagnetic sensor to her IBM ThinkPad laptop through one of two PCMCIA slots on the side of the system. She planned to use this instrument to measure the electromagnetic activity in the area during the next event, eight hours from now. A large electromagnetic field had been detected by an Air Force satellite cruising over the region during a previous event, prompting Susan to bring along additional hardware in the hope of picking up new clues.

Last night's event, which Troy Reid and the rest of the high-tech team in Washington had monitored by releasing the Scent-Sniffer programs, had pointed to the exact spot where they were now. Susan had learned this and much more during the Internet chat she'd had with her superior using the SEALs' portable satellite link. Reid had E-mailed her a copy of last night's virus, which she'd compared to the copies from the previous nights, noticing the ongoing trend of the 260 bytes of undecipherable binary code always changing from day to day, while the rest did not.

Susan used the sleeve of her T-shirt to wipe the perspiration off her forehead. Like Cameron, she also wore shorts and a plain white T-shirt—a lot more comfortable clothing than the fatigues Lobo had forced them to wear on their way in. She couldn't understand how the SEALs wore so much gear in this humidity, but none of them seemed to mind. In fact, none of them said much at all, except for Lobo, who would come by periodically to see if they needed any assistance.

The computer engineer used her second PCMCIA slot to connect a temperature and humidity meter. She had already installed the software drivers for each of the two probes in her ThinkPad. Two windows on her screen displayed the current status of the external sensors. Ambient temperature measured 29°C, or around 84°F. Humidity read at eighty-nine percent. Based on the way she was sweating, Susan did not question the readings. EM activity read at less than 0.01 decibels (dBs) across her selected frequency spectrum, ranging from 1 megahertz (MHz) to 1 gigahertz (GHz). The information was displayed on a bar graph with frequency on the horizontal axis in increments of 100 MHz, and EM noise level on the vertical axis in increments of 1 dB. Electromagnetism existed everywhere electrical current flowed through a conductor, from lightning and power lines to electric toys. Classic EM specifications in the computer industry, controlled by strict FCC regulations, provided commercial limits for computer-generated electromagnetic interference at specific frequencies, up to a gigahertz, to keep the electronic noise generated by a home computer from interfering with other household items, like wireless phones, pagers, remote control units, and even pacemakers.

In the middle of the jungle, her systems told her all was calm.

"Not a creature was stirring," she mumbled.

"Not even a mouse."

Susan turned around, startled to see a grinning Cameron Slater. Perspiration had formed an inverted triangle on his T-shirt at sternum level, visible through the open vest. The soaked fabric clung to Cameron's upper chest, outlining his pectorals. Susan founds herself staring, then looking away.

"You seem to be in a cheery mood," she said.

"This place is amazing. So much like the Maya, but in some ways very un-Maya."

She shut off her system and stood. "Un-Maya? How so?"

"The *tumbaga*, for–" he began, but stopped, momentarily glancing at Susan's chest, only he didn't look away but actually pointed while whispering, "You might want to cover those."

Susan glanced down and noticed that, like Cameron, her T-shirt was also wet with perspiration and sticking to her chest, clearly outlining her breasts through the thin and soaked fabric. She blushed, immediately crossing her arms to cover her protruding nipples.

Cameron removed his vest and put it over her shoulders. "Don't want to send a bunch of Navy boys the wrong message." He winked.

Susan smiled, embarrassed.

"Keep it," he said while helping her with the buttons. "I've got another one in my backpack."

"Thanks." The vest felt comfortable, letting air through but providing an additional layer to conceal her bosom.

"The *tumbaga*," he repeated.

She recovered her composure, narrowing her eyes. "Excuse me?"

"*Tumbaga* artwork is very un-Maya. Unlike the Aztecs or the Inca, the Maya had little interest in gold, preferring to work with the hard and challenging jade. Yet, there's plenty of both here. Enough *tumbaga* to make me feel that I was at an Incan site in Peru, but then plenty of jade work classic of the Maya. One of the stelae has turquoise inlaid with the *tumbaga*, which is more Incan than Mayan. Very strange. Anyway. I think I've found the entrance to the temple."

"You did! Where?"

"I'll show you."

She followed him to one of the corbel vaults, which separated the steps from the temple's terrace, almost a hundred feet long by around thirty wide. Slabs of limestone formed the floor of this covered terrace, as well as the walls of the main building. Sunlight shone onto the porch through the opening between columns. The wall opposite the corbel vaults had no apparent openings that could provide access to the interior. Cameron pointed at one of the vertical slabs that formed the front wall. It was slightly different from the other because it had a row of holes drilled along its two long sides, from the floor to the ceiling.

"Looks like finger grips," he said, sticking his fingers in the holes.

"Should we get Lobo's men to help us try to move it?"

He rubbed his chin, frowning. "Maybe later. I still have to do a little more homework before deciding how to proceed. This place is full of warnings."

"Warnings?"

He nodded and walked off the terrace, climbing down the steps, stopping halfway, sitting down. Susan sat next to him. He pointed at a series of glyphs in a row, which he read from left to right. "These, as far as I can tell, appear to be warnings of some sort to respect the sanctity of the place, which is also quite strange because the Maya used glyphs mostly to record historical events, the movement of the stars, specific dynasty affairs, and also as a powerful propaganda tool."

"What kind of warning?"

"Can't tell. Deciphering Mayan glyphs has been a real challenge because we're missing too many codices. We usually can only decipher around sixty to eighty percent of them. But today, with so many new glyphs, I'm barely scratching fifty percent."

"What are codices?"

"Codices are the Mayan equivalent of our modern books. They were made of either deer hide or bleached fig-tree paper. After the trained scribes completed one, it would be covered with a film of plaster and folded like an accordion, a process that would have preserved them to this day. Unfortunately, the Spanish destroyed most of the codices during the sixteenth century. One Franciscan missionary by the name of Diego de Landa was personally responsible for burning the majority of the Mayan codices. Only three codices survived those terrible days, saved by Spaniards who took them home as souvenirs. They are named after the cities in Europe where they eventually surfaced. The Dresden Codex, the Madrid Codex, and the Paris Codex. A fourth codex, the Grolier Codex, was found in a cave in Chiapas, Mexico, and exhibited at the Grolier Club in New York in the early seventies. So, due to the narrow minds of the Spanish invaders, the modern archaeologist is left with only a fraction of the information required to solve the many mysteries left behind by the Maya. That's why I can't understand the exact meaning of this warning, which is the case with most of our work. The lack of enough background information—contained in those lost codices—leaves the field open to a lot of opinions, theories, interpretations. These warnings, for example, could be nothing but ancient bluffs of the Mayan priests to scare off enemies. Or they could be quite real and to be taken seriously. But I can't tell which. Either way, a warning in glyphs is just another unusual finding in a most unusual place. There's also the question of the land keepers. Where are they?"

Susan glanced about her. Dense jungle looked down upon the site from all angles. "Good question. Is it possible that they only come here for their rituals but actually live elsewhere?"

He nodded. "That's my current guess, actually. They probably live within walking distance. It's possible that they might even have a post nearby that watches the place closely."

"In case of intruders?"

He nodded. "That's a big part of the reason why I'm unwilling to touch anything. The Mayan civilization made incredible achievements in mathematics, astronomy, and architecture, but they were also superb warriors, and quite ruthless with their enemies, oftentimes using them as human offerings to their gods. They liked to break their backs at the sacrificial altar before pulling out their beating hearts."

"We covered that yesterday, thank you."

He put a hand on hers and gave it a soft lingering pressure. She didn't mind the contact. "Just trying to make my point for not wanting to desecrate this place. Don't want to tick them off."

"What about the SEALs? They should be able to protect us, right?" Susan also thought of her gun, shoved in her shorts by her spine.

He shrugged. "They sure look mean and lean with their weapons and uniforms, but I'm not sure how they would stand up to an attack by the Maya. Like I said, they are phenomenal warriors and this is their home turf. I doubt Lobo and his men would last very long."

Susan suddenly didn't feel all that secure, even as she felt the cold steel of her PPK.

They sat by the steps and shared a canteen of purified water. Cameron told her about his past. The son of the U.S. ambassador to Guatemala, he'd grown up in this country until the age of sixteen, when his father retired from the government and settled in San Diego, California. By then the young Cameron Slater had become an amateur archaeologist, having spent much of his free time going on field trips to nearby Mayan sites.

"So I went to UCLA and got my bachelor's and also my master's in archaeology, but with a specialization in pre-Columbian cultures. Eventually I got my doctorate from Stanford and began teaching, while going on more field trips, writing papers, attending conferences, and essentially living and breathing my work. Before I knew it I was moving from college to college, following research grants, teaching some, also writing a few textbooks along the way, but spending a lot of time on field trips. That's why I left my post at Georgia Tech and headed to Georgetown. A couple of fat research grants."

"Are your parents still living in San Diego?"

He shook his head while glancing at his mountain boots. "Dad passed away almost ten years ago. He was only sixty-three." He paused. "Cancer. Mom mourned herself to death. She died a year later, even though she had been in perfect physical shape at the time of Dad's death. They had been married almost forty years."

Susan nodded, putting a hand on his shoulder. "I'm sorry."

He inched his shoulders up and down. "I've never seen two people so close in my life. I truly believe they were soul mates. She simply couldn't go on living without him. It was like a part of her had really died. She lost the will to live and died in her sleep one night. Natural causes, they said—if you call mourning a natural cause. But let's not get all depressed here," he added cheerfully. "Let's talk about you. I'm sure your story's not quite as gloomy."

Susan almost laughed, settling for a sigh. "I wish." In a way she wanted to tell him how much she could relate to the pain that his mother had gone through. "My parents are still alive, though I don't see them as often as I would like to, especially after . . . well, my husband and daughter were killed in an auto accident two years ago."

Cameron put an arm around her shoulders. "I'm so sorry, Susan. I didn't know. Metcalf never mentioned it when he called the night that you came by my place."

She nodded. "It's not the kind of thing that I want advertised. In fact, aside from my parents, Metcalf, and Reid, not too many people know. Jonathan Metcalf helped me get back on my feet after the accident. He put me in contact with Reid at the FBI when I expressed a desire to do something else."

"Susan, I'm *really* sorry. I'm also very impressed that you have been able to bounce back the way you have. I can only imagine how terrible you must have felt."

"I have my moments," she said, getting up. "Anyway. I'd better get back to my gear."

He also stood. "I hope I didn't offend you. I—"

"I don't think you're capable of offending me, Cameron Slater. And thanks for this." She gave him a brief smile while pointing at the vest. Then she walked away.

3

Covered with a cape of moss, Antonio Strokk removed his headphones and glanced at his sister, also cloaked with moss, lying next to him behind the thick underbrush tangled with the trunks of the stately ceibas and mahoganies encircling the impressive site. The former Russian Spetsnaz operative had deployed his troops around the area efficiently, just as he had been taught many years before. His team covered every SEAL in the area. At his command the two dozen seasoned warriors would fire their silenced weapons and eliminate the threat before they knew what had hit them. The trip wires the Americans had left behind to warn them of intruders would have tricked most of the operative community, but Antonio Strokk and his team had seen too much action to fall for them.

Celina, also wearing headphones, lowered the small dish antenna of their eavesdropping equipment. Thanks to the incredible acoustics of the Mayan site, they could listen to the conversations while setting the receiver to the lowest setting, which pleased Strokk because it conserved batteries.

She also removed her headphones.

"What do you think?" she whispered in the murky bush.

"I'm not sure what to think. For now we must continue to wait. See how the situation develops." The Venezuelan-Russian veteran knew the value of waiting and observing. By issuing a single command, Strokk could take control of the site in less than a minute, sparing the scientists and their equipment from the silent fusillade that would end the lives of the SEAL team. But he feared doing so would have adverse effects. Slater and Garnett were apparently making progress in the investigation. Strokk's intervention now would only slow down that process.

The former Spetsnaz officer had learned the hard way that patience was a weapon far more powerful than the Sig Sauer automatic strapped to his utility belt. In his lifetime, Antonio Strokk had to exercise extreme patience not just in the field, but also with his superiors at the KGB, which had dictated the missions of Strokk's Spetsnaz team during the Afghanistan campaign. After the collapse of the Soviet Union, he had decided to become his own boss and contract out of his services, rather than offering them to the new Russia for slave wages and a small apartment in Moscow. In the ten years since he had gone independent, Strokk had amassed a large fortune, which he used not only to live like a king, but also to finance the deployment of a force like the one surrounding this bizarre Mayan site on this hot and humid afternoon. And it was getting hotter. Sweat poured down his face, stinging his eyes. The moss cape not only weighed down on him, but also felt like a furnace. But he endured it, just as he had withstood his nightmarish years in the Afghan mountains . . .

Afghanistan.

The rugged operative frowned, remembering the pain, the unmitigated terror. He tightened his groin muscles as his ears detected the high-pitched wail of the Afghan women, their faces veiled, hateful eyes burning him. Many hands reached down, lowering the pants of his fatigues, pressing his own blade against his testicles. Horror seized him as the blade ruptured the skin, like ripping Velcro, severing them.

The agony had been unequaled. He had shouted out in raw, savage pain, wrenching out bloodcurling howls, his arms and legs numb from the pressure he'd put on the restraining rope, blood jetting between his legs. Through his tears he had watched the silhouette of an Afghan woman, back-lit by the sun, one hand clutching the bloody knife, the other gripping his manhood high up in the air, all the while bellowing the same wicked cry that still chilled him with the power of a thousand Russian winters. Then she had thrown them on the ground and stepped on them.

Scourged, castrated, dying, Antonio Strokk breathed in short sobbing gasps, feeling hands securing his face, pressing it against the ground, fingers stabbing the sides of his jaw, forcing his mouth open. The women shoved his testicles in his mouth, shouting incomprehensible words.

He tasted himself; tasted sand, dirt, his own blood. His convulsing stomach forced bile up his gorge. He vomited, spitting them out. But the knife returned to his groin, pressed against his member as more hands shoved the dusty testicles back in his mouth. His pain-racked mind had understood the message, triggering the command to chew, to ignore, to accept, and to chew again, over and over. But his mind detected something else, the sound of nearing helicopters, the downwash of hovering craft, the screams of the Afghan women as machine guns came alive, as the ground around him exploded, as figures dispersed in the bright sunlight, as the pressure on his groin vanished.

Strokk blinked out of the flashback, breathing deeply, staring at his sister, who had put on her headphones and continued monitoring the camp. He fixed his headphones back over his ears and listened to the distant conversation, but mixed with the small talk he could still hear the Afghan women, shouting, laughing, cursing him.

Antonio Strokk knew he would continue to hear their voices until the day he died.

Chapter Thirteen

001101

1

December 16, 1999

Cameron Slater had always been fascinated by ancient history. From an early age he had dreamed of becoming an archaeologist, losing himself in the history of a place, peeling back the layers of time, searching, digging, piecing together the ancient past, bringing back the legacy of past civilizations, saving the work of generation upon generation. His passion had driven him through school in UCLA, in Stanford, in Georgia Tech, earning degree after degree, slowly becoming an authority in the subject, traveling to distant places in search of the past, probing beyond the surface, formulating his own theories, however controversial and unconventional they may have seemed.

Cameron Slater was a diffusionist, believing that the ancient world was quite intercultural, cross-pollinated, with distant civilizations having been in contact at some point in their pasts. He had found evidence of this claim everywhere he had looked, in the graceful lotus motifs decorating the necks of Incan vessels, found not only on the frieze of the Great Ball Court at the Mayan city of Chickén Itzá, but also adorning the towering granite columns at Karnak, Egypt. Cameron had also found evidence in Mayan structures built in the shape of the Egyptian letter M, called ma, signifying country, the universe. In the practice of mummification, originating in Egypt, diffusing throughout the world, through India, Indochina, Polynesia, and the Americas. In the Egyptian god Horus showing a remarkable resemblance to Quetzalcoatl, the feathered serpent of ancient Mexico. In their daily lives, sharing passions for similar entertainment, like wrestling, phallic cults, respect for dwarfs, and building stepped pyramids. From linguistic parallels to burying rituals. Where Egyptians placed small strips of papyrus in burials, the Aztecs included a lot of paper with their dead. Or the bearded Phoenician oarsmen carved on a

700 B.C. relief, striking an incredible resemblance to a pre-Columbian incense burner discovered in Guatemala. And the list went on and on, the parallels unending, mind-boggling, challenging, but also evident, undeniable.

Cameron Slater gazed at the dark temple, across the moonlit cenote, remembering his trips, his excursions, the mountains of Peru, the jungles of Venezuela, the mangroves of Guyana, inhospitable to all but those who had chosen to learn to live from the land. He remembered the primitive expeditions, the intense heat, the mixed rewards of sweet successes and the heartbreaking disappointments of failed excursions. He recalled the villages, the natives, their customs, their dances, their hospitality. His mind traveled back to his earlier archaeological days, the romance of the field drawing him with savage power, controlling his will, blocking out the outside world, just as it did tonight, possessing him with intoxicating force.

He had found a unique site, a virgin location, untouched by outsiders for millennia, surviving so many waves of invaders, of destruction, of subjugation. Cameron Slater took in the magnificent sight, the ornate roofs, the corbel arches, the geometrically perfect pyramid. He listened to the sound of the night, mixed with the incessant clicking of Susan's laptop as she put the finishing touches to her search routine.

Susan Garnett.

Cameron wasn't sure why he felt so attracted to this stranger. An attraction that went well beyond the short-lived relationships with females in the archaeological circle, or the occasional adventure with locals during an expedition, like the daughter of the coffee merchant in Venezuela, the adventurous sister of his Peruvian mountain guide, or that unforgettable dancer outside Brasília, who taught him a thing or two about the most ancient of human pleasures.

Perhaps he should just keep it professional to make it easy for him to walk away when this was over. Cameron Slater, world traveler, noted author, distinguished speaker, had never entertained the notion of being tied down, of belonging to someone. His life had always revolved around archaeology, around his work. Even his own brownstone in Georgetown was nothing more than an extension of his office, a base of operations, easily moved to another school if the right grant came through for the right research project. In the twenty years since obtaining his Ph.D., Cameron had moved dozens of times, from the East Coast to the West, and back to the East Coast, and many places in between, living the nomad life of a modern archaeologist, living out of a suitcase, always going where the field research of the moment was, where the grants sent him, sometimes for months at a time, without having to pick up the phone and explain his sudden decision to anyone.

So what makes you so special? He thought, shooting Susan Garnett—busily tapping the keyboard of her laptop—a puzzled look.

God, she's lovely.

He looked at all of her, under the moonlight, at her delicate arms, bent at the elbows, long fingers tapping the keys with that familiar comfort that came from repetition. A thin neck, fine features, captivating hazel eyes that drew him in every time she locked them on him. And that smile, honest, welcoming, yet mysterious, with a secret past, which only kindled his feelings.

Inhaling deeply, Cameron shook his head, looking away, trying to let it go, forcing the Brazilian dancer into his mind, remembering her glistening body, soaked from swimming in jungle pools, cool water dripping onto him. *Let it go, Slater. You won't be able to give her the time.*

Just let it go.

2

The electromagnetic meter on her screen began to move a few seconds before the event, almost imperceptibly, but strong enough for Susan Garnett to notice. The bars in the upper frequency range stirred into life, reaching the two-decibel level.

She had wondered if her system would freeze, and now she realized that it would not, perhaps because she stood in the center of this celestial force, like in the tranquil eye of a hurricane, safe from the storm, isolated from the winds, but still very much within the path of the virus.

Cameron Slater sat next to her, by the edge of the cenote, the gray light from an orange moon high in the sky casting a wan glow across the site, mixing with the off-white glow of her screen. Lobo stood behind them, peering at the screen over their shoulders.

The digital counter on her system kicked in, marking the start of the event, due to last fourteen seconds. EM activity flurried, particularly in the upper frequencies. The bar identifying frequencies between 900 MHz and 1 GHz peaked at the 20 dB mark. She noticed no changes in temperature or humidity. The hard drive in her system whirled, downloading a digital image of the EM noise, sampled once every millisecond, creating a huge file of binary code fourteen million lines long and largely reflecting the upper end of the selected frequency spectrum.

As the event ended, right before the EM activity vanished, the entire frequency spectrum bounced up to the 20 dB mark for a fraction of a second.

"Let's see what we've got." She worked the keyboard, pulling up the binary file. Rows and rows of ones and zeroes filled her screen.

She activated her custom disassembler in an attempt to translate the huge binary file into assembly code.

The screen changed to:

STATS
LENGTH: 42, 342, 021 BYTES
COMPOSITION: 0% ASSEMBLY CODE 100% UNKNOWN
ORIGIN: UNKNOWN
HOST STATUS: UNKNOWN
UNFILTERED STRAIN FOLLOWING . . .

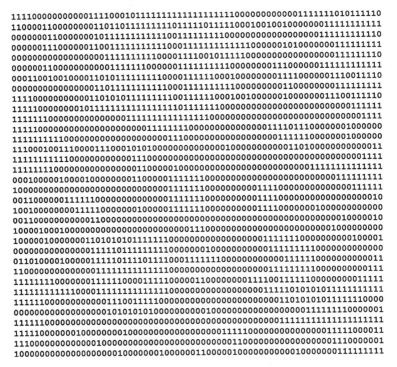

CONTINUE BROWSING? Y/N

"Great," she said, hitting N before looking at Cameron. "My disassembler doesn't recognize it. Let me try something else."

Susan remote-logged in to the FBI network using the Navy's dedicated satellite link and followed the path of the Sniffers, which, as on previous nights, had converged on the Hughes satellite and down to her current location. She launched her custom petri dish software to dissect the virus captured tonight by her software cocoons.

PETRI DISH SOFTWARE
FEDERAL BUREAU OF INVESTIGATION
©1999 BY SUSAN J. GARNETT
12-16-99 21:03:00

```
CC1 01011010.10101010.01011001.01110100.10111010.01000110.11010101
CC2 01111011.00101000.01011001.01110110.01111010.01000110.11010101
CC3 01001010.11101010.01011111.01101100.10111011.01000110.11010101
CC4 01101011.10101010.01111001.01110100.00100010.01000110.11010101
CC5 01110010.10101100.01001001.01111100.11111001.01000110.01010101
CC6 01111110.11101010.01111000.01110100.10111010.01000110.01010101
```

Susan reviewed the first six iterations of the mutation sequence of this virus, quite similar to the ones she had seen in previous days, with every replication showing a completely different signature.

"Nothing different here," she said more to herself than to her small audience. In addition to Cameron and Lobo, two SEALs also watched her work the system.

She ran her software against the main body of tonight's captured virus.

STATS
LENGTH: 1270 BYTES
COMPOSITION: 7% ASSEMBLY CODE 93% UNKNOWN
ORIGIN: UNKNOWN
HOST STATUS: INTACT
UNFILTERED STRAIN FOLLOWING . . .

```
1000101101010100101100111110101010101001100011110001110101010101011001101
1010110101110101100101010101010100101011101010110010101010101110101010110
1010011011010010101001010010101111001011100101010101110100110110110111010100
0100010010010010101001010010101011011111001010010101001111001010100100010
0101100110110101101011101011001010101010101010010101110101011001010101011
1010101011010100110110100101010100101011110010111001010101010101101001101
1101010001001101010010100101010010100101011011111001010010101001111001
0101100110111010110101110101100101010101010100101011101010110010101010101011
1010101011010100110110100101010100101011110010111001010101010101101001101
1101010001001101010010100101010010100101011011111001010010101001111001
1000101101010100101100111110101010101001100011110001110101010101011001101
1010110101110101100101010101010100101011101010110010101010101110101010110
1010011011010010101001010010101111001011100101010101110100110110110111010100
0100010010010010101001010010101011011111001010010101001111001010100100010
0101100110110101101011101011001010101010101010010101110101011001010101011
1010101011010100110110100101010100101011110010111001010101010101101001101
1101010001001101010010100101010010100101011011111001010010101001111001
0101100110111010110101110101100101010101010100101011101010110010101010101011
1010101011010100110110100101010100101011110010111001010101010101101001101
1101010001001101010010100101010010100101011011111001010010101001111001
1000101101010100101100111110101010101001100011110001110101010101011001101
1010110101110101100101010101010100101011101010110010101010101110101010110
1010011011010010101001010010101111001011100101010101110100110110110111010100
1101010010010010101001010010101101111100101001010100111100101010010010
0101100110110101101011101011001010101010101010010101110101011001010101011
1010101011010100110110100101010100101011110010111001010101010101101001101
1011101010001001101010010100101010010100101011011111001010010101001111
0101100110110101101011101011001010101010101010010101110101011001010101011
1010101011010100110110100101010100101011110010111001010101010101101001101
1101010001001101010010100101010010100101011011111001010010101001111001
```

CONTINUE BROWSING? Y/N

"It's all the same as before," she said, shaking her head. "Only seven percent can be disassembled. The same *damned* seven percent that I've been looking at for the past five days!"

She did a sanity check anyway, pulling up each of the disassembled sections, finding the daily counter, which triggered the activation of the virus at the exact same time every day, with a daily adjustment to compensate for the decreasing duration of each event as the virus counted down to the end of the millennium. She reviewed the section managing the duration of the daily freezes and watched in disappointment as the routine that defined the event to take place at one A.M. GMT on January first remained undecoded.

She brushed back her damp hair. Humidity levels had reached eighty-two percent. Susan began to get concerned about the reliability of her system in such a moist environment. If the humidity reached the inner workings of her laptop, it could short circuit something, killing her work.

She chose to keep going until it reached eighty-five percent. Then she would shut everything off and wait until the morning sun burned off the haze.

Lobo and the other SEALs lost interest and walked away. Cameron remained by her side.

"Got to hurry," she said, going on to explain the incompatibility of high humidity and electronics while she continued tapping keys.

Susan compared the undecoded routine from tonight's virus with that of the previous days, finding that it had not changed. All ones and zeroes were in the exact same location. She performed a multiple DIFF between tonight's virus with that from the previous nights, finding that once again, 260 bytes did not match with any of the previous viruses.

"Odd," said Cameron, leaning forward. "So within the virus released each night there are 260 independent bytes?"

"I think I forgot to mention that. Why?"

"Well, the Maya had two calendars. I told you about the Long Count calendar, which is based on solar movement, like our Gregorian calendar. But there's also a religious Calendar, which had thirteen 20-day months, or 260 days."

Susan sat sideways to him. "That is odd. Do you think there's a clue somewhere in there that might help us decode it?"

"How many of these independent binary segments do you have?"

"The events started on the eleventh, but my cocoons didn't go into effect until the twelfth, which means I have five, including tonight's."

They spent a few minutes reviewing the strings on the screen, but nothing seemed obvious. Then Susan noticed the humidity level rising to eighty-five percent.

"That's as much as I want to push the hardware," she said, powering down the system.

He helped her put away the high-tech gear in waterproof hard cases, leaving out only the solar-cell electric generator to begin charging the batteries at first light.

They sat side by side looking at the stars. By then all the SEALs were sleeping, save for the two on guard duty. They stood in between the small temple and the courtyard, covering both entrances to the site from a safe distance.

Moonlight continued to glow, casting a gentle shine on the polished limestone. The resonance of the site echoed the distant howling of monkeys and the chirping of birds in a rain forest serenade that changed pitch according to the gentle breeze blowing down from the mountains to the south.

"Sounds beautiful," she said.

"The Maya used their skills to build objects not just of architectural beauty, but also of harmony with the land. This place abounds with harmony. It flows with a hidden, yet powerful energy that emanates from the very stone used to build it, from the arrangement of buildings around a cenote, simple but with amazing resonance to capture the natural sounds of their jungle, to make it a *part* of the jungle. In our societies we want to delineate between civilization and the wild. We have concrete and we have grass, skyscrapers and parks, parking lots and meadows. We always like to polarize, to divide, to set up boundaries. The Maya believed otherwise, carrying their fenceless concept to other senses, like these natural sounds bouncing off the limestone that also came from the same jungle, like the sweet smell of the orchids growing out of those magnificent ceibas, like the way light bounces off the structures, reflecting it to the surrounding vegetation, providing unity to their world."

Susan remained quiet, wondering about a man who could see so much, who could articulate such thought-provoking words, just as he had done the night she'd met him, letting her inside his mind so naturally, without dominance, in the same manner with which he had been looking at her in the past two days, never obvious, never intrusive, yet always courteous, respectful, oftentimes out of his peripheral vision, even as he regarded the stars beyond the circular opening in the trees.

She interlaced her fingers while hugging her knees, glancing at her fingernails, suddenly wishing they were better cared for, perhaps with just a little polish. Susan narrowed her eyes at the thought. Until now the shape of her fingernails had not mattered.

Cameron pulled out the pack of Camels and leaned it in her direction. "One is not going to kill you."

Susan regarded him strangely. "How did you know I—"

"The way you looked at me when I used one for the ticks. The way you handled it when I gave it to you to burn the ticks off of your other leg after you got uncomfortable."

She pulled one and held it between her index and middle fingers, the filter brushing against her lips. Cameron produced a lighter and extended it toward her while lighting it with a single flick of his thumb, holding the flame steadily in front of her. She leaned forward, her fingers brushing the side of his hand, drawing with forgotten pleasure. Then she watched him light one for himself, automatically cupping the cigarette with one hand while holding the lighter in the other, the pulsating flame showering his rugged features with yellow light. He did this with the same fluidity that she had observed earlier, when he had studied the glyphs, or when he had saved that soldier from a horrible death. Who was this man, who made her feel so secure, so comfortable? Who would risk his life to save another's without hesitation one instant, and the next would notice little things, like the expression on her face when he had pulled out the pack of Camels the day before, or the way her fingers handled the cigarette?

"It's been a very long time," she said, filling her lungs, holding it, slowly releasing it.

"I know."

She turned to him. He had not said *how long has it been?* Or, *why did you quit?* He had said *I know.* He was reading her once more, understanding just by the way she acted that it had been a very long time since she had smoked. "Why do I get the feeling that I can't really keep secrets from you?"

"I hope you don't find that intrusive."

She continued to regard him with intrigue. "I don't find anything you do intrusive."

3

Ishiguro Nakamura disassembled a six-inch telescope on a large boulder breaking the dense vegetation, where they had decided to spend the night. Jackie had set up her instruments next to him, including a microwave receiver that scanned the same frequencies as their radio telescope back at Cerro Tolo, but lacking an astronomical range. According to their calculations, once they got beneath the celestial beam, they would not need anything but the receiver to pick up the transmission.

The petite Japanese-American woman unplugged her battery-operated equipment and carefully stored them in waterproof containers before stowing them away in their oversize backpacks, disappointment hardening her soft features.

"We'll be there tomorrow night," Ishiguro said reassuringly.

Jackie continued to frown, admonishing eyes turning to Kuoshi Honichi, peacefully snoring inside his sleeping bag. The corporate liaison had twisted his ankle just a half hour after leaving the riverbank, slowing down their progress to a crawl as the muscular Porfirio had to help him walk while Jackie navigated and Ishiguro hauled both Kuoshi's and his own backpacks. Ishiguro had wanted the guides to take him back to the boat, but the obstinate junior executive would not hear of it, demanding that if he didn't come along, the mission would have to be canceled.

"Why is he here anyway?" she said, crossing her arms and pouting.

Ishiguro wrapped his arms around her. She continued to hug herself but did rest her head on his shoulder. "There's no reason for him being here," she added. "And I don't understand why you let him stay. We usually don't let him get away with this crap back in Chile."

"He's armed," Ishiguro whispered. "That's why I didn't just order the guides to take him back to the boat."

Jackie made a face, glancing back at the short, lanky, and nerdy specimen of a man. "*Armed?* Are you serious?"

"A pistol. I first spotted it on him in the boat, and again when we had to wade through the mangrove after leaving the boat."

She tilted her head. "I guess it is not a bad idea out here. Who knows what we will encounter. I'm just surprised that he has one. He just doesn't fit the type."

"I get the feeling that our corporate liaison may be something more than just a plain corporate liaison."

"Yeah," she said, nodding. "He's a royal pain in the ass. The little bastard can't even pull his own fucking weight."

"Now, now," Ishiguro said, rubbing a hand against her back. "That language is unbecoming of an eminent astronomer like yourself, discoverer of the first confirmed message from outer space."

"*Right.*"

"I just hope you still remember me when you're rich and famous."

"Stop it."

"You'll look great on the cover of *Newsweek* and *Scientific American*."

"Watch it, mister."

"Maybe you'll let me hang around and clean up the lab after you."

"I'm warning—"

He kissed her. Jackie resisted for a few seconds. Then her soft lips parted, welcoming him. A moment later they gazed at the stars. Moonlight glowed around them, standing at the top of the large limestone boulder that protruded from the jungle like a gleaming island in a sea of hunter green.

"What a magnificent sight," he said, observing the stars of the Northern Hemisphere, quite a different view from the cosmos visible at the south end of the continent. Together they made out the Big and Little Dippers, Perseus, Cassiopeia, the lonely Castor, almost directly above them, and the Deneb of the Swan, just barely grazing the horizon.

"From the Andes to the Petén," he said.

"So vastly different," she added. "Yet, the stars glow just as beautiful."

"And someone from one of those stars is trying to make contact with us. Amazing."

"I wonder what kind of message it is."

"My dear Jackie, I get the feeling that we'll find that out very, *very* soon."

4

Susan Garnett woke up to the strange sounds echoing between the stone structures. Sloe-eyed, half asleep, she unzipped her sleeping bag and sat up, wondering if she was dreaming. Everyone around her slept, including the two SEALs supposedly on guard—something that Susan found quite odd.

Strange.

She went to reach for Cameron, sleeping just a couple of feet away, but decided against it, not certain why, just that she shouldn't. Instead, she stood and put on her sneakers.

Subtle voices bounced off the limestone, the baritone pitch reminding her of an opera singer. For a moment Susan could have sworn that it was calling her name, but it could have been the breeze sweeping down from the mountains. The voice seemed to come from far ahead, but she couldn't tell for certain.

Moonlight continued to glow, spreading its half-light across the ethereal-looking architecture. But something else gleamed at the site. It came from the temple, beyond the vine-laced columns and corbel vaults, past the limestone terrace, within the heart of the ornately decorated edifice. Susan stood, the voices carrying a hypnotic force that made her begin to walk. And as she did the voices became more distant, increasingly vague, but urging her to move faster, to come closer.

She did, in a half trance, walking around the edge of the cenote, listening now to voices emanating from the waterhole, like an enchanted chorus, rising out of the dark waters and going straight to the heavens.

She reached the twenty intricately carved steps and began to climb them, slowly, with unexpected serenity, reaching the stone columns, walking beneath the triangular arches, stopping in the middle of the terrace, staring at the back-lit silhouettes of three figures wearing loincloths and large feathery headdresses. They didn't speak, yet Susan knew what they wanted, what they thought, and she followed them inside, past the same indented limestone slab that Cameron had noticed earlier, now pushed aside, exposing the cavernous interior of the Mayan temple.

The computer scientist took her place around the fire, bluish smoke spiraling skyward from its pulsating flames, revealing many wall carvings, murals etched in stone, depicting dozens of Mayan scenes, rituals, games, wars, crops, all encircled by mosaiclike carvings containing numbers in Maya. Limestone reliefs of plumed serpents and werejaguars danced in the pulsating light, in the azure haze that enveloped the elderly men as they removed their headdresses, revealing the alienlike elongated heads and flattened brows that she had seen so many times in the past days. The shamans rocked back and forth in the sapphire smog to the rhythm of silent drums. The one closest to Susan had a number of gold earrings plus a jaguarlike tattoo on his left forearm. He also had tattoos in the shape of bands around his upper arms. Another man had a colorful bird painted on his left shoulder, resembling a quetzal. Moths danced around them, chasing the light in an unavoidable deadly dance, fizzling in midair, vanishing within crimson tongues of fire.

Susan inhaled the sweet-smelling fumes coiling out of the crackling flames, warming her, soothing her, clouding her mind. She closed her eyes, the warmth spreading to every inch of her body, in and out of her pores, controlling her senses, her very soul. She felt carried away, unable to resist this compelling force, like the moths, following a primal directive, surrendering their fate to their instincts.

She opened her eyes, smoke layering the limestone floor, dancing over it, staining it green, like the jungle, like a vast landscape, slowly resolving irregular islands of stone within the ocean of trees. The hazy panorama gained resolution, the images becoming sharper, in focus, revealing temple pyramids, palaces, ball courts, great plazas, all bustling with activity, with growth, with prosperity. City-states emerged out of the jungle, like in time-lapse video, stone block after stone block, erected by a swarm of skilled laborers at incredible speed.

Days and nights revolved around Susan Garnett, the passage of time, the seasons, the centuries, the millennia. Temples rose from the dense vegetation, reaching toward the heavens, triggering the study of the sky, of the cosmos. The development of mathematics, of architecture, of astronomy flourished, exploded, peaked. Noble scribes, armed with porcupine quill brushes, recorded their advancements on bleached fig-tree paper, painting chronologies, inscribing their history, their experiences, their beliefs, their fears, encoding their knowledge in numbers, in sequences, carving them onto mosaics.

The scarlet flames spread through the smoke, staining it, robbing it of its cobalt hue, of its purity, of its life. Cities fell, civilizations vanished, flourishing again at distant sites, momentarily regaining their lost momentum. Scribes recorded their final days, their darkening future, the fear of the men from the sea.

The smoke became bloodred, deep crimson. Cries echoed in her mind, followed by the sounds of thunder, of war, of destruction. Armored men razed the land, spreading terror and disease, decimating its inhabitants, enslaving them, burning their records, their codices, attempting to erase their very history, their traditions, their beliefs. Susan felt their pain, their agony, their despair. She saw wives losing husbands, husbands losing wives, children orphaned, women raped, men tortured, books burnt—all in the name of Spain—mass exterminations shamelessly justified under the umbrella of Christianity.

The terrible visions flashed beneath the smoke faster than she could register them, one after the other, again and again, as conflict ravaged harmony in the New World, in the mangroves, in the mountains, in the jungle. But through the harrowing sights, through the whirling, bloodstained smoke, through the desperate cries of a dying civilization, Susan Garnett felt another presence, another entity next to her, soothing, gentle, soft, delicate, like the embrace of a child, or the touch of a cherub. Susan breathed this cloud with all her might, filling herself with the floating essence of her daughter, with her innocence, her love, her purity. And as she began to recharge her emotions with the light force emanating from the presence of Rebecca, as her maternal instincts resurfaced with unequivocal clarity, Susan Garnett perceived another being around her, one that brought unity, completeness, security. She felt overwhelmed by the presence of her husband, of his strength, his masculinity, his possessive nature. Drowned by the totality of her experience, by the joy of this mystic reunion, Susan sensed a powerful force, one that reminded her that she didn't belong to this hazy world, to this surreal land of wondering souls, of psychic encounters. Her life belonged in the landscape portrayed beneath the mist that continued to swirl, continued to gyrate, like a giant nebula, its colors shifting with the times, with the seasons, always gaining clarity, enhancing resolution, defining patterns of pixels conforming to the contours of hills and valleys, of new and ancient metropolises, of meandering rivers and crystalline lakes.

The haze continued to whirl, like a heavenly cyclone, turning, changing, improving focus. The pixels gained definition according to their position in the tri-dimensional map beneath the spinning smoke, becoming slightly elongated at the hills and rounder at the valleys, like a contour map, increasing precision. Concentrations of elongated pixels grew in numbers as the terrain sloped upward, overwhelming their round counterparts conforming to the flatlands, like a binary map, charting the land, defining it, outlining its uneven features, its eclectic topography.

The azure smog spun even faster, becoming obscure, pushing images to its periphery, leaving the core alone, empty, dark. Susan felt her companions departing, sensed their happiness, their encouragement to go on, to seek the truth, to see beyond her scientific mind, to explore, to dream, to open her mind, to pray for strength.

The murky vapor continued to spin, flashing images across her field of view, one after the next, in rapid succession, overpowering her senses, her mind, her soul, exhausting her. Dizziness fell upon her, clouding her thoughts, dulling her, pushing her to the edge of consciousness, to the edge of an insurmountable abyss, a cenote of universal proportions, distancing her from her loved ones.

Susan fought this overwhelming force, trying to remain near her husband, her daughter, but she felt the futility of her effort, her energy draining, her will vanishing, fading, collapsing into a brief, whirling, black mass of conflicting thoughts, before that too vanished.

ooooooo t>t>t>eeeee

Chapter Fourteen

001110

1

December 17, 1999

Dawn in the lowlands of the Petén.

A bloodstained sun broke the horizon, staining the star-filled night with fists of gold and orange, swallowing the stars, erasing the moon, turning the indigo sky into ever-lighter shades of blue, burning the hissing fog rising off the thick vegetation.

Low clouds covered the land like a cotton mantle, slowly moving with the light breeze sweeping from the south, thinning with the increasing temperature. Night creatures receded into the darkness of the jungle as sunlight pierced the canopy, like laser beams, finding small tiny openings in the tangle of branches to touch the leaf-littered ground. Moths, horseflies, and mosquito hawks danced around these luminous rays, absorbing the sun's energy before continuing on their search for sustenance. Crawlers also searched for these patches of warmth on the ground, using them to regulate their body temperature. Warmth-seeking insects also pursued hosts to feed their survival needs, ready to attach themselves to anything of substance, like a deer sleeping in a thicket, or a wild turkey hiding in the brush, or the human beneath the layer of moss at the edge of the jungle.

Antonio Strokk cringed when feeling a sharp sting on his upper thigh. He inhaled deeply through his mouth and slowly exhaled through his nostrils, rapidly losing his patience, something that seldom happened, for he knew quite well the consequences of those lacking the stamina to wait for the right opportunity before making a move. But a night sleeping with bugs crawling into his fatigues was pushing his tolerance envelope. Celina, on the other hand, seemed to have endured the night quite well, despite finding an assortment of colorful bugs crawling inside her pants, including one she had to dig out of her vagina.

The former Russian Spetsnaz officer remained still, eyes surveying the site, getting regular status reports from his team, all enduring the same jungle treatment as they waited for his signal to raid the area. That was another reason why Strokk, despite his bug problem, could not afford to complain. He led a team of mercenaries, whom he controlled through fear, plus generous financial compensation. His men feared him, and through that fear, they respected him, obeyed him, *killed* for him. Complaining about mundane things, even something as painful as a tick feeding off his thigh, would be seen as a sign of weakness, unbecoming of his position, injecting doubt in his men about his ability to lead them.

Although he could not intervene in the scientists' progress without negatively impacting their investigation, Antonio Strokk looked for ways to get them moving faster. And he was convinced that as long as the Garnett woman remained sleeping, they would not make progress, which translated in more time spent with bugs crawling up his—

Ouch!

Another bite, this one in his groin. He reached down, shoving his hand into the pants of his cammies, crushing the offending bug.

Strokk sighed. A few minutes ago his sister had thought of an idea to wake up the scientist without telegraphing their position to the rest of the team, which had been up for at least an hour.

Strokk lined up the sights of his scope with the computer scientist, setting the crosshairs on her face. Then he activated the laser beam on the scope, zeroing in on her closed eyelids. No one should notice the tiny red spot on her face unless they happened to be looking right at her from a very close distance. The nearest group was having breakfast a couple dozen feet from her.

Wake up, sleeping beauty.

2

Susan Garnett woke up with a piercing crimson light stabbing her eyes. She rolled over, away from it, filling her lungs with the smell of the MREs—meals, ready to eat—being consumed by a half-dozen SEALs. She felt the extreme humidity, heard the buzzing of mosquitoes hovering overhead, recalled the memories of last night's bizarre dream.

A headache pounding her temples, Susan opened one eye, halfway. Streams of sunshine forked through the circular opening in the trees, casting the now familiar golden glow on the limestone structures. A light fog lifted off the cenote, resembling an awakening volcano.

Her eyes mere slits of stinging pain, Susan peered at the rising mist, glowing with sunlight, swirling in the morning breeze.

Swirling mist. Strange dream.

She looked around her, confused, a bit light-headed, her temples aching, throbbing. Her mouth was dry, pasty.

Cameron's sleeping bag was already folded and stowed against his backpack, as well as the rest of the team's. Lobo and two SEALs manned their satellite gear, wearing headphones, probably updating the Pentagon.

Susan unzipped her bag, finding it odd that she was wearing her sneakers. She stood, stretching her light frame, once again checking her surroundings, spotting Cameron squatting by the ornate temple's front steps, scribbling in his field notebook, the floppy hat shadowing his features. As she inhaled, her lungs burned, as well as her throat. Was it from the three Camels she had smoked with Cameron? Was that also the reason for her headache? Or could it be from . . .

Susan shook the thought away, reaching for her backpack, producing a plastic bottle of Excedrin, popping three in her mouth, and washing them down with a sip of purified water from her canteen. She poured a handful of water in her cupped hand, splashing her face, her skin tingling, waking up. She followed that with a breath mint, inhaling deeply once more, ignoring her sore throat, massaging her temples.

Lobo looked up from his work and nodded. She nodded in return while walking toward the temple, around the foggy cenote, careful to remain far away from the edge, barely visible in the haze. Glaring sunlight drilled her eyes, magnifying the headache. Susan endured it, passing a pair of SEALs standing guard next to the temple, by the ornate pillar marking the original entrance to the site.

"Ma'am," one of them said, tipping his camouflage floppy hat. This was the same blond that Cameron had saved by the river. Since then the kid had managed to stay close to the archaeologist—something that Susan had found amusing. The SEALs were here to protect Cameron and Susan. Yet, so far, Cameron Slater had done the bulk of the protection. *And he is the only one without a gun.*

"Morning," she replied, her throat raspy.

She reached the steps a moment later and tapped Cameron on the shoulder. "We gotta talk. Up there." She pointed at the terrace with one index while rubbing her left temple with another, her hoarse voice also carrying an edge. She desperately needed to get out of the sunlight.

The archaeologist lifted his hat, running a hand through his dark, shoulder-length hair, grinning. "And good morning to you too." He winked. "What makes you think I want to be alone with a moody woman who also has a headache—no matter how *lovely* she looks in the morning."

In spite of the searing pain behind her eyeballs, she managed a brief smile. "That bad, huh?"

He nodded, mockingly extending an open palm up the steps. "Let's just say it's all uphill from here."

"Don't go there, Cameron," she whispered, heading up the steps. "I can be a real *sweetheart* in the morning."

"Just remember, I'm probably the only one willing to share my cigarettes without asking for anything in return."

She made a face as they headed up to the temple. The thick columns and corbel arches blocked most of the glare. The coolness of the murky terrace had a soothing effect on Susan, allowing her to inch her eyes open beyond narrow cracks.

"Something happened last night," she said, glancing at the limestone slab blocking the temple's entrance.

"What?"

"I—I don't know where to begin," she said, suddenly unsure of herself.

He tapped her on the arm. "How about starting at the beginning?"

Susan regarded this rugged, yet gentle man, his brown eyes warm, welcoming, encouraging. She told him everything she remembered, to the last detail, including the intricate stone carvings, the plumaged headdresses, the way they communicated without words, the swirling smoke. She took almost ten minutes to do so, also describing the curious binary code defining the land. Cameron listened intently, an intrigued look on his square face.

When she finished, he walked over to the large slab and inspected the floor around it. "If I had to guess, I'd say this stone has not been moved since yesterday, at least not according to the surrounding layer of dust on the floor. There are no track marks."

Susan frowned. "Then how in the—"

"But," he added. "That doesn't mean it didn't happen. Though that would mean that Lobo's men fell asleep at their post."

"Maybe it was a dream, but it sure feels that it was real."

"Why didn't you wake me up?"

"I almost did . . . but something made me not want to do it."

"What?"

"I'm not sure. It just didn't feel right for me to wake you. And the voices . . . they kept luring me into the temple . . . and, well, you know the rest."

Cameron crossed his arms, his gaze on the floor, obviously considering what he had heard. "The men who greeted you . . . describe them to me."

Susan stared off in the distance. "Aside from the deformed skulls . . . they were fairly old, maybe in their sixties, with wrinkled skin and bald heads. They all wore these blue and green loincloths, and their hats were quite elaborate."

"Any special markings? Tattoos? Body piercing?"

"Yes. One of them had several earrings, but just on one ear. He also had the tattoo of a jaguar. Another man had one of a quetzal."

"Anyone else?"

"I don't remember."

"The smoke. What did it smell like?"

"Can't remember. It just made me feel very relaxed."

"Probably a hallucinogen," he said, leaning forward and taking a good whiff from the same gear vest that he had given her yesterday. "Smells like the Camels we smoked last night. And you said you had your sneakers on this morning?"

"Yep. And I do remember taking them off last night."

He raised his eyebrows. "Strange, Susan. Very strange."

Her headache began to recede, a mix of the coolness of the terrace plus the Excedrin. Her logical mind gathered momentum. "There's one thing that may prove if this really happened."

He lifted his eyes.

"Follow me." She stepped outside and headed down the steps with Cameron in tow, walking around the cenote, still veiled in haze, but much lighter as the morning sun burned it off.

They reached her stowed gear. Cameron helped her set it up, including hooking up the main battery connected to the solar power generator.

Sitting on the stone floor, her laptop on a portable bench, Susan powered it up.

"You going to tell me what you're doing?" Cameron asked, sitting next to her, his right shoulder against hers as he peered at the screen.

Susan pulled up the file containing last night's digitized version of the electromagnetic activity.

STATS
LENGTH: 42,342,021 BYTES
COMPOSITION: 0% ASSEMBLY CODE 100% UNKNOWN
ORIGIN: UNKNOWN
HOST STATUS: UNKNOWN
UNFILTERED STRAIN FOLLOWING . . .

CONTINUE BROWSING? Y/N

"Look familiar?" Susan asked.
"Yep."
She typed Y and kept looking at the large file, reaching the end.

```
0000000000000001111101111111110000000100000000000111111111100000000000000
0110100001000001111101111011110001111111000000000000111111100000000000011
1100000000000000111111111111110000000000000000000011111111110000000000111
1001000000001111000000010000011111110000000000111000000001000000000000000
0011000000000000110000000000000000000000000000000000000000000010000010000
1000010001000000000000000000000000011100000000000000000000000001000000000
0000000000000001111101111111110000000100000000000111111111100000000000000
0110100001000001111101111011110001111111000000000000111111100000000000011
1100000000000000111111111111110000000000000000000011111111110000000000111
1000001000000011010101011111110000000000000000000011111110000000000100001
0000000000000001111101111111110000000100000000000111111111100000000000000
0110100001000001111101111011110001111111000000000000111111100000000000011
1100000000000000111111111111110000000000000000000011111111110000000000111
0000000000000001111101111111110000000100000000000111111111100000000000000
0110100001000001111101111011110001111111000000000000111111100000000000011
1100000000000000111111111111110000000000000000000011111111110000000000111
1111111100000001111100001111100001100000001111001111110000000011111
1111111111110000111111111111110000000000000000000111110101011111111111111
```

```
11011011  00011000  00011000  00011000  00011000
00000000  00111100  00111100  00111100  00111100
11111111  00011000  00011000  00011000  00011000
00000000  00000000  00000000  00000000  00000000
11111111  00000000  00000000  00000000  00000000
```

"Why are there spaces?" Cameron asked.

She shook her head. "Don't know. I never did look at the bottom of this file. It doesn't make sense. It's also separated in eight-bit sections, or bytes. Strange that the disassembler didn't decode that. They look like a simple string of numbers."

Cameron stared at the five blocks of numbers. "It is a string of numbers ... but in *Maya*."

"What?"

He pointed at the first block.

```
1 1 0 1 1 0 1 1
0 0 0 0 0 0 0 0
1 1 1 1 1 1 1 1
0 0 0 0 0 0 0 0
1 1 1 1 1 1 1 1
```

"That's three dots over two horizontal lines. Remember what I told you the other night about their numbering system."

Susan nodded. "Each dot represented a one. Each line a five. So this number is a thirteen?"

"Correct," he said.

"What about the other blocks? They're all the same."

"The Maya understood the concept of zero and used a large oval-shaped symbol, or the shape of the shell of a slug or hermit crab to describe it. I've seen their symbology for so long that it comes very naturally. But if you use your imagination, you can see the ones in the block taking up that shape."

00011000
00111100
00011000
00000000
00000000

"If that is the case," she said. "Then we're looking at a string of five numbers." She wrote them on her engineering notebook, also separating them by spaces.

13 0 0 0 0

"That's a Mayan date," Cameron offered. "And I don't have to look it up to translate it to our Gregorian equivalent. It's the end of the Mayan thirteenth *baktun*."

In spite of the humidity and the rising temperature, Susan felt a chill sweeping through her as she remembered the discussion she had had with Cameron the night they had met. The end of the thirteenth *baktun* coincided with . . .

"Zero one, zero one, zero zero," she said.

"We better figure out the rest of this message, and quick. I get the feeling that we're being told what is going to happen at one A.M. on January first."

"All right," she said, controlling her excitement to remain focused. "According to the experience I had last night, this file could be a contour map, with the hills represented by concentrations of ones and valleys by concentrations of zeroes."

"Interesting. When you look at the array that way, you can almost begin to see a pattern forming in front of your eyes," Cameron said, staring at the binary code above the Mayan date. "You can follow the terrain, with the zeroes representing flatland and the ones peaks."

"Let's see if we can clean it up a little."

"What are you going to do?"

"Run an averaging program to sharpen the edges and filter out some of the noise inherent in the translation of EM to binary code." She typed several commands and the system churned away for around twenty seconds, finally displaying:

STATS
LENGTH: 42,342,021 BYTES
COMPOSITION: 0% ASSEMBLY CODE 100% UNKNOWN
ORIGIN: UNKNOWN
HOST STATUS: UNKNOWN
FILTERED STRAIN FOLLOWING . . .

```
1111000000000001111111111111111111111111111000000000000111111111111111
1100001100000000110110111111111011111011111000000000000000011111111111
0000001100000000101111111111111001111111110000000000000000111111111111
0000001100000011001111111111110001111111111111000000000000000111111111
0000000000000000001111111111100011111111111111000000000000000111111111
0000011000000000001111111000000111111111110000000001110000011111111111
0000000000000011010111111111100001111111111000000001110000001111111111
0000000000000011011111111111100011111111111000000001100000001111111111
1111000000000011010101111111110011111111111000100000010000001111111111
1111100000000010111111111111111110111111100000000000000000000000111111
1111100000000000000000011111111111111110000000000000000000000000001111
1111100000000000000000000001111111000000000000001110111000000000000000
1111111111000000000000000000011100000000000000001111110000000000000000
1111111111111110000000000000000000000001000000000011010000000000000011
1111111111000000000000011000000000000000000000000000000000000000001111
1111111100000000000000011000001000000000000000000000000001111111111111
0000000000000000000000000001100001111110000000000000000000000111111111
0000000000000000000000000000001111110000000000111000000000000000111111
0000000000111110000000000000001111110000000000111000000000000000000000
0000000000001111000000000000001111110000000000111000000010000000000000
0000000000000011000000000000000000000000000000000000000000010000000000
0000010000000000000000000000000000000000000000000000000000001000000000
0000000000000011111111111110000000000000000011111100000000000000000000
0000000000000011111111111111100000010000000000111111110000000000000000
0000000000000011111111111111110000000000000000111111111110000000000111
1000000000000011111111111111000000000000000000111111110000000000001111
1111110000000011111111111111000000000000111111111111110000000001111111
1111111111000011111111111111000000000000000111111111111111111111111111
1111000000000000111111111100000000000000000000111111111111111111000000
0000000000000011111111110000000010000000000000000111111100000011
1111100000000000000000000000000000000000000001111111111111111111111
1111000000000000000000000000000000000111110000000000000111110000111
1100000000000000000000000000000000000110000000000000000011100000011
0000000000000000000000000000000000000100000000000000000000111111111
```

CONTINUE BROWSING? Y/N

She went to the bottom.

```
00000000000000011111111111111110000000100000000000111111111110000000000000
00000000000000011111111111011110001111111000000000000111111110000000000011
11000000000000001111111111111110000000000000000000001111111110000000000111
00000000000111110000000000000011111110000000000111000000001000000000000
00000000000000011000000000000000000000000000000000000000000000000000000010
10000000000000000000000000000000011000000000000000000000000000000000000000
00000000000000011111111111111110000000100000000000111111111110000000000000
01100000000000011111111111111110001111111000000000000111111000000000000011
11000000000000001111111111111110000000000000000000001111111110000000000111
10000000000000111111111111111100000000000000000000011111110000000000000001
00000000000000011111111111111110000000110000000001111111111110000000000000
01100000000000011111111111111110001111111000000000000111111000000000000011
11000000000000001111111111111110000000000000000000111111111110000000000111
00000000000000011111111111111110000001100000000001111111111100000000000000
01100000000000011111111111111110001111111000000000000111111000000000000011
11000000000000001111111111111110000000000000000000111111111110000000000111
11111111000000011111111111111110000000000000000011110011111100000000011111
11111111111110000111111111111111000000000000000000001111111111111111111111
```

```
11011011  00011000  00011000  00011000  00011000
00000000  00111100  00111100  00111100  00111100
11111111  00011000  00011000  00011000  00011000
00000000  00000000  00000000  00000000  00000000
11111111  00000000  00000000  00000000  00000000
```

"Amazing," Slater said while looking at the filtered image, after the averaging program had eliminated some of the noise.

"The technique is pretty common in the photo enhancing industry. The military also uses it quite extensively to improve the quality of its images."

"It also looks as if the averaging program didn't change the Mayan date."

Susan regarded the screen for a moment, considering the possibility of blank spaces. The way her software detected the end of the string was by finding three or more blank spaces. She placed the cursor on the blank line and tapped on the right arrow key of her laptop, counting ten spaces before the cursor reached the end of the blank line and dropped to the beginning of the Mayan date.

She explained that to Cameron, also adding, "That's why my software never detected the Mayan date. It thought that was the end of the file."

"Well, it certainly looks like there's an image in there, and I can see how it could be interpreted as the topography of a region."

Susan agreed. "*Now* you believe me?"

"Why do you think there are still some ones sprinkled in the valleys?" Cameron pointed at a few ones among zeroes. "Boulders?"

"Could be. Or maybe it's just noise. First thing we have to do is find the region of the land that matches it."

"How are you going to do that?"

Susan grinned. "Trade secret."

3

"I think they're on to something, *hermano*," came the voice of Celina Strokk through his earpiece.

Antonio Strokk, one hand battling a bloodsucking parasite having a feast on his groin, kept the other clutching a pair of binoculars. "Did she say that last night's event resulted in a binary map of some piece of land?"

Celina nodded beneath the moss. "Correct. Now she will try to find a match."

"A match? How?"

"Most likely by either E-mailing the file to the FBI headquarters to get them to run it against a 3-D contour map, or by downloading the 3-D map software on her system and doing the comparison here."

"I see," he said, finally snatching the insect between his index and thumb and crushing it, exhaling with relief. "Which way is faster?"

"Depends on how extensive the search needs to be. The hardest part will be finding the correct region. Then they have to run it against that area while making allowances for scaling differences between the binary image and the 3-D map. That could take a while if the search area is, say, the entire American continent. But if they can narrow it down to a small area of a few hundred square miles, then the task becomes much simpler and capable of being handled in any good laptop, like the one she has down there."

Strokk watched the scientists confer with the SEAL commander, Lieutenant Lobo, before making the cable connections to the satellite gear. Strokk hesitated about giving the order to strike now. The more he waited, the better the chances of the scientists making a breakthrough, but at the same time, the more the FBI back in Washington learned about how to defeat the virus, which was exactly what he was trying to prevent. However, if he was to strike too soon, eliminate the SEALs, and force the scientists to feed misinformation to Washington, he could actually slow down the investigation because the scientists might be unwilling to put up a real effort just to have him profit from their research.

Act too soon and risk losing. Wait too long and risk losing.

In addition, his team was growing impatient after almost thirty-six hours of surveillance. Based on the sporadic complaints he'd heard on the operational frequency, the former Spetsnaz officer knew they would not stand this much longer and feared that one of them might open fire to force the rest of the team to commit itself.

But his instinct told him to wait—the same instinct that had kept him alive during contracts in Bogota, London, Rome, Istanbul, Zurich, and so many other places. Strokk listened to this inner voice and abided by it, for it represented the combined knowledge of his operative years, the sum of his professional wisdom. And that wisdom told him that in spite of the heat, in spite of his men complaining, in spite of the relentless insects making a banquet of his body, the international contractor should remain put. Strokk also instructed his team to do likewise, indirectly warning everyone that he would personally shoot the first man who dared challenge his command.

The Americans had finished making the wireless connections and were now dialing into Washington.

4

Susan Garnett watched the percent meter on her screen increase as her powerful ThinkPad downloaded a 250-megabyte 3-D map of the American continent, figuring that it would be a reasonable place to start. She'd had a discussion with Cameron on the probable location of the area outlined by the binary topography and decided that they should first search the entire region once occupied by the Maya, including the western section of El Salvador, all of Guatemala and Belize, and southern Mexico, plus the Yucatán Peninsula.

She now viewed both North and South America, from the Northwest Territories of Canada to Cape Horn, at the southern tip of Chile. Using the pointer, she outlined an area covering the Classic Mayan kingdom, not only zooming in, but also selecting that area as the first search region of a custom program that she had hammered out in the past thirty minutes, while establishing contact with Washington and downloading the large file. The program would take the suspect binary code and attempt to overlap it on the selected portion of the 3-D map to find a match. To accomplish this, Susan had to define certain parameters.

The first was the relative scales of the binary map and the 3-D map. She assigned the value of one to the scale used by the 3-D map. She eyeballed the relative size of her binary map and opted for an initial scaling value of 0.001, thus making the 3-D map one thousand times larger than the binary map, to make certain that she started with something that was on the small side of the scale and work her way up to the matching scale.

Her second parameter was the relative orientation of the digital map with respect to magnetic north. As a starting point, she made the top of the binary file zero degrees, or magnetic north, just like the 3-D map.

Her third parameter was the resolution of the search. What would qualify as a match, considering the possibility of noise injected in the conversion of the electromagnetic field to binary code during last night's event, even after filtering some of the noise out? Susan chose the value of fifty percent match to generate a flag. She could adjust that parameter later on, based on the number of matches that occurred during the initial search. She didn't want the resolution to be so loose that it generated too many "false" matches. On the other hand, she didn't want it so tight that she would not generate any matches.

Finally, she had to define what constituted one full search. She encoded this in the program, making the first "stepped" comparison of the binary map against the 3-D map at the initial settings of relative scale, orientation, and resolution. After one complete pass, the program would adjust the scale of the binary map in increments of 0.001, all the way up to 1. Then the program would reset the orientation of the binary map relative to the 3-D map by one degree, slightly shifting its definition of magnetic north. Then the relative scale would be reset back to 0.001 and start over.

She reviewed this simple but critical portion of the program.

```
10 ORIENT = 0; MATCH = 0
11 SCALE = 0.001
12 CALL COMPARE
13 IF MATCH = 1 THEN GOTO 21
14 SCALE = SCALE + 0.001
15 IF SCALE > 1 GOTO 17
16 GOTO 12
17 ORIENT = ORIENT + 1
18 IF ORIENT > 360 GOTO 20
19 GOTO 11
20 DISPLAY NO MATCH; GOTO 22
21 CALL ADD NEW MATCH; GOTO 14
22 END
```

"All right," she said to herself. "If a match is found, it will be logged in and the search will continue through the nested loops of ORIENT and SCALE until they perform a full scan of all parameter combinations."

"How long will it take to go through one full iteration of orientations and scales?" Cameron asked, once again sitting by her side. Lobo and another SEAL knelt behind them, listening with interest. It was just past ten in the morning and the sun had burned off most of the fog rising above the cenote. According to the sensors connected to her system, temperatures had already climbed to the mid-eighties and the humidity was just below eighty percent. They were all sweating. Susan had promptly put on the vest that Cameron had loaned her yesterday.

"The actual time to compare the information in the digital map with its equivalent frame in the 3-D map is about seventy microseconds of compute time. At the initial scale settings of 0.001, the binary map will have to be stepped around ten thousand times to cover the selected area in the 3-D map. That means that a single pass at one orientation and one scaling factor will take ... let's see." She jotted some numbers on her engineering notebook.

ONE COMPARE STEP = SEVENTY MICROSECONDS OR 0.00007 SECONDS
ONE SINGLE PASS = 10,000 COMPARE STEPS
TOTAL COMPUTE TIME = 0.00007 SECONDS X 10,000 = 0.7 SECONDS

"So, less than a second," she said. "Now, keep in mind that's just with one set of orientation and scale settings. There are one thousand scaling factors, from 0.001 to 1, and 360 orientations per scaling factor." Again, she jotted down the numbers.

LENGTH OF SINGLE PASS: 0.7 SECONDS
NUMBER OF SCALE SETTINGS: 1000
NUMBER OF ORIENTATIONS: 360
TOTAL COMPUTE TIME: 0.7 SECONDS X 1000 X 360 = 252,000
    SECONDS

Cameron made a face. "That's ..."

"Around seventy hours of uninterrupted computing time. But it won't be nearly as long because as the scaling factor increases, there will be fewer comparison steps between the binary map and the 3-D map because the size of the binary map will increase in relation to the 3-D map."

"So, what's your estimate?"

"Around fifteen hours, which is still a long time. That's why Reid's also going to be doing it at the FBI using our HP workstations, which should finish in minutes instead of hours. However, Reid's task will be a little longer because in addition to searching in this area, he's also running the routine across the entire continent. That should take him most of the day. And at a fifty percent match we're bound to generate more than just one match, which means we'll have to run the compare again on all of the highlighted matches using a finer resolution. I'm estimating that the elimination phase will take just as long as the initial phase because the higher resolution across fewer sites requires just as much computing time as a lower resolution search across the entire region."

"When do we start?"

"Right now. I'm going to do a few test runs to adjust the resolution setting before I E-mail the program to Reid to run on the HPs." She then launched her routine. A window popped up on her screen, giving her the basic statistics of the search, currently set to the default starting values.

```
CURRENT ORIENTATION: 0
CURRENT SCALE: 0.001
CURRENT MATCHES: 0
RESOLUTION: 50%
ELAPSED TIME: 0 HRS 0 MIN 0 SECONDS
% COMPLETE: 0.00
PRESS S TO START
PRESS H TO HALT
PRESS R TO RESTART
PRESS F TO FINISH
```

Susan pressed s and the hard drive began to whirl. Within seconds, the screen changed to:

```
CURRENT ORIENTATION: 0
CURRENT SCALE: 0.007
CURRENT MATCHES: 120
RESOLUTION: 50%
ELAPSED TIME: 0 HRS 0 MIN 5 SECONDS
% COMPLETE: 0.00
PRESS S TO START
PRESS H TO HALT
PRESS R TO RESTART
PRESS F TO FINISH
```

Frowning, Susan pressed H. The system halted its search.

"Why did you stop it?" Cameron asked.

"Look at the number of matches," she replied. "The resolution is too vague."

She pulled up the source code for the program, changed the matching resolution to sixty percent, and kicked it off again. This time the number of matches dropped to forty after ten seconds.

"Let's try again." She halted it once more and changed the resolution to seventy percent. This time there were only eight matches after fifteen seconds. One final adjustment and the number further dropped to five after thirty seconds. Susan let that run continue while she performed a small calculation, projecting about three thousand matches for the entire search, a manageable number for a follow-up finer resolution search. She E-mailed the revised program and instructions to Reid, requesting that he run it first on the selected area in Mesoamerica before the rest of the continent, and to be sure to send the results back to her immediately for her and Cameron's review.

She glanced at her screen one more time:

```
CURRENT ORIENTATION: 0
CURRENT SCALE: 0.265
CURRENT MATCHES: 31
RESOLUTION: 75%
ELAPSED TIME: 0 HRS 3 MIN 6 SECONDS
% COMPLETE: 1.03%
PRESS S TO START
PRESS H TO HALT
PRESS R TO RESTART
PRESS F TO FINISH
```

She did a quick calculation and decided that her projection of three thousand matches was right on target with thirty-one matches at just over one percent complete. Now she just had to wait. With a little luck, Reid would finish this initial search in fifteen minutes or less, sending her the results. But she decided to keep her system running as a backup. Worst case, she would halt her search after reviewing Reid's results and kick off the finer resolution search.

Standing and stretching, she turned to Lobo and Cameron. "What about getting a lady something to eat? I'm starving."

The SEAL commander brought her one of their MREs.

5

Ishiguro Nakamura's legs burned from the stress as Luis continued to hack his way through the jungle under the direction of Jackie, who followed the Guatemalan from a respectable distance to keep out of the way of the swinging machete and the flying debris it created. Behind Jackie staggered Kuoshi with the help of Porfirio. Ishiguro went last, hauling twice his normal load because of Kuoshi's wound.

Ishiguro's shoulders throbbed. Beads of perspiration stung his eyes. Ticks and other bugs continued to attack his legs, despite the bug repellant he had brought with him. Jackie and Kuoshi had the same problem. Luis and Porfirio, however, appeared immune.

They had been marching since first light, trekking almost two miles since, and getting awfully close to their destination, according to Jackie's GPS receiver.

This had better be worth it, he thought, continuing down the trail, too tired to admire the local flora. The towering trees indeed concealed an entire ecosystem conditioned to living with little sunlight. Lush ferns grew out of fallen logs. Colorful orchids and other flowers decorated the trees, amid curtains of hanging vines and moss. But to the Stanford Ph.D. they represented just more jungle. His initial admiration for the virgin rain forest had rapidly degraded to his current state of exhaustion and annoyance. All that seemed to matter was his next step, and the one after that, slowly advancing past ravines, through mangroves, across streams, closing the gap to the coordinates that had resulted from a satellite triangulation that at the moment seemed like a long time ago.

The astrophysicist inhaled deeply, the warm air stinging his lungs. It even hurt to breathe, but he endured it, checking his watch once more, calculating that they had less than thirty minutes before they reached their target.

6

"That was fast," Cameron observed the moment Susan displayed Reid's E-mail.

```
CURRENT ORIENTATION: 360
CURRENT SCALE: 1
CURRENT MATCHES: 2978
RESOLUTION: 75%
ELAPSED TIME: 0 HRS 14 MIN 6 SECONDS
% COMPLETE: 100%
PRESS S TO START
PRESS H TO HALT
PRESS R TO RESTART
PRESS F TO FINISH
```

"That's what happens when you have a couple of dozen Hewlett-Packard workstations working in parallel," Susan said, munching on her half-eaten MRE. "Fifteen hours becomes fourteen minutes." She stopped her own comparison and kicked off a new one on the matched sites but with a resolution of ninety percent, and asked Reid to do the same. She went back to her meal after receiving an acknowledgement from her superior.

She had projected three thousand matches, and the actual number had been close, giving her a warm feeling about their prospects of zeroing in on the location.

Lieutenant Lobo and another SEAL walked away. Cameron sat sideways to her while she ate.

"You're brilliant," he said.

He caught her with a mouthfull of processed chicken. Pointing at her jaws, Susan nodded, chewed some more, and finally swallowed. "Thanks," she replied, taking a sip of water. "But most of it's the tools and a little luck."

His square face, framed by the long dark hair, softened as he said, "Don't ever sell yourself short, Susan Garnett. You're something very special." He put a hand on her right shoulder and gave it a soft squeeze.

For a moment Susan forgot all about computer algorithms and viruses, about binary codes and countdowns. She liked the physical contact and smiled while holding his hand. "That's the nicest thing anyone's said to me in some time."

He didn't reply—*didn't need to reply*. His eyes conveyed his feelings for her, more direct than ever before. The eye contact lasted several seconds, but Susan felt that they had communicated for hours. In that brief, unexpected moment, her palm pressed against his knuckles, she knew *exactly* how he felt. She could read his mind in the same manner that she could read her husband's after years of marriage, only she had known Cameron for less than five days.

Cameron Slater.

Susan filled her lungs, conscious of her nipples pressing against the white cotton T-shirt. Ever since meeting Cameron Slater, Susan had felt like a woman again, had felt alive again. Sunlight became brighter. Colors came alive in her eyes as she gazed about, as if Cameron had lifted a veil off her face, allowing her to enjoy the world as she had done long ago.

A beep on her system returned their attention to the screen. Another message from Troy Reid. The search with ninety percent resolution had resulted in zero matches.

She lowered her gaze. "I was afraid of that."

"What?"

"Too loose a resolution and we get many matches, most of them false because too many topologies conform to the binary map. Too fine a resolution and we get zero matches, probably suggesting that the translation of the EM event into binary code was too noisy, too coarse even for the image-enhancing algorithm. I'll recommend we drop to eighty percent and try again. See what we get." She tapped the keys of her laptop and sent the instruction to Reid.

"What else could it be?" asked Cameron.

"The frequency range," she said. "Last night I performed a wide-area scan from one megahertz to one gigahertz in increments of one hundred mega-hertz. So I essentially had ten listening channels open, each being sampled once per millisecond. Most of the EM activity occurred in the nine hundred megahertz to one gigahertz range, meaning that the frequency being trans-mitted from the source is likely to be in that high-frequency range. The res-olution of the binary conversion could be immensely improved if I narrow the range and increase the sampling rate of the conversion algorithm within that smaller range while also decreasing the width of each listening channel."

"I see," replied Cameron. "So if you were to narrow the search frequency to a range of nine hundred megahertz to one gigahertz, and then divide that range into ten listening bands of ten megahertz each, it should reduce the noise and improve the resolution of the conversation, right?"

She nodded. "Exactly. It's kind of like trying to tune in to a radio station but you don't know the frequency. All you know is that the station broadcasts only once per day for several seconds. That forces you to perform a broad scan of the entire range of interest at a lower resolution. Each of my listening channels last night was one hundred megahertz wide. For tonight I'm plan-ning to narrow the listening channel width to around ten megahertz, with the entire range being only one hundred megahertz wide. That's a ten X improvement in the frequency selection."

"Which you hope would result in a ten X improvement in the resolution of the binary map."

"You've got it. The problem, of course, is that even that may not be enough to get a clean conversion. Keep in mind that sometimes there is a difference of less than one megahertz between radio stations. You have to play with the tuner to get a specific station, and that's after you *know* the station's number. Imagine trying to find a station without knowing the number and of course the station only broadcasts once a day for several seconds."

"Sounds like we may have a few iterations to go."

"The problem is that we don't have that many bullets left in our gun. Today is the seventeenth. We only have fourteen more chances to find the frequency, map it, and figure out what the message is."

"What if the selected frequency is not within this new frequency range? What if it's higher that one gigahertz? Should we try to perform a search at a higher frequency than that?"

She shrugged. "Again, it boils down to the resolution. Widen the search and drop the resolution. For now it appears that there was a lot of activity in this upper frequency. Let's try the proposed narrowed range tonight and go from there."

"I'm in, but there's still something that doesn't make sense."

"What's that?"

"If the resolution of the binary map is so way off, why is it that we got such crisp information on the date of the event?"

Susan thought about that for a moment and quickly went back to her system, pulling up a window that showed the electromagnetic meter right before the event. She clicked the PLAY button at the bottom of the window, replaying the event, looking at the graphical record of the EM meter as the event progressed, pausing often, noticing the intensity of the activity in the upper frequency range, up to the last instance, right before the event ended, when a single pulse of EM activity filled every frequency in the selected range for a fraction of a second. She clicked REWIND for a second and then STOP, followed by PLAY. This time, when the frequency-independent EM pulse appeared on the screen, she clicked PAUSE. At the time she had not thought much of it. But now she understood.

Tapping an unkempt fingernail on the plasma screen, Susan said, "This last pulse corresponds to the bottom of the binary file, the Mayan date. Looks like it was broadcast across all frequencies."

Cameron grinned while nodding. "You're an amazing woman."

"Save that for when we're out of the woods, *literally* speaking. Also, don't forget that we still have to figure out the meaning of the 260 bytes of data in the captured viruses. Each has been different so far."

"Do you think you might also have a resolution problem there?"

She shook her head. "That code is extracted directly from the body of the virus. There is no translation from the outside world into the digital world. It's all digital. It should be already clean. We just have to figure out what it means. And I get the feeling that the answer to that puzzle is somewhere around us."

Susan looked at the beautiful temple, at the pyramid, at the smaller palace, marvelous works of stone, so much in harmony with its surroundings, looking not like something erected *on* the land but coming *out* of the land, like an extension of the jungle, like her unkempt fingernails, different from the rest of her hand but very much a part of it.

Breathing the warm and humid air, Susan returned her attention to the laptop to review the recorded event once more.

Chapter Fifteen

001111

1

December 17, 1999

Antonio Strokk was the first to hear it, vegetation being hacked away. He listened intently for another moment, eyes closed, hoping that the sounds would reveal an animal, but the slashing sound was human, and it was coming toward them.

For a moment his instincts failed him. With all of his preparations, he had not thought of the possibility of someone noisily approaching from behind. He had set up booby traps beyond the perimeter hot-wired by the SEALs in case one of the American soldiers decided to take a stealth tour of the jungle around the site. But he had not expected this.

Celina was already moving off the moss, seeking the cover of a ceiba's wide trunk. She had personally set up the charges and knew what kind of blast to expect. Strokk also rolled off the moss and behind an adjacent tree, keeping his silenced weapon aimed at his personal target, the SEAL commander.

In seconds the intruder would reach the trap, not only blowing himself to pieces, but also telegraphing Strokk's team's presence to the SEALs. If he allowed the elite American fighting force the opportunity to vanish into the jungle, Strokk knew that his chances of coming out alive were drastically reduced. As seasoned as his team was, Strokk knew that it could not match an alert SEAL unit on the hunt. His only advantage against the highly trained naval force was the element of surprise, of being able to give an order and shoot them all at once, before any of them knew what had hit them.

And Antonio Strokk, former Russian Spetsnaz commander, gave the order, leading the strike by firing three silenced rounds into the head and chest of the SEAL commander. Celina did the same with her target.

2

Susan jumped away in shock the moment Lieutenant Lobo's head blew apart, spraying her and her equipment with a crimson mist. In the same instant, all SEALs within her field of view dropped to the ground, silent bullets ripping open their craniums. Before she could react, Cameron was on top of her, forcing her down on the stone courtyard, shielding her with his own body.

"Everybody down!" a distant SEAL screamed moments later, raising his silenced submachine gun at the jungle, shooting several rounds before falling to his knees, blood spurting from his chest. Then he collapsed.

A surreal mantle descended over the entire area as the surviving SEALs returned fire in all directions while seeking shelter behind stelae and pillars, but the enemy seemed to be everywhere, firing from all angles, catching the Americans in a deadly cross fire, rapidly decimating the naval team.

Susan and Cameron rose to a deep crouch, gazing at the havoc around them. Most SEALs were down, limbs twisted at unnatural angles, blood pooling around their bodies.

"We have to get out of here!" she said, a sudden burst of confidence gripping her, flushing out the initial shock, forcing her to look past the slain figures sprawled across the courtyard.

Together they raced the twenty feet separating them from the nearest SEAL, Lieutenant Lobo.

Susan forced back the vomit reaching her gorge at the sight of Lobo's face, eyeballs out of their sockets from the internal pressure of the round that tore his head in half, splashing the limestone around him with gray matter and bloody foam.

Cameron grabbed the SEAL's large side arm. Clenching her teeth, gunpowder assaulting her nostrils, she followed him around the cenote as a powerful blast shook the jungle to their right, followed by screams.

They reached the stone pillar, the one by the large temple, near the main cavelike entrance to the site. Susan stopped, pressing her back against the stone reliefs of the pillar, Cameron standing next to her, also breathing heavily.

A SEAL ran in their direction, the ground around him exploding from a fusillade of silent rounds. The warrior, the bulky blond Cameron had saved from the caiman two days ago, zigzagged as he sprinted across the front of the temple, by the steps. Then he suddenly arched back, a bullet stabbing his chest. He hit the ground just a dozen feet from Susan, rolled toward the steps, and miraculously surged back up to his knees, as if he were praying. The soldier lifted his weapon toward the trees beyond Susan and Cameron, but before he could fire, a round tore into his neck. As the young man's body remained kneeling for a few grotesque moments, his nearly severed head leaned back to a sickening angle, before ripping cleanly off his upper torso, hitting the ground with the thump of a sack of potatoes.

Susan cupped her mouth as she ran away, led by Cameron, feeling another convulsion, tasting the MRE in the back of her throat, her heavy breathing mixing with the howling of monkeys and squawking of birds. Moss dangled from high branches as she kicked her feet against the uneven terrain, the ground suddenly exploding in front of them, bullets walloping against the trees leading to the jungle.

They stopped, looking around them, nearly dropping to their knees as a powerful explosion shook the ground, followed by the terrified screams of a woman.

"What—who is that?" Susan asked, panting.

"Don't . . . don't know. But someone . . . wants us alive!" Cameron replied, nearly out of breath, scanning their surroundings with Lobo's gun, unable to find a target. She kept her Walther PPK hidden from view.

"You're . . . right," she replied. "Otherwise we'd also be dead by—"

"Don't move!" a voice echoed by the edge of the site, mixing with the female screams emanating from the jungle to their immediate right. "And drop that gun!"

3

Antonio Strokk received a status report from each of his fire teams surrounding the site. All SEALs had been terminated and the scientists had been intercepted by the temple.

Staring at Celina who was currently reloading her submachine gun, he gave the order to terminate the intruders with extreme prejudice. He also ordered two of his men to hold the scientists at the temple until he got there.

A moment later he heard four of his men racing through the jungle in the direction of the screams.

4

Ishiguro Nakamura rushed to Jackie's side the moment a deafening explosion blasted Luis's body into a cloud of human debris, spraying the jungle around him, as well as Jackie, who had braced herself in the thick underbrush while screaming out loud.

"Are you okay?" he shouted, grabbing her shoulders, the loud explosion ringing in his ears.

"Oh, God! Oh, my God!" She stared at her hands, stained with the blood and tissue of Luis.

"Jackie! Are you hurt?"

"Oh, Sweet Jesus!"

"JACKIE!"

She froze, staring at him, eyes blinking in recognition. Then she hugged him.

"Are you all right?"

"Ye—yes. Yes, I'm fine! Oh, God, he just blew up!"

He embraced her. "I know, baby! I know!"

Kuoshi staggered toward them, clutching his weapon. "Get away!" he told them. "Get out of here!"

They both looked at him. "What are you talking ab—"

"No time to explain! Get away!"

The second guide, Porfirio, dropped his backpack and took off, rapidly losing himself in the jungle.

"You too!" the corporate liaison shouted. "Get out of here!"

Shadows moved in the jungle. Incoming soldiers, their silhouettes momentarily becoming alive against the backdrop of the triple-canopy jungle as they crossed a beam of sunlight filtering through the heavy vegetation. Dark olive fatigues and silenced Uzis turned to black phantoms cruising through the bush as they left the narrow shaft of light behind.

Kuoshi leveled the pistol at the nearest shadow and fired twice, the reports echoing loudly, stabbing Ishiguro's eardrums. The figure arched back from the impact.

"There isn't much time!" Kuoshi warned. "You must get out of here! Save the equipment! Save yourselves!"

Ishiguro grabbed Jackie's hand. "What about you?"

"I'm doing my job!" he shouted. "I'm protecting you! Now get out of here and go do *your* job!"

A bullet zoomed so close to Ishiguro's head that the sound rang in his ears long after it had lodged itself in the tree with an explosion of bark.

That was all the encouragement the scientists needed. They hurtled into the jungle, shoving moss and vines aside, jumping over a fallen log, through thick vegetation, around trees, increasing the gap.

Kuoshi fired again, and again, buying them time.

They had to get away ... *but where?* Ishiguro thought. They were in the middle of the Petén. The closest place was many miles away.

Jackie tripped on something and tumbled out of control across the leaf-covered terrain, also making Ishiguro fall, his torso burning from the impact against a clump of boulders.

They struggled back up, eyes frantically searching for a path through the dense bush. They had to put some distance between them, get away from their pursuers, make it to—

Kuoshi's agonized outcry echoed in the jungle.

"Oh, God!" Jackie said. "Kuoshi—"

"He did ... what he had to," Ishiguro said, breathing heavily, shoving branches aside, reaching a large opening between the towering ceibas, the large backpack slowing him down, burning his—

The earth dropped away.

Ishiguro and Jackie tried to find a foothold, but there was none. Everything seemed to collapse around them. The trees disappeared as they fell into the ground, almost as if swallowed by it. They flapped their arms and legs in a desperate effort to reach for anything to break the fall as their senses filled with fear, as the smell of damp earth enveloped them before losing consciousness.

5

Joao Peixoto quickly covered the four-foot-wide hunting trap with a pair of palms and leaves, before hiding behind a rock as three soldiers approached the area.

The men stopped ten feet from his trap, scanned the area with their automatic weapons, and turned around.

6

Wearing a set of jungle fatigues, Celina by his side, Antonio Strokk stood in the middle of the courtyard inspecting the damage his well-trained troops had inflicted on the unsuspecting platoon.

The Venezuelan-Russian, the sleeves of his uniform rolled up to his elbows, slowly walked among the slain SEALs, wondering how he was going to get rid of them. In spite of all their preparations he had not thought of that one, and in this heat and humidity those corpses would start decomposing very soon.

A muscular man with a crew cut approached them. "At least two got away. We lost track of them."

Celina sighed.

"You said earlier that there was some equipment left behind?"

"Two large backpacks. Looks like an assortment of personal gear, nonperishables, and a disassembled telescope. There is also some electronics equipment that I do not recognize."

"Keep looking," he ordered. "And get those bodies out of here."

"What do we do with them, sir?"

"Tie rocks around them and throw them in the water hole," Celina said.

Strokk glanced at his sister, her short brown hair contrasting sharply with her ghostly skin and dark eyes. He nodded approvingly.

The stocky mercenary rushed off.

"Now," he said, "why don't we go meet our new friends? After that I also need you to inspect the captured equipment in the backpacks for clues."

Strokk and Celina walked toward the temple while his men dragged the bodies of the SEAL team to the water hole, stripping them of weapons and ammunition before shoving rocks into their fatigues and kicking them over the edge.

Three heavily armed mercenaries, belts of ammunition slung across their chests bandoleer style, stood ominously over the captured scientists, who sat on the steps leading up to the temple. The Garnett woman resembled a model, tall, thin, like Celina, but with finer features, dark olive skin and catlike, almost Asian eyes. Slater, who'd appeared rugged from a distance, looked even rougher close up. Hard-edged features, piercing eyes as dark as his long hair, and very muscular, but lean.

Slater began to stand, but one of the mercenaries, a man with a bull neck, grossly muscular arms and shoulders, and a green-dyed crew cut, shoved a gloved palm against his shoulder, forcing him back down.

"Good morning," Strokk said, standing in front of the couple, motioning his men to stand them up. "My name is Antonio Strokk, you are my prisoners, and you will do *exactly* as I say."

The same hand that had shoved Slater down now grabbed his vest and yanked him up. The archaeologist threw his arm back, forcing Greenhair's hand off of him. In the same fluid motion, he also pushed the hand of a second mercenary as he reached down to grab Susan. "Get your hands off of her!" he warned. The hypermuscular mercenary was about to retaliate when Strokk raised a palm.

"Enough."

The mercenaries backed off, reluctantly, Greenhair letting Slater know with his blue-eyed stare that this little episode was not over.

"You have big *cojones* to act this way, *cabron*," Celina said, measuring Slater. "Petroff could break your back just like that!" She snapped her bony fingers.

The archaeologist gave the gaunt female terrorist a contemptuous glance before grabbing Susan's hand and giving it a reassuring squeeze. "What do you want with us?"

"The same thing that your government wants, Dr. Slater," replied Strokk. "Information on the global virus."

"You want to know how to kill it?"

"Something like that."

"You're the ones responsible for the deaths in Washington," said Susan in an accusatory tone.

Strokk shrugged. "People die, Miss Garnett."

"And I suppose you're just going to kill us as well after you get what you need from us?"

Celina walked up to Susan. "You have no idea what we could do to you, *puta*. How would you like for every guy here to fuck you in every position known to mankind until your skin turns as raw as those stone statues? You think you felt bad enough when Bloodaxe killed your pathetic family?"

"Hey!" Slater snapped, getting in between the two women. The massive mercenaries stepped forward again, aiming their weapons at the archaeologist.

"I said, ENOUGH!" barked Strokk, moving his sister aside. "This is how we're going to do this. You two go back to your research. Celina, who is very technically capable, will oversee your work to make sure that you don't try to warn your people in Washington. All information goes directly to me. I'll decide what gets fed to Washington to keep them from getting suspicious. If you do as I say, you'll live. If you don't... you will wish you were never born. Do we understand each other?"

"How do we know you'll keep your end of this deal?"

"You don't, *puto*," replied Celina.

"Then what makes you think that we'll—" Slater began.

Susan cut him off, squeezing his hand while firmly stating, "We will do as you say."

Strokk grinned. "I know you will."

7

Susan spent the next hour making minor repairs to the computer equipment. In spite of the terrorists' best efforts to spare the hardware, stray rounds had damaged one of the solar cells and a communications radio, breaking the satellite link to Washington. After a few patches, involving activating redundant gear, she had the system back on-line and now sat in front of the laptop in the middle of the stone courtyard, horseflies buzzing overhead. Cameron sat next to her. Two of the large mercenaries—one of them Cameron's green-haired friend, Petroff—remained a dozen feet away, their large machine guns hanging from their shoulders, their Slavic features softened by camouflage cream. Celina stood right behind the scientists as the PC rebooted.

Over two dozen men in camouflage gear had entered the site, many of them sat around with their pants down picking insects off their skin. Others walked around inspecting the dazzling display of pre-Columbian art. Some of them pointed at the precious metals and stones adorning edifices and stelae. One of the tick-picking brutes caught her gazing in his direction and promptly dropped his underwear while grabbing himself and yelling something in what sounded like Russian, drawing laughs and howls from his comrades-in-arms nearby. Susan just turned away and ignored it. She not only had plenty of reason to hate the crude terrorists for what they had done, and for what they were attempting to do, but she had a special contempt for the borderline anorexic woman who called herself Celina, standing behind them, her gaunt features and dirty hair adding a dimension of evil to her persona.

The display came alive. A message on the screen informed her that reidt@fbi.gov wanted to start an Internet chat with her.

"Go ahead," replied Celina, pulling out a huge pistol, which look ridiculously large at the end of her pencil-thin arm, but which Susan felt the gaunt terrorist could use with expert marksmanship. She pointed the gun at Cameron's groin.

The archaeologist frowned.

"Remember, *puta*," Celina added in an accent that could have been Slavic or Hispanic, or both, "if you try anything funny—including trying to attach any hidden files to your transmission—your boyfriend here loses his ability to fuck you. And from the looks of it, I'd say that'd be quite a loss."

Susan clenched her teeth at her crudeness, but chose to ignore her as she had ignored the tick-picking jerk. She also chose to play it straight for now. The female terrorist seemed to be computer literate.

Cameron patted Susan's forearm. "Stay calm."

"Don't worry," she replied, eyes on her screen, his touch as reassuring as her PPK, still shoved in her shorts, by her spine, covered by the T-shirt and the gear vest.

REIDT@FBI.GOV:	WHAT HAPPENED? THE CONNECTION WENT DOWN.
SG@RLOGIN.NET:	JUST A GLITCH. WE'RE BACK ON-LINE.
REIDT@FBI.GOV:	ANYWAY . . . TOO MANY MATCHES AT EIGHTY PERCENT.
SG@RLOGIN.NET:	HOW MANY?
REIDT@GBI.GOV:	ONE HUNDRED AND NINETY-TWO, AND NONE OF THEM MAKES ANY SENSE. THEY ALL SMELL LIKE DEAD ENDS. I'VE ALREADY KICKED OFF A CHECK AGAINST THE ENTIRE WORLD. I'VE GOT ALL OF THE BUREAU'S MACHINES, PLUS WE'VE PATCHED IN THE TREASURY DEPARTMENT AND ALSO LANGLEY. IT'LL STILL TAKE AN HOUR OR TWO. WILL LET YOU KNOW.

Susan explained to Reid her theory about narrowing the frequency range to increase the resolution of the acquired EMI activity to get a cleaner baseline.

"So many matches," said Celina, her large pistol still aimed at Cameron. "Intriguing . . . but what does that mean?"

"Too early to tell," said Cameron.

"You keep that up and you won't be able to get it up ever again. Your girlfriend here will have to get satisfaction somewhere else, perhaps with Petroff. He has quite the reputation back in Kiev." She pointed at the steroid-fed Ukrainian, clutching the largest machine gun Cameron had ever seen. The green-haired mercenary regarded the archaeologist with contempt. "I suggest you try to answer my question one more time."

Cameron sighed, looking at Susan, realizing that the terrorists would not only be using him to force Susan to cooperate, but also using Susan to get him to obey, capitalizing on their affection for one another. "All right," he finally said in a resigned tone. "Last night's transmission did provide us with a Mayan date corresponding to zero one, zero one, zero zero at the bottom of what we suspect is a binary landscape. This leads me to believe that a major event will take place there at the end of the millennium. That's all I know at this point. You have seen Susan's theory about improving the resolution, but for that we need to wait until tonight's event. In addition, the FBI's going to extend the search area to the entire world."

"Much better," Celina said. "Ask Reid what is the FBI doing next."

At Susan's hesitation, the terrorist pressed the gun against his groin. Susan watched Cameron gazing down at the huge muzzle shoved in between his legs and opted to comply, reading her superior's reply a moment later.

REIDT@FBI.GOV:	WE'VE ALREADY CONTACTED THE WHITE HOUSE TO BRING THEM UP-TO-DATE. I'LL LET YOU KNOW WHAT HAPPENS NEXT. IN THE MEANTIME, WE'LL KEEP ON SEARCHING FOR A MATCH WITH WHAT WE'VE GOT. YOU JUST GET READY FOR TONIGHT'S EVENT.
SG@RLOGIN.NET:	WE'RE READY.
REIDT@FBI.GOV:	LET ME KNOW IF YOU NEED ANYTHING ELSE. THE SEALS BEHAVING THEMSELVES?
SG@RLOGIN.NET:	NO PROBLEMS ON THAT FRONT. WE HAVE EVERYTHING WE NEED.
REIDT@FBI.GOV:	ALL RIGHT. WE'RE STILL INVESTIGATING THE MURDERS. NOTHING YET. WILL KEEP YOU POSTED. BYE NOW.
SG@RLOGIN.NET:	BYE, SIR.

Susan frowned and broke the connection. "Now we wait," she said. "Until tonight at seven, for the next event."

"Well done." Celina lifted the gun, brushing it gently against Cameron's left cheek. "I'll be checking on *you* later."

Susan didn't like the sound of that.

"If it's all right, I'd like to continue my study of the glyphs. They're a good source of clues."

The female terrorist, wrapped in incredibly tight black jeans and a black T-shirt, nodded. "Petroff has been ordered to never leave your sight. You are free to go about the area. But don't even think about going into the jungle. You'll never make it past the first dozen feet. And you're not allowed to connect to the satellite link unless I'm present."

Susan watched her give Cameron a slow female wink before leaving.

"Skinny-ass bitch," she mumbled, a strange feeling of possessiveness clouding her judgment.

"Now, now," said Cameron, leaning against her, rubbing shoulders. "If I didn't know any better I'd say that you are jealous."

"Don't you have work to do?" she snapped.

Cameron's grin broadened.

"What's so funny?"

"Come," he said, standing. "Why don't you give me a hand with those." He pointed at a small knapsack next to the few books on glyphs that he had brought along. "There's some of my tools in there. Let's go do some more—" His gaze shifted to Petroff. The mercenary was using a hunting knife to dislodge a large piece of jade adorning the headdress of one of the ball players carved on the stelae at the edge of the courtyard. "Hey!" Cameron shouted. "Don't touch that!"

Petroff, rocking the tip of the knife between the limestone and the jade, waved him off and continued his work.

Cameron's features tightened into a mask of rage as he sprung with the ferocity of a jungle cat, pushing the mercenary back. "I said, don't touch them, you imbecile!"

Just as Susan stood, Petroff smacked the stock of his machine gun across Cameron's head, dropping him cold on the stone floor. He then swung his leg back to kick the unconscious archeologist, but Susan shoved herself in the way, shielding Cameron. "NO! Stop! You animal!"

Petroff hesitated, breathing heavily, not certain what to do. He took a step back as Strokk and Celina rushed toward them, shouting in Russian. Petroff replied angrily in the same language, pointing at Cameron and then at himself.

Strokk knelt by Susan's side, inspecting Cameron's head wound, checking for a pulse. "Petroff says that Slater attacked him." He spoke more Russian and Petroff handed him the canteen strapped to his belt.

"The animal was desecrating the stelae! Cameron tried to stop him, but he wouldn't listen!" Susan shouted, gently placing Cameron's head on her lap after crossing her legs and sitting by him. She softly ran her fingers over a patch of red skin between his left eye and temple.

"Fool," commented Celina, watching with indifference.

Susan locked eyes with the female terrorist, burning Celina with her stare, before returning her attention to Cameron.

Strokk poured some water on the wound. Susan rubbed the water on the archaeologist's face and neck. "These men are trained killers, Miss Garnett," said Strokk. "Their reactions are deadly. Slater's lucky that Petroff didn't shoot him . . . he's coming around."

Cameron moaned and stirred, Susan held his head in place, looking into his eyes as he blinked, his face twisting into a mask of pain.

"My . . . head . . ."

"Easy," she said, rubbing his face, cupping water in her hand and wetting his cheeks, his wound. "Don't talk."

Strokk stood. "He'll be all right. Keep him awake. And by all means, keep him from taunting any of my men. I can't be responsible for his foolish acts."

"The statues . . ." Cameron began, inhaling and exhaling, bringing a finger to his temple and rubbing. "Don't touch the–"

"Dr. Slater," Strokk said. "I suggest you stay out of my team's way. If my men wish to take some souvenirs with them, they should be allowed to do so. I'm certainly not going to stop them if it helps their morale, as long as they stick to the main objectives of this mission. Is that understood?"

Cameron's eyes became mere slits of anger as he sat up and spoke with amazing calm. "Look, this site is the find of the century. It's untouched, and more important to me than my life. If your men touch so much as a single statue, I will refuse to help you. And if you kill me, you know that Susan will not help you any further–and without us, you have no hope of learning about this virus to stop it before the deadline expires."

Strokk regarded the archaeologist first with surprise, then with contempt. He unholstered his sidearm and aimed it at Susan's face. "Is this site more important to you than her life too?"

Cameron shifted his gaze from Strokk to Susan.

"Don't interfere, Dr. Slater," said Strokk, cocking the gun while pressing the muzzle against her left temple. "Or you'll be staring at her brains on your lap for a long time. Now, do we understand each other?"

Cameron exhaled heavily.

"Good." The terrorist turned to Susan. "Be sure to get ready for tonight's event. My patience is running thin. I want answers on this global event. You do *not* want to disappoint me."

Chapter Sixteen

010000

1

From time immemorial, outsiders had come and taken from Joao's land. The first Spaniards arrived on the shores of the Yucatán in the early 1500s, not only claiming a soil that didn't belong to them, but also ushering Old World diseases into the New World. Smallpox, influenza, measles, unknown illnesses among the Maya that claimed more lives than the steel of the conquistadores' swords, killed over ninety percent of Mesoamerica's native population within a century. Outsiders had come and taken from the Maya. They had robbed them of their land, of their women, of their traditions, of their dignity. They had come and imposed an alien way of life, a different religion, strange beliefs. They had raped the women, enslaved the men, indoctrinated the children. They had burned their codices, desecrated their temples, looted their palaces, stolen gold and precious stones, ridiculed their culture, and enforced a way of life that valued the accumulation of wealth rather than the enhancement of the human spirit. But the Maya had fought back with surprising vigor, bravely refusing to be subdued, resisting the incessant waves of invaders, inflicting fear in their hearts. Their valiant efforts, however, could not push back the overwhelming tide drowning their land, razing it with the rage of the most violent of forest fires, attempting to uproot their culture like an unwanted weed in the gardens of another Spanish-claimed territory. Only this garden was too vast to be fully controlled. The surviving natives retreated to the lowlands of the Petén, deep within the protection of the vast jungle, of mangroves, of swamps, of jaguars and caimans, safe from the unyielding fist of the Spaniards. But the ancient warriors remained alert, ready to launch jungle-style warfare on any invader foolish enough to enter their green sanctuary. Many did come in, following Mexico's independence from Spain in 1821, when the new government tried to subdue the Maya into laborers on cash-crop plantations, triggering the beginning of what became known as the War of the Castles. Armed by the British in neighboring Belize, the rebelling natives not only expelled the Mexican army, but managed to gain control of the entire Yucatán Peninsula until 1901, when a new wave of government strikes destroyed many aspects of Mayan cultural traditions and agricultural methods. And the true Maya retreated once again to its beloved Petén, hiding beneath its thick canopy, beyond impenetrable terrain, past treacherous swamps, preserving their core beliefs, their heritage, their culture. But they also remembered the invaders, never forgetting their atrocities, their wickedness, the brutality with which they had attempted to eradicate their entire civilization.

Wickedness. Brutality.

Joao Peixoto's heart filled with anger as he surveyed the site from the lush branches of an opulent ceiba. The wrath of his ancestors boiled inside of him, a fury kindled by the sight of so much death, so much blasphemy. He had seen the new soldiers dump the bodies of the first team into the pure waters of the cenote, defiling the virgin pool. Now the same men desecrated the holy temple of Kinich Ahau, the jaguar sun god. They also carved out the precious stones and metals from the stelae of Chac, rain god and cosmic monster, and of Ix Chel, the moon goddess of medicine and childbirth.

Joao closed his tearful eyes, controlling the urge to attack the invaders, to avenge this unforgivable crime, to appease the angry gods. But he couldn't do so without permission from the high priests, without their consent. He was a *nacom*, a Mayan military leader, loyal to the shamans, the carriers of his people's traditions, keepers of his culture's unstained values, of the secret ways to enter the limestone structure, and of its deadly traps.

The Mayan warrior noticed the shadow of the trees shifting across the cenote. The sun had began its decline toward the western horizon, which meant the strangers he had captured should have been delivered to his village by now. He hoped to learn much from them, perhaps even enough to generate a recommendation to the high priests.

Before he returned to his village, Joao watched with personal satisfaction that the long-haired man who had been respectfully inspecting the area for the past two days was now standing. The stranger had made a valiant effort to prevent the desecration of the large stelae honoring Hunahpu and Xbalanque, the hero twins engaged in a game of *pokatok*.

Honor lived within that man, as well as within the woman who had come
to his defense.

2

Ishiguro Nakamura watched the body of Luis being splattered over the jungle's leaf-covered terrain. He heard Jackie scream, saw her contorted face
reflecting her horror. The dark jungle came alive with the sounds of the
enemy. Kuoshi clutched a weapon, warning them to run away, to find a way
out, to preserve their research. He saw faceless figures bearing automatic
weapons nearing, heard the multiple reports from Kuoshi's gun, listened to
his agonizing scream. Ishiguro watched the trees rush past as Jackie and he
raced through the thick underbrush. He felt the ground giving beneath him,
heard Jackie shriek once more. The heavy backpack pulled him back, nearly
flipping him in midair as he fell into a black hole.

Drenched in perspiration, Ishiguro woke up with a monstrous headache. In
spite of the relentless pounding against his temples and behind his eyes, he
opened them and found himself staring at the sagging breasts of an old
woman. She was kneeling across the room in front of a flat rock while using
her hands to mold a yellowish, soggy mass. Flies droned around her.

Jackie, he thought. *Where are you?*

The woman slowly raised her stare until her weathered eyes met his. She
studied him for a few seconds before going back to her work while mumbling
something that sounded more animal than human.

Ishiguro brought a finger to his right temple and slowly rubbed it, feeling
as if he'd been asleep forever. He managed to sit up and take a better look
at what appeared to be the inside of a stone shack, in the center of which
stood a tripod made of sticks. A clay dish hung over two small burning logs.
Smoke curled up to the top of the bullet-shaped roof, escaping through a tiny
opening. He saw no sign of his wife.

He inspected his body and noticed he only wore the khaki slacks and shirt.
His gear was gone. *Even the boots,* he thought, staring at the straw and dirt
caught in between his toes.

How long have I been out?

He looked at his left wrist, but his G-shock Casio was also gone.

Ishiguro frowned as he recalled hitting his head right before passing out.
He brought a hand up and felt a lump between his left temple and the back
of his skull, letting out a sigh of relief. The wound had not bled. His hair still

felt smooth, not clumped and knotted as it would have been if it was caked with dry blood.

Slowly, very slowly, his mind kicked in. They had been ambushed and were being chased when the earth had given way under them.

He had to find out what had happened. Was Jackie all right? Where was she?

Ishiguro tried to stand but felt light-headed and collapsed back on the bed, his mind drifting to the faceless strangers who had attacked them. His skin tightened at the thought of Jackie being hurt, the thought renewing his desire to stand up, to look for her.

Ishiguro pushed himself and stood, ignoring the overwhelming headache. He staggered toward the shack's entrance. The toothless woman began to speak the dialect again. He shrugged and left her.

Sunlight assaulted his eyes, stinging them, flaring his headache. Squinting, using a palm to shield his eyes, Ishiguro realized that he had indeed been taken in by a native tribe. There were a dozen similar limestone shacks with hatched roofs scattered around a small clearing, mostly shielded by ceibas, mahoganies, and rubber trees, creating jagged patches of sunlight across the entire village. Children dressed in short skirts played with a black ball while two dozen women, wearing either loincloths or just short skirts, breasts exposed, worked near a small fire twenty feet to his left. A small stream flowed in from the jungle, sectioning the village in half, and disappearing back into the woods. He saw no men anywhere.

One of the women turned in his direction. She was of light olive complexion, very muscular, and with dark hair dropping to the middle of her back. In fact, after another inspection of the group, he decided that all of the women were athletically built, with particularly strong legs.

The woman began to walk in his direction. The muscles on her legs pumped against the skin with every step. Her face didn't look like that of a typical native. Her nose had some resemblance to the flat and wide noses typical of the region, but hers was thinner and smaller. Her lips, although cracked and dry, were full, and her eyes . . . they were not green or hazel, but light gray, crowning her high cheekbones. She was definitely the product of generations of European and native Indian interbreeding. The woman carried an infant strapped to her loincloth. The baby was sleeping.

She came up to him, took his right hand, and guided him to a shack at the other side of the clearing, motioning for Ishiguro to go inside.

The interior was murky. A dirt floor, a tripod with a hanging clay pot, and a single bed. Blinking to adjust his eyes, Ishiguro saw Jackie lying on her back, eyes closed.

His stomach knotting, he rushed to her side, sitting in bed, noticing the large lump on her forehead, feeling for a pulse, exhaling in relief when he found one.

He inspected the nasty bruise right above her left eye, also noticing the clay pot filled with water and a white cotton rag next to it. The astrophysicist immersed the cloth in the water, soaking it, then wringing it before applying it to her forehead. She stirred and moaned. He repeated the process many times for the next thirty minutes. At one point in time she opened her eyes but quickly fell unconscious again.

Ishiguro forgot all about the mission, the celestial signal, the strong possibility of an extraterrestrial contact. At that moment, sitting on a straw bed inside a stone shack in the middle of nowhere, his thoughts focused on Jackie, realizing that she was indeed the most important thing in the world to him. Nothing like being threatened with the possibility of losing her for Ishiguro to put things in the right perspective. And so he cleaned her face, her neck, her forearms, her dirty hands, feeling frustrated that he could do nothing more for her, wishing that she had stayed behind, back in Cerro Tolo, safe within the protective walls of the observatory.

Just then he felt a presence behind him.

In the twilight of the room, Ishiguro stared at a thin but very muscular native dressed in a dark skirt. His shoulder-length hair was tied in a ponytail. There was an air of confidence, intelligence, and lack of curiosity in his dark eyes, encased in purplish sockets.

The man stopped a few feet from Ishiguro. "What are you doing in this land?"

Ishiguro was momentarily surprised. "You ... you speak English ... quite well." He detected a mix of Spanish and British accents.

"Please answer my question."

"My wife ... she needs help. I need to find a—"

"This land belongs to my people," the stranger interrupted. "Strangers are *not* welcome. The people of your world kill just to kill. The people of my world only kill to eat. I saw the attack on the soldiers, the way they are now desecrating the temple of Kinich Ahau. So I ask you again, what are you doing here?"

Ishiguro narrowed his eyes. "Temple of Kini ... Soldiers? I—I don't understand."

"Tell me what you are doing here."

Ishiguro looked at Jackie before returning his attention to the native, realizing he had some explaining to do before he would be in a position to ask anything. He decided that honesty was his best alternative. After all, he had done nothing wrong. He even had the papers from the Guatemalan government providing him access to this region to conduct his work. But, should he be *truly* honest? Should he stick to his story of seismic research? He frowned, realizing how silly that sounded in light of the recent events. And who had tried to kill them? Why were there soldiers at this temple? Why was there a temple in the first place? Ishiguro took a chance and opted for the real truth.

"I'm a scientist, an astronomer." He watched the native's face closely, looking for a reaction.

"The study of the heavens," the half-naked man said. "My people have also studied the heavens. Go on."

The comment caught Ishiguro by surprise. Perhaps he should have brushed up on the findings of the ancient Maya on his way here, but at the time he had been too concerned about the scientific aspect of the celestial contact.

He spoke slowly, with moderation, always pausing to make sure that the native understood everything that he had said. He mentioned his findings at Cerro Tolo, the signal from outer space, its synchronization to this global event that froze computer systems, the satellite triangulation that pointed to the coordinates in the jungle. When he finished, the native appeared perplexed. Although Ishiguro had made a good effort at keeping his explanation as simple as possible, he sensed that he may have lost the English-speaking native somewhere along the way.

"Where is the origin of this signal?" he asked.

Ishiguro raised his brows at the question. "You mean, you want to know *exactly* where the signal came from?"

"That is correct," he replied in the accent that Ishiguro found intriguing, almost surreal, considering the haggard appearance of this half-naked man and the primitive surroundings.

"I . . . well, yes. I could show you if I had a map of the cosmos."

"You need a chart of the heavens?"

The Japanese astrophysicist nodded.

"Wait here." The Maya left. Two similarly dressed men took his place, regarding him with poker stares.

Perplexed by the unexpected conversation, Ishiguro exhaled heavily before going back to tending Jackie, still unconscious. This time, as he softly rubbed the damp rag over her head, she opened her eyes, staring at nothing in particular, just gazing, finally shifting them to him.

"Hi there," he said, smiling, a sense of relief washing down his anxiety.

She opened her mouth but nothing came out.

"Don't try to talk," he said. "Nod if you can understand me."

She did.

"You've got a nasty bruise over your left eye, probably from the fall back in the jungle. Do you remember that."

She nodded, also adding a barely audible, "Ye—yes," followed by, "Where?"

He told her, spending five minutes explaining their situation. By the time he had finished, Jackie had gained enough strength to sit up.

"Strange . . . very weird," she said.

"You're telling me." He put a hand to her china-doll face. "You had me worried. For a moment there . . ."

"You won't be getting rid of me *that* easily," she replied, half smiling, closing her eyes. "My head . . ."

"Welcome to the club," he said. "When they return I'm going to beg them access to our stuff. I brought some painkillers."

"What do you think is going to happen to us?"

"Not sure. They seem reasonable. I think as long as we stick to the truth we should be fine."

The haggard Maya returned, along with three elder men dressed in colorful loincloths. He blinked twice at their deformed skulls, alienlike, as well as their prominent brows, reminding him of the drawings he'd seen of cavemen in some book long ago. All were completely bald, their elongated heads glistening in the wan light filtering through the shack's entryway. Several earrings adorned one of them, along with the tattoo of a jaguarlike figure on his left forearm. The second man had tattoos in the shape of bands around his upper arms. A third man had a colorful bird painted on his left shoulder. Behind them stood the same woman who had taken him here, the infant still strapped to her loincloth. She held what appeared to be a rolled-up yellowish poster.

Ishiguro remained seated, next to Jackie. "This is my wife," he said. "She is also a scientist."

Joao nodded, turning to one of the elders and saying something incomprehensible. The women yielded the poster to the alienlike Maya, who unrolled it and handed it to the rugged native. He set it at the foot of the straw bed.

"Where?"

Ishiguro and Jackie looked at the drawing, at one another, and back at the drawing.

"Incredible," she said.

Ishiguro was at a loss for words. The map depicted the northern sky surrounding the southern constellation Centaur, drawn with amazing detail, including systems not visible with the naked eye. "Do you own telescopes?"

The Maya shook his head.

"Then how did you do this?"

"We have other means for recording the sky. Where is the origin of this signal?"

Jackie stretched her arm, her index finger pointing at the lower right side of the constellation. "Right *here.*"

Ishiguro nodded.

The Maya turned to the elders.

"Hunab Ku," the one with the earrings mumbled, eyes opening wide in obvious surprise.

"Kuxan Suum," replied the priest with the banded tattoos.

"What's going on?" asked Ishiguro.

The elders added more incomprehensible phrases before the woman stepped forward, rolled up the papyruslike astronomical chart, and followed the elders out of the shack.

"What was that all—" Jackie began.

"I am Joao Peixoto," the native interrupted. "This is my tribe. Those were the high priests. I am charged with their protection. The temple of Kinich Ahau is sacred, untouched by outsiders until a few days ago, when an English-speaking team arrived and set up a camp at the site. Then a second group arrived, killing most of the members of the first team, as well as yours."

"Why?" Ishiguro asked.

"I hoped you would be able to tell me that."

Ishiguro frowned. "How did we escape? All I remember is falling down some hole."

"A hunting trap," he explained. "You were lucky. No one else survived, aside from the long-haired man and his woman at the site."

Ishiguro was now utterly confused. Joao must have noticed this because he explained everything that had happened during the shooting, as he recalled it.

"Seems like others have detected this signal as well," observed Jackie, looking more and more alive, eyes alert. She managed to stand.

"And they want to keep it a secret bad enough to kill for it," said Ishiguro, also standing.

"What about the first team? The one with the surviving couple?" she asked.

"Probably a competing party who got there first but wasn't able to defend itself."

Ishiguro turned back to Joao, standing in the center of the murky interior. "What was the significance of the origin of the signal on your astronomical chart?"

"It came from the Hunab Ku."

"One of the priests mentioned those words," Jackie said. "What do they mean?"

"The center of the universe, from where all things come."

The two scientists exchanged a puzzled glance. "What do you know about these daily events I've mentioned?" Ishiguro asked.

He shrugged. "The high priests claim that our ancestors are sending us a message."

"For what reason?"

"They have not said. I do not believe they know for certain."

Ishiguro saw this as a perfect opportunity. "Perhaps we can help you figure it out."

"How?"

"That was our mission," he said. "To capture this signal from the heavens in the hope of deciphering its meaning. We brought some equipment to accomplish this task. If we can set it up at this site before the next event, we'll be able to tune into the message. Of course, there is the problem with the soldiers."

Joao nodded, looking in the distance, his eyes suddenly glistening with anger. "You will be allowed to access your equipment."

Ishiguro felt like pressing his luck. "What about getting to the site? We need to be close enough in order for our equipment to pick up the message."

"I will discuss this with the high priests." He turned to leave.

"Joao?"

The Mayan warrior stopped.

"How did you learn English?"

"From British missionaries in Belize. Many years ago."

"Thanks for saving our lives," said Jackie. "My husband and I are very grateful."

He nodded once and left.

3

Antonio Strokk listened with forced patience to one of his subordinates as he told him about the broken branches leading deep into the jungle, toward the river.

"Get a search party together. Take five . . . no, seven men. I want all survivors found and shot on the spot. I want no witnesses. Understood?"

"Yes."

His subordinate gone, Strokk approached his sister, sitting by the steps of the temple admiring a pear-size piece of jade shaped like a heart.

"Quite exquisite," she said, breathing on it before rubbing it against her jeans. "Especially for a bunch of savages."

"Where are our two guests?" Strokk asked.

Celina extended a thumb toward the temple's entrance. "In there, for the past hour."

"Is Petroff with them?"

She nodded, setting the jade down and picking up a mask made of gold, another artifact dislodged from one of the statues. "How much do you think something like this is worth?"

Strokk regarded the detailed mask, feeling its weight. "This is at least five pounds. Just the gold alone is worth a small fortune, but add the historical value and offer it to the right buyer . . . who knows, perhaps a few hundred thousand . . . maybe more."

"Consider this our bonus," she said, waving at a couple dozen precious objects scattered around her. "For having to sleep with the bugs."

"That may be the only payment we get if those scientists don't get a breakthrough soon. Time is against us. Our employer needs to learn how to break the virus."

Celina frowned. "If we fail, we must return our advance payment."

"This may also affect our future contracts."

"Then you also better hope that those imbeciles catch the rats who got away. The man we shot was Asian, probably meaning that another country has also figured out the location of this place, especially judging from the gear we captured."

Strokk remembered Celina's explanation of the six-inch telescope plus a microwave receiver and other assorted electronics that could be used to monitor electromagnetic noise, just like the American scientists.

Glancing up the steps, Strokk recognized Petroff's bulky figure under one of the triangular arches leading into the temple's terrace. The mercenary kept his weapon pointed at the unseen scientists, probably dusting off more ancient glyphs in search of clues.

He exhaled. Celina was right. Right now they had the situation under control from the American point of view. Washington felt that the operation was proceeding as normal. But the runaways from the second party were a wild card. If they managed to get away, Strokk had a feeling that this place would soon be crawling with new rats.

4

Sitting on the stone terrace facing a wall of glyphs surrounding larger carvings, Susan Garnett handed Cameron an assortment of brushes and fine picks as he attempted to interpret the ancient reliefs.

"What are we going to do?" she whispered, even though Petroff, twenty feet away, did not speak a word of English.

"Bide our time," he said reassuringly. "We're safe as long as they need us, so we must continue to make them feel that we are making progress in our investigation."

"But that means giving our work to the enemy, to the other side . . . whoever that is."

"That's going to be an interesting balancing act," the archaeologist replied. "Give them enough to keep them happy, but not too much to provide them with a true lead over our side. Meanwhile, we look for the chance to escape. You still have that gun with you, right?"

She nodded. "Escape? Where?"

"Out there. In the jungle."

"But . . . we're at least fifty miles away from the closest town. How are we going to . . ." She let her words trail off when she remembered his tales from previous research trips. "I forgot. We would live off the land, right?"

"The jungle will protect us, once we get there. But first we need to find a way to escape, and that's when your gun may come in handy."

"But there's so many of them, and that animal over there won't let us out of his sight."

Cameron nodded, touching the side of his face. "And it's not just the sheer quantity of brutes. The bastards sure know how to fight."

"That was very stupid of you," she said in the admonishing tone of a mother scolding her son.

He shrugged, using a small brush to get the dirt off the fine crevices of the carving of a woman who not only had the elongated shape and brows typical of Mayan nobility and high priests, but also sported exaggerated jaws and cheekbones, reminding Susan of body builders on steroids.

"I couldn't help myself. Guess I've always been on the reckless side of life," he commented, switching to a fine pick, which he used to dislodge ancient dirt and grime from the monsterlike face, thoroughly cleaning it. "There," he added. "Susan Garnett, meet Lady Zac-Kuk, mother of the legendary Pacal Votan."

Susan elbowed him for changing the subject, but went along with the conversation anyway. "Pacal Votan? Didn't you mention something about him before? He ruled Palenque, right?"

Cameron Slater, the professor, nodded approvingly. "Very good. Palenque is in Chiapas, Mexico, roughly two hundred miles away. What else do you remember?"

"Wasn't his body the one found at the Temple of . . ."

"The Inscriptions."

"Right."

"Pacal is considered by many to be perhaps the greatest Mayan chief of all times. His death marked the end of the Classic Period. In other words, things went downhill after him."

"Tell me about his mother," said Susan, staring at the stone relief.

"Lady Zac-Kuk, a Palenque princess, married her consort, Kan-Bahlum-Mo, also royalty, but not from Palenque, so he couldn't rule. Their first son was Pacal, born in A.D. 603. When Lady Zac-Kuk's father died, she ruled Palenque until Pacal was twelve years old, at which time he became the new ruler. She coached him for some time, publicly showing her support for him to keep other relatives from trying to gain control of Palenque. She ran a very tight ship and was able to outmaneuver many ploys to kill her and her young child. Pacal grew as savvy as his mother, ruling until his death in A.D. 683. Based on paintings and carvings, his mother is believed to have suffered from an overactive pituitary gland, resulting in the grotesque deformation of her facial bones. For the Maya, however, that was seen as celestial, godlike, probably helping her keep control of the government until Pacal became of age."

"So . . . why is Pacal's mother depicted here, so far from Palenque?"

"Excellent question. But not only that," he said, "for the glyph of Pacal is just about everywhere in this place, almost as if it were an extension of Palenque itself."

"Do you know why that is?"

The college professor shrugged, noncommittal. "Chiefdoms," he began, his voice turning official, "like Palenque and Tikal, for example, were erected during the Classic Period, as well as in many other sites in the Chiapas and Petén lowlands. Following Pacal's death and the beginning of the post-Classic Period, those cities were abandoned and new cities were erected in the northern Yucatán Peninsula, like Uxmal, Copán, and Chickén Itzá. Now, this site is between Palenque and Tikal, both Classic Period city-states. One would think that perhaps some of the inhabitants of Palenque, following the decline of that city, may have moved north, toward the Yucatán. Some may have stopped here and erected this site in memory of their great chief and his mother. However, I've also found signs of post-Classic work here, like that feathery serpent."

Susan looked to their right, almost at knee level, where the limestone had been carved to give the appearance of mosaics, over which a serpent with feathers was poised crawling toward the ceiling.

"Feathery serpents are later additions to the Mayan mosaic design. They were first sculpted in Uxmal, a post-Classic city-state. You mentioned one of the priests in your dreamlike experience the other night had one tattooed, right?"

She nodded, impressed with his recollection. "Why did the people of Uxmal, hundreds of years after Palenque, opt to build this place?"

"Another conflicting finding in a most intriguing place. In the past two days I have gathered enough information to keep archaeologists busy debating suppositions for generations."

"What do you think?"

"During the Classic Period, there were long-standing Mayan alliances between chiefdoms, like Palenque and Tikal. But after the death of Pacal, this trade between city-states began to decline, sparking interstate conflicts. During the post-Classic Period this conflict evolved into full-fledged warfare between the new chiefdoms in the Yucatán. Why would the warring people of Uxmal, five hundred years later, venerate such relatively ancient rulers like Pacal Votan, whose contributions were not in the development of war but of science and the arts? It would be like Benito Mussolini building a large shrine in memory of Michelangelo or Leonardo da Vinci."

In the half-light of the terrace, Susan regarded him with an admiration that stemmed not from his knowledge or his ability to apply it to figure out this puzzle, but because of the unpretentious, almost humble way in which he talked, stating the facts as he knew them, and letting his audience decide for themselves.

"We obviously still have more homework ahead of us," she offered. "Now, why don't you let me take another look at that bruise."

Reluctantly, almost like a child embarrassed at a black eye he'd received at school, Cameron turned his head sideways to her. The purple blotch covered most of his left temple. Impulsively, she kissed it, startling him.

"What was *that* for?"

She shrugged, grinning. "I couldn't help myself. Guess I've always been on the reckless side of life, especially as of lately."

"I can't imagine you being reckless."

"You have *no* idea."

Cameron put a hand to her face, offering comfort in the ruggedness of his touch, his callused hands reflecting the life that Susan Garnett found so intriguing. She put a hand over his, gently pressing it against her cheek while closing her eyes, imagining him in faraway places, alone, living off the land, surviving on nature, becoming one with the jungle, searching for mystic sites, digging, unearthing, discovering, living by his rules. The images awakened dormant feelings in Susan Garnett.

A grunt from Petroff made Cameron withdraw his hand. The large Ukrainian grinned while making a swinging motion with the stock of his weapon at head level.

Cameron ignored it, standing. "Let's go over there next," he said, pointing to the wall next to the slab blocking the entrance to the temple. Hundreds of mosaics, each about eight inches square and sporting a different Mayan number, had been carved on the limestone wall. "I've been meaning to try to study the number sequence. Since I first saw it."

The mosaics started at floor level and extended halfway up the eighteen-foot-high wall. Susan recognized numbers from one to nineteen. She also noticed mosaics containing the oblong shape representing zero with one or more dots over it. In some cases there was one or more lines topped with a few dots over the oblong symbol. "What numbers are those?"

"Beyond nineteen, the Maya used the symbol of zero at the bottom, plus dots above it to represent each additional sequence of twenty numbers. Remember, their system is vigesimal. Two dots over zero means two times twenty, or forty. Three dots means sixty, and so on." He pointed at one symbol that had zero at the bottom, then one dot, then two horizontal lines, and finally two additional dots. "That's thirty-two. Twenty is depicted by the zero topped by a single dot. Then we have two horizontal lines, each representing five, plus two dots at the top."

"Twenty, plus ten, plus two. I see," she said, pointing to another mosaic with a zero topped by three dots and a single line. "That would be sixty-five, right? Three dots times twenty, plus five for the line."

"I'd offer you a teaching assistant job but I'm afraid my students would stop paying attention to my lectures if you're up on the podium with me."

She shook her head, studying the array of Mayan numbers. "They don't seem to be following any particular sequence. Besides, in which order are you supposed to read them?"

"Mayan glyphs are normally read left to right and top to bottom."

"Oh, like our language."

"Right, but that's for glyphs. These are numbers, so they may be arranged differently."

They stepped back and studied the array of what appeared to be twenty mosaics horizontally and thirteen vertically.

"Looks like the middle row is all the same number, twenty," Susan observed. "As well as the two center columns, dividing the matrix into four quadrants."

"Good eye. The Maya loved symmetry."

"Any significance there?" she asked.

"The four quadrants could represent the four magnetic headings, north, south, east, and west. The number four also represents the number of primary wave functions of the Maya's form-giving principles of energy: attraction, radiation, transmission, and receptivity. Four is also the number of times that thirteen needs to be multiplied to get fifty-two, the number of years of Pacal Votan's galactic rule, from A.D. 631 to A.D. 683. There's all kinds of other possibilities," Cameron added.

Susan regarded him for a moment. Something didn't quite add up. "Hold on," she said. "You mentioned earlier that Pacal Votan was born in A.D. 603 and began to rule when he was twelve, right?"

He nodded.

"That would mean that he became Palenque's ruler in A.D. 615, not A.D. 631. He should had ruled for sixty-eight years, not fifty-two."

Cameron's grin told Susan that the renegade professor was about to disclose another one of his controversial theories.

"Pacal Votan was indeed born in A.D. 603," he began. "He became ruler of Palenque when he was twelve, under the close supervision of his mother, Lady Zac-Kuk. But something wonderful happened in A.D. 631, when he was only twenty-eight. That is the year when Pacal, for reasons not yet understood, achieved synchronization with the galactic core. He declared himself a serpent, a possessor of knowledge. He devoted most of his remaining fifty-two years of life to the development of ideas and mathematics, to charting the cosmos, to erecting the Temple of the Inscriptions, which is itself fifty-two feet high in commemoration of his rebirth. But more on Pacal later. Do you see any other numerical patterns?"

She nodded. "There's different types of decreasing and increasing sequences. The number thirteen is at each corner of the array, marking the starting point for the decreasing sequences moving horizontally as well as vertically. Then it looks like there are some sporadic numbers of various sizes sprinkled around. There might be a pattern in there, but I'm going to have to translate them into decimals in order to make some sense of them. You mentioned that the Maya were skilled mathematicians, right?"

He nodded.

"Let me go get my laptop."

"Why?"

"I can enter this sequence and then kick off a program that will go through many permutations in an attempt to find a mathematical formula that describes the ordering sequence."

Cameron regarded the numbers with narrowed eyes. "Just remember that the Maya had very peculiar ways of arranging numbers, unlike the numerical sequences of today. They may not fit any linear formula but more a geometrical expression, so keep that in mind when trying to find a pattern, it may be more in space than linear. It's certainly worth a try, though."

Susan shrugged. "It'll give me something to do before tonight's event, and also give the jerks the appearance that we're attempting to make progress."

Cameron nodded and moved on to the reliefs on the opposite side of the terrace, which resembled Mayan priests dressed in ceremonial gowns praying in front of a stone wall. Next to the priests it appeared as if the earth had opened up, swallowing several men dressed like regular Maya, with simple skirts and a few feathers. He began to make notes in his field notebook, obviously more interested in the pictorial reliefs than in the numerical ones.

Puzzled by the complexity of the drawings, and rapidly developing an appreciation for the enigmatic investigative work that was archaeology, Susan left the temple, walking past Petroff, ignoring his mumbling of something in Russian that sounded obscene. Susan headed down the steps, noticing Strokk and Celina listening intently to a handheld radio.

5

Strokk heard the voice of the leader of the search team crackling through the static of his encrypted radio. Celina stood next to him.

"The trail led us to a small village."

"What kind of village?"

"Looks very primitive. A dozen stone shacks. Some natives walking about, mostly women and children."

"Any sign of the runaways?"

"Negative, but they could be in the shacks."

"Search the entire place. If someone gets in your way, shoot him."

Chapter Seventeen

010001

1

December 17, 1999

Ishiguro was the first to hear the multiple screams, ear-piercing, agonizing. He and Jackie had been inspecting their surviving gear inside one of the stone shacks, disheartened to find that over half of their equipment, although carefully packed in well-padded containers, had been damaged during the fall. The rest they had left behind during the shooting.

He rushed outside, blinking in the late-afternoon sun filtering through the trees. Jackie followed him, the shouts and screams intensifying. Four armed men dressed in guerrilla-style clothing shoved women and children aside as they inspected one of the huts at the opposite end of the clearing. Many natives rushed into the jungle. Children cried. Women screamed. Joao and his men were nowhere in sight.

The village's elders, all three of them, approached the armed strangers, shouting over the cacophony of sounds created by the women and the children. Two of the guerrillas swung their weapons at the incoming old men, firing silenced rounds into two of them, also hitting two women and a child. A guerrilla knocked the third elder unconscious with the stock of his rifle, and was about to fire into his elongated head when another soldier spotted the scientists across the dusty clearing, his features tightening.

He shouted something that sounded Russian and his comrades pointed their weapons at Ishiguro and Jackie. In that same instant one of the armed men dropped to his knees, letting go of his weapon, hands on his neck, before collapsing on his side and going into convulsions. Two more guerrillas also collapsed, victims of this invisible force. His comrades convulsing on the ground, the fourth armed man took off toward the jungle, firing blindly into the trees. He fell forward a moment later, crashing headfirst into the light underbrush bordering the jungle, his body twitching, dust boiling up around him.

"What in the hell was that?" asked Jackie.

Before Ishiguro could even speculate, Joao Peixoto entered the clearing holding a long tube. Ishiguro went up to meet him, but the Mayan warrior ignored him, kneeling by the fallen elders, the high priests, blood pooling around two of them. The rest of Joao's men materialized at the edge of the jungle, like shadows coming alive from the bush, a few of them dragging the limp bodies of three more guerrillas, piling them up on one side of the clearing. Women and children reemerged from the tree line, some cautiously peering at the clearing, others racing to the aide of the slain women and a child no older than six or seven. Three men carefully lifted the only priest who did not get shot. He appeared unconscious. They took him inside one of the shacks.

"Jesus," Jackie said. "What do we do?"

"Nothing," said Ishiguro, watching the Mayan warriors pile up the guerrillas at the edge of the clearing. Some of them were still alive, trembling, foaming at the mouth, glassy eyes staring at the sky. "Two of the elders have been killed, plus two women and a kid. The third elder was knocked unconscious. There will be hell to pay for this."

The film of hate burning in Joao's eyes confirmed his comment. The Mayan chief stood in the middle of the clearing, surveying his tribe, looking at the dead women, tensing at the sight of a young mother clutching her dead child, an agonizing wail wrenching out of her lungs while staring at the sky.

Ishiguro chilled at her weeping, at her suffering. Two other women escorted her to a nearby shack.

The scientists remained still. Nothing they could say or do would make the situation any better. The soldiers had likely tracked them down to the village. In a way Ishiguro felt responsible, accountable. He wished he could do something for the dead Maya, bring them back, reverse the clock, never have come here in the first place.

Shafts of crimson and yellow-gold forked through the trees, casting a half-light gloom over the dusty clearing, over the dead. But through the mournful cries, through the hazy dust dancing in the blazing, late-afternoon sunlight, through the veil of terror enveloping the small village, Ishiguro saw Joao walking toward them, ire shimmering in his glistening stare. The scientist sensed his anger, his rage, his desire to achieve total and utter retribution.

"The sacred temple," Joao said, the conviction in his stolid gaze fueled by the power of a hundred ancient civilizations. "Get your equipment ready. We're leaving immediately."

2

Antonio Strokk breathed in deeply, controlling the urge to slam the radio against the rocks. Instead, he calmly handed it to Celina after three failed attempts to raise the search team, which had gone off the air minutes ago, right after Strokk had given the order to search the village. Now nothing.

Nothing!

"What could have gone wrong?" Celina asked.

Strokk didn't reply, the situation not making sense. The team was to maintain radio contact during the search. Four men would go in the village and carry out his orders while the other three remained hidden in the jungle, providing cover and also updating Strokk real time.

The former Spetsnaz officer invoked his training, his field experience, the hell he'd endured in Afghanistan, to control his emotions, to study the situation from an objective perspective, like the battlefield commander who realizes that the enemy has annihilated his first wave of attack. Strokk had to assume the worst, that the search party had been compromised, somehow. Questions piled up in his mind, one after the other. Who did this? The villagers? Were they armed? But so were his men, both in the clearing and in the jungle, providing cover from the trees. And what should be his next move? Should he stay put and wait for the enemy to come to him? Should he send another search party? Was a new team doing to him what he had done to the Navy SEALs less than twelve hours ago? Perhaps this had been the handiwork of another contingent of SEALs, sent here to reinforce the first team.

Possibilities.

Strokk considered them all and then made his decision, shouting orders, forming three assault groups with orders to fire on anything that walked on two legs. This time the Venezuelan-Russian would lead the assault, coordinating operations while also running the center team of the three-pronged attack. Celina and Petroff would remain behind to cover the scientists while Strokk pulled everyone else into the strike teams.

3

Joao Peixoto moved silently and swiftly through the dense jungle, his bare feet cold as he made his way across the dew-covered leaves, late-afternoon sunlight filtering here and there through the dense canopy.

Joao was angry, but he didn't let his emotions interfere with his focus. His mind followed a primal instinct, a single objective, the same directive that had driven him back to the jungle and away from the killing fields of southern Guatemala a decade ago: the survival of his tribe, the avoidance—or elimination—of a threat to his people.

And that threat now advanced noisily through an assortment of bonelike trees and thick underbrush, across curtains of vines and moss, moving directly toward his village. He had detected three groups of men, four or five soldiers per group. He currently followed the one to the far left.

Joao abruptly stopped and closed his eyes, letting his ears tune to the sounds of the dark jungle, listening to the language of his world. Slowly, he dropped to a deep crouch, his gaze narrowing as it landed on a giant fern hanging off the side of a twisted rosewood.

The Mayan chief remained immobile for several moments, listening, before quietly reaching for the blowpipe secured to his waist and sticking one end behind the deep green leaves.

A gaboon viper, one of the regions deadliest and most aggressive snakes, leaped through the fern leaves and landed next to Joao, who quickly stepped on its leaf-shaped head before the snake could get its bearings, applying just enough pressure to hold the poisonous reptile in place while he grabbed its head with his left hand.

The dark brown snake, roughly two feet in length, wrapped itself around Joao's forearm. The Maya tied the head to his wrist in order to free up his hand, and once again went in pursuit, stopping once more several minutes later. This time he turned over a medium-size rock next to a clump of boulders bordering a swampy creek and was rewarded by a colony of giant centipedes, their venom far more powerful than the viper's. Hundreds of crawlers, ranging in size from tiny larvae to adults measuring up to three inches in length, wormed their way through a labyrinth of holes dug in the humid soil beneath the rock.

Carefully selecting only adult males, which he identified by the red coloring of their heads, Joao used a large leaf to scoop them up. The aggressive insects nearly stood on their hind legs while exercising their deadly pincers protecting their mouths, ready to inject any intruder with the toxic contents in the sacks behind their eyes.

Joao placed a dozen of them inside a small deerskin pouch hanging off his waist. Then, just as carefully, he turned the rock back over to preserve the colony.

A deep breath and a brief scan of his surroundings, and the jungle warrior dashed forward, cutting left as he neared his quarry, quickly running a semi-circle around the slow and noisy soldiers, positioning himself two hundred feet in front of them, right next to a tall ceiba with long and thick moss-draped branches protruding in every direction for fifty feet.

Joao climbed up the tree with ease and crawled across a two-foot-wide branch, the viper still wrapped tightly around his arm, enjoying the warmth of the Maya's skin. Wrapping himself with the moss, he removed the string over his forearm while once more holding on to the viper's head. Slowly, Joao uncurled the reptile off his limb and held it over the trail just as five soldiers neared, their scraping and creaking as they walked across the jungle mixing with the clicking of insects and the hissing of the snake.

Joao let go of the viper just as the soldiers marched roughly thirty feet below. In the same instance, he reached for the bag filled with the deadly centipedes, briefly shook it to anger them, and untied the knot.

Screams suddenly filled the jungle as the viper landed on one soldier and bit him in the face before slithering away. The soldier dropped to his knees as the others frantically looked in every direction. Joao, protected by the thick branch and the draping moss, emptied the bag over them.

Half of the centipedes landed on the soldiers. The deadly drop found an exposed wrist, the base of a neck, and a forehead. As pincers broke through the skin of three soldiers, tiny muscles squeezed the venom sacks, forcing the toxic liquid through microscopic channels. The paralyzing chemical reached the soldiers' bloodstreams seconds after contact.

More screams followed. The surviving soldier opened fire on the rosewood as one of his comrades convulsed on the ground from the viper's venom and the other three dropped to their knees in shock, their mouths foaming.

Joao waited until the firing stopped before aiming his blowpipe at the surviving soldier, who spoke on the radio while surveying the grounds with an automatic rifle.

From such short distance, Joao scored an easy hit to the upper back. The soldier bent like a bow while dropping his weapon and struggling to reach behind him. In seconds the powerful venom paralyzed him, and he collapsed next to his fallen comrades, two of whom were still alive but unable to move as the poison from the centipedes gained control of their motor and nervous systems.

4

Antonio Strokk was the first to reach the left team and felt his stomach filling with molten lead. The five mercenaries making up the rest of the center team caught up with him seconds later.

"Look at them," one of his men mumbled, fear straining his words.

Four of the operatives were dead, froth oozing from their mouths and nostrils, their dead eyes staring at the solid roof of branches above them. One was still alive but convulsing, as if he had an epileptic seizure. A few moments later he too died.

"This one has bite marks on his cheek," said one of the soldiers while leaning down over one of the corpses.

"Here is a dart," said another one while pointing to the small object imbedded in a soldier's upper back.

Strokk rubbed the stubble on his chin, swallowing hard. "Damned savages."

"Over here," another mercenary said, pointing to branches broken over a moss-slick boulder surrounded by lush ferns. "Look."

Strokk nodded. "Call the other team. Tell them to come over immediately. There is a change of plans."

"Ye—yes, sir. Right away."

The seasoned operative silently cursed his luck. He was not fighting professional soldiers anymore. Strokk's team of mercenaries was being confronted by a new enemy, who didn't follow the rules of engagement that the former Spetsnaz officer had learned to master in the world of independent contractors. In order to not only survive, but also prevail, Strokk had to further alter those rules, define his own strategy, force the savages to react to *his* moves—and do it immediately, while he still could. The enemy had already cut the size of his team in half. At this rate he would run out of men by morning.

5

Moss-draped, the Mayan chief crawled down the rosewood as the last soldier disappeared from view. He gave his victims a brief glance. In less than an hour the first scavengers would arrive. By tomorrow morning only bones and uniforms would remain.

Nothing went to waste in the jungle.

Since he now knew where they would head, Joao chose not to follow them. Instead he took another route to get to the rendezvous point, where his people were already hard at work making the necessary preparations to welcome their uninvited guests.

6

Under gleaming moonlight, Antonio Strokk stood in the middle of a field of ferns surrounded by thick vegetation. Four of his mercenaries were with him. The rest he had ordered to make a wide semicircle ahead of him, in an effort to catch the savages who had left such an obvious trail for his team to follow, undoubtedly to a second ambush. But the natives had chosen the wrong person to mess with this early evening.

Strokk's caution had paid off, measured by the three natives his men had managed to seize while working on making the trail. Two had attempted to escape and had been shot, much to Strokk's detriment. He wanted a prisoner, someone whom he could use not to interrogate, because Strokk doubted the natives spoke any of the languages he knew, but simply to send the rest of the savages a clear message. To his relief, the third one had been captured alive.

Wearing a pair of night-vision goggles, Strokk walked with an air of command as he approached the bruised, half-naked man, young and muscular, perhaps in his early twenties. His back was against the ground as two soldiers grabbed him by the ankles and held him in place.

The native remained silent, dark eyes staring at his captors with an air of defiance. The mercenaries gathered around Strokk and his hostage. Strokk glanced down at the Maya. "Bring a dead one over," he ordered the man next to him.

"Excuse me, sir?"

"Bring me one of the natives you just killed."

Two soldiers did, pulling a limp, brown body across the ferns and dropping him next to the live Maya, who glanced over to his dead comrade, eyes widening in mourning.

"Castrate the corpse," Strokk said, pointing to the dead Indian.

No one in the group whispered a word. One of the mercenaries unsheathed a hunting knife, lifted the dead man's skin flap secured to his waist, and emasculated the body. Blood pooled in between the Indian's legs. The mercenary then tossed the severed member at the live Maya, who jerked back, slapping it off his chest, blood dripping to his abdomen, his gaze shifting between his dead comrade's groin, the bloody knife, and Strokk, who grinned at him.

"Now you're getting the picture, Moctezuma. Pluck out the corpse's eyes."

Again, one of his men performed the macabre ritual on the maimed corpse, also flinging the eyeballs, attached to the end of long nerves, at the terrified Maya.

"Now," Strokk said, grinning at his hostage before surveying the faces of his men. "It's time to send these Indian bastards a message."

7

Joao Peixoto crouched over a thick rosewood branch overlooking a small clearing. The moon hung high in the crystalline sky, its gray light dancing on the leaves as a breeze swirled the canopy overhead. Monkeys hooted in the distance, their raucous mixing with that of a pair of red macaws squawking on an adjacent tree.

The noise abruptly stopped and the birds took flight, their sounds replaced by Joao's own, a warning to his men that their guests had arrived.

The Mayan chief readied his blowpipe, inserting a poisoned dart and bringing one end to his lips while aiming his deadly weapon at the ground below.

Through moss and scattered leaves, he saw the figure of his own man under the moonlight using his hands to feel his way through the jungle. No soldiers were with him. The young Maya tripped on an exposed root and fell, quickly getting up and reaching out with both hands to feel for his surroundings.

Joao felt an anger boiling deep inside of him. His man was blind. Upon closer inspection, he noticed the bloody tracks down his cheeks and neck.

Climbing down from the tree, he reached the moss-slick path next to his subordinate and was horrified at the sight. The soldiers had plucked out his eyes.

Controlling his emotions, Joao emitted a hooting sound. *It's us, your family. You are safe now.*

The wounded Indian opened his mouth to reply but could only make guttural noises mixed with bloody froth. The savages had also cut off his tongue.

Enraged, Joao called for his men, who materialized in the jungle moments later, along with several women and the two scientists hauling their backpacks.

Jackie Nakamura looked away in terror, burying her face in her husband's chest as he hugged her.

Joao turned to the women and ordered them to take the maimed warrior to safety. One of the women began to cry, the young Maya's mother, and so did another woman, his sister, but they complied with Joao's order and took the trembling warrior away.

Joao Peixoto tried to focus on his predicament, shoving the scourging anger aside. Two of the elders were dead. The third was still unconscious. He had no one but himself to consult, to review his plan prior to implementing it. But like his father, and his father before that, Joao Peixoto's blood carried the genes of the region's finest warriors, the ones who proudly and bravely defended their land against wave upon wave of invaders, even in the face of overwhelming odds.

The Mayan chief wondered what had happened to the soldiers. Why weren't they following his man, who in spite of being blind had managed to reach the clearing? Did they realize that they were headed for a trap and decided to send Joao a message? Did they return to the temple of Kinich Ahau?

Joao was convinced that he was up against a dangerous and ruthless adversary, but nevertheless he gathered his men and laid out his plan of attack, determined to purge his land from such creatures.

8

The numbers in the laptop browsed down the screen as a custom C++ script tried to find the mathematical formula defining the order of the numbers in the array of mosaics carved on the far wall of the temple's terrace. Susan sat by the edge of the steps, beneath the corbel arches, the laptop resting on her thighs, the light from the pulsating screen mixing with that of the hissing lantern next to her. Cameron worked on the reliefs carved on the left wall of the terrace, with the assistance of another gas lantern, its yellowish light washing the ancient inscriptions. Petroff stood guard at the bottom of the steps, by the stone pillar on the left side of the large limestone edifice, his concerned expression matching Celina's. Something was very wrong, but the terrorists kept it to themselves while ordering the scientists to continue their investigation.

So far her search for a pattern in the number sequence had been in vain. She couldn't make any sense of them, and the more she tried to reorder them before restarting the sequence-matching algorithm, the less they made any logical sense. She returned the screen to their original order, staring at them with diminishing confidence.

13	12	11	10	9	8	7	6	5	20	20	5	6	7	8	9	10	11	12	13
12	66	2	3	4	5	6	7	8	20	20	8	7	6	5	4	3	2	66	12
11	2	56	0	66	13	66	56	0	20	20	0	56	66	13	66	0	56	2	11
10	3	0	0	0	0	0	0	0	20	20	0	0	0	0	0	0	0	3	10
9	4	33	33	56	0	56	33	33	20	20	33	33	56	0	56	33	33	4	9
8	5	20	20	20	66	20	20	13	20	20	13	20	20	66	20	20	20	5	8
20	20	20	20	20	20	20	20	20	20	20	20	20	20	20	20	20	20	20	20
8	5	20	20	20	66	20	20	13	20	20	13	20	20	66	20	20	20	5	8
9	4	33	33	56	0	56	33	33	20	20	33	33	56	0	56	33	33	4	9
10	3	0	0	0	0	0	0	0	20	20	0	0	0	0	0	0	0	3	10
11	2	56	0	66	13	66	56	0	20	20	0	56	66	13	66	0	56	2	11
12	66	2	3	4	5	6	7	8	20	20	8	7	6	5	4	3	2	66	12
13	12	11	10	9	8	7	6	5	20	20	5	6	7	8	9	10	11	12	13

"Find anything?" Cameron asked, kneeling next to her, his rugged features softened by the moonlight. He dimmed his lantern and set it next to hers.

"Just more geometrical relationships," she said, tapping the screen. "Each quadrant, as defined by the rows and columns of number twenty, is almost a mirror image of each other. Beyond that, my mathematical models detected a few sequences, but they don't propagate beyond a few numbers before becoming erratic, random. Any luck on your end?" She saved her work and closed her laptop.

"Lots of pictorials but very little meaning on the surface. There's enough new data here to keep the likes of me occupied for the next decade."

Susan Garnett checked her watch. "I was afraid you would say something like that."

"Why?"

"Because we only have fourteen days to figure it all out."

Chapter Eighteen

010010

1

December 17, 1999

Standing at the edge of the cenote with Cameron by her side, Susan Garnett gazed up at the evening sky, star-filled, majestic. Moonlight diffused through the mist rising out of the water hole, gaining a sublime presence, a glowing life of its own. Grayish beams waltzed with the fog, gently swirling to the rhythm of a light breeze sweeping across the lowlands of the Petén, to the sounds of insects clicking, distant monkeys howling, birds chirping.

Susan watched it with intrigue, but could not bring herself to enjoy it despite its mystic overtone because of the dark cloud veiling her life for the past day, since the Russian brutes had arrived. For a moment she had held some hope, when the team led by Strokk had taken longer than planned to return to the site. She had hoped for a miracle, for a supernatural force to come in and make the mercenaries vanish, leaving her biding her time, waiting for the right moment to use the Walther PPK still tucked in her shorts, by her spine. But the Russian terrorists had returned to the jungle, albeit short five men.

She sighed, staring at the moonlit, swirling haze, alive with fluttering moths. Perhaps a small miracle did occur, for the Russian commander seemed angry, disturbed, concerned, shouting orders to his men, deploying them to the surrounding jungle, out of sight, leaving her and Cameron once again alone with Petroff and Celina.

"It's time," Cameron said, pointing at his watch and then at their gear.

She nodded. "Let's do it."

2

The night breeze sweeping through the thick jungle caressed Joao Peixoto's face and neck with the same tempo as the moss swaying overhead. Joao, his skin glistening with sweat, moved across the terrain quietly but swiftly, his senses tuned to its sounds, easily imitating them. He walked in a deep crouch, moving through the dense bush with ease.

Joao stopped, closing his eyes, moving his head in every direction, scanning the area, listening, moving forward again, slower now as he closed in on his target.

He continued his stealthy advance for fifteen more minutes before stopping by a large, moss-draped ceiba, backlighted by the pulsating glow from a distant fire streaming through the jungle. If he listened very carefully, he could also hear voices no more than a thousand feet away. The ceiba's opulent trunk fenced one edge of a small clearing, layered with animal bones, mostly mammals, but also a few reptiles—all unfortunate to have come within the killing zone of the cartiga ants, their large mound, resembling a mud obelisk, standing six feet tall next to the ceiba, almost hidden from view.

Joao carefully stepped around the clearing, unwilling to trigger the mound's alarm. Cartiga ants were as fast as they were voracious, capable of skinning a deer in minutes. He continued his advance, moving only when the breeze picked up and rustled the branches and enshrouding moss, stopping when it died down. His callused feet provided him with added friction, reducing the stress on his muscles as he worked his way around the edge of the clearing, spotting a man in dark olive fatigues hiding in the thick brush holding an automatic weapon.

Joao unsheathed the knife belonging to one of the soldiers he had killed at the village, firmly curling the fingers of his right hand around its rubber handle. The stranger turned the weapon in his direction as Joao dropped to the ground behind a mahogany tree and let a curtain of moss shield him.

The sentry, his face darkened by the night and also by camouflage cream, remained still in the tangled brush bordering the courtyard end of the sacred site, twenty feet away, looking almost directly at Joao, but keeping the weapon pointed to his right, toward the flickering specks of light filtering through the dense jungle.

The armed stranger took one step toward the mahogany tree where Joao hid. The Maya slowly began to crawl around the trunk to remain out of sight, coming around the other side, taking advantage of the opportunity to catch his quarry sideways.

He lunged from behind the shield of moss and tangled vines with the speed of a jungle cat, the blade pointed at the neck. The stranger reacted like a worthy warrior, pivoting on his left leg, avoiding Joao's initial strike. The blade missed its intended target and the Mayan chief had to settle for a blow with his shoulder into the man's stomach.

Joao heard the quick expulsion of air as he landed on top of him. The man's weapon flew off as both figures rolled over the leaves for a few moments before separating.

The man reached for his side arm, but Joao didn't give him the chance to use it, slashing his knife down and across the stranger's neck, the blood rhythmically jetting from the deep cut spraying him.

The sentry fell to his knees, collapsing face first, his life over.

Joao leaned down to hide the corpse in the foliage behind the mahogany before resuming his hunt.

3

EM activity filled Susan Garnett's system, the vertical bars of the digital meter dancing on her screen, jolting up and down the decibel scale according to the intensity of the activity in each 10-MHz-wide frequency channel, from 900 MHz to 1 GHz. Like yesterday, the electromagnetic activity began before the official start of the global event, which lasted fourteen seconds, as expected. Susan watched the single EM pulse across all frequencies at the end of the event, before all returned to normal.

"That was it?" asked Celina, standing behind Susan and Cameron, a big gun in her left hand. Petroff stayed back, in the background, but very much alert, keeping an eye not just on the trio by the glowing computer hardware, but also on the deserted site.

Susan nodded without turning around. "Good things come in small packages. Let's see what was dumped tonight."

STATS
LENGTH: 42, 342, 021, BYTES
COMPOSITION: 0% ASSEMBLY CODE 100% UNKNOWN
ORIGIN: UNKNOWN

HOST STATUS: UNKNOWN
UNFILTERED STRAIN FOLLOWING . . .

```
1111000000000001111111111111111111111111111000000000000000000011111111111
1111000000000001111111111111111111111011111000000000000000000011111111111
0000000000000000011111111111110011111111110000000000000000000011111111100000
0000000000000001111111111111110001111111111000000000000000001111111111
0000000000000001111111111111001111111111111000000000000000001111111111
0000000000000000001111111001100111111111100000000111000000001111111111
0000000000000001111111111111101101111111110000000011110000011110001111
0000000000000001111111111111100011111111111000000000110000010111111111
1111000000000001111111111111111001111111000000100000010000001111111111
1111000000000101111111111111111101111111000000000000000000000000111111
1111111000000000000000111111111111111100000000000000000000000000001111
1111100000000000000000001111111100000000000000001111011100000000000000
1111111111000000000000000011000000000000000111111110000000000000000
11111111111111110000000000000000000000010000000111111110000000001111
1111111111100000000000111000000000000000000000000000000000000111111111
1111111100000000000000001100000100000000000000000000000000000111001111
0000000000000000000001100000111111000000000000001110000000000000111001111
0000000000000000000000000000000111111100000000001110000000000000111111
0000000000011111000000000000000011111110000000000011100000000000000000000
0000000000000111110000000000000011111100000000000111000000010000000000
0000000000000001100000000000000000000000000000000000000000000010000000
0000010000000000000000000000000000000000000000000000000000001000000000
0000000000000011111111111111000000000000000001111110000000000000000
0000000000000011111111111111100000001000000001111111110000000000000
0000000000000011111110011111110000000000000000011111111111100000000000111
1000000000000011111111111111100000000000000000011111111100000000001111
1100011000000011110001111111100000000000001111111111111100000000001111111
1111111111100001111111111111110000000000000011111111110000001111111111
1111000000000000011111111110000000000000000000000111111111111111111111111
0000000000000001111111111000000000010000000000000000011111111100110011
1111100000000000000000000000000000000000000111111111111111111111111
1111000000000000000000000000000000000011110000000000000111110000111
11000000000000000000000000000000000000011100000000000000011100000011
000000000000000000000000000000000000000011100000000000000000111110000
```

CONTINUE BROWSING? Y/N

She went to the bottom.

```
0000000000000011111111111111100000010000000000011111111100000000000000
0000000000000011111111101110001111110000000000011111100000000000011
1100000000000001111111111111100000000000000001111111110000000000000111
0000000000011111000000000000011111110000000111000000010000000000000
0000000000000011000000000000000000000000000000000000000000000000010
1000000000000000000000000000001110000000000000000000000000000000000
0000000000000011111111111111000011100000000011111111100000000000000
0110000000000001111111111111100011111100000000001111110000000000011
1100000000000001111111111111100000000000000000011111111100000000000111
1000000000000011111111111111000000000000000001111111110000000000001
0000000000000011111111111111000000011000000011111111100000000000000
0110000000000001111111111111100011111100000000001111110000000000011
1100000000000001111111111111100000000000000000011111111100000000000111
0000000000000011111111110000001110000011100000011111111100000000000
0110000000000001111111111111100011111100000000001111110000000000011
1100000000000001111111111111100000000000000000011111111100000000000111
1111111000000011111111111111100000000000000001111001111110000000011111
1111111111100001111111111111110000000000000000001111110011111000000111
```

```
11011011  00011000  00011000  00011000  00011000
00000000  00111100  00111100  00111100  00111100
11111111  00011000  00011000  00011000  00011000
00000000  00000000  00000000  00000000  00000000
11111111  00000000  00000000  00000000  00000000
```

"What do you think?" she asked Cameron.

The archaeologist shrugged, the glow from the color screen washing his sharp features, as well as the purple lump on the side of his face. "Looks about the same, and the date hasn't changed."

"Let's clean it up with the averaging program. Then I'll perform a DIFF." She typed a few commands and let the system take it away, returning seconds later with,

STATS
LENGTH: 42,342,021 BYTES
COMPOSITION: 0% ASSEMBLY CODE 100% UNKNOWN
ORIGIN: UNKNOWN
HOST STATUS: UNKNOWN
FILTERED STRAIN FOLLOWING . . .

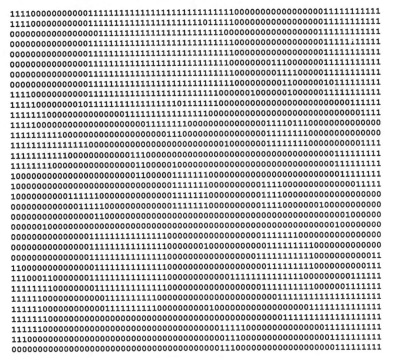

CONTINUE BROWSING? Y/N

She went to the bottom.

```
0000000000000001111111111111111000000010000000000011111111110000000000000
0000000000000001111111111111111000000000000000000001111111111110000000000011
1100000000000000111111111111111000000000000000000001111111111110000000000111
0000000000000000000000000000000000000000000000000001111000000010000000000000
0000000000000001100000000000000000000000000000000000000000000000000000000010
1000000000000000000000000000000001110000000000000000000000000000000000000000
0000000000000001111111111111111000011100000000000011111111110000000000000
0110000000000000111111111111111000111111100000000011111111110000000000011
1100000000000000111111111111111000000000000000000001111111111110000000000111
1000000000000001111111111111111000000000000000000011111111110000000000001
0000000000000001111111111111111000000011100000000011111111110000000000000
1110000000000000111111111111111000111111100000000011111111110000000000011
1110000000000000111111111111111000000000000000000001111111111110000000000111
0000000000000001111111111111111000000011100000000011111111110000000000000
1110000000000000111111111111111000111111100000000011111111110000000000011
1110000000000000111111111111111000000000000000000001111111111110000000000111
1111111100000001111111111111111000000000000000011111111111100000000011111
1111111111110000111111111111111000000000000000000011111100111111000000111
```

```
11011011   00011000   00011000   00011000   00011000
00000000   00111100   00111100   00111100   00111100
11111111   00011000   00011000   00011000   00011000
00000000   00000000   00000000   00000000   00000000
11111111   00000000   00000000   00000000   00000000
```

"Doesn't appear to be that much different from yesterday's," she mumbled.

"It may be different enough to get a match," offered Cameron.

Susan tilted her head from side to side, not certain if she bought that. "Let's see just how different it is."

She launched the DIFF program. The hard drive whirled for a minute as her C++ script compared the two large files. The system displayed:

```
DIFF
VERSION 4.0.1.

FILE              BYTES
1217              42,342,021
1218              42,342,021
DIFF_0            9,230
DIFF_1            2,101
TOT_DIFF          11,331
% DIFF            0.0267%
```

Susan frowned. "Less than point zero three percent. Not much of a difference."

"I see the difference, but how do you read the other lines?" asked Cameron.

"The first file, from December seventeenth, GMT, is compared against the second file, from moments ago. Any zeroes in the first file that changed to ones in today's file will be noted under the DIFF_0 category. Likewise, any ones in the first file that changed to zeroes, will be noted under the DIFF_1 file. The sum of the two represents all of the zeroes and ones that switched states between yesterday's dump and tonight's, likely as a result of the narrower search."

"So now we run the map comparison program, right?"

"After I connect with Reid. No sense in us trying to run these comparisons when the FBI's computers can do it so much quicker." Susan turned around. "I'm going to dial into the FBI now," she told Celina, who gave her a nod, her eyes barely acknowledging her request. Like Petroff, the slim terrorist seemed preoccupied with her surroundings. Obviously something terrible must have happened to the missing members of their team that now the surviving terrorists seemed on edge.

Susan remote-logged into the FBI system and started an Internet chat with her boss.

REIDT@FBI.GOV:	HOW DID IT GO?
SG@RLOGIN.NET:	I'M ABOUT TO E-MAIL YOU THE NEW FILE. ANY LUCK TRYING TO GET A MATCH WITH LAST NIGHT'S MAP AGAINST THE ENTIRE WORLD?
REIDT@FBI.GOV:	NOPE. SAME STORY AS WITH THE AMERICAN CONTINENT. HOPEFULLY WE'LL GET LUCKY TONIGHT.
SG@RLOGIN.NET:	YOU'LL HAVE TONIGHT'S IN A FEW MINUTES. SUGGEST YOU START UP AT SIXTY PERCENT AND SEE WHERE THINGS LEAD FROM THERE. WHAT ABOUT TONIGHT'S VIRUS?
REIDT@FBI.GOV:	FIGURED YOU'D ASK. CHECK YOUR E-MAIL. I'VE HAD ONE OF YOUR SUBORDINATES DO ALL OF THE LEGWORK READING THE CONTENTS OF THE COCOONS. HE'S E-MAILING YOU THE RESULTS TO KEEP YOU FROM SPENDING TIME ON THAT. I'VE GLANCED AT IT. NOTHING EXCITING. JUST MORE OF THE SAME. HOW'S THE ARCHAEOLOGICAL ANGLE COMING ALONG?
SG@RLOGIN.NET:	MAKING PROGRESS, BUT NO BREAKTHROUGHS YET.
REIDT@FBI.GOV:	KEEP ME POSTED. BTW, IS THERE SOMETHING WRONG WITH THE SEALS' LINK TO THE PENTAGON? THE BRASS HASN'T RECEIVED THE TEAM'S REGULAR UPDATE IN THE PAST TWELVE HOURS.

"Watch how you answer that," warned Celina from behind.

Susan sighed. Preoccupied or not, the female terrorist *was* paying close attention.

SG@RLOGIN.NET:	WILL CHECK. SAW THEM EARLIER WORKING ON THEIR SCRAMBLER BUT DIDN'T HAVE TIME TO ASK QUESTIONS. THE PROBLEM HAS TO BE WITH SOMETHING SPECIFIC TO THEIR SETUP BECAUSE WE'RE USING THE SAME EQUIPMENT FOR THE UPLINK AND OUR COMMUNICATIONS IS WORKING FINE. I'LL CHECK WITH THEM RIGHT AFTER THIS. IF THEIR SCRAMBLER'S DOWN I'LL OFFER THEM OURS IN THE INTERIM.
REIDT@FBI.GOV:	GREAT. WILL PASS THAT ALONG TO THE PENTAGON. ANY PROBLEMS WITH THE SEALS? NAVY BOYS BEHAVING?
SG@RLOGIN.NET:	NO PROBLEMS. BTW, LIEUTENANT LOBO'S STANDING RIGHT HERE. WANT TO ASK HIM SOMETHING?
REIDT@FBI.GOV:	AH . . . NO, BUT IF THEIR GEAR IS NOT UP IN ANOTHER FEW HOURS, A COUPLE OF COLONELS WILL COME HERE TO TALK LIVE TO THEIR TROOPS DOWN THERE SINCE OUR CONNECTION APPEARS TO BE MORE STABLE.
SG@RLOGIN.NET:	WILL PASS THAT ALONG. ANYTHING ELSE?
REIDT@FBI.GOV:	NO. WILL E-MAIL THE RESULTS OF THE SURFACE MAP COMPARISON IN TEN TO FIFTEEN MINUTES, DEPENDING ON HOW LONG IT TAKES TONIGHT.

Susan suspended the Internet chat but kept the connection open to share files. She reviewed the contents of tonight's captured virus, verifying that the mutation sequence looked just as it had in previous days and also that there was a 260-byte section of undecipherable code that was different from any other captured virus. She added this code to a file that contained the 260-byte sections from the other files, displaying them on the screen back to back.

"And it's always in the same location," she said, pulling it up on the screen. "Starting at byte number 367 to byte number 627 of the virus. Here's the string from the first day that we captured the virus, which corresponds to the second daily event. There are eight bits in a byte, or 2,080 bits in 260 bytes. That's what follows, arranged in rows of 71 bytes each, except for the last row."

```
100010110101010010110011111010101010100110001110001110101010101011001101
101011010111010110010101010101010100101011010101100101010101110101010110
101001101101001010101001010101111001011100101010101110100110110101011010100
010011010100101001010100101001010110111111100101001010100111100101010010
010110011011010110101111010110010101010101010100101011010101100101010101011
101010101101010011011010010101010010101111001011100101010101011101001101
010110011011010110101111010110010101010101010100101011010101100101010101011
101010101101010011011010010101010010101111001011100101010101011101001101
101110101000100110101001010010101000101001010101011011111100101001010101001111
010110011011010110101111010110010101010101010100101011010101100101010101011
101010101101010011011010010101010010101111001011100101010101011101001101
010101100110101101010101001010110010101011110101010101010010101010101010
011110100111001010100101010010101001010010001100101001010100101011000010101010
101010010110011001010010100101011001010101010101010010100100110110010101010
101010101010010101010101011010101001010101010010110100111100101010010101010
010100010101010010010010100001010101001010010101010101011001010101010101011
101110101000100110101001010010101000101001010101011011111100101001010101001111
010110011011010110101111010110010101010101010100101011010101100101010101011
101010101101010011011010010101010010101111001011100101010101011101001101
100010110101010010110011111010101010100110001110001110101010101011001101
100010110101010010110011111010101010100110001110001110101010101011001101
101011010111010110010101010101010100101011010101100101010101110101010110
101011010111010110010101010101010100101011010101100101010101110101010110
001101010001100101010010010110100101010101011101010101010101011010101010101
011011010010111101010110101010101010101010010101111001011111101010101010100
101010110100101010100100101001001101010100101001010010110101101010010101
001010100101100101001010010101010101010011011100101001010100101001010010101
101010101010101001100101010101011010110010101100101010010100101010000111001101
010110101100101011001101001101101001010101001010111100101110010101010101
110100110110111010100
```

"Looks pretty random," commented Cameron.

Susan nodded, staring at the undecipherable string of characters that resembled neither assembly language instructions nor a binary map, like the
one Reid was currently trying to match to a topography anywhere on the
planet. "Not sure what to make of it."

"It'll come to us," he replied. "I'm sure it'll come to us. We've just got to
keep chipping away at it."

4

Joao spotted another figure in fatigues clutching an automatic weapon, near
the tree line, one leg resting on a fallen log, the other immersed in a sea of
ferns bordering the petrified wood.

The Mayan chief wasted little time. The moment he'd killed the first sentry
he had committed himself, realizing that the soldier would be missed in the
next radio check. He had to hurry and take out as many men as possible
while he still had the element of surprise on his side.

He reached for his knife, grabbing the steel end between his index and
thumb, throwing it at the soldier with expert ease. The black shape dashed

across the fifteen feet separating them, striking a direct hit in the side of the
neck.

The soldier dropped the weapon and whipped both hands to his bleeding
neck, unable to utter a sound. Joao followed the knife with matching speed,
palm-striking the handle, driving the serrated steel through the windpipe,
nearly severing the head. The soldier fell to the ground a corpse, blood squirt-
ing like a fountain, spraying Joao's short skirt.

Thirty seconds later he moved silently again, maintaining a rhythm, reaching a spot twenty feet from the edge of the clearing, spotting the dark silhouette of another man against the lighter background of the moonlit clearing
extending beyond the lush vegetation. He also noticed a small fire under a
coffeepot hanging from a tripod. Beyond that he recognized the couple who
had put themselves in harm's way to protect the sacred site. He felt relieved
that they were still alive, and wished he could do more for them, but at the
moment the Mayan chief had plenty to keep him busy.

Lowering himself over the branches of a fern growing out of the side of
a tree, two rocks flanking him as he used his knees to inch forward, Joao
locked his predator's eyes on a man who stood a few feet from the edge of
the jungle holding a machine gun.

Joao dropped to the ground, moving forward like a snake, silently approaching the motionless sentry facing the clearing. Joao estimated him at
over six feet tall and with wider shoulders than he had. He assumed that the
machine gun in his hands was not the only weapon the tall sentry had, feeling
certain that if the guard was as careful as the guerrillas fighting government
troops back in the eighties, the sentry would most likely be packing at least
a handgun and perhaps a knife or two.

The hunter approached his prey from the side, firmly clutching his knife
while hiding under the light underbrush that gently swirled in the warm
breeze. Files droned in the darkness. Mosquitoes buzzed near his ears. Joao
kept his eyes fixed on the sentry, who was looking in the opposite direction.
Inching forward once again, he stopped abruptly when his right knee rested
on what felt like a weathered branch. Quickly, he tried to shift his weight but
the light branch gave.

Snap!

Joao froze as the sentry, twenty feet away, automatically brought the
weapon around and pointed it in his direction, moving it back and forth,
obviously not sure of the exact origin of the noise.

Joao waited, the knife, still bloody from his first two victims, clutched in his right hand.

Hesitant, the sentry remained motionless, like a wax figure, the weapon aimed at a spot a few feet to the Maya's left. The guard was being cautious, not amateurishly reacting to what could have been just a forest creature, but determined to check out the noise. He took two steps forward and scanned the terrain ahead with his weapon at the ready. Joao, now less than ten feet away, inched closer while hiding in the dark underbrush.

At eight feet, the Mayan chief surged forward, arms stretched out, covering the few feet that separated them in less than a second, not giving the guard a chance to react. The sentry's head was still facing the opposite direction when Joao drove the ten-inch steel blade across his throat, instantly severing the windpipe. Startled, the sentry dropped the weapon, bringing both hands to his neck as he collapsed.

Joao pulled out the knife, stepping back as a spray of blood reached his face.

The sentry convulsed momentarily before going limp, his eyes fixed on Joao, who stood a few feet away, the bloody knife clutched in his left hand.

Wiping the blood off his cheeks, he leaned down and grabbed the corpse's feet, dragging it behind the heavy foliage, noticing as he did this that the sentry wore a headpiece, a radio, which he removed and briefly listened.

"Sergei? Hans? Alex?"

Joao frowned, moving away from the corpse. The message told him two things. One, his men were also making progress going around the clearing, methodically eliminating the threat. Two, word of the missing men was getting out. Filling his lungs, he gave out a war cry.

5

Susan Garnett snapped her head toward the strange howl, sounding part human and part animal. "What was *that*?" she asked.

Before Cameron could reply, Petroff was on his knees, clutching his neck, pulling out a black dart, looking at it with surprised eyes, collapsing on his side, eyes rolling to the back of his head, froth forming in his mouth. Celina rushed for the cover of a stelae while rapidly speaking into her small radio. Although Susan couldn't understand what the terrorist said, it was obvious that they were under some kind of attack.

Everything turned surreal. Cameron jolted up, pulling Susan along, racing away from their gear, toward the small limestone palace, the jungle coming alive with animal-like sounds, with screams, with sporadic gunfire, followed by more screams and more gunfire, the multiple reports echoing across the site, masking the origin of the sounds. A battle was under way beyond the edge of the clearing, and the two scientists were caught in the middle.

Two bullets struck a column to their immediate right, exploding in white clouds of bursting limestone. Cameron dove for the cover of a small stone wall, dragging Susan down with him, cushioning her fall with his own body. The howls intensified. The gunfire subsided. Multiple steps preceded blurred movement from beyond the short columns of the ancient palace. The slim figure of Celina Strokk raced across the clearing between the temple and the palace, directly toward the scientists, her gun pointed at them, its muzzle flashes conveying her intentions.

Limestone exploded around them, the debris striking Susan on the shoulder, the smell of gunpowder assaulting her nostrils.

Susan screamed, falling back, caught by Cameron, who lifted her light frame with incredible ease, carrying her away from the boiling white cloud momentarily hazing the incoming terrorist.

The archaeologist pressed Susan against his body as he raced back toward the courtyard, bullets striking stone with the sound of a dozen hammers. He clutched her even tighter, reaching the safety of a large stelae, setting her down.

Her shoulder burning, her temples throbbing from her beating heart, Susan grimaced, ignoring the pain, reaching for the Walter semiautomatic, flipping the safety, sitting up, her back against the lumpy reliefs of the ancient stone, Cameron next to her, chest heaving, sweat filming his forehead.

The terrorist fired several rounds before her weapon ran out of ammunition. Susan stood, leveling the PPK at Celina, catching her reloading, one hand on the spare ammunition clip, the other holding the empty weapon.

"Drop it!" Susan warned, lining the front sight on the terrorist's upper chest, imagining the silhouettes at her old shooting range.

Celina grinned, opening her palms, unceremoniously letting go of the machine gun and the clip, which clattered on the limestone floor. The terrorist then slowly reached for her side arm, pulling on the Velcro strip securing the gun in the holster.

"Stop!" Susan shouted, remembering her husband's warning about limiting her speech to short words versus long sentences during this type of situation, otherwise it would take her longer to fire because her brain would first have to stop controlling speech before sending the command to pull the trigger.

"Do not worry," Celina said, grinning, her hand resting on the holstered weapon. "I am just disarming myself."

"Hands off!" Susan screamed, hoping her loud voice would convey her determination.

Celina curled the fingers of her right hand around the gun's stock.

Out of options, Susan Garnett slowly released her breath while squeezing the trigger three times in rapid succession, the multiple reports echoing loudly and repeatedly across the site, like that of a machine gun.

The rounds transferred their energy as they struck the terrorist right below the throat. She arched back, landing flat on her back, white dust curling out from under her body as she impacted the limestone hard, blood immediately pooling beneath her, fixed pupils staring at the canopy overhead.

Susan lowered her gun, swallowing hard, realizing what she had done, what she'd had to do, silently cursing the terrorist for forcing her to fire the weapon. For several seconds she just stood there, staring at the slim body sprawled over the stone floor, catching her breath. Slowly, she flipped the safety.

"She left you no other choice," Cameron said, softly but firmly, pulling her aside, under the cover of the palace's short columns. The echo from the Walther's report died out, yielding to the high-pitched war cries from the warriors who had apparently claimed the lives of many mercenaries.

Then an eerie silence descended on the site. Gone were the animal howls, the firearm discharges, the agonizing screams, replaced by the hooting of monkeys, the chirping of birds, the clicking of insects, the natural sounds of the jungle covering the swift battle.

"What happened?" she asked, her shoulder throbbing, her hand still clutching the PPK, thumb on the safety lever, ready to flip it back up. She had fired three rounds, leaving five in the weapon, enough to defend themselves if another terrorist threatened them. But not one mercenary ever made it out of the jungle.

"Your shoulder," Cameron said, pointing to a bloody patch beneath the cotton shirt. "Let me take a look at it."

"Later. Right now it looks like we have company," she said, watching a native emerge through the tangled bush, a long tube held in his left hand. Then another one emerged, wearing a short skirt.

"Maya," commented Cameron, inspecting the strangers from behind the shadows of the palace's small terrace. Slowly, several Mayan warriors entered the site, many of them taking up posts around the pyramid, or the temple. Only one walked toward the palace, a medium-height, slim man with intense dark eyes, blood staining his chest and short skirt.

"I mean you no harm," he said. "Come out, please. The threat is now past."

Susan and Cameron exchanged puzzled stares.

"He speaks English?" she asked.

The archaeologist shrugged. "Beats me."

As they stepped outside the palace and onto the courtyard, an Asian couple entered the clearing from the east side, through the path made by the SEALs three days ago. They hauled large backpacks similar to the ones Strokk and his team had brought from the jungle the day before.

"What's going on?" Susan asked.

As the Asian couple approached them, Cameron said, "I get the feeling we're about to find—"

A gunshot echoed through the night, coming from deep in the jungle. All heads swung in that direction. The warrior closest to Susan glanced at two of his comrades, snapping his fingers. Both natives sprinted into the jungle.

"One got away," the Maya said. "I believe it is their leader."

"Get the bastard," said Susan.

Cameron turned toward Susan, as did the Asian pair. The native regarded the computer scientist with an air of respect. "He will *not* get away. Wait here," he said, before disappearing in the bush.

6

Antonio Strokk fired at a shadow made by a swinging branch under the moonlight. His senses clouded by the fear of these silent, undefeatable warriors, the former Spetsnaz officer raced across the thick jungle, toward the boats. He still had a chance if he could make it to the river.

Carrying a few spare clips for his Sig Sauer pistol, plus his many years of experience, gave Strokk a surge of confidence about his prospects of coming out alive, of making it back to civilization, of surviving. He had enough money stashed away to buy himself a small island and live like a king for the rest of his life. Perhaps this was his signal that the time had come to retire.

And so he ran, following the glowing readings of his sister's GPS unit. His team was dead. He could not reach anyone on the operations frequency. Celina also had to be dead, probably killed while in the clearing, along with Petroff and probably the scientists as the savages reclaimed their site.

And they can have it! he thought, regretting ever taking on this assignment, wishing he could turn back the clock. At the time it had seemed so easy, a straightforward surveillance operation, which had rapidly escalated into this mess from which he now tried to escape, tried to flee, one leaping step after the next, past clumps of moss-slick boulders, beneath hanging vegetation and cluttered vines, across mangroves, dashing through a small clearing, noticing the bones scattered across the dirt.

Momentarily distracted, Strokk tripped on the carcass of some creature, crashing headfirst into a tall mound of dirt at full speed, stabbing the crusty surface, cracking it, going through, stopping when his shoulders struck the mound. His head inside, like an ostrich's, the mercenary tried to break away but could not on the first backward jolt, taking him several vital seconds to bring his legs under him, pressing them against the base of the mound, finally breaking free, but at the price of shoving both feet into the mound. His stomach knotted as a swarm of ants spread across his head, stinging him with the power of a thousand white-hot needles, scourging his face, his nostrils, his ears, his neck, his shoulder.

Eyes shut tight, pain-maddened, the terrorist kicked his legs, already covered with a thick layer of ants rapidly propagating up his thighs. He managed to free them, crawling back while slapping his face, his neck, struggling to wipe away the angered bugs crawling under his fatigues, down his back, across his chest, up his pants. He shouted in agony, only to give the ants another place to go, filling his mouth, biting his tongue, the ceiling of his mouth, reaching his throat. Dropping to his knees, coughing, Strokk made the mistake of opening his eyes, trembling from the blinding pain of dozens of insects stinging his eyeballs. His fingers brushed away the bugs as fast as others replaced them, in a vicious cycle that rapidly weakened him with the terrifying notion of being eaten alive, as he thrashed among the bones that had originally distracted him.

Through the harrowing pain quickly robbing him of his sanity, Antonio Strokk half watched, half heard two natives approaching him, one from each side, keeping a safe distance as he convulsed over the ant-littered ground, shoving bones aside by the large mound, unable to coordinate his body, quivering from the savage pain, from the sanity-stripping madness that made him wish for instant death. He wished for the torture of a thousand Afghan women, for a dozen castrations, for anything but this devouring pain flaying him, consuming him.

But the natives remained there, long after Strokk lost the ability to speak, his tongue swelling from hundreds of bites, filling his mouth, choking him. His left eye a bulging mass of ants and blood, Strokk managed to crawl back, to roll away, constantly slapping his face, ripping off his shirt, exposing a layer of ants feeding off his chest, shoving them away, feeling more ants crawling up his pants, onto his chest, tearing at his flesh.

Racked by inconceivable pain, feeling his entire body ablaze—but much worse because the insects would not consume him fast enough to bring death—the terrorist reached for his side arm, turning it on himself, beneath his chin, his thumb fumbling with the safety, struggling to flip it, unable to do so as the ants continued to feed, continued to strip him of his flesh one bite at a time, making him lose control of his bladder and his bowels.

Scourged, twitching, blind, trembling, he dropped his weapon, listening to it strike a rock, the sound mixing with the incessant clicking of insects crawling into his ears, shooting beams of raw pain straight into his brain. He wished for death, coveted it, begged for it to come, to take him away, for anything—absolutely anything—was better than the infernal reality of his situation.

7

Joao watched what was left of the terrorist, whose trembling limbs still conveyed life. The Mayan chief maintained a safe distance from the swarm of ants flowing out of the mound, glistening under the moonlight, resembling a river of molasses, rapidly enveloping its prey, claiming it, picking it apart, before returning to their mound with the nourishment needed for their young.

Joao nodded. Nothing, not even the lowest, most despicable kind of human beings, went to waste in the jungle.

Chapter Nineteen

010011

1

December 18, 1999

The new day brought along a new alliance, not just across cultures, but across time. As the crimson sun loomed over the canopy of trees to the east, the jungle stirred to life. Night creatures receded into the darkest corners of this tropical habitat, giving way to the morning shift, to the hooting monkeys hurdling across a hanging sea of branches, losing themselves in the lush vegetation, and suddenly reappearing again, leaping through space, snatching limbs with Olympic grace, doubling back, and disappearing again, their blaring howls adding to the jungle concerto of chiming birds.

Susan Garnett listened to the natural sounds echoing across the ancient Mayan site, the sacred temple of Kinich Ahau, according to Joao Peixoto, the remarkable Mayan chief who had delivered them from the terrorists.

Joao conferred with Cameron Slater at the edge of the cenote. Joao's men were busy replacing the gold and precious stones to their rightful places.

The computer scientist rubbed her eyes and yawned, breathing the cool and humid morning air. Sleep had not come for some time last night. Instead, she had spent hours comparing notes with the astrophysicists, now peacefully snoring in their joined sleeping bags next to their gear. Susan stood and stretched. Cameron looked in her direction and waved. She waved back, before he returned to his discussion with Joao. Susan had also contacted Reid soon after the terrorists had been eliminated. A new team of SEALs was on the way, expected to reach the site by early afternoon.

Reaching her gear a dozen feet away from the sleeping bags, Susan powered up her laptop and began to make changes to the electromagnetic search range, which she had tuned from 900 MHz to 1 GHz in increments of 10 MHz. According to the E-mail exchange she'd had with Reid last night, following the short-lived skirmish, Susan had learned that the binary map search resulted in no better matches than the night before last. Last night, however, the Japanese-Americans had provided her with great insight to fine-tune her frequency range. Their search for extraterrestrial intelligence (SETI) at Cerro Tolo had been focused on the frequency emitted by hydrogen atoms, 1.420 GHz, following the accepted theory among the SETI community that since hydrogen was the most abundant element in the universe, other intelligent worlds would likely choose this frequency to communicate.

"And they were probably right," she mumbled, pulling up the C++ script commanding the search routine she had written a few nights ago.

"Talking to yourself?"

Susan turned around. Ishiguro Nakamura stood behind her, arms crossed, hair sticking up, his slanted gaze on her laptop's color screen.

She smiled. "Morning."

"Hello," he said, kneeling beside her.

"Jackie still sleeping?"

He nodded, blinking rapidly to clear his sight. "She's had quite an exciting past few days. It's best to let her rest. But then again, so have you. How's that shoulder?"

"Better," she said. Both Ishiguro and Cameron had used some of the SEALs' first-aid equipment to disinfect the superficial wound and dress it last night. "Thanks."

"You're very welcome."

She turned back to her screen, fingers tapping the dark keyboard. "Hopefully this change will help clean up the binary dump," she said, adjusting the frequency range of her sensors to just two 100-KHz bands below the 1.420 GHz center frequency, and two above it.

"Who do you think is out there?" he asked, eyes shifting skyward.

"Whoever they are, there's certainly a relation to the ancient Mayan beliefs. The origin of the signal you intercepted matches the Hunab Ku, the so-called Galactic Core, which also matches the celestial origin of this global virus," Susan replied, modifying the decibel scale to avoid missing any high-amplitude peaks. Her current scale went up to twenty decibels. She cranked it up to thirty dB while also increasing the resolution, which she could now do because of the much narrower frequency search, similar to increasing the volume of the radio after tuning it to a single radio station.

"This Hunab Ku, however, appears to be a planet—at least based on the way it moves around HR4390A. That would tend to suggest an advanced civilization."

Just then Cameron joined them. "Hey, gang." He sat to the right of Susan. "Sleep well?"

Ishiguro nodded.

"Like a baby," Susan replied, tilting her head toward the archaeologist. "A very happy baby," she whispered.

"Anytime," he replied, kissing the side of her face.

Susan and Cameron had joined their sleeping bags and held each other all night. Although no sex had resulted, Susan had enjoyed his nearness as he'd hugged her from behind, comforting her in a way that she had missed since her husband passed away.

"Learn anything new from Joao?" Ishiguro asked.

Cameron frowned. "Bad news is that Joao doesn't know how to enter the temple. He says that knowledge resided solely with the elders, the shamans, until the time came to pass it on to the new priests. Unfortunately our terrorist friends killed two of them, and the third is unconscious from a head wound." He touched his purple patch for effect. "So nobody can tell us for now. This is especially bad because according to Joao, the shamans were getting ready for what they called the moment of total synchronization, thirteen *kin*, or days, away. I think they would have helped us tremendously in solving this puzzle because that date coincides with—"

"Zero one zero one zero zero," said Susan.

"Right."

"Does he even have a clue where they went prior to entering? Was it by the terrace? A secret tunnel?" asked Susan.

"That's the good news. Remember the numbers in the mosaics?"

"How can I forget?"

"Well, according to Joao, at certain ceremonies, the three priests would go up the steps by themselves. Joao and his warriors always remained outside, unable to see what it is that the priests did to go in."

"*That's* the good news?"

Cameron squeezed her hand. "You're as impatient as you are beautiful."

Susan wasn't sure if she should thank him or punch him. Instead, she said, "Well?"

"One time Joao said that the sun was at such an angle that he was able to see the shadows of the priests as they gathered by the slab next to the matrix of numbers in the terrace. They were pressing their hands against them."

"*Pressing* them?" asked Ishiguro.

Cameron nodded.

"Like ... a combination for a vault," Susan said, her eyes shifting to the limestone structure.

"Exactly," replied the archaeologist. "There is a sequence of numbers that will somehow either unlock or move the slab out of the way."

"What if we can't figure out the combination?" she asked, remembering her frustrating attempts to find a pattern that made sense.

"Maybe the SEALs can blast their way in when they get here later today," offered Ishiguro.

Cameron shook his head emphatically. "Can't do that, not only because it would further despoil this place, which has already been desecrated enough, but it would also put us at odds with the local Maya. As you have seen, you don't want these guys as your enemies."

Susan nodded. "I've also got Reid's word that after we finish our work here we would leave them alone. Everyone who knows about this place is either here or has been killed."

"My government knows about it," offered Ishiguro.

"That's also covered," said Susan. "The White House should have already contacted your superiors to keep a lid on the whole thing."

Ishiguro grinned. "That shouldn't be too difficult. My government is quite good at keeping lids on things."

"What about the terrorists? There's a chance that they contacted their headquarters to inform them where they were going," asked Susan.

"We'll have to figure a way to deal with that," said Cameron. "Don't forget that Joao and his men are quite capable of taking care of themselves. If someone arrives uninvited and starts grabbing for the gold, they will be toast in seconds. Anyway, there's a couple more reasons why we don't want to just blast our way in. First because it would alter the investigative sequence of this mysterious event. So far we have been given clues, which we must use wisely to figure out the meaning of this celestial contact. We have to solve the puzzle, not brute force our way through it."

Susan and Ishiguro nodded.

"Besides," the archaeologist added, looking solemn, "there is also a catch with trying to dial in the combination."

"What's that?"

He shook his head. "I'm not sure. Joao mentioned to me that a couple of young men, who were slotted to be trained by the high priests, decided to go up the steps once and try to get inside the temple. Joao was nearby at the time and heard the scraping sound of rock against rock, mixed with the screams of the young men. By the time he reached the temple, there was no signs of the pair. That observation adds clarity to the large mural on the east side of the terrace, where some men are being swallowed by the earth, near the shamans. That pictograph was a warning: you get only one chance to dial."

Susan swallowed.

"Which means," Cameron continued, "*I* only get one chance to dial since I'm the only qualified person to attempt this."

"You can't do this," Susan said immediately, grabbing his forearm. "We hardly know anything about this puzzle, much less a combination of numbers that's either going to grant you access . . . or *kill* you."

"I'm sure we can come up with something."

She made a face. "With *something?* What? I've spent a long time messing with those numbers on my system and have nothing to offer to you."

"Do you remember anything else from the other night?"

Susan shifted her gaze to the large stone edifice, beyond the swirling haze, under the shade of opulent ceibas, remembering her dreamlike encounter with the high priests who resembled the descriptions given by Ishiguro and Jackie. Closing her eyes, she visualized their elongated heads, their peculiar tattoos, their body piercing, again, all matching the elders seen by the Japanese-American couple at the Mayan village, further reinforcing the reality of her experience. She struggled to remember the surreal interior of the temple, the wall carvings, the murals of so many Mayan scenes, of plumed serpents and werejaguars. She repeated everything she remembered to Cameron and Ishiguro, who listened intently as she kept her eyes closed, focusing on remembering every last shred of detail, including the numbers carved on the mosaics, the numbers that Cameron now believed held the key to unlocking the ancient door to the interior of the temple. When she finished, Cameron was staring at the temple, Ishiguro at his hands.

"That's all I can remember, but obviously not enough to get us in there."

"Get us in where?" said a female voice from behind. All three turned around. Jackie Nakamura regarded them with slanted, sleepy eyes.

"Good morning, dear," said Ishiguro, standing, giving her a hug.

The petite Japanese-American woman rested her head on her husband's shoulder and closed her eyes. "So tired," she mumbled.

Cameron and Susan also stood.

"Can we get you anything?" Susan offered.

"Maybe some water?" Jackie asked.

Cameron reached in one of the SEALs' backpacks, which the terrorists had gathered next to their own supplies, and produced a canteen, handing it to the female astrophysicist.

"Now," Cameron said. "Why don't you join me on the terrace for a bit of ancient lock picking? Susan, bring your laptop. I think we're going to need it."

2

On the terrace, Cameron stood in front of the mosaics. Susan sat cross-legged just to his right, the PC on her lap. Ishiguro and Jackie walked about, admiring the reliefs.

Susan magnified the decimal version of the matrix to fill the entire screen. Cameron didn't need the conversion, being proficient with the Mayan numbering system.

13	12	11	10	9	8	7	6	5	20	20	5	6	7	8	9	10	11	12	13
12	66	2	3	4	5	6	7	8	20	20	8	7	6	5	4	3	2	66	12
11	2	56	0	66	13	66	56	0	20	20	0	56	66	13	66	0	56	2	11
10	3	0	0	0	0	0	0	0	20	20	0	0	0	0	0	0	0	3	10
9	4	33	33	56	0	56	33	33	20	20	33	33	56	0	56	33	33	4	9
8	5	20	20	20	66	20	21	13	20	20	13	22	20	66	20	20	20	5	8
20	20	20	20	20	20	20	20	20	20	20	20	20	20	20	20	20	20	20	20
8	5	20	20	20	66	20	24	13	20	20	13	23	20	66	20	20	20	5	8
9	4	33	33	56	0	56	33	33	20	20	33	33	56	0	56	33	33	4	9
10	3	0	0	0	0	0	0	0	20	20	0	0	0	0	0	0	0	3	10
11	2	56	0	66	13	66	56	0	20	20	0	56	66	13	66	0	56	2	11
12	66	2	3	4	5	6	7	8	20	20	8	7	6	5	4	3	2	66	12
13	12	11	10	9	8	7	6	5	20	20	5	6	7	8	9	10	11	12	13

"All right," said Cameron, flipping through his notes, excitement straining his voice. "The center of the array shows the number twenty, which also expands to divide the matrix into four quadrants, each almost identical mirror images of the others, but not quite."

"That's right," replied Susan, looking at the center of the array, dominated by the number twenty. Just to the left of this cluster of identical numbers,

Susan spotted the number twenty-one. On its mirror image location on the upper right quadrant, it became twenty-two. "Going clockwise from the upper left quadrant, the number goes from twenty-one, to twenty-two, twenty-three, and finally twenty-four on the lower left quadrant. All other numbers in each quadrant are an identical mirror image of each other along the vertical and horizontal axis. What does that tell you?"

"A sequence. Remember, the Maya lived and died by sequences, but mostly geometrical ones. This tells me that the first number of our combination comes from the upper left quadrant."

"How can you be so sure?"

The archaeologist shrugged. "I'm never sure, Susan. Archaeology is not a sure science. But I do have another clue. The number twenty in Mayan mythology represents the Hunab Ku."

"The galactic core."

"That's right. The Maya also believed that the universe moved in a clockwise motion. That matrix represents part of that universe, with the Hunab Ku at its center radiating its energy across the galaxy, defining the four form-giving principles of energy, according to the Maya."

"Attraction, radiation, transmission, and receptivity," Susan said.

Cameron grinned. "I'll make an archaeologist out of you before this is over." He knelt by her side and gave her a kiss on the lips, short, but certainly meaningful. Although they had cuddled in bed the previous night, they had not really kissed beyond a good-night brush of the lips. Susan tasted him, feeling like a woman again. But she quickly forced her hormones to remain put so that she could give Cameron her undivided attention. Half blushing, half smiling, running a hand through his long hair, she said, "I'll take it that was the right answer, Professor?"

"You're even getting the extra credit," he said, kissing her forehead before standing, opening his weathered notebook, thumbing through yellowish pages. "Anyway," said Cameron, turning businesslike, "those subtle hints, combined with the known fact that Mayan codices read from left to right and top to bottom, suggests the order of the combination."

Susan's engineering mind returned with amazing clarity. "I want you to think things through before you start dialing the combination, which, by the way, we have not really discussed exactly how that might be done."

"We'll get to that in a moment, though I've got a pretty good idea. Now, this temple, which we have come to learn and love, was constructed in memory of Pacal Votan."

"Right."

"All of the glyphs that I have been able to decode tell me this."

Susan nodded.

"Two dates are crucial in Pacal's life, aside from his birth in A.D. 603 and his death in A.D. 683. They are the start of his earthly rule in A.D. 615, and the start of his galactic rule, in A.D. 631. Those dates constitute our first clue in figuring out the combination. I should have noticed that earlier when I first inspected the numbers, but at the time I'd been too preoccupied with the murals. However, the murals did point me straight back to this matrix of carved mosaics, for here lies the clue to entering this temple, where we hope to find further insight into this puzzle."

Ishiguro and Jackie now flanked Susan, still sitting with her PC on her lap. Cameron addressed his small audience, which grew to four when Joao approached the temple, remaining standing beneath one of the corbel vaults.

"A.D. 615, the beginning of Pacal's earthly rule," he repeated, flipping through his notebook, "represents 1,366,560 *kins*, or days, since the beginning of the last Great Cycle, which will come to an end on December thirty-first."

Jackie raised her hand, as if she were in school. Susan and Ishiguro grinned.

"Yes?" Cameron asked.

"What is the Great Cycle?"

Cameron spent five minutes explaining to the Japanese-American team how the Maya kept time using the Long Count calendar, and how that system was used to keep track of thirteen *baktun*-long cycles, or 5129 years on the Gregorian calendar.

"So," he continued, having brought his audience up to speed, "the Maya were so obsessed with numbers that they oftentimes assigned them to their chiefs, according to their birth date. Furthermore, they would break up the numbers to make them easily represented in their numbering system. Pacal then became 13 66 56 0, a number with great harmonic resonance."

Jackie raised her hand again. "Harmonic resonance?"

"In simple terms, a number is considered to be harmonically resonant when it can be converted to other significant numbers with simple mathematical operations. Just to give you a taste of this, 1,366,560 divided by 360, the number of days in a year according to the Maya Long Count or Haab calendar, minus the vague 5-day period, yields 3796. The same number divided by a full 365-day period yields 3744. The difference between 3796 and 3744, is 52, the exact number of years of Pacal Votan's galactic rule, from A.D. 631

to his death in A.D. 683. Now, the Maya had a second calendar, called the Tzolkin, which consisted of 260 days. This calendar, derived by multiplying the number of the Hunab Ku, 13, by another familiar sacred number, 20, was used for a variety of religious purposes. Now, if you align day one of the Tzolkin with day one of the Haab, you will start what the Maya called the 52-year cycle, meaning that fifty-two 365-day years will go by before day one in both calendars line up again. That's what I meant by a number that has harmonic resonance, and Pacal Votan's number is by far the most resonant of all Mayan numbers."

Everyone remained silent, grasping the significance of Cameron's words, of his incredible explanations.

"Now," he continued, obviously quite used to speaking to an audience, "look at Susan's screen, at the matrix."

Susan's eyes returned to her screen, as well as the astrophysicists'.

```
13 12 11 10  9  8  7  6  5 20 20  5  6  7  8  9 10 11 12 13
12 66  2  3  4  5  6  7  8 20 20  8  7  6  5  4  3  2 66 12
11  2 56  0 66 13 66 56  0 20 20  0 56 66 13 66  0 56  2 11
10  3  0  0  0  0  0  0  0 20 20  0  0  0  0  0  0  0  3 10
 9  4 33 33 56  0 56 33 33 20 20 33 33 56  0 56 33 33  4  9
 8  5 20 20 20 66 20 21 13 20 20 13 22 20 66 20 20 20  5  8
20 20 20 20 20 20 20 20 20 20 20 20 20 20 20 20 20 20 20 20
 8  5 20 20 20 66 20 24 13 20 20 13 23 20 66 20 20 20  5  8
 9  4 33 33 56  0 56 33 33 20 20 33 33 56  0 56 33 33  4  9
10  3  0  0  0  0  0  0  0 20 20  0  0  0  0  0  0  0  3 10
11  2 56  0 66 13 66 56  0 20 20  0 56 66 13 66  0 56  2 11
12 66  2  3  4  5  6  7  8 20 20  8  7  6  5  4  3  2 66 12
13 12 11 10  9  8  7  6  5 20 20  5  6  7  8  9 10 11 12 13
```

"Pacal's number is the secret to this mysterious sequence of numbers. The sequence of 13 66 56 0 is everywhere, once you know how to look for it."

Susan felt a chill. The archaeologist was correct. She immediately spotted the sequence not just starting at each corner and moving inward in a diagonal line, but also across, where the sum of certain adjacent numbers would yield the magical sequence.

"This is amazing," said Ishiguro. "In all my years, I never imagined such harmony."

Cameron nodded. "The Maya were indeed amazing. And in the middle of Pacal's sequences, the Hunab Ku, the number twenty, also symbolizing zero one, zero one, zero zero, gloriously spreads its wings, dividing the galaxy according to the four form-giving forces."

Susan set her laptop down and stood. Ishiguro and Jackie did the same. "All right, Professor. What's the next step?"

"Simple, I hope, for my sake anyway. You start clockwise. Four numbers, four quadrants."

"But which of the numbers do you use?" asked Jackie.

Cameron grinned. "Yet another puzzle within the original puzzle. To answer that you must understand the sense of extremism that the Maya had when it came to order, to harmony. Upper left meant *radical* upper left, meaning that the first number of the sequence must be the upper left-most thirteen in the upper left quadrant."

Susan nodded. "The same applies to the other quadrant. Upper right, lower right, and lower left."

"Exactly."

"How do you dial it in?" Susan asked.

Cameron pointed at a hair-wide gap between the mosaics. "You wouldn't know they were there unless you knew what to look for."

"So you just press them?"

The archaeologist nodded. "But just in case, why don't you all back off to where Joao is, by the steps."

Ishiguro and Jackie exchanged glances and complied. Susan remained by him.

"You too, Susan. Don't want anything to happen to that little face."

"You should have thought about that before hugging me last night, before kissing me just now. Now we're in this together one hundred percent, so start pressing. I'm staying right here."

Cameron shook his head. "Do you know how irrational this is? If something were to happen to me, at least you would survive to—"

Susan Garnett put a hand to his lips. "Don't go there, please. I've *been* there."

"But this is not very logical, Susan. We can't afford for both of us to—"

"I've always been a little on the reckless side of life," she interrupted, drawing a heavy sigh from Cameron, who cupped her face, kissed her, and turned around, facing the ancient array of mosaics.

The archaeologist placed the palm of his right hand on the ancient relief of the upper left-most mosaic, two bars beneath three dots identifying it as decimal number thirteen.

"The stone's cold," he said, before planting his left foot back and leaning into the rock. The mosaic gave, caving in almost six inches, its grinding sound, echoing lightly inside the terrace, reminding Susan of large clay pots being dragged over concrete.

She held her breath, waiting for something to happen, but nothing did. The mosaic remained depressed. Cameron stepped to the right side of the array, placing his palm on the next number in the sequence, sixty-six. Again, he pressed, and again, the stone gave.

"Two more to go," he said, positioning his palm over the correct mosaic in the lower right quadrant and pressing hard, pushing it back.

"Now for the last one," he said, locating the lower left-most mosaic with the number zero in it and placing his hand on the shell-like carving of the Mayan numeral.

He turned to Susan. "Last chance to get away."

She stepped up to him, holding his left hand. "I lost someone I loved dearly. This time I'm going with him, anywhere."

Cameron regarded her for a brief moment, his dark eyes deep, absorbing. Then he pressed the stone.

3

Cameron and Susan stepped back as the massive slab began to recede into the wall, like the mosaics, but rumbling much farther back while pivoting on its left side, revealing not just the cavernous hall that Susan remembered from the other night, but also the incredible thickness of the exterior wall, almost six feet of solid limestone.

"And you wanted to blast through this?" he muttered to himself, cool air streaming out of the ample room, swirling his hair as he peered at the dark interior, Susan by his side, still holding his hand. "We're going to need lanterns."

A couple of minutes later, armed with three lanterns, the group went in, slowly, Cameron leading and Joao trailing, their sounds amplified inside the stone chamber, echoing off the ancient walls to the rhythm of the pulsating light. A heavy feeling of dread formed in Susan's stomach as she peered at the interior. She found it difficult to breathe, feeling as if the thick walls closed in on her as she stepped away from the entrance. She forced her mind to focus, to shove her fears aside. She watched the archaeologist at work, lifting the gas lamp toward the nearest wall, shining its light onto the intricate reliefs, exposing a phenomenal mural that ran the entire length of the rear wall. The combined light from the three lamps revealed a rectangular-shaped room, roughly fifty feet wide and thirty deep.

"Hold it there," Cameron said, the dampness chilling Susan as she stood next to him, as much surprised by the elaborate reliefs as by the serene expression on his face, on his eyes as they swept the mural, the ancient carvings. Once again, she found reassurance by being close to him.

"Dear God," he mumbled, backing away a few steps, looking toward the left, then to the right, returning his focus to the figure in the center.

"What?" Susan asked. "What do you see?"

Cameron pointed at the far left, where a young mother was shown holding a baby surrounded by fire, flying quetzals, and feathery serpents. Common people, dressed in simple loincloths or short skirts, knelt by her feet as she held the baby toward the sun.

"That's Lady Zac-Kuk, Pacal's mother, and the famous chief himself at birth, in A.D. 603."

Cameron angled the hissing lantern toward the next life-size relief, showing a boy of around twelve years of age in a ceremonial gown and ornate headdress sitting on a throne, a woman with deformed features on his right. Once more commoners knelt by his feet.

"Young Pacal ruling," Cameron said. "With mother nearby for counseling and for ratification of his power, just as described in the glyphs all around the terrace and the steps, which matches the reliefs from Palenque."

"Why does she look like that?" asked Ishiguro, a finger pointing at the enlarged jaw and prominent brow ridge.

"Pacal's mother suffered from the clinical syndrome known as acromegaly. Her bones and soft tissue were progressively enlarged as a result of a malfunctioning pituitary gland.

"Next is an older Pacal, venerated by his people for his wisdom, fairness, and vision. Over there he is shown building the Temple of the Inscriptions. Now, this is very strange. Come," he said, walking toward the right side of the mural.

"Pacal did die in Palenque, in A.D. 683, as shown by this date beneath his body lying on an altar and encircled by flying quetzals. But he is never carried inside the Temple of the Inscriptions, in the tomb built especially for him and unique to all of Mesoamerica. No other Mayan edifice has ever been used as a tomb, like in Egypt, except for the Temple of the Inscriptions."

Susan squinted, struggling to keep up with Cameron, watching the pictorials of Pacal being taken away from Palenque, away from the temple where he was supposed to be buried. "But, if Pacal was not buried there who did Ruz find in 1952? Who was in Palenque?"

Cameron nodded. "That sure explains it," he mumbled.

"Explains what?" asked Susan.

"Remember what I told you about Mayan royalty? About how they deformed their skulls and filed their teeth?"

"Yes."

"The mummified remains found by Alberto Ruz at the Temple of the Inscriptions had neither of those. Why was Pacal Votan, the greatest Mayan chief that ever lived, lacking the elongated skull and the filed teeth that were the norm of the day? Archaeologists have debated the question for generations. Now I finally understand why. He wasn't buried at Palenque."

"Where was he buried then?" asked Ishiguro, standing next to Cameron now, extending the lamp toward the right-most section of the mural.

Cameron pointed at the last two pictorials, one showing a procession of men carrying a coffinlike object across the jungle, and another depicting the same group reaching a clearing in the middle of the jungle, shielded by the branches of towering trees—all surrounding a cenote.

"You mean that—"

"He's buried here," Cameron said. "According to this last relief, and the accompanying glyphs."

"But where?" asked Joao, stepping forward for the first time. The Mayan chief had remained in the background, but obviously listening careful. "I do not see a tomb."

"Neither do I," said Ishiguro, looking about, holding the lantern high in the air, washing the interior with yellow light. His wife stood beside him, also checking for a sign of a burial.

Cameron shook his head. "You got to give Pacal's subjects a little more credit than that. They wouldn't have buried him up here. If they went through so much trouble at Palenque, burying an impostor in a chamber that was four floors belowground, they certainly would have done something similar here, where apparently the real Pacal was buried—again, according to the glyphs."

"But where?" asked Susan.

Cameron also looked about, grinning as he pointed at yet another matrix of numbers, on the far right side of the room, adjacent to the 3-D pictorial of the Maya carrying Pacal's body to this site. "There's our next safe, and its combination is probably also booby-trapped."

Approaching it, Susan saw to her relief that the numbering sequence appeared to be the same as the one outside. "Same key for both locks?"

Cameron didn't reply, rubbing the stubble on his chin while regarding the array, also thirteen down by twenty across.

Susan jotted them down on her engineering notebook anyway, taking a few minutes to complete the array.

```
13 12 11 10  9  8  7  6  5 20 20  5  6  7  8  9 10 11 12 13
12 66  2  3  4  5  6  7  8 20 20  8  7  6  5  4  3  2 66 12
11  2 56  0 66 13 66 56  0 20 20  0 56 66 13 66  0 56  2 11
10  3  0  0  0  0  0  0  0 20 20  0  0  0  0  0  0  0  3 10
 9  4 33 33 56  0 56 33 33 20 20 33 33 56  0 56 33 33  4  9
 8  5 20 20 20 66 20 24 13 20 20 13 21 20 66 20 20 20  5  8
20 20 20 20 20 20 20 20 20 20 20 20 20 20 20 20 20 20 20 20
 8  5 20 20 20 66 20 23 13 20 20 13 22 20 66 20 20 20  5  8
 9  4 33 33 56  0 56 33 33 20 20 33 33 56  0 56 33 33  4  9
10  3  0  0  0  0  0  0  0 20 20  0  0  0  0  0  0  0  3 10
11  2 56  0 66 13 66 56  0 20 20  0 56 66 13 66  0 56  2 11
12 66  2  3  4  5  6  7  8 20 20  8  7  6  5  4  3  2 66 12
13 12 11 10  9  8  7  6  5 20 20  5  6  7  8  9 10 11 12 13
```

"Slightly different," she said, noting that the unique number in each quadrant was shifted one quadrant in the clockwise direction. "Nifty little trick, to see if you're paying attention."

"That's the Maya, always taxing the human mind. And if I know anything about their way of thinking, my guess is that the wrong combination will immediately shut the main door, trapping us inside. We would be dead from asphyxiation within a couple of hours. So just in case I do get it wrong, why don't you all wait outside? That way, if I get trapped inside, not only will I last longer, but you can dial the combination again to reopen the door."

Ishiguro and Jackie nodded, stepping outside. Joao followed them out, leaving his lantern on the floor. Susan remained put, grabbing Joao's lantern.

"No way I can talk you out of it, huh?"

She smiled and shrugged. "We're a team, remember?"

He didn't reply, pressing his palm against the first number. It caved. He followed with the second, third, and fourth.

The massive slab to the side of the entryway moved back with alacrity, almost as if it were spring-loaded, giving Cameron and Susan no time to react and try to sneak out of the room. At once, vaultlike, the accurately cut stone slammed shut, a tire-deflating sound marking its airtightness, sealing the entrance, leaving the scientists staring at one another in the glowing yellow light.

The walloping sound had an air of permanency that made Susan's skin goose-bump. She rubbed her hands over her forearms. "What are we going to do?" Her voice was now amplified by the acoustic resonance of the large anteroom.

"Conserve oxygen." Cameron immediately dimmed his lantern and switched off Susan's.

The sudden murkiness did not feel reassuring, further inciting a panic that she struggled to control, something about being locked inside hundreds of tons of ancient stone with no apparent way out. "Do you have matches to light it back up again if we need it?"

"Ex-smokers always carry a lighter," he said, adding while grimacing, "I guess I guessed wrong."

Susan opened her mouth to reply but was instead momentarily jolted by the now-familiar rumbling noise, like rock against concrete. "I—I don't think you did," she said, a trembling finger pointing at the floor to their right, a five-foot square of shiny limestone began to sink, exposing a passageway.

Cameron approached her, putting a hand to her face. "Relax, would you? I'll be the first to tell you when to start praying, all right?"

She nodded.

When all motion ceased, Cameron and Susan slowly, cautiously, approached the gap on the floor, the glowing lantern leading the way.

"Steps," she said, noticing a stairway heading down into the darkness. A dry and cool draft of air rose out of the hole. "The Maya *were* quite clever."

"Now you're getting the picture."

"If I really *had* the picture we wouldn't be trapped."

He glanced at her with that scholarly-like look that always conveyed a sense of control. In her current predicament, Susan appreciated it, for it brought comfort in this cold and dead place. "Who says we're trapped?"

Susan regarded him quizzically, not certain what to think sometimes. *"Sweetheart,"* she said, "the main door is *shut.* Get it? Closed. Locked. I call *that* being trapped."

"We're not trapped until we can't move forward anymore. That way," he said, extending a thumb over his shoulder, toward the temple's blocked entrance, "is going *back*, not forward."

"Have I told you how *strangely* you think sometimes, Cameron Slater?"

"Have I told you how *tempting* you look in the dim light of a Mesoamerican temple?"

She couldn't help a laugh, which brought a sense of relief in spite of her growing fear of being trapped in this place, like the ancient wives of pharaohs, buried alive to be with their husbands in the afterlife. The thought struck her as ludicrous, until she also thought of her life following Tom's death. For all practical purposes she might as well have been in the coffin with him.

Susan took a deep breath of the dead air rising out of the hole, pointing at the darkness projecting beyond the first few steps. "I'm right behind you, honey."

"Count them as you go. I'll do the same," he said, holding the lantern in front of him as he took the first step.

4

"They're trapped!" Jackie said, standing on the terrace, running her hands against the hairline crack between the massive limestone slab and the walls. "How are we going to get them out?"

Ishiguro turned to Joao, who shook his head. "My job was to protect the priests. I was trained for that since birth. I have no knowledge of the inner workings of this structure. I'll have one of my men go back to the village and check on the high priest. Maybe he has awakened."

While Joao shouted something at one of the Mayan warriors guarding the site, the Japanese astrophysicist looked about him, not knowing what do to. Cameron Slater and Susan Garnett were the real experts here, and they were currently trapped inside the temple, running out of air.

He turned to the mosaics, but found the four numbers of the combination still depressed. The stone shifting back had not reset the combination lock. Checking his Casio, he clicked the digital chronograph. Cameron had estimated no more than an hour for all of them, meaning that he and Susan had probably three hours at the outside.

"Come," he told Jackie. "Let's go set up our equipment. Perhaps we can be of help by picking up clues from tonight's event."

"I don't like this," Jackie said. "I feel like we're just abandoning them. Poor Susan must be panic-stricken in there."

Ishiguro took his wife's hand. "She's in the best possible hands. If I were to be trapped inside one of these, what better friend to have on your side than a seasoned archaeologist? Now come, I got the feeling that Cameron and Susan are hard at work in there. We also have work to do. We'll come back in a half hour or so, to see if something has changed."

With a reluctant backward glance at the colossal limestone slab blocking the entryway, Jackie Nakamura followed her husband out of the terrace.

Chapter Twenty

01‾01‾00

1

December 18, 1999

The walls flanking the ancient staircase came alive under the glowing light from Cameron's lantern, his archaeological eyes taking in the beauty of the intricate chiseled work that had turned vertical slabs of rock into stunning murals depicting various facets of the life of the Maya's chief ruler, atop a ceremonial altar, sitting on his throne, presiding over a game of *pokatok*.

Cameron thought of Alberto Ruz Lhullier, the man who discovered Pacal Votan's first crypt in Palenque back in 1952. He thought of the excitement, of the fear, of the breathless anticipation that must have gone through Ruz's mind as he first descended down steps similar to these, toward the heart of an edifice from another time, from another culture, during a very different period in history.

He moved cautiously down the limestone steps, one at a time, slowly, with respect, absorbing the details of the reliefs, a continuation of the story in the anteroom. Actually not a continuation, but additional information, more insight, depicting the ruler Pacal actually being buried in the Temple of the Inscriptions at Palenque upon his death by his son, Chan-Bahlum. But a dark future loomed beyond the horizon for the once-bustling city, a future of invasions, of desecration, of looting, of destruction. And so Chan-Bahlum had ordered the exhumation of his father in A.D. 688, just five years after Pacal's death, and the search for a distant place, protected by the Petén's lush jungles, beyond the reach of the nearing wave of invaders. He had ordered that no records be kept of his decision to preserve the memory of his father, of his works, of his mortal remains. Scouts departed to all corners of the Yucatán, searching for the ideal site, settling on this one. By the end of A.D. 689 the crypt had been finished, and Pacal's body transferred to its final resting place, as depicted by the last pictograph in the anteroom.

Cameron continued to interpret the carvings, struggling to contain his excitement, the euphoria that must have also swept through Ruz in 1952, the realization of making the discovery of a lifetime, the climax of his career. He spoke out loud, clearly, explaining to Susan everything he saw, everything he felt, how the site was finished by A.D. 693 and ordered to remain guarded through the centuries, across the millennia, by generations of high priests under the protection of skilled warriors.

"For how long? Forever?" Susan asked.

Cameron shrugged. "I can't tell."

After twenty steps they reached a landing with a U-turn, followed by another flight of thirteen steps, where Cameron saw more iconographic reliefs, detailing the early post-Classic Period, according to the dates, ranging from A.D. 792 to around A.D. 1201.

"That explains the feathery serpent and other post-Classic artwork. The descendants of Pacal and Chan-Bahlum continued to record their history for some time," he commented, reaching the second landing, staring down a wide corridor beneath a triangular, corbel-shaped ceiling, amazed that the essence of the Maya Classic Period had survived the test of time, uninfluenced by the advent of technology, by the waves of invaders that razed Mesoamerica, eradicating its native culture. But the temple had not been fully isolated. Through the centuries other civilizations had somehow influenced Joao's ancestors, however subtly, maybe as a result of the Mayan military leaders' tradition of traveling beyond their land to learn about the outside world. That explained the Uxmal influence, as well as the influence of other ancient civilizations, including the works with gold from the Incas in Peru and the Aztecs in central and northern Mexico."

"I can understand being influenced by the Aztecs, who weren't that far away. But the Incas, down in Peru?" Susan asked with amazement. "That's quite a ways down there."

"You forget that almost five hundred years passed since this place was built to the time when the first Spaniards set foot in Yucatán. That's a long time. Much can happen in that many years."

"Never thought about it that way," Susan said, peering down the dark staircase. "I didn't realize how deep this place is," she added, walking beside him, her hazel eyes gleaming in the dim light, a hand tucked in one of the pockets of the khaki vest Cameron had given her a few days ago.

"Let's see, thirty-three steps is about thirty feet below the level of the anteroom. This temple is taller below ground than above ground, built this way to keep it hidden from outsiders. They probably used all of the limestone they dug up to build the structure above ground, as well as the pyramid, the small palace, and the courtyard."

"I feel a breeze," Susan said.

Cameron nodded. "That's what I was hoping for. Like in Palenque, the architects who designed and built this place have included ventilation tubes from the outside to help control the moisture buildup."

"Boy, do I feel lucky," she commented, bracing herself.

"You should. That means we won't be asphyxiating anytime soon."

"No, but we'll probably die from hypothermia."

"Are you cold?"

She nodded.

"Show you a trick," he said, reaching for the left sleeve of his own vest, tugging on a zipper partially covered by fabric. "Do like I do." He unzipped a bag of folded material beneath the sleeve. He pulled on the fabric and it turned the short sleeve into a long sleeve of thin nylon lined with cotton. He did the same to his right sleeve.

She smiled and also quickly turned her vest into a light jacket. "Clever. Thanks. That feels better."

"And that's not all." He approached her, unbuckling the four straps of her vest, turning them inside out, and revealing a long zipper running from her waist up to her neckline. He zipped it up and then moved to the collar, Where another zipper released a hood, which he put over her head, securing it with straps.

"That's the thing about my job. One moment you're in the scorching heat, and the next you're walking in some cave in subzero temperatures. These vests are great to make those environmental changes a little more bearable."

They moved down the corridor, past long tables packed with offerings, shells full of pearls, jade beads, dozens of pottery dishes, gold arrowheads, and several jade figurines. "Just like in Palenque," Cameron commented, explaining how Ruz had found similar offerings beneath the Temple of the Inscriptions, as he neared Pacal's crypt.

They reached the end of the corridor, finding yet a third slab blocking the way. Another wall of mosaics covered the wall next to the limestone slab. Once again, the scientists went to work.

```
13 12 11 10  9  8  7  6  5 20 20  5  6  7  8  9 10 11 12 13
12 66  2  3  4  5  6  7  8 20 20  8  7  6  5  4  3  2 66 12
11  2 56  0 66 13 66 56  0 20 20  0 56 66 13 66  0 56  2 11
10  3  0  0  0  0  0  0  0 20 20  0  0  0  0  0  0  0  3 10
 9  4 33 33 56  0 56 33 33 20 20 33 33 56  0 56 33 33  4  9
 8  5 20 20 20 66 20 23 13 20 20 13 24 20 66 20 20 20  5  8
20 20 20 20 20 20 20 20 20 20 20 20 20 20 20 20 20 20 20 20
 8  5 20 20 20 66 20 22 13 20 20 13 21 20 66 20 20 20  5  8
 9  4 33 33 56  0 56 33 33 20 20 33 33 56  0 56 33 33  4  9
10  3  0  0  0  0  0  0  0 20 20  0  0  0  0  0  0  0  3 10
11  2 56  0 66 13 66 56  0 20 20  0 56 66 13 66  0 56  2 11
12 66  2  3  4  5  6  7  8 20 20  8  7  6  5  4  3  2 66 12
13 12 11 10  9  8  7  6  5 20 20  5  6  7  8  9 10 11 12 13
```

"The pattern is the same, but always with a slight change," she offered.

Cameron smiled. It was not often that he encountered a woman who was not only beautiful and smart, but also someone with whom he could connect. "Do you want to do the honors this time?"

Susan readily accepted, pressing the harmonic numbers, starting with the lower right quadrant and continuing clockwise. The first rock-grating sound came from above, echoing down the stairs they had just taken.

"The floor," Cameron said. "It's lifting back up."

Her eyes widened.

"Relax," he said, setting the lantern by his feet and hugging her. She hugged him back, hard, conveying a mix of affection and fear. "Remember the first rule in archaeological exploration," he whispered in her ear. "You're never trapped as long as you can keep moving forward. Besides, whether there is one slab blocking our way back, or a thousand slabs, the end product is the same, you can't go back that way unless we find something ahead that can reset the stones, or show us another way out."

Just then the slab in front of them disappeared in the wall, its rumbling amplified by the enclosing stone, ending in a hissing sound as air escaped out of the next chamber, momentarily swirling their hair while the relative air pressures equalized. His ears popped.

Cameron went in and froze. In front of him stood a replica of the burial chamber, roughly thirty feet square, found by Alberto Ruz Lhullier in Palenque, down to the large sarcophagus lid depicting Pacal at the controls of a spaceship headed toward the stars. During his lifetime of archaeological work, Cameron had literally memorized many works of Mesoamerican art. One such masterpiece was the carving on Pacal's sarcophagus, a five-ton block of limestone eight feet in width by twelve in length and almost a foot in thickness. It included the glyphs running along the border, surrounding the main relief, which told the primary mission of the Mayan chief.

Cameron walked all around the sarcophagus, inspecting the glyphs, verifying their similarity to the ones he'd committed to memory long ago.

"What do they say?" Susan asked.

"Pacal Votan, galactic agent 13 66 56 0, was ordered by those above him to leave his homeland by the Hunab Ku and go to the Yucatán, the land of the Maya on Earth, traveling through the Kuxan Suum. He arrived to a place by the Usumacinta River, near the site that became Palenque, which he then founded. Pacal built the Temple of the Inscriptions, designed for his return trip to the Hunab Ku, where he was to report that the terrestrial Maya were ready to receive the harmonic synchronization during its passage through the 5129 years of the Great Cycle ending at the completion of the thirteenth *baktun*, or zero one, zero one, zero zero."

Susan frowned, her expression telling Cameron she was not certain what to make of the explanation. She pointed to a hole roughly ten inches in diameter on the far side of the chamber. It appeared to go up, toward the surface. "What's this?"

"Amazing," Cameron said. "They even built what archaeologists have termed a psychoduct, or a speaking tube, just like the one in Palenque, connecting the crypt to the temple above us."

"A speaking tube . . ." she asked, almost to herself. "Where does it go?"

"To the . . . hmm," he said, rubbing his chin.

"Do you think it still works?"

"Only one way to find out." He pointed to the opening. "Be my guest."

2

Jackie Nakamura heard it first, a faint cry emanating from the terrace, amplified by the incredible acoustics of the ancient edifices.

"Up there," she said, pointing to a dark hole on the left side of the temple, where they had returned a few minutes ago after spending the last twenty setting up their equipment for tonight's event.

Ishiguro, who had been inspecting the mosaics, walked over to his wife, standing at the far left corner of the shadowy porch, where the carvings of two shamans showed them with their heads turned toward the foot-square hole, as if listening to it.

"That's Susan," Jackie said.

3

While Susan shouted for help, Cameron continued to inspect the interior of the crypt, looking for differences between this place and Palenque, finding one on the left wall, a painting of the cosmos, depicting the southern constellation Centaur in the center, surrounded by other galaxies.

"Cameron," Susan said, waving him over, pointing at the speaking tube. "Listen."

" . . . *you all right? We can hear you clearly.*"

"We are fine," Susan replied to Jackie, whose voice came through the hole with amazing clarity, as if she were talking from the next room. "Can you use the same combination of numbers to reopen the entrance?"

"*Can't. The four numbers are still depressed. The returning slab did not reset them.*"

In the twilight of the room, Cameron saw Susan frown. That probably also meant that the mosaics controlling the moving floor in the anteroom were also depressed.

"We'll figure a way out of here," he said, a hand on her shoulder, pressing gently. "Trust me. I've been in tight spots before. If I know the Maya, there is something in this chamber that either resets the previous doors so that others can use them, or maybe it reopens them. The trick is figuring out what it is while avoiding activating decoys, traps meant for those who do not belong in here."

"Like us?"

"We'll be all right, Susan."

"Do you really have any idea how to get out of here?"

Cameron nodded. "I have my suspicions, but it's too early to tell."

"That means you have *no* idea."

"This map of the sky, for example," he said, shooting her a look. "Notice how there are fine cracks containing clusters of stars. One such cluster corresponds to the Hunab Ku. That's one possibility. Another one's over there." He swung the lantern to the section of wall flanking the entrance to the chamber, where a number of wall indents followed a hairline crack in the shape of a square. "Those look like finger grips. They could be for a drawer built into the wall, perhaps housing more offerings for Pacal to take with him in the afterlife. And over here, these reliefs depict the body of Pacal being lowered into his new resting home. Also notice the fine cracks around the shield of Lord Pacal." He pointed to a mosaic six inches square. "Problem is, unless I'm quite sure, I can't just start pressing and pulling."

She nodded. "Because they could be traps."

"Right."

Susan braced herself, inhaling deeply. "All right, Cameron. I believe you."

"That's a relief," he said, grinning.

She opened her mouth to reply but Jackie's voice filled the crypt.

"We're going to try to lower a couple of water bottles," Jackie said.

"Thanks," Susan replied. "We can certainly use them."

"You got it. Anything else?"

"Yeah. In case we don't make it out before tonight's event, there's some gear that I need you to get ready. Do you have pencil and paper?"

"In a moment."

While Cameron continued to inspect the burial chamber, Susan provided the astrophysicists with step-by-step instructions on how to operate her equipment, the required access passwords, which programs to bring up on her laptop, and how to set it up in receiving mode in preparation for the upcoming event. She had already made the necessary changes for the selected frequency range in the morning, following a night of discussions with the Japanese team. Ishiguro and Joao were able to lower a canteen and a pack of plastic-wrapped beef jerky—which Susan and Cameron consumed quickly, neither of them having had any breakfast and just a light dinner the night before. While they ate, Ishiguro had informed them of the help on the way, including a medical helicopter for the unconscious shaman and other wounded natives, plus two dozen SEALs for protection. It was then that Susan had learned that Troy Reid was also coming, along with a half-dozen members of her team plus more computer gear.

Now they sat on the stone floor, tired, cold. Cameron had further dimmed the lantern to nothing more than a vague glow, enough to break the total darkness that would otherwise engulf them. He could barely make out the carvings on the opposite wall of the chamber.

"Hold me," Susan said in the near darkness, scooting over, resting her head on his chest. He hugged her, closing his eyes, her nearness making him forget about computer viruses and ancient temples. Cameron savored her touch, her arms reaching behind him, pressing him against her, close, very close, the intimacy amplified by their surroundings. They were alone, isolated, a hundred tons of stone shielding them from the outside world.

Cameron Slater, eminent archaeologist, field expert, distinguished college professor, realized that for the very first time in his busy life he had developed strong feelings for someone else—despite his best efforts to use past relationships to force such alien emotions aside. He didn't have the time, the desire, the need to get involved like this, with something that went so far beyond anything he had experienced before, that he felt exposed, sailing in uncharted waters, trekking through unfamiliar jungle.

But primal feelings had already begun their slow outward motion, released from the deepest corner of his soul, slowly turning, radiating outward, gaining control of his senses, of his mind. His logic told him to let go of this, to walk away, to seek comfort elsewhere. But Susan Garnett had already burst into his life, awakening feelings he didn't know existed, making him long for a life much different from the one he had lived. He wasn't sure what it was about her that drew him in with a power far stronger than the Brazilian dancer, or the Peruvian beauty. Susan Garnett was beautiful, but so were so many others, and some even more gorgeous and exotic. Perhaps it was her smile, or the way in which she focused those hazel eyes on him, honest, profound, conveying comforts beyond those of the flesh, offering friendship, companionship, love.

Susan's breathing grew steady, serene, peaceful. She curled up like a baby, head on his chest, legs tucked over his thighs. He kissed the top of her head and also fell asleep.

4

The electromagnetic meters on both the SETI gear and Susan's jumped to life at the frequency of 1.42 GHz, peaking at an amplitude of 30 dBs, providing Ishiguro and Jackie with a clear representation of the EM energy bombarding the area.

Troy Reid, the bald and overweight official from the Federal Bureau of Investigation, stood behind them, swabbing his forehead with a handkerchief inside one of the dozen tents that the Americans had pitched in the courtyard following their arrival in the middle of the afternoon. Close to thirty people roamed the site now, including a small army of Navy SEALs, deployed quite efficiently around the site. A medical helicopter had also flown to the nearby village. Word from Joao was that the local Maya had refused to let the strangers take away their surviving high priest and had forced them to tend to him on site. The last update he'd gotten from the Mayan chief was that the medics had stabilized the priest but weren't certain when he would regain consciousness. Reid had spent a long time chatting with Susan through the speaking tube, which the SEALs now used as a ventilation duct, to force air into the burial chamber. In the tent next door, the Americans had set up three HP workstations, fed by the generators, and networked back to Washington via dedicated satellite links.

The puttering from a pair of portable electric generators echoed to the rhythm of the tent's canvas flapping in the evening breeze. Ishiguro kept his eyes glued not just on the meter on the screen, but also on the bar next to it, which indicated the number of megabytes of hard drive being consumed as the analog-to-digital translators converted the waveforms into binary code.

At the same time, Jackie used their undamaged SETI gear, which included a portable ten-foot-diameter radio telescope, to gather additional information on the event by searching the microwave range, snapping radio images of the southern constellation Centaur. This part was really a long shot, because if their 350-foot radio telescope back at Cerro Tolo could pick up nothing but a faint violet haze surrounding the distant star, the ten-footer outside the tent stood little chance of capturing much beyond terrestrial EM noise.

The event lasted twelve seconds, and Ishiguro shut down the sensors.

"That was it," he said, turning to Jackie, her china-doll features washed with amber light. "Just over forty-two megabytes. Like Susan predicted. Did you snap any pictures?"

Jackie nodded. "I'm not sure what we'll get with this little telescope. I've captured two images, both aimed at the expected origin of the source, based on its location for the past few days, as it follows an elliptical orbit around HR4390A. Each file's around 150 megabytes in size. It's going to be a little while before our portable system can convert them to images."

"Let's look at the EM conversion first," said Reid, sitting next to Jackie and beginning to work the keyboard of Susan's computer, pulling up the binary data dump. "Then we'll turn the HPs loose on your radio telescope images."

```
STATS
LENGTH: 42, 342, 021 BYTES
COMPOSITION: 0% ASSEMBLY CODE 100% UNKNOWN
ORIGIN: UNKNOWN
HOST STATUS: UNKNOWN
UNFILTERED STRAIN FOLLOWING . . .
```

```
0000000000000000000000000000000000001111111111111111111111000000000000000
0000000000000000000000000000000000001111111111111111111111000000000000000
0000000000000000000000000000000000001111111111111111111111000000000000000
0000000000000000000000000000000000001111111111111111111111000000000000000
0000000000000000000000000000000000000000000000000000000000000000000000000
0000000000000000000000011111111110000000000000000000000000000000000000000
0000000000000000000000011111111110000000000000000000000000000000000000000
0000000000000000000000011111111110000000000000000000000000000000000000000
0000000000000000000000011111111110000000000000000000000000000000000000000
0000001111110000000000000000000000000000000000000000000000000000000000000
0000001111110000000000000000000000000000000000000000000000000000000000000
0000001111110000000000000000000000000000000000000000000000000000000000000
0000000000000000000000000000000000000000000000000011111111110000000
0000000000000000000000000000000000000000000000000011111111110000000
0000000000000000000000000000000000000000000000000011111111110000000
0000000000000000000000000000000000000000000000000000000000000000000000000
0000000000000000000000000000000000000000000000000000000000000000000000000
0000000000000000000000000000000000000000000000000000000000000000000000000
0001111111111000000000000000000000000000000000000000000000000000000000000
0001111111111000000000000000000000000000000000000000000000000000000000000
0001111111111000000000111111111111111111111111000000000000000000000000000
0001111111111000000000111111111111111111111111000000000000000000000000000
0001111111111000000000111111111111111111111111000000000000000000000000000
0001111111111000000000111111111111111111111111000000000000000000000000000
0001111111111000000000111111111111111111111111000000000000000000000000000
0001111111111000000000111111111111111111111111000000000000000000000000000
0000000000000000000000111111111111111111111111000000000000000000000000000
0000000000000000000000111111111111111111111111000000000000000000000000000
0000000000000000000000111111111111111111111111000000000000000000000000000
0000000000000000000000111111111111111111111111000000000000000000000000000
0000000000000000000000111111111111111111111111000000000000000000000000000
0000000000000000000000111111111111111111111111000000000000000000000000000
0000000000000000000000111111111111111111111111000000000000000000000000000
0000000000000000000000111111111111111111111111000000000000000000000000000
0000000000000000000000111111111111111111111111000000000000000000000000000
0011111111111111110000000000000000000000000000000000000000000000000000000
0011111111111111110000000000000000000000000000000000000000000000000000000
0011111111111111110000000000000000000000000000000000000000000000000000000
0011111111111111110000000000000000000000000000000000000000000000000000000
0011111111111111110000000000000000000000000000000000000000000000000000000
0011111111111111110000000000000000000000000000000000000000000000000000000
0011111111111111110000000000000000000000000000000000000000000000000000000
0011111111111111110000000000000000000000000000000000000000000000000000000
0000000000000000000000000000000000000000000000000000000000000000000000000
```

CONTINUE BROWSING? Y/N

He went to the bottom.

"The same date," Reid said.

Ishiguro nodded. "Zero one, zero one, zero zero."

"But the general pattern is much different from previous dates," said Reid. "Much more defined."

"I think we're now listening at the precise frequency," Ishiguro offered.

"Let's see what it yields," Reid said, forwarding the binary file onto the HP workstations.

5

Susan Garnett had her eyes closed, but she was not sleeping. Her mind was in a faraway place, in another time, when the night's cool air had filled her lungs with peace and comfort, bringing with it the sweet memories of Rebecca, of Tom, of a life that would never be again, a life that she now found herself remembering with affection, but no longer with *obsession*, also realizing that hope once again filled her.

Susan had felt alone then, but she didn't feel alone now, in the quiet and murky chamber, in the arms of Cameron Slater. Her body had belonged only to her husband, but he was gone, had been gone for a very long time, leaving her alone.

Alone.

Susan hated being alone. She had longed for the touch of a man, for the embrace of that stranger who had so suddenly come into her life, for the man who understood her pain and was willing to lend more than a helping hand during her worst moment of need.

Susan opened her eyes and turned in the direction of Cameron, who smiled.

A decent man.

"Hey, I thought you were—"

She put a finger to his lips and slowly shook her head as she sat over his thighs, facing him, her knees pressing against his sides, her fingers digging into the hard muscles of his shoulders. Cameron closed his eyes, surrendering himself to her touch.

Leaning down, she kissed him, enjoying his taste, his lips, soft, unlike the rest of him, hardened by years of fieldwork. He cupped her face and returned the kiss, passionately, but with the gentleness of a partner, of a husband.

"Thank you," she said, a hand on his cheek.

"No. Thank *you*," he replied. "I'm enjoying this as much as—"

"Sue? Dr. Slater? You guys down there?"

They looked up, toward the speaking tube.

"Where else can we be, Troy?" she replied, standing, but not before kissing Cameron once more.

"Rain check?" he whispered.

"Absolutely."

"We have a match," Reid said, his voice sounding surreal.

"We do? *Where?"* Cameron now stood by her side.

"Palenque. We got a perfect match with the Maya site at Palenque."

Susan and Cameron exchanged a puzzled glance.

"What does that mean?" she asked Cameron, who turned up the intensity of the lantern and began to pace around the crypt.

"It certainly suggests that the point of contact on zero one, zero one, zero zero is Palenque, not here."

"What do you think is going to happen there?"

"Well, according to Mayan mythology, the completion of the Great Cycle, at the end of the thirteenth *baktun*, will be a moment of global harmonic realignment, when the spirit of Pacal Votan, galactic agent 13 66 56 0, will return to Palenque to bring unity to his people. There are some parallels here with the Christian belief of a second coming of Jesus."

"On the day of final judgment?"

"Correct. But for Christians, that day symbolizes the end of the world, the final chapter of the Earth."

"The apocalyptic message in the Book of Revelation," Susan said.

"How do you know about—"

"I'm Catholic. In the Book of Revelation the angels of the Lord come to Earth to set the stage for the second coming of Jesus Christ."

"In Mayan mythology this day is supposed to symbolize a new beginning, a refreshing of the spirit to begin a new Great Cycle."

"But the Maya have all but disappeared," said Susan. "The modern world has eradicated their culture to a few isolated spots. You yourself told me that Palenque is nothing but a tourist attraction these days, plus whatever digging archaeologists like yourself might be doing. Whose spirits is Pacal going to renew? The terrorists even killed two of the priests and wounded the third."

Cameron sighed. "Good question." Then he spoke directly into the hollow duct connecting them to the surface. "Reid?"

"Yes, Dr. Slater?"

"Was there anything else translated? Anything at all?"

"The date was the same. The only odd thing was that although the Temple of the Inscriptions is not geographically at the center of Palenque, it was at the center of the binary map."

Cameron looked about him. "There's something else that's missing. We now have the place and the time, and I also think we may have the message, but I fear that something else must be done to replace the fact that Palenque is not the same place Pacal left in A.D. 683. Much has changed since."

"We've contacted the White House," said Reid. *"The President is currently in conference with the Mexican president to figure a way to isolate the area for the next couple of weeks, if that helps in any way."*

"It will likely help once we know what else must be done."

Susan stepped up to the speaking hole. "What about the body of the virus? The 260 bytes of data that are always different on each daily event?"

"I checked them, Sue. They're still following the same pattern since we began tracking them on the twelfth."

"That may be the last piece of this puzzle," Cameron said.

"But how are we going to figure it out?"

Cameron didn't answer, his eyes shifting back to the ancient carvings.

6

Cameron Slater wasn't a gambler by nature, but he certainly knew how to mitigate risks, how to gather all available information before making a decision. He knew that the global event on 01-01-00 would take place in Palenque. He also knew that Pacal Votan was due to return to Palenque on this date to refresh the human spirit and prepare it for the next Great Cycle. Around the crypt were stone buttons that he could press, one of which, he felt certain, would not only reveal a passage out of the crypt, but also provide another clue on what work remained to be done prior to the end of the thirteenth *baktun.*

"But what?"

"Cameron? Did you say something?"

He turned around. "Just thinking out loud." Susan sat beneath the speaking tube while he continued to inspect his options, also certain that while one would free them, the others would kill them. That was the way of the Maya.

"These 260-byte files," he added. "You looked at them, right?"

Susan nodded.

"And saw no possible pattern?"

"My disassembler could not decode it, and there is no apparent surface pattern like with the binary map."

"The Maya, however, were masters at geometrical sequences, as you have come to find out recently. Have we really analyzed these files under that eye?"

"Doubt it."

"See, we need to think geometrically. Whatever the message, it's related to the end of the thirteenth *baktun.*"

"To zero one zero one zero zero."

He nodded. "Is there a way to get a small laptop down here?"

Susan stared at him for a moment before saying, "My laptop's too big, but let's call Reid. See if he brought something smaller that can be networked."

7

Ishiguro Nakamura watched with a sense of awe as the nineteen-inch monitor of one of the FBI's HP workstations displayed the first of the two captured images by the portable radio telescope, showing an incredibly clear picture of the planets circling HR4390A.

"It . . . it *can't be,*" Jackie said.

"How in the hell . . . ?" he asked.

"This is impossible," Jackie said. "This place is 139 light-years away. Even a Cerro Tolo mounted on a rocket at the edge of our solar system could not capture such an image."

"I'm counting thirteen planets," said Ishiguro, forcing his mind to focus, to get past the unexplainable circumstances and focus on the gathered data.

Jackie Nakamura, sitting next to him in front of the workstation, tapped a fingernail on the screen. "Same here. Thirteen planets. Son of a—"

"How can you tell them apart from nearby stars?" asked Reid, standing next to them, eyes narrowed while also staring at the screen, his face glistening with perspiration. Reid's massive bulk was not compatible with the tropical weather.

"A combination of many factors, including coloration, shape, and degree of pulsation. I guess after you stare at the universe like we have, planets and stars look radically different. Trust me, *those* are planets."

"And these little ones are their moons," added Jackie. "All twenty of them."

Ishiguro frowned. "Thirteen planets and twenty moons?"

"Just like the rows and columns of those arrays of numbers in the temple. Could that be just a coincidence?" asked Jackie.

"We'd better let Dr. Slater know. Perhaps he can make some sense of it," offered Reid.

"Hold on," Jackie said, zooming in on the five closest planets to HR4390A, which was almost five times the size of the Sun. "Let's see what else we can learn here."

The Japanese astrophysicist nodded. "The orbits are too close to HR4390A. Surface temperatures must be well beyond those that can sustain life."

"At least as we know it," she added.

"True."

"Still," Jackie said, pulling down a few menus to measure the wavelengths of the captured image, whose wide-frequency spectrum provided them with information not just in the visual range but also in the ultraviolet and infrared ranges. "According to the IR signature, the closest planet might as well be a star. Its surface temperature is over nine hundred degrees." She continued to tap the keys and information kept on browsing. "The temperature decreases steadily. The fifth planet has an average temperature of around three hundred degrees, still too hot to sustain life . . . as we know it."

"What about the rest of the planets?" asked Reid with growing interest.

She panned across the image. "Here are the next five planets, ranging in temperature from 190 degrees to 22 degrees."

"From boiling hot to freezing," said Reid. "Any of them close to our Earth?"

Ishiguro pointed at the last one. "The tenth one is. The temperatures that

Jackie's quoting are in degrees Celsius, not Fahrenheit. Twenty-two Celsius is room temp, or around seventy-two Fahrenheit."

"That's an average temperature, of course," said Jackie. "I'm sure there is a range, like on Earth."

"So number ten might be the one, huh?" asked Reid, pointing at it on the screen, a bluish-green circle surrounded by darkness.

"What about the rest of the planets?" asked Reid.

Jackie pulled them up on the screen. "From minus five to minus ninety, Celsius."

"Now *those* are freezing," said Ishiguro.

"What's on the second image?" asked Reid.

Jackie worked the pull-down menu and retrieved the second file, already translated into a digital image by the HP workstations.

"Oh, my God," she said, leaning into the screen as the second image materialized. It was a close-up of the tenth planet, its bluish hues and cloud coverage resembling those of Earth.

"How in the hell? How did you *get* this shot?" asked Ishiguro.

"I ... *I don't know!*" she said. "I thought I was just taking shots at one resolution ... I ... the microwave signal must have come preset with these images. I can't think of any other explanation."

They stared at it for several minutes, admiring its similarities to Earth, including snow-covered polar caps, bluish-green oceans, and dark brown continents, though none of the shapes even came close to matching those of Earth.

"Close in on that," Ishiguro said, pointing at a spot of land between breaks in the clouds, close to the equator. "Looks like peculiar irregularities in the landscape."

Jackie worked the keyboard and the mouse, zooming in while also running a program to enhance the image by averaging the pixels to keep the picture from getting grainy.

None of them said a word as the new image came alive on the screen. Right there, in front of them, with undeniable clarity, from a planet 139 light-years away. The trio saw the landscape in utter disbelief, reading the sequence of numbers etched on the land, across what appeared to be a massive mountain range, larger than the Andes and the Himalayas combined.

"The millennium clocks," hissed Jackie Nakamura. "They're counting down to this sequence!"

"We need to get this information to Susan and Dr. Slater!" said Troy Reid, sweating profusely. "After that, I have to call Washington!"

8

The portable computer system turned out to be a small NEC mini notebook, just seven inches long and four wide, easily lowered to the burial chamber while also attached to an Ethernet cable, electronically linking Susan with the powerful workstations in the courtyard. The tiny system came loaded with a pocket version of Windows98 and with limited memory, but fortunately the files captured from the daily virus, at 260 bytes each, were small enough that they could all fit at once inside the system's memory card.

Susan sat with her back to the crypt, the NEC on her lap, its bright display casting an eerie glow inside the crypt, bringing thousand-year-old carvings to life.

"The technology from the modern world illuminating the works of the ancient world," Cameron mumbled in a poetic tone, marveled by the moment.

Susan regarded him with admiration, wondering about a man who viewed life so much differently than anyone she had ever met, a man who drew satisfaction from moments usually ignored by others, who saw beauty in things that often escaped the eye.

She leaned over and kissed him on the cheek.

"What was that for?"

"For adding perspective to my life."

The small system churned away, its relatively slow microprocessor working to display the requested information on the small screen.

Susan looked at the first file, scanning the lines of code. "Looks pretty random. Any words of wisdom from the world of archaeology?"

```
10101010110101001101101000101010100101011111001011100101010101111101001101
10111010100010011010100101001010100101001010110111111001010010101001111
01011001101101011010111010110010101010101010010101110101011001010101011
10101010110101001101101000101010100101011111001011100101010101111101001101
01010110011010110101010100101001011001010111101010101010100101001010101010101
01111010001110010101001010100101010010001100101001010100101011000010101010
10101001011001100101001010010101100101010101010100101001001101100101010
10101010101001010101010101001010010101001011011001111100101010010010101010
01010010101010010010101001010000110101010010101010100101001010101010101011
10111010100010011010100101001010100101001010110111111001010010101001111
01011001101101011010111010110010101010101010010101110101011001010101011
10101010110101001101101000101010100101011111001011100101010101111101001101
10001011010101001011001111101010101010010011000111100011101010101011001101
10001011010101001011001111101010101010010011000111100011101010101011001101
10101101011101011001010101010101001010110101011001010101011101010101010110
10101101011101011001010101010101001010110101011001010101011101010101010110
00110101000110010101001011010010101010111010101010101011101010101010101
01101101001111010101101010101010101010010111110011111101010101010100
10101101100101001001010100100110010010010010011010110110101101010010010101
00101010010110010101001010010100101001010110111001010010101010010101010101000101
10101010101010100110010101010101101011001101011001010010101010000011100101
01011010110010101100110100110110100101010100101011111001011100101010101
11010011011011101010100
```

"From the world of archaeology *and* also from the world of astrophysics."

She nodded. It had taken them several minutes to come to terms with the incredible revelation about the planets circling HR4390A. The parellels were indeed amazing, beyond anything she could have imagined. "Thirteen planets and twenty moons," she said, still in awe.

"Just like the Tzolkin, the Mayan sacred calendar, divided into thirteen months of twenty days each, which multiplied together yields 260 days. Let's divide this file in the same way. Split it up into thirteen rows of twenty bytes each."

Susan did the math. "That would mean creating rows of 160 bits each. Here's the first two segments."

```
01000101101010101011011001111101010101011011000111100011101010101011001100
11010110101110101100101010101011101001010111010101100101010101011101010101011
010101110110001010
```

```
11010001011111001011100101010101110100110110111101011101001101010100101001
01010110100101011011111100101001011100111100101010110010110011011010110
101110101100101010
```

"See anything?" she asked.

Cameron studied the screen for several moments. "The last five bits are the same for both strings," he commented.

"Zero one zero one zero," she said. "It's missing the last zero."

"You indicated that this was the string for the *second* day of the virus, right?"

"Correct. We missed the first day."

"Let's shift the entire search to compensate for this. Place the first bit of the array as the last one and redo the segmentation."

She did, promptly displaying the new 160-bit rows.

```
1000101101010101011011001111101010101011011000111100011101010101011001101
1010110101110101100101010101011010010101110101011001010101011101010101101
101011101100010100

1010001011111001011100101010101011101001101101110101110100110101001010010
1010110100101011011111100101001011100111100101010101100101100110110101101
011101011001010100
```

Cameron tapped on the last six bits of each segment. "Do you see what I see?"

Susan nodded. "The missing zeroes. I'll be damned. It now matches all of the observations from the SETI team. The number of planets, the number of moons, and also the sequence of numbers spotted on the tenth planet." She displayed five more segments, noticing the pattern.

```
011010101011111101001101010101011011100110110011011101011011101100010011
1010110100101011011111100101001011100111100101010110010110011011010101
1010101011010010100

0000110101110101100101010101011101001010110101011001010101011101010101
10001010111110011100110011100110011000110101010101011001100011100111101100
1010101011010010100

0110101010111111010000011100011011110011011001101110101101110110001001
110010101111100111100111001010101110001101010101011001100011100111101100
1010101011010010100

111010101011111101001101010101011011100110110011011101011011101100010011
1001010111110011100110011100110011000110101010101011001100011100111101100
1010101011010010100

0100111111010111111010011010101010110111001101100110111010110110111011000100
1110011111100000001100111001100111011001101010101011001100011100111101100
1010101011010010100
```

"Now," Cameron said. "I'll bet you anything you want that the 260-bytes segments on the following days will reveal a similar segmentation pattern, after you shift the bits to compensate for the day that it was received in relation to the starting date, December eleven."

"Then we should align them based on these boundaries?"

"Good. You're thinking geometrically, like the Maya. Now, create a file that is formed by rows as defined by the zero one, zero one, zero zero code, concatenating the following days also segmented based on this code and let's take a look at the resulting binary map."

She did, creating 91 binary segments, or rows, 13 for each of the seven days that they had intercepted a virus. Each segment contained 160 bits, lined up according to the 010100 code, creating an array of ones and zeros 160 bits wide and 91 bits long. Susan rotated the array by ninety degrees, making it 91 bits wide and 160 bits long. Still, her small screen could not display all 91 bits in each row, leaving the last two out.

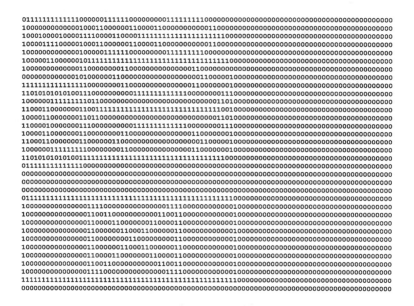

CONTINUE BROWSING Y/N?

"Great," Susan said, inspecting the array, quickly detecting a set of geometrical patterns. "Let me transfer the file to Reid. See if he can display the entire array on the HP and then get it to match another landsca—"

"Not so fast." Cameron ran a finger over the screen, tracing the ones over the background of zeroes. "I don't think this is a landscape."

"Oh? What is it then?"

"Glyphs. The last piece of the puzzle."

Susan narrowed her eyes and inched closer to the screen. "Can you read them?"

"Looks like they're in a row, like a cartouche."

"Cartouche? You said those were the equivalent of a modern sentence, with the glyphs making out the individual words, right?"

"That's right." He reached for his field notebook, tracing out the first one. He grinned. "That's the symbol for the city of Palenque. Send Reid an E-mail. I'm going to be needing my decoding books down here."

9

The cartouche was incomplete, as expected, since they had only downloaded seven of the first eight messages and they still had twelve to go before 01-01-00. The binary file so far contained seven and a half glyphs, which Cameron had managed to decode, putting together a story that complemented the reliefs in this secret temple. He began with what he already knew from the ancient carvings.

"Pacal was exhumed by his son, Chan-Bahlum, as depicted in the reliefs adorning the walls of this temple, and brought over here, again as shown by numerous glyphs and pictographs etched in the limestone. This information, as I stated earlier, explains why the mummified body found by Alberto Ruz in the Temple of the Inscriptions lacked an elongated head and filed teeth, as was so typical with Mayan leaders. Chan-Bahlum, in his rush to get his father's body out of the city and to a safe location, probably grabbed the first body he could find and shoved it in the crypt, beneath the famous mask of jade and the other precious offerings found in 1952. Then this site was founded and construction began immediately under extreme secrecy. That's how far the story goes according to the reliefs in this temple. What we were missing was the continuation of this incredible story. And here we have it, in this final cartouche. Problem is, that we're getting it piecemeal, a couple of glyphs per day. Also, the Maya are still being the Maya and are giving us the story backward, with the ending first, which explains why the first glyph in the sequence is for the city of Palenque, where it all converges on zero one, zero one, zero zero. The rest of the glyphs provide instructions on the necessary arrangements to be made to the original crypt in Palenque, including relining the interior of the tomb with cinnabar, the reddish material always found in Mayan tombs, on the walls, or on objects accompanying dead persons. In Mayan cosmogony this coloring symbolizes resurrection and hope of immortality. The other glyphs provide clear instructions on additional arrangements to be made around the Temple of the Inscriptions in preparation for the celebration of the end of the Great Cycle and the beginning of the new one, like the relative position of certain stelae and other small structures."

"What about the tomb itself? What is supposed to go in there if the body found by Ruz was not the real Pacal?"

"The glyphs stop before telling us that, though I'm quite sure it'll be included in the captured viruses over the next week and a half." His eyes shifted to the large sarcophagus monopolizing the center of the crypt. "But I do have a pretty good guess who needs to be moved back home."

Susan nodded. "Problem is, it won't be as easy as clicking your heels three times and saying the magic words."

"Maybe," said Cameron, walking over to the relief of Pacal being lowered into his current resting place, placing his hand on the mosaic of the Mayan chief's seal, and pressing it. The stone caved in almost a full foot. Several things happened at once. First, the door to the crypt slid shut with the force of a steel safe. Next the sarcophagus's lid scraped back, reaching the back wall, which also began to move out of the way, revealing a tunnel that seemed to angle up, toward the surface.

"Then again, maybe not," added the archaeologist in a triumphant tone, inspecting the coffin's reddish interior, finding a human skeleton, its face covered by a mosaic mask of jade quite similar to the one found by Ruz at Palenque. Dozens of jade necklaces adorned him, as well as several bracelets.

Susan was speechless, inspecting Pacal's mortal remains as well as what appeared to be their way out of this place. "How—how long have you known that this was the way to get out?"

He tilted his head toward her. "Like I told you before, I had my suspicions, but it was too early to tell for certain. The glyphs describing the preparations needed at Palenque gave it away."

10

The tunnel led them to another flight of stairs, this time flanked by plain stone walls. After thirteen steps they reached a landing with a U-turn, similar to the one they had taken on the way down. After twenty more steps, they reached the top of the stairs and another landing. A stone slab blocked the way. Next to it was another array of mosaics.

13	12	11	10	9	8	7	6	5	20	20	5	6	7	8	9	10	11	12	13
12	66	2	3	4	5	6	7	8	20	20	8	7	6	5	4	3	2	66	12
11	2	56	0	66	13	66	56	0	20	20	0	56	66	13	66	0	56	2	11

```
10   3   0   0   0   0   0   0   0  20  20   0   0   0   0   0   0   0   3  10
 9   4  33  33  56   0  56  33  33  20  20  33  33  56   0  56  33  33   4   9
 8   5  20  20  20  66  20  22  13  20  20  13  23  20  66  20  20  20   5   8
20  20  20  20  20  20  20  20  20  20  20  20  20  20  20  20  20  20  20  20
 8   5  20  20  20  66  20  21  13  20  20  13  24  20  66  20  20  20   5   8
 9   4  33  33  56   0  56  33  33  20  20  33  33  56   0  56  33  33   4   9
10   3   0   0   0   0   0   0   0  20  20   0   0   0   0   0   0   0   3  10
11   2  56   0  66  13  66  56   0  20  20   0  56  66  13  66   0  56   2  11
12  66   2   3   4   5   6   7   8  20  20   8   7   6   5   4   3   2  66  12
13  12  11  10   9   8   7   6   5  20  20   5   6   7   8   9  10  11  12  13
```

"The way out," said Cameron, starting on the lower left quadrant and working his way counterclockwise.

The slab at the bottom of the stairs closed as this one creaked open, revealing thick jungle, along with a stream of fresh night air, which Susan inhaled deeply.

"Freedom," she whispered as they stepped away from the edifice, realizing that they had exited at the other side of the temple.

A moment later the slab shifted back, as if controlled by an ancient timer, closing the passageway.

Cameron pointed a thumb at it. "The reset mechanism. Now we know the secret to completing the whole cycle."

Susan kissed him on the cheek. "Thanks," she said.

"Why?"

"For the greatest and scariest experience of my life."

Cameron smiled. "Stick around, Susan. And you'll be kissing me every day."

The couple walked around the temple, reaching the tunnellike entrance to the left side, by the stone pillar, where only two days ago they had been threatened by Strokk and the terrorists as they tried to make their way into the jungle. Now that same spot was being guarded by a pair of Navy SEALs, who turned their camouflaged faces at them, eyes narrowing in suspicion.

"Hi," Susan said. "We're the ones who were trapped down there."

One of the SEALs looked toward the temple and back at the scientists in their soiled clothes. "Ma'am?" he said. "How did you . . . ?"

"Long story," said Cameron, putting an arm around Susan, who also ran an arm behind him as they walked side by side, her thumb stuck into his back pocket.

"But quite a story," said Susan as they walked past the startled SEALs and waved at Reid and the Japanese team.

Epilogue

In the Year of our Lord, 1999, the Earth continued to rotate along its longitudinal axis relative to the Sun, just as it had for the past 4.5 billion years, along an eternal path defined long before the Solar System was born, long before a spinning nebula of boiling gas shot away from billions of exploding stars and became its own galaxy, the Milky Way; long before the entire universe, an infinitesimal mass of super-heavy matter, began to expand following the cosmos's most phenomenal and unequaled release of galactic energy.

Planet Earth continued to spin as the new millennium neared, continued to radiate the crimson energy of thousands of digital clocks counting down to the sequence of numbers that would bring total planetary alignment with a distant life-form, one whom none of the scientists involved in this historic quest could even begin to dream about, for it existed far before everything else known to mankind, and it would exist long after the Sun expanded at the end of its life and swallowed the Earth, before shrinking to a dark, smoldering mass of heavy metals.

In the days that followed what Cameron Slater called the single most important discovery in the history of pre-Columbian studies, much activity took place both at the temple of Kinich Ahau as well as in Palenque, all directed by the original four scientists, whom together had unlocked the key to achieving galactic synchronization. Even the special envoy of scientists, deployed to the site at the request of the U.S. president to witness and record the event, followed Cameron and Susan's direction.

As the days leading to 01-01-00 unfolded, adding more glyphs to the cartouche, Cameron made further adjustments to the site deep within the Temple of the Inscriptions, making sure that not only the true mortal remains of Pacal Votan were deposited in the stone coffin, just as it had happened over twelve hundred years before, but also positioning the right offerings according to the information downloaded from the virus each day.

The millennium clocks froze across the Earth, the succession of numbers required for total planetary synchronization washing the heavens from Washington, D.C., to Seoul, from Tokyo to Rio de Janeiro, from Singapore to Moscow, from Delhi to Paris. The visual energy propagated across the sky, scattering through the galaxy, acknowledging a state of readiness that matched the recent events taking place in a remote clearing in the Yucatán Peninsula, also matching a similar series of numbers from a previously unknown planet 139 light-years from Earth.

As thousands of clocks flashed the final series of numbers, presenting it to the firmament with undeniable clarity; as the millennium came to a close, also completing the Great Cycle, the thirteenth *baktun*, the heavens filled with a new kind of energy, one that was immeasurable by man's systems, but which did pulsate across the galaxy at infinite speed, crossing the boundaries of space and time, rushing through the scorching core of the Sun, and striking the third closest planet with uncanny accuracy.

Cameron and Susan were sitting on the steps of the Temple of the Inscriptions when it hit, blinding at first, like a thousand high beams, but much more powerful, and warm, but not the warmth that's associated with ambient temperature. Susan felt an inner heat, one that warmed her core, her very soul, as the light enveloped her, vanishing her surroundings, swallowing the jungle, the limestone edifices, the sky itself.

Then a vision came to Susan Garnett, from the very distant past, and then another, this one more recent, and yet another from ten years ago. The back flashes came with no relative order, rapidly, one after the next, like in fast-forward video, but much faster and far clearer too, for every vision carried its own set of feelings, of emotions. Susan watched them all not as she had remembered or perceived that they had occurred, but as they had *actually* occurred, without her personal bias, envy, greed, or pride to distort reality. She found herself reliving each image, smoldering guilt or overwhelming joy expanding through her in exhausting, alternating cycles. She saw in vivid detail the pain she had inflicted on others, knowingly or not. And she also experienced the happiness that she had spread during her lifetime. But another realization chilled her, for she was judging not just what she had done or said—or failed to do or say—but also what she had *thought*. In fact, thoughts carried far more weight in this hazy, self-assessing courtroom than her actions, for the level of pain or joy seemed stronger, sharper.

Consummating guilt struck her with the power of a thousand bad dreams not just from the mere acts themselves, but from *witnessing* the effects of such acts, of such words, of such thoughts on the people she had touched during her life. Susan's visions came in various levels, the highest dominated by the visual memory of her life, but right beneath it, snippets of the lives of

others as a result of her actions shocked her mind. Some visions were pleasant, satisfying, for there were many times when she had acted out of love,
without the dark veil of selfishness, of anger, of greed. But other apparitions
raked her mind, like a white-hot claw, slowly turning, scourging her. She saw
the effects of not returning phone calls from friends, of her offending driving
style, of failing to come through on a promise, of lacking benevolence as a
college professor, of ignoring her parents, of forgetting to call on holidays,
of being judgmental. She saw with uncanny detail every single opportunity
in her life where she could have done good to others and had not, from a
homeless person on the side of the road, to the old widow lady next door
who just wanted company, to the collection basket at church that she would
sometimes just pass on. She watched with horror how a vagrant killed himself
following Susan's stoplight speech about getting a job and not being a bum.
The guilt ravaged her, eating her alive, like a predator. No, more like a cancer,
for it came from within. Her heart cried out for the visions to stop when she
saw that old woman next door returning to her apartment heartbroken every
time Susan had pretended not to be home to avoid wasting time talking
nonsense with her. And there were so many other unexpected visions that
shocked her, visions from school, from her childhood, from her early married
days, during her pregnancy, during the trial, when Hans Bloodaxe was carried
away from the courtroom. She felt ashamed of the joy that she had felt at
the time, finally achieving retribution for the murder of her family.

Susan Garnett found that there was no place to hide from such torturing
apparitions, no place to run, no way to explain or justify, no room to apologize, just unconditional acceptance of past behavior, just guilt or joy, two
commanding feelings that wove themselves in a repeating cycle as her life,
as they so often say, flashed before her eyes. This period of self-evaluation,
reserved as the starting point of the afterlife, flooded her senses with constant
appraisement, followed by either joyful praise or utter reprimand, depending
on the vision.

The swirling haze, of similar composition as the one in her dreamlike
experience, spun faster and faster, like a whirling cyclone. The celestial tor-
nado swept through Susan Garnett violently, not only exposing all of the
wrong in her life, but also extracting it, like a filter, purging the bad while
letting the good continue through as a part of her. Every pain-racked vision
of wrongdoing, even at the smallest levels, was followed by a growing feeling
of relief, of forgiveness, of renewed hope, of a promise to change.

Only then, after she had been distilled in mind and spirit, after she had mentally atoned every impure act, or word, or thought, after her whole self had been purified to the innocence of a child, was she ready for the next step, for the next vision, one of indescribable peace, comfort, exultation. She felt a powerful being around her, within her, providing total unity, total harmony, absolute molecular synchronization. She also felt the presence of Tom and Rebecca, but their memories no longer hurt, no longer crushed her senses. They spun around her like an ethereal fog, encouraging her to go on, to fulfill her life, to remember this moment, to preserve the immaculate state of her soul.

The mist began to recede, like the morning fog, thinning under the power of the sun, until all that remained were crystalline star-filled skies, and the peaceful serenade of the surrounding jungle as she sat on the steps of the Temple of the Inscriptions at Palenque, Cameron Slater next to her.

The scientists stared at each other, not certain what to say or how to say it.

"Did you . . . ?" she began, not sure what to call the experience.

"Yes," he replied, holding her hand. "Every *last* thought."

They stood and gazed down at the large site, white tents pitched among the ancient ruins. People walked about in a daze, staring at the stars. She saw Troy Reid, as well as several members of her FBI team and most of the scientists from the presidential envoy, stepping out of tents, their faces looking about, gazing upward, toward the cosmos.

"Look at them, Cameron. Look at them all."

"They experienced it too. All of them."

She checked her watch, amazed that such a deep, life-enriching experience had lasted but a minute; one minute and one second to be exact, though she wasn't sure how she knew that. She just did, and she also knew that everyone else did as well. The sequence of numbers frozen in the millennium clocks around the world had been the final progression that had unlocked this magical experience, achieving galactic synchronization with a distant civilization. Or was it something beyond just a civilization?

"What about out there?" she asked, pointing beyond the jungle. "Do you think everyone experienced it?" she asked, suddenly realizing that this event, like the global daily freezes, had touched every corner of the world, but not with the same intensity as in the heart of the ancient Mayan world. "It faded as it spread. We felt the full effect, but those far away did not. In fact, those in distant places may have only sensed a brief feeling of warmth, of harmony, like that of an infant being kissed by its mother. But nothing that comes close to what we've just witnessed. But how do I know that?"

"Total harmonic synchronization," said Slater, also staring in the distance.

"The Maya knew this thousands of years ago, having received the entire message, like we just did, while also realizing that those from distant lands did not, and also sensing the urge to spread the word, to carry on that message across space and time. There's even a parallel here to Jesus Christ and his apostles. Only very few got the Holy message and were asked to spread the good news to the rest of the world."

Susan filled her chest with the magnitude of the experience, and also with the possible explanations that it brought. "If only the Maya experienced it in its fullness, back at the beginning of the last Great Cycle, do you think that could explain the bizarre similarities between the Maya and other cultures?"

Cameron nodded, his eyes on the starry sky. "I . . . I think you might have something there. It certainly fits the observations. Many people experienced this at some point back then, at the beginning of the last Great Cycle, just as we know it now. But only some civilizations were able to preserve this celestial gift, this vision, this prophecy, like the Maya. For the rest, it was lost, probably after a few generations, if that long, either because they were too far away from the source, or just because they stopped caring, or maybe got conquered by another civilization, or because of one of a thousand other reasons."

"Do you think mankind can keep it alive longer this time?"

The archaeologist shrugged. "Who knows? By tomorrow I'm sure there will be some people who will offer a logical explanation for the event and try to shove it aside." He leaned closer to her while whispering, "I wouldn't be surprised if one of those scientists down there twists the entire thing to fit some kind of scientific model just to get himself on the cover of *Newsweek*." He straightened and added, "Anyway, probably some groups will go along with that and some will not, choosing instead to hang on to the true message. I'm sure many religious groups will put their own spin on what happened here as well, trying to fit the facts with their own beliefs, though I suspect that there might be a fair degree of truth in their thinking. A part of me feels that what we experienced here today was of a supernatural nature."

Susan nodded. "I feel it too. Only something omnipotent could have triggered such a self-evaluating journey . . . I even knew how other people felt because of my actions."

"I know," he said. "And some of them weren't pleasant. But maybe . . . maybe it *wasn't* supernatural. Perhaps it was extraterrestrial. Maybe on that tenth planet lives such an advanced civilization that we cannot even begin to imagine it, opting instead for the supernatural explanation."

"Perhaps," said a female voice from behind.

The scientists turned around and watched Ishiguro and Jackie descending the steps, hand in hand. Susan had forgotten all about them. The Japanese-Americans, who had set up their equipment at the top of the temple, the highest structure for miles around, sat next to them, their faces awash with the same trancelike glow that radiated from Cameron Slater and which no doubt she also wore.

"From a scientific perspective," said Ishiguro Nakamura, "the technology to attempt to communicate with other civilizations is less than fifty years old. Given the age of the universe, the odds are that if another civilization could receive our messages, that civilization is quite likely to be much ahead of ours, probably *thousands* of years ahead. If you take what we have accomplished in the past one hundred years and extrapolate it out to a thousand, you can easily see why our world would seem like the stone age to theirs."

Jackie nodded. "And even a thousand years is insignificant in the larger scheme. Some civilization could have existed for much longer than that, mastering disciplines that may seem even beyond science fiction, like some of the myths that you have told us about the Maya."

"Mind control, transportation to other galaxies without the assistance of today's imperfect mechanical surrogates," said Cameron. "That's what the Classic Maya had mastered. Galactic agents like Pacal Votan were able to comprehend this incredible gift and use it to build an entire civilization."

"Until the Europeans came," said Susan, frowning. "Their arrogance prevented them from understanding this incredible blessing, choosing instead to burn, to enslave, to eradicate."

"But Pacal's son foresaw this and used his ruling years to build a secret temple to preserve the gift from the likes of Diego de Landa, who burned so many records, so much history." Cameron looked up the steps, toward the temple atop the pyramid.

"What's going to happen to the hidden site in the Petén?" asked Jackie.

"It never existed," replied Susan. "It's back in the hands of its rightful owners. One of the priests survived, but more than that, everyone in that village experienced what we just did. They have been injected with the gift to preserve it for another 5,129 years."

Ishiguro frowned. "But shouldn't we offer them some protection, to make sure that the tradition is not lost?"

Cameron grinned, shaking his head. "Just the opposite, my friend. That temple is probably the best chance that our world has of preserving the gift for future generations, because it will remain pure, without the distortions of reality likely to be injected by our world as it gets passed down from generation to generation. I guarantee you that for most of the world, what took place here today will be quite forgotten in a hundred years, and a vague memory at best in five hundred years. But with the Maya, the gift has endured over five *thousand* years, and it's likely that, if left alone, it may endure five thousand more. But if we try to help them out, we would be doing to them just what the Spaniards did five hundred years ago, staining their pure culture with our imperfect ways. Trust me, they're much better left alone."

Ishiguro did not look convinced. "What's preventing another terrorist group from looting the place?"

"The Maya warriors were able to neutralize that terrorist group in minutes, just as they probably did through the centuries, as other threats neared it. They have been able to protect it since it was first erected in A.D. 690. That's over 1,300 years. You tell me what other civilization has lasted that long. Our own United States has only been around for a couple hundred years. How can we provide them with long-term protection when we haven't been around that long in the first place?"

The Japanese scientist nodded. "I never thought of it that way."

"Most people don't," Cameron said. "We're trained from birth to think in terms of the next ten, maybe twenty years. The Maya are trained to think in terms of thousands of years. Take the temple back in the jungle, for example. It was built thirteen hundred years ago, and yet, those slabs slid back and forth on mechanisms that performed as smoothly as when they were first constructed. That kind of longevity is quite alien to our way of thinking. Most automobiles and appliances won't go much beyond ten to fifteen years, and that's with a lot of maintenance. Our technology doesn't age well. It's a reflection of our McDonald's society. Everything is like fast foods, want it now, get it now, but it won't last long. However, that doesn't matter because you can always get a new one down the road, and another one later on. I tell you with the utmost certainty that we have little to offer to the Maya in terms of protection or assistance in preserving the gift we received today. We must leave them alone, that's the best present we can give them in return for allowing us to experience this soul-cleansing event."

"And that's exactly what will happen," said Susan. "All records of those coordinates are being deleted. I learned the other day that the reinforcements that we got a couple of weeks ago at that site had been blindfolded to prevent any of them from knowing the exact location of the site. The pilots were told that this was just a SEAL training exercise in conjunction with the FBI high-tech crime unit. As for the medics at the village, none of them ever saw the site, just a harmless village in the jungle. Right now the secret is preserved, for as long as we choose to keep it preserved."

"At least the world has the celestial observations," said Ishiguro, recalling the image of the tenth planet, now called Maia, displayed on the covers of many magazines and newspapers around the world, including *Newsweek, Time,* and *U.S. News & World Report.* "Now the SETI community has something concrete to focus their efforts on."

"Problem is," said Jackie, "that with our current technology, all we can do is observe. We can't communicate real time because our transmissions can't exceed the speed of light, meaning it will take 139 years before they reach Maia."

"They do have the capability of communicating with us," said Cameron. "If they choose to do so, like in their daily transmissions, or with the way in which they scanned our millennium clocks, reading our sequence of numbers almost real time, somehow, using a technology that we may not discover for centuries."

Susan smiled. "Speaking of undiscovered technologies, Reid told me yesterday that the word in Washington is that NASA's trying to come up with a proposal for a voyage to Maia."

Ishiguro frowned. "How? We barely got to the moon, and Mars is still on the drawing board at NASA."

Susan shrugged. "Back in 1961 reaching the moon seemed like an impossible task too. Yet, we got there eight years later. You know the old saying, when there's a will . . ."

Cameron raised an eyebrow. "It would certainly bring unity to the world, just as it did to this nation back in the sixties."

They remained silent, considering the possibilities of such a project.

Two days later, Cameron and Susan were driven to a nearby airport, where an Army C-130 Hercules transport flew them to New Orleans. There they boarded a commercial jet to Washington. The morning papers were already packed with speculation as to the true meaning of the surreal, worldwide event, including several speculative articles on Maia, the recently discovered planet in the southern constellation Centaur.

Everyone from radical religious groups and heads of state to talk-show hosts had an opinion, and most were as far apart as the galaxies in the universe. It didn't surprise Susan and Cameron to learn that the experience did fade as it left the limestone shelf of the Yucatán Peninsula. People in northern Mexico and the southern United States experienced a few seconds worth of a back flash, in many ways almost like an intense daydream. By the time it reached Canada, the effect had faded to a warm feeling of sudden comfort. It also didn't surprise them to see that news of the event was competing with the initial results of the Year 2000 transition, which had not gone nearly as badly as everyone had forecast it would. Some systems had gone down, but others had picked up the load. Countries in South America and the Middle East were having the worst problems, but they were already being addressed as they flared up. In all, computer industry experts felt that the worst Y2K problems would be corrected within a couple of months, and most issues addressed within the next eight months.

"It's already happening," Cameron said, pointing to several articles in the paper he had picked up at the airport. "Everyone's got his own spin on what happened, and although many mean well, the variety of opinions will only distort the true meaning of what took place."

They remained silent for a moment.

"What's next for you?" she asked, gazing out of the window, watching the swamplands surrounding New Orleans disappear beneath the clouds.

Cameron Slater took her hand and kissed it. "With some luck our names will never make it to the papers, meaning we get to return to our normal lives." At the scientists' unanimous request, the United States and Japan had worked out an agreement to keep their names out of the media. Both countries had also shred all evidence of the site in Yucatán, except for two time capsules, which housed the files containing the descriptions of the event as witnessed by the presidential envoy. One capsule would be kept in the White House, not to be opened for five thousand years. The other, under a similar time stipulation, would be buried at a secret location in Japan.

"A normal life?" Susan sighed. "That sounds too good to be true."

"I think if we both work at it we have a good shot of making it, don't you?"

She stared into Cameron's dark eyes and smiled, peace filling her for the first time in two years. A normal life did seem within her reach, and Cameron Slater was certainly someone with whom she could share that life.

Susan Garnett took his hand and placed it over her heart while staring out of the window. A layer of clouds extended toward the blazing horizon as the morning sun spread its luminous beams on the new millennium.